THE WINE-DARK THRONE

DAMIEN J. COLUCCIO

Damien Joseph Coluccio is the owner and publisher of this work.
ISBN: 978-1-7635940-1-2 Print
ISBN: 978-1-7635940-2-9 eBook
Year of first publication: 2025

Published with the assistance of Authors Own Publishing Services Pty Limited
Edited by Danikka Taylor and Henry Sinclair
Cover design & Internal Illustrations by Casey Grills
Map Design by Angeline Trevena

For more information visit:
www.damienjcoluccioauthor.com
authorsownpublishing.com

To those who must live with difficult choices.

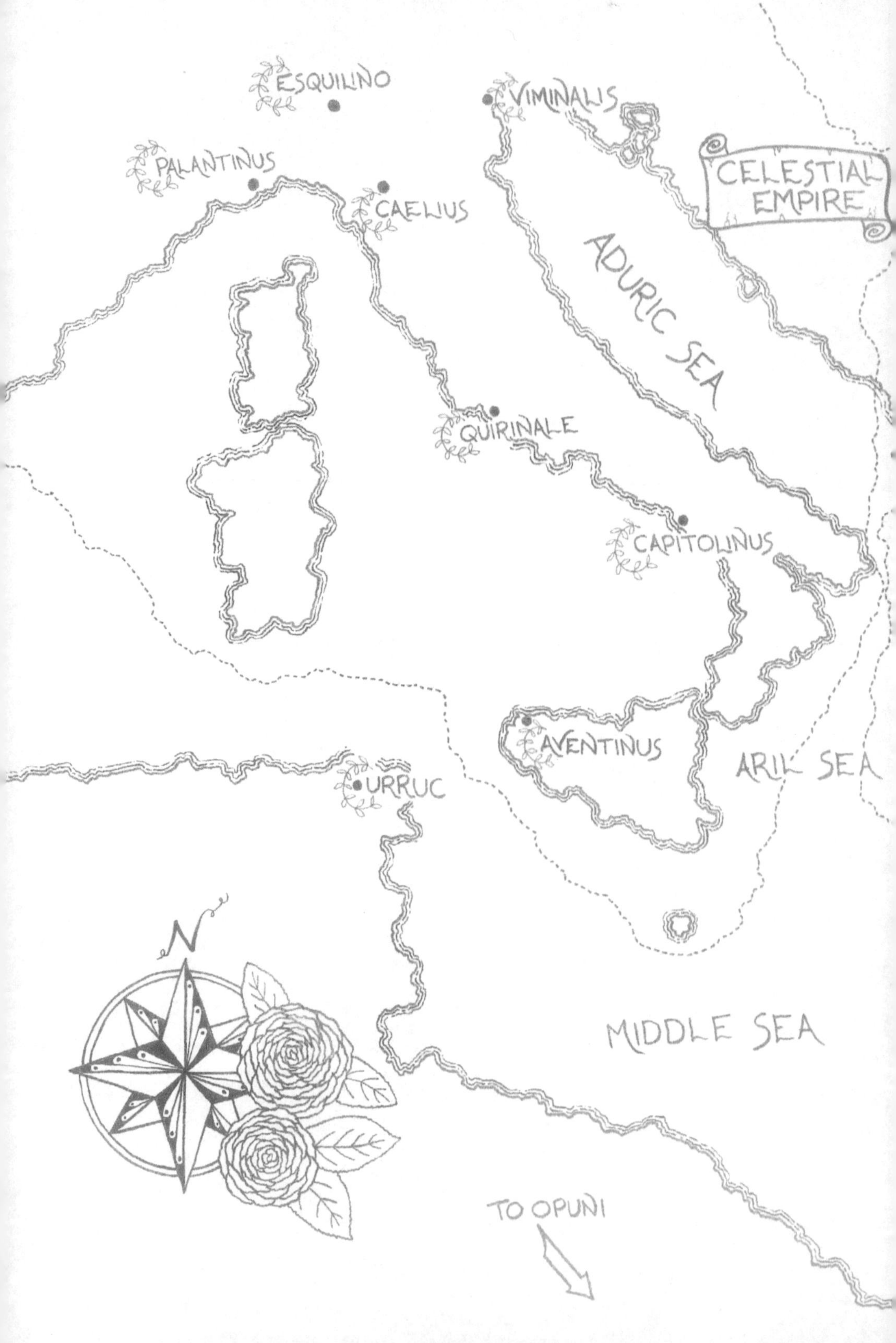

ESQUILINO
VIMINALIS
CELESTIAL EMPIRE
PALANTINUS
CAELIUS
ADURIC SEA
QUIRINALE
CAPITOLINUS
AVENTINUS
ARIL SEA
URRUC
N
MIDDLE SEA
TO OPUNI

THE LEAGUE OF KINGDOMS
TO ARYDOR
COLD SEA
DRAMAKI
ARTAS
TETHALIA
THEVAI
DELPHON
TRILOS
ATHANAI
APASA
KORIITHOS
PHORONIA
PALLAN
ICARII SEA
SOLMATHUS
ANAMA
KONOSO

Content Warning

This story has been written with a mature audience in mind and contains strong themes and occasional descriptions of violence. Readers should exercise discretion and prioritise their well-being.

BOOK THREE:
SACRIFICE

CHAPTER ONE

A salt breeze drifted through the tall, thin windows, rustling scraps of parchment on the desk and stirring strands of hair the colour of the rough sea on a dangerous dawn.

Desma blinked blearily at the shards of sunlight that lanced across the room like spears, her mouth dry with the taste of wool and her eyes crusted with drunken sleep. She peeled her head away from the table where she had slumped sometime in the early morning. A large jug stood empty beside her. As much as she could say against her captors, they kept her well supplied in wine.

She shuffled over to the washbasin and splashed water on her face, soaking the front of her dress. With a groan, she shed her peplos to the floor and approached the open wardrobe to pull out a drab grey dress. Such garb seemed to be favoured among Koriisthosan women, but how she wished to see the flash of a gem on her hand or the swirl of a peplos whose colour reminded her of joy.

Grabbing a couple of figs, she dragged herself to the window that offered the best view of the city and harbour.

Koriithos was filled with the scent of herb bundles hung outside temples and shrines; the streets around the palace were strewn with orange and almond blossoms, and garlands of ivy and pine boughs tied between buildings.

The city was preparing for a wedding. Her wedding. To King Gylippus' son, Prince Lycon.

She dropped the fig stems on the floor, crossed the room, and collapsed onto her bed heavily, sighing into the soft pillows. It was past noon. The servants would not arrive until near sundown for her evening meal and bath. If she ignored the presence of the guards at the door, she could almost imagine herself an actual guest of the kingdom, instead of a captive being forced into marriage.

The prince was inoffensive to look at – younger than thirty, with windblown sable hair, coppery skin, and well-muscled calves. But both times she had laid eyes on him, he had glared at her with such anger. He was being made to marry the prophesised saviour of his own kingdom. How he must hate her! And she knew nothing of him. Was he cruel? Cold? She swallowed harshly. He would be her husband, and she doubted Koriithosan law would be as beneficial to women as Apasan. Would he be allowed to strike her, punish her, keep her locked away?

She screamed into the pillow, letting the fabric muffle her helplessness. Five weeks she had travelled from home to Trilos and finally to the famed canal city. She had been shunned by society, forced to crawl and eat sand, made to relive the moment she killed her father to save his soul. And for what? To have but seconds of freedom as a cleansed woman before being caged again, this time in walls of stone as opposed to Tinia's laws.

How long had it been since she had been carried from the megaron and left here? The second astronomer Hyllos had visited once, but that was it. He had said her crew were safe, but could he be trusted? She hadn't been allowed to see them or send a message. All requests to speak to war leader Actor or first astronomer Kalchas were denied. As too were her pleas to speak with King Gylippus.

She had even sent a note to the priestesses of Uni in the city below, knowing that her request could not be denied as it was a holy plea. She had begged the temple to stop the marriage, claiming that it was a sham in the eyes of their goddess, Queen of Marriage and Keeper of Social Order, since she was unwilling. History was filled with stories of men and women being punished for breaking the sacrality of marriage vows.

But their response had been that their goddess saw no reason to interfere, and the marriage would proceed with her blessings.

She considered deserting her marriage as soon as she was able, but she had only just escaped the anger of Tinia, King of the Gods. The rage of his queen was known to be worse. Desma saw no way out, and even if she did, it would leave her crew in danger of Gylippus' retribution. She had no family to defend or claim her, and her crew could not save her from this fate. She was alone in the world.

So, Desma would marry Lycon and one day become queen, would become a wife. Bile rose in her throat at the thought.

She rolled out of bed and asked the guards for more wine.

Desma's thoughts stumbled over each other as the night wore on, her lips stained with rich Thevan wine. It was the only relief she had from the constant nothingness and dread. Even the servants avoided talking to her. When she asked one of the maids when the wedding was meant to be, the woman had smiled kindly and whispered, 'Very soon'.

A clatter in the hallway roused her from her brooding. Were they changing guards again? It seemed every hour new men came to the door. Someone cursed outside. Gods, these guards had rough tongues on them.

Her swimming head began to spike like someone was driving needle-thin shards of ice into her brain that then melted. Another curse from the guards. She growled inwardly. Why did the king not choose men who could be quiet? It must have been after midnight, judging by the moon – moons? – in the sky. These men had no consideration for good people who needed peace and sleep!

She stumbled to her feet to give them a tongue lashing, collapsing against the door, where she held herself up by the latch, taking several steadying breaths until the world stopped spinning.

Something heavy thumped against the door.

Her toes felt wet. Someone had spilled wine in the hall; it flowed under the door and lapped at her bare feet. Not only were these guards rowdy, but they were drunk on duty. When she was queen, she would teach them how to behave properly. She paddled her toes in the wine. Strange ... it did not feel right. It was thick and hot, and there was a coppery smell in the air.

Desma gagged. It was blood.

She pushed herself away from the door, tripping over an apple and falling into a heap on the floor. Bloody footprints followed her across the room. Scrambling across to the window, she pulled herself up and grabbed the largest clay amphora from the table.

Heart pounding in rhythm with her head, breathing fast, she watched the door. There was no lock on the inside. The king wanted her kept *in* and was not worried about her keeping anyone *out*. She swore at herself for drinking so much. Not that she had thought there was a chance she was going to be assassinated.

The fighting grew quieter, then the door swung open.

She raised the amphora high.

The hall was filled with Koriithosan soldiers, her dead guards at their feet. She might have felt relieved had the men not stepped casually over her fallen guards, one bending deftly to clean the dripping blood from his blade with the sleeve of his fallen comrade.

One of the men gestured with his sword. 'Come quietly.'

She frowned at his thick accent that she could not place. 'What do you want with me?' she asked, stalling. Who were these men? She made to lower the amphora, eyes downcast, but when two soldiers came towards her, Desma hurled the jug at one of them.

With a wild scream, she spun and kicked the other's stomach, her foot barking in pain as it hit his hardened leather armour. He crumpled to the ground.

More soldiers rushed forward.

She grabbed a bowl and smashed it into a face, continuing her momentum to punch another soldier in the side of the neck. They had put their weapons away. It appeared they did not want to risk hurting her. She had no such prohibition. Letting one get close enough to grasp her shoulder, she relieved him of his large knife, stabbing his thigh and shoving him into another man.

All the time she kept screaming, only pausing to take another breath. Gods, let someone hear her!

She ducked beneath a punch, stumbling dizzily. Someone kicked her legs out from under her and she fell on her back. She rolled and stabbed a foot, its owner bellowing as she was wrenched away.

More hands grabbed her. She bit fingers, clawed eyes, ripped at ears. She flailed and kicked and elbowed, but was soon clasped by hands everywhere, twisted and trussed in the air with ropes. Someone stuffed a cloth in her mouth to gag her, before she was thrown over the shoulder of a man who rivalled Bion in size.

Desma could not keep the tears from her face as she was carried from her rooms, past her dead guards, to find more bodies piled at the hallway intersection. Two women and a man in armour. Had they heard her screams?

She did not believe these men were Koriithosan, but then who? And why were they taking her?

They descended through the heart of the palace, sticking to the smaller halls and little used stairs to avoid notice. Twice they came across a servant and two more bodies joined the shadows.

They passed a room stacked with barrels and came to a tunnel, leading to a small stone pier with two lanterns on a canal. To the left, in the middle distance, she could see the harbour. To the right was darkness. It must be a small inlet from the main canal, carved to allow goods to arrive directly to the palace rather than into the harbour.

Two men in Koriithosan garb were waiting on the pier. They nodded to the lead man before leaving. One looked vaguely familiar; he glanced at her in disgust.

Their group boarded a small barge and it was soon pushed off, heading for the harbour.

She had given up struggling, hanging limply as they sailed out of the tunnel and into the moonlight. They rowed past moored ships until they were at the southern end of the harbour, where men called out from a small vessel and cast down ropes. Her carrier grabbed a rope with one hand but slipped and they both briefly dipped under the waves before they were hauled up.

Once onboard, Desma was discarded roughly to the deck, her already throbbing head banging against the wood. Her vision blurred red for a moment as copper filled her mouth, salt lining her lips. She closed her eyes.

'Hello, Desma,' a cruel voice said above her.

Her eyes slammed open. *It couldn't be ...*

A man clad in ornate robes of red and white, shining under the moon. Eyes the colour of burnt cinnamon sat above a vainglorious smile that still haunted her dreams at times. He bent down to remove her gag.

'Camillus,' she breathed.

He raised a finger. '*Bishop* Camillus,' he chastised. 'But we will have plenty of time together to train you in some proper manners.' He turned to the captain. 'The quinquereme is waiting just beyond Koriithos' waters. Whip the rowers, as we need all speed.'

The captain left, barking orders, the ship buzzing with movement.

Camillus knelt down beside her, grabbing her face roughly. 'This is not going to be a pleasant voyage for you,' he said calmly. 'But it will be immensely pleasurable for me.'

She huffed snot from her nose into his face.

That wiped the grin away. Eyes wide with rage, he slapped her so hard light flashed across her vision.

'Vile harridan,' he hissed. 'Let's see how well you keep this spirit. Your mother did not last long at all, so I hear. Take her below. Once we are on the quinquereme, put her in the cell.'

Desma struggled, but it was no use. She was hauled back over the giant man's shoulder. As they descended the stairs to the hold, she craned her neck a final time. The palace, softly aglow with golden firelight and the silvery moon. Her friends were up there. She had to believe they were safe. The king had to know that she would not abandon them, that she would not sacrifice their freedom for her own.

She did not know what the Empire wanted from her, or why Camillus would risk war with Koriithos for her. She had nothing for them. Why could the world not leave her alone?

Scant minutes ago, she had been angry to have her freedom taken away by Gylippus. Now she would give anything for him to send his warriors to drag her back to her room.

The palace vanished from view.

Her tears, mixed with seawater, continued to fall as darkness surrounded her.

CHAPTER TWO

Khufu's fist banged against the door again, the wood vibrating under the impact.

It had been four days since the crew were arrested and thrown into a well-decorated prison, supplied with sumptuous meals, fresh linens, and rich wine.

Four days without Desma.

Each time the door opened, one of the crew leapt up and harassed the guards. They had to see Desma, or talk to her, or send her a message. They only wanted to know she was alive and well, to let her know she was not alone, no matter the separation in marble and stone.

Every request was rebuffed with either silence or a rattle of spears, as were their requests to speak with Actor or the king.

But today Khufu had caught a glimpse of Hyllos, second astronomer and one of several chief advisors to the king, lingering at the end of the hall when the servants had entered with breakfast. He had shouted after him, but the Koriithosan man had stepped away. Khufu continued to shout his name, ignoring the orders to quiet down from the guards. The crew had learned quickly that, unless they actually tried to escape, the warriors would not touch them.

Once the door was shut, he had switched to banging with his fist.

It had been five minutes and his hand throbbed, the pain biting against the pine planks. They would answer him, or the next thing hitting the door would be Bion's shoulder.

He felt a soft tap at his elbow.

He looked down at Cela who was holding an apricot.

'Yes?' he said, never ceasing his knocking.

'Apricot?' she said, offering the fruit.

'Thank you.' He took it with his unoccupied hand and bit into the sweet flesh, eyes returning to the door.

Cela leant against the wall and watched him, eyes shining. For that is what Cela was – bright. Skin like honey-kissed milk. Hair like golden wheat in the height of summer. Voice like silver ringing.

'You know, the knocking is getting slightly annoying.'

'Good,' he grunted. 'Let us hope it is also irritating to our captors.'

As second-in-command to Desma, Celadine outranked him as captain, and he was honoured to serve the two of them. She was the brightness of their crew, the unwavering sun that never set. But sometimes one had to step into the darkness, to feel its weight, its solemnity, its tempting freedom. She needed to remember that the world was filled with both laughter and tears.

'I think Arete might stab you with the fruit knife before they open the door,' Cela said, nodding towards the shipwright. Khufu glanced over his shoulder and saw the small, solemn woman staring daggers at him while she sliced a pear thinly.

'A fruit knife is small. I will be alright.' Khufu was an imposing man, with skin the colour of earth dug deep from a riverbank, black hair cut short, and eyes rich as evening. His chiton of muted green was slightly too small, making him appear taller than he was. They were all dressed in sombre Koriithosan colours, for their clothes had been taken away to be washed and never returned. Only Cosmas kept his own clothes and somehow still smelled fresh. Khufu had long ago given up questioning the strange quartermaster.

'Depends on where she sticks it,' Cela murmured.

Before he could respond, there was shouting and clattering from the other side of the door. A voice called through the wood. 'The King approaches. Step away from the door!'

Khufu and Cela stepped back while the rest of the crew gathered from the other rooms and courtyard. The seven of them stood together, limbs tensed and faces set.

The doors opened and guards flooded the room, swiftly securing the space, despite the fact the crew were all clearly standing in one place.

Once the guards were satisfied, they banged their spear butts three times on the floor and in swept Gylippus, King of Koriithos.

He was an old man, having ruled the city-state for over forty years. His black hair had twin streaks of grey at each temple, and his skin was lined as though he spent his life in salt and spray. His dark grey robes bordered with gold were at odds with his bare feet.

Atop his brow was the sapphire crown centred with Nethuns' four-prong fishing spear. Koriithos had been the home of Nethuns, Hoar-God of the Deeps, favoured of the Sea Lord, until he abandoned his people to take up residence in the Empyrean city of Viminalis.

The king surveyed them all, his face harsh and lips twisted into an almost-snarl. 'Where is she?' he barked.

Khufu moved to ensure he was standing in front of Arete, Cela, and the crew's overseer, Kassandra, ignoring their indignant looks. 'Who, King?' he asked cautiously.

'I will cut your nose from your face,' Gylippus growled. 'Do not toy with me! Where is Desma?'

His heart went cold.

'What do you mean?' Khufu snapped, fear pushing iron into his words. 'You took her from us, and we've been locked in this room. What has happened?'

'Guards, stab him in the thigh if he dares speak to me like that again,' the king ordered. Two guards stepped forward, spears raised in readiness.

Khufu held out an arm to stop Bion from retaliating. 'I mean no disrespect, King. Only we know nothing of Desma since she was purified. We have been asking but have received no response. Please, tell us.'

'If I may, my king?' Hyllos said, stepping from behind him.

Gylippus nodded tersely.

Hyllos was tall with slim shoulders. Freckles scattered across his face like pollen on parchment, drawing attention to his intelligent brown eyes. His hair was shorn close at the sides, but the crown spilled long and loose, tied back in a short tail, and when he spoke his voice unfurled, deep and warm as cedar smoke.

'Last night,' he said, calmly and factually, 'whether willing or not'—the king grunted—'Desma was taken from her rooms. Our guards were slain around her door and throughout the palace. We followed their trail and believed she boarded a ship.' He met Khufu's gaze, his eyes wiser than his years suggested. 'An Empyrean ship.'

Cela exploded, shaking her fist at the astronomer, while the others clamoured in protest. Desma would never leave them willingly. And she had no love for the Empire – not after the atrocity committed against her family. They had destroyed her home and stolen the sacred treasures of Urruc, a bounty that should have guaranteed her place in history but had been relegated to a paragraph in the great burning of the Grand Temple.

The king's shout brought Khufu back to the room. The guards rapped their spears against their bracers, stepping forward threateningly. Khufu barked his own order, bringing his crew to heel.

Hyllos continued. 'We are hoping you would have some information regarding her rescue.'

Khufu shook his head. 'You are wrong, star-seer. You know what Aventinus did to the Apasan temple. Desma's mother ... her father. She would never go with them by choice. I do not know what they want from her, but her life now dances the spear tip.'

Cela spoke. 'We know nothing of this. Please, she needs us. You must let us go after her.'

Gylippus laughed. 'What fool do you take me for? You arranged her rescue to ensure she'd escape, so you could turn around and pretend you were the only ones who could save her. Suddenly, you are not just heroes – you are free. And I've lost the queen my kingdom needs. But rest assured, I will get her back. I will kill those who assisted her escape. And to teach her a lesson, I will kill one of you.' He turned his back on them and left, feet slapping on the green-streaked marble floor.

Hyllos turned to follow.

'Wait,' Khufu called.

The star-seer paused, glancing after the king before turning back to them.

'You must listen,' Khufu said. 'Desma would never leave us, and she would not have had those men and women killed just to free herself. You know this.'

Hyllos' eyes revealed nothing. 'I advise the king. The king makes his decisions. If you know anything, you must tell me.'

'Can we speak with Actor?' Cela asked. The war leader had accompanied them during their search for the monster terrorising the city. The monster Desma had slain – an act that gave her a chance to seek the king's purification, cleansing her of the blood crime of killing her own father. The same man Cela had once called father, too.

'War Leader Actor is busy organising ships to pursue,' Hyllos answered. His eyes moved across the group. 'But I will ask.' He left, the guards pulling the doors shut firmly.

As soon as the Koriithosans were gone, the crew erupted in discussion.

'Why would they take her?' Kassandra asked.

'We need to escape ourselves,' Bion said, his large arms crossed until his bronzed muscles bulged.

'And steal back our ship,' Delphinus added, his sea-green eyes flashing dangerously.

'How can we escape?' Kassandra said. 'We have no weapons and only one door.'

'The door is no obstacle.' Bion eyed the wooden barrier as though he were tempted to break it then and there.

'Quiet,' Khufu said, his voice cutting through the babble. 'They are already a night ahead of us. Let us see if Actor comes. If he does not, then we escape. Arete, find us a way out,' he ordered their shipwright and strategist. The small woman nodded and stepped away, her hazel eyes growing distant as her mind worked.

'There is no sense in wasting energy with mindless worry,' Khufu said to the rest of them. 'Calm your minds and pray to whatever god will bring you comfort right now. Be ready to move.'

Once the crew had dispersed, Khufu caught Cosmas' eye and nodded towards the small courtyard. The quartermaster unfurled himself from the wall he was leaning against and followed him outside.

Cosmas' pale blue eyes narrowed as he approached. He defended Desma and Cela with a viciousness that was only equalled by Delphinus' barbarity in battle, and had never faltered in his duties, but ... there was something about him Khufu could not quite enunciate. There was something in his voice that made Khufu's hackles rise, in his gaze that made others shudder. He had joined the crew despite Khufu and Cela's objections. Desma had stood firm against them both and said she trusted him as one would trust the tide, declaring that the stranger – who had tried to *poison* them – would be their new cook.

Once they were alone under the lemon trees in the courtyard, surrounded by high walls pockmarked with small windows, Khufu hardened himself to hold Cosmas' eyes.

The quartermaster did not seem perturbed by the stare, his face impassive as he plucked a lemon from a nearby branch. He punctured the skin with his nail and slowly peeled a strip off the fruit. He held it to his nose and pinched it sharply, releasing the oils from the skin. He breathed deeply, eyes never leaving Khufu.

'You have escaped already,' Khufu said. It was not a question.

Cosmas gave a small smile. 'Yes.'

'And I imagine it is a route open only to you?'

'I barely managed the climb myself.'

Khufu glanced towards the tall windows inside that opened to the seaside cliff. The window was too narrow to allow anyone but Cosmas, and possibly Arete, through. And no one but the quartermaster could have scaled down the cliff face. And back up again.

'What did you find out?'

'Nothing. I was looking for Desma, but it is a large palace and I only had a few hours each night to look.' Cosmas' lips thinned in annoyance. 'I must have been on the other side of the palace when Desma was taken. Otherwise,

I would have heard or seen something. I had to decide whether to start east or west and tossed a coin. The gods are not always generous with their favour.'

It still made no sense to Khufu. The king was a typical Koriithosan man: suspicious of foreigners, including other League kingdoms, and dismissive of women. Yet, once the purification ceremony was over, they had swiftly separated the crew from Desma and announced her marriage to his son and only heir.

'Did you find out why they want her to marry their prince?'

'I heard whispers of a prophecy, but I have no details.'

'A prophecy ...' Khufu whispered to himself. What god had ordained this new path for her? He stepped away from the quartermaster to one of the nearby windows, his eyes falling to the sails below, white gashes in the sea as ships moved to and fro in the harbour. The lines of sunlight drew his gaze to the horizon, conjuring the feeling of freedom he had cherished since he first laid eyes on the Middle Sea.

Almost five years had passed since he was first approached by Desma and Cela. He had been visiting Apasa for the Periomic Games, held every six years, which drew men from all over the League to compete in various events. He himself was there for the sailing event, leading the crew of a small bireme.

They travelled the Middle Sea, following the Games held in different kingdoms of the League and cities in the Empire. In between the major games, they would spend a season or two in a city, sailing in local races or taking part in far more dangerous, underground events that would risk life and limb but reward richly.

Khufu's crew had won splendidly in Apasa, far outstripping their competition with a fierce grace – but he had not been able to attend the award ceremony. He had watched from afar as his second was awarded the myrtle and bay wreath, the crew a small golden rose, and later the bag of gold.

He could compete, but he could not be acknowledged, for he was not a citizen of the League.

A few days later, he had been drinking in an Apasan tavern when he found two young women standing in front of him, one like bright sunshine and the other dark like his wine. He knew that they were what his people called *mobok-ranatim*, sister-scales. They were the balance of each other, like the moon and the tide.

After one afternoon talking with them, Khufu left his crew and became captain of the girls' newly constructed trireme. Within six months, he was granted Apasan citizenship. He taught his commanders all they needed to sail a ship, to be calm in a storm, to be fierce against pirates. They were the sisters he had left behind in Opuni. And he would die breaking the world before he let harm come to them.

'If we do not succeed with talking our way out of here, we will need to fight,' he said eventually, turning back to the quartermaster. 'Either one of us dies when they retrieve her, or we all die when they fail. Someone needs to escape to go after Desma.'

Cosmas peeled another strip from the lemon. 'It will be me.'

Khufu nodded. 'If we are not out of the room by tomorrow's sundown, then you must save her.'

'Many will die,' the quartermaster said quietly. 'You do not understand what you are unleashing.'

'I unleash nothing,' Khufu said.

It was true. Cosmas would go after Desma whether he ordered him to or not. And he would do whatever was necessary.

'Let us pray, for both our sakes and the city's, that the War Leader is wise,' Cosmas said before biting into the sour flesh.

Let us pray, Khufu agreed silently.

CHAPTER THREE

'What do you mean they want to see me?' Mynta asked incredulously, stifling a yawn as she scratched at a stubborn piece of sleep still stuck in her eye.

The sun was already well above the walls of the house, and it promised to be a clear, blistering day. She was only awake because Anesidora had stood over her with a bucket of water ready to tip over.

'I can read their message a third time if you did not comprehend it the first two,' Anesidora replied.

'I have not been up long enough to have to deal with your snarkiness,' Mynta said coolly, sipping her lemon syrup water.

Her nursemaid lifted a brow. Anesidora had been Mynta's closest companion since she was in swaddling; now she was an old woman with grey-gold hair in a long tail, sharp eyes, and a wry mouth, wearing her usual conservative chiton of warm brown with a cream himation over it. Mytna owed her life to the older woman – in more ways than one.

Waving a fan of flexible bronze – a marvel from the Clevers at Sethlans' Forge – to try and dispel the sweat that lined her forehead, Mynta relented. 'I do not understand why these merchants have requested to see me. They have always dealt with my father. Pass the request on to his secretary.'

'It would seem,' her nursemaid said, holding out a hand to stop a maid from carrying out her order, 'that they have been trying to speak with Councilman Linos to no avail. Your father has lost much power within the Council, and Galen's star is on the rise. His time is taken up with gathering his supporters to oppose Galen's growing influence on King Hilarion.'

'You know much for a simple nursemaid, Anesidora.'

'The elderly are forgotten as quickly as a wave after it has crested,' she replied with a sniff. 'Their request for an audience would appear to be a final, desperate attempt to gain access to this household. They believe you may be the foot in the door they need.'

Mynta considered. 'When do they wish to come?' she asked, plucking the last fig from the plate as a maid took it away.

'They are available at a messenger's notice,' Anesidora read. 'Which means today, if not sooner. They're desperate indeed.'

Mynta chewed the fruit slowly, her mind – and stomach – churning. This was all so sudden. She needed time to think, to prepare. Why did they want to see her in the first instance? She would not be able to get them a meeting with her father, though they would be unaware of their current relationship. So why bother to meet with them at all? Perhaps there was an opportunity here ...

'Tell them they may see me tomorrow at lunch,' she said.

'Very good, my lady,' the older woman said with a proud smile.

Mynta was silent as her maids moved about her, cleaning up the breakfast dishes, wiping her hands and face, and preparing her hair. It had been a couple of weeks since she began to run the house alone, out from under the ever-disapproving eyes of her mother. But she had not received any guests in that time. Now her first would be a group of merchants. She hated entertaining when it was not Desma and Cela visiting. She had no true friends in Trilos, for all the other maidens were seen to be rivals for the hands of prospective husbands. Over the last year, she had been viewed as less of a threat, less of a prize ... just less.

A polished copper mirror was brought from her bedroom and propped across from her so she could comment on her hair if needed. Her eyes instinctively slid away from her reflection, but she caught herself and purposefully moved them back.

She remembered when her face was tight, stretched, every bone as sharp as a razor and covered in cosmetics to create an illusion of warmth and health. Now, her cheeks were flush on their own, her eyes bright and clear, and her smile came unbidden and unforced. She had been freer with her meals since her mother and father had vacated the house for their palace apartments, and she noticed some of her dresses had become a little tighter.

Running a hand over her body, feeling the folds where over a year ago had been a smooth, uninterrupted plane of skin, she squeezed her thighs, each wide enough so she could not touch her fingertips on the other hand. She was large, there was no dispute. But why, when a man was described as being large, was it considered an admirable trait? Even if he was not muscular but fat, other qualities would be listed. But for a woman, for her, it was the first thing in people's minds and on their lips. For so many years, her body was slowly dying, deprived of the blessings of Horta it so desperately craved, her strength and vitality withering like ghosts. All to please her parents and the lust of a prospective husband.

But ever since she stood up to her father – finding the strength she knew was inside but was too terrified to let out, drawing her courage from Desma and Cela – she had been left alone. She had never known what a blessing it was to be alone, to only have oneself to praise or blame for choices and mistakes.

And if a man did not want her because she was large and healthy, instead of a twisted sense of skeletal beauty, then she was glad when they averted their gaze and stepped quickly away. She had no time for ignorant fools.

Usil was in fine form again the next day, the sky blue without blemish, the sea so clear the sailors could see the bottom a hundred meters from the shore, counting the fish before they caught them. The breeze was hot and lazy, gently brushing against bodies as it flowed from the west.

Trilos, first home of the Smith-God Sethlans, was famed for its innovations and creations. The Clevers of the Thinkery and the priests of The Forge dedicated their lives to crafting new inventions, from household items to terrifying warships. Mynta sat in the relative cool of the courtyard garden, feet submerged in the water of the small artificial creek that flowed from one end of the garden to the other, before being pumped back to the beginning underground.

She had donned the lightest peplos she owned that could still pass as acceptable in front of company. The colour of lavender leaves with a scattering of amethysts sewn along the bodice, it left her arms bare and had slits rising above the knee that allowed as much skin as possible to be free of cloth. Her hair was piled atop her head, more to keep it off her neck than for style, but her maid had done an admirable job making it look presentable.

A boy fanned her with a large palm, trying to shift the air slightly with each wave and bring some relief from the heat. Even still, sweat made her skin slick.

It was close to noon. They would be arriving soon.

She had witnessed countless meetings her father had held in the house and in their apartment, had seen how he cajoled and twisted the other party. Oftentimes, it appeared to mean little to him whether they were a partner or a rival. His sole focus was only ever gaining the greatest advantage. One thing he always did was ensure the meeting began with a demonstration of his power, his position. It was not dissimilar to when she had confronted him, seated in his chair in his own hall. It had served her well.

Her stomach rolled as though filled with snakes, her throat tightening and forcing her to constantly swallow, as if trying to clear dust that coated her tongue. She had searched her father's records for past dealings with these merchants, or some hint of what they may wish to discuss, but had found nothing. So she must be ready for anything. Where the bird landed decided the fate of the ant.

She turned to her fanboy, who was trying to hide his huffing breath even as his sweat pattered the ground by his feet. Pity blossomed in her heart. 'Take a break,' she said with a small smile. 'I am feeling much refreshed. Go to the kitchen and ask for some cooled fruit.'

The boy gave a tired but grateful bow of his head and darted away, the palm bobbing behind him.

The shade had begun to move. Soon she would be in the direct sunlight and would either burst into flame or melt into a puddle. Both options were undesirable, so she pulled her feet from the water and moved across the garden, leaving her sandals behind.

Her home was built of the same yellow stone as the majority of the city, surrounded by a high wall that provided shade from most of the sun's journey through the sky. The garden graced the centre of the house. All rooms opened to a covered walkway held up with slender pillars that allowed one to step directly into the garden.

She had just settled on a marble seat beneath a pomegranate tree when a maid hurried up the path. 'My lady, the merchants have arrived.'

May Turms guide this meeting, Mynta prayed silently.

'Is it noon?' she asked.

'Not quite, my lady. They did not want to give offence by being late. They are waiting outside the walls.'

'Very well. Admit them once it is noon.'

The maid hesitated. 'But, my lady, they are standing in the sun without shade. Would it not be more hospitable to bring them indoors? I can offer them lemon water and fruits until lunch is served.'

Mynta shook her head. 'No. My invitation was for noon. Admit them into the courtyard then only, then come inside to serve my lunch.'

The maid looked confused but bowed before leaving to inform the merchants.

Mynta rose and walked through the courtyard to the inner doors, the mosaic of the welcoming hall cool beneath her feet.

Anesidora was supervising the food being laid out, scolding a maid for placing two plates of the same cheese down. She moved to her lady's side.

'Do you think it is wise to keep them without? The day is hot, and we have wine aplenty,' Anesidora asked in a whisper.

Mynta laid on the only dining lounge and plucked a piece of crumbling goat cheese and a slice of warm flatbread. 'Time is in short supply for them, not for me,' she said. 'They need to be aware that it is by my grace whether I grant their request, whatever it be. For why else would they desire to speak with me?'

'It is better to show the bloom before the thorns,' her nursemaid warned.

Mynta frowned but waved her away. As she chewed, she could hear men talking in the courtyard, a strain of discontent in the air. The maid she had sent to greet them slipped through the door, leaving it ajar. Mynta's lounge had been positioned just so that she could see the flustered merchants in the small gap. And they could see her lounging in the shade eating a meal.

The maid returned and shut the door in their faces.

'They are without, my lady,' she said with a shallow curtsy.

'Thank you,' Mynta replied, taking a sip of watered-down wine. Not only did she want to keep a clear head, but wine always made her face hot, and the day's heat would no doubt last well into the evening.

Mynta savoured her meal, taking her time with a small bunch of grapes as she plucked and chewed each one thoughtfully, planning her next morsel. She then picked up several slices of smoked sausage and segments of fennel that left her mouth cleansed and sweet, followed by some figs stuffed with rosemary ricotta and honeyed carrots. Squeezing fresh lemon juice over cold roast pork, she enjoyed the crunch of the crackling and the herby marinade.

Finishing her wine, she raised her cup and the maid filled it again. As she went to grab some more pork, there was a loud bang on the courtyard door. She paused, brows raised as her hand hovered over the plate. An argument flowed over the courtyard wall, but the words were indistinct.

Another bang as someone knocked three times.

Mynta resumed filling her plate. 'Anesidora, please welcome our guests and invite them inside for shade and water.'

CHAPTER FOUR

Anesidora moved at a stately pace and slowly pulled open the doors, revealing a group of six men crowded at the entrance, looking as though they were ready to trample over her. 'My lady, Amynta of Trilos, daughter of Councilman Linos who is Emissary to Apasa, welcomes you to her home and bids you enter. We offer shade and water and safety until you depart. Under Tinia's eye.' Her nursemaid stepped aside after the traditional greeting and waved for them to approach.

The merchants crossed the small space from the door in haste. Each let out a relieved sigh at the coolness offered by the shade. Servants appeared with cups of water and bowls of fruit slices. It gave Mynta a moment to observe them.

They were men of classic Trilosii stature: bronze skin, dark hair, and eyes that tilted slightly. Their rich clothing of silk and fine wool was somewhat marred by sweat stains. And though they wore perfume, Mynta had to struggle to not wrinkle her nose at the strong body odour that pushed past the jasmine and oud and spices.

One man stood slightly apart. His earth brown eyes were watching her intently, a cup in one hand, while the other mopped at his brow. His long, yellow chiton was edged in green thread, a gold earring dangled from an ear, and one arm was filled from wrist to elbow with bracelets.

Mynta met his eyes as she placed another piece of pork in her mouth and chewed slowly. She took a distracting sip of wine as she nodded to her nursemaid, who hurried to her side. 'My lady requests your names, good men, and your reason for visiting.'

The man in the yellow chiton stepped forward before any of his companions could speak. 'I am Duris, master merchant of the eighth generation. These men are my colleagues and sometimes rivals.' His voice was smooth and forthright, his eyes never leaving Mynta's face. 'We have been trying for several days now to contact your esteemed father to propose a business opportunity. Alas, affairs of state occupy much of his time. My friend, Ancus,' he gestured to a younger merchant wearing a red chiton, 'suggested perhaps the beautiful lady of the house may be able to offer some assistance to our cause.'

Mynta felt a blush begin to creep up her face and blamed it on the wine. The very watered-down wine. For Uni's sake, she was not a child with a head full of air. 'I am surprised that such an opportunity would remain after so much time has elapsed,' she said. 'Would it not have been more economically prudent to seek investment elsewhere, rather than risk the chance of it slipping away, or worse, being taken up by another merchant?'

Duris' lips twitched. 'I was unaware my lady was so well versed in business to be able to ask such sage questions.'

Her nursemaid let out a huff that bordered on impoliteness. Mynta shot her a look. 'It does not take a master merchant to realise that when a golden opportunity arises, you need to seize it quickly.'

'Truth continues to fall from your lips, my lady,' Duris replied. 'Fortunately, we have so far managed to keep news of our discovery quiet. Though for how much longer, I do not know. We are hoping that once we have secured your father's support and investment, we can move rapidly to secure the rights from the Fifth Advisor.'

'My father is a busy man, master merchant. I'm afraid that his attention is focused solely on Council and kingdom.' She saw them deflate at her words, two at the back muttering about wasting their time. 'However,' she said slowly, drawing their attention back to her, 'this matter brings me interest. Please, continue.'

The other merchants began to talk among themselves. Young Ancus pulled at Duris' sleeve, whispering in his ear. The master merchant kept his face smooth, but she caught the glint in his eye. Mynta raised a brow at him and waited.

Duris smiled. 'The opportunity we bring is sensitive and comes at great cost. While I appreciate your ... enthusiasm, I'm afraid we will need to seek what we require elsewhere. This is not the time for a dabbler to try her hand in trade and business. With respect.'

A flare of annoyance rose at the undercurrent of condescension in his voice, but she bit her tongue. 'I agree wholeheartedly, Duris, and I hope you are not implying that I, daughter of Linos, would be so unknowledgeable of my father's business that I could not – or have not – conducted my own?'

On cue, her nursemaid scowled fiercely at the master merchant for the perceived insult to her mistress.

Duris gulped and bowed his head. 'Of course not, my lady, and please grant me your forgiveness for any implication or insult I unwittingly gave. Perhaps you may be interested in our small venture.'

Ancus opened his mouth to disagree, but Duris silenced him with a sharp wave of his hand, his bracelets ringing. 'We have discovered a deposit of tin approximately three days ride south of the city, near the village of Sabate. It is mostly on the land of an older farmer.'

'And yet, here you are speaking to me,' Mynta quipped. 'It appears the farmer is whom you need to be speaking to.'

The corner of Duris' mouth lifted. 'Of course. We have already assured him that, considering his advanced age, it was in his best interests to accept our offer rather than try to secure the mining rights from the king and attempt to harvest the ore himself. He saw reason, and agreed to sell. However, that took up most of our collective liquid assets. We still require funds to obtain the right to mine from the fifth advisor, the permit from the leader of Sabate, and then money for equipment and to pay for the labourers.'

'A significant investment, indeed,' she said, unable to keep the surprise from her voice. Without knowing the details, even she knew it was an incredible sum they were investing. 'And this is all for tin? I assume there is a sudden need for it, or you would not be so eager to secure the mining rights.' A thought struck her. 'And from what you said, *most* of the ore is on the land you have purchased. Which means some is located elsewhere, perhaps on neighbouring farms or on the king's land. If so, you either need to buy all the surrounding land – for which you do not have the capital – or receive the rights from the advisor, which grants you ownership of the entire mine no matter under whose land it spreads.'

Duris gave her a warm smile. 'Exactly. We have kept the buying of the land quiet as best we could. And the tin is for The Forge. They have put out a call across the kingdom and are willing to pay handsomely for it. Having a new-found tin mine so close to the city could mean riches many times over for our investments.'

'And how much is it you are seeking from our household?' She held her breath.

The master merchant turned to Ancus and conferred briefly. Duris whispered something which made the younger merchant shake his head. He said something else, to which Ancus thought briefly on before giving a single nod and stepping away.

Duris turned back to her. 'Two thousand gold drachmae.'

Her eyes bulged and her nursemaid coughed roughly. *Two thousand gold drachmae!* An incredible sum indeed. Enough to keep a prominent household in the city running on wine and meat and song for two years, with some to spare. And it far outstripped the monthly allowance her father gave to run the house and the little extra she had aside. She sank lower on the dining lounge, unable to keep the disappointment from her face. 'I am afraid that is too steep for me, master merchant. And I will confess that while I do not know the particulars of mining, I find it difficult to believe this amount is required.'

'I will admit, my lady,' Duris said carefully, 'that I erred on the side of opportunity and asked for more than less. The rights from the king would be within the realm of two thousand. The permits from Sabate could easily be another five hundred. Equipment from the Thinkery – for mining is not where you want to cheat on lesser machinery, as one cave-in could ruin the entire endeavour – would be at least four thousand. Initial layout for labourers before we start turning a profit is another five hundred. Smelting fees – unless we want to build or buy a forge ourselves – would be another thousand. These are all conservative estimates. That leaves us at eight thousand. And we have pooled another thousand into an emergency fund to draw upon if required. The total cost of investment comes to nine thousand gold drachmae. Given the lateness of the proposition, we've also decided to waive the requirement for you to match the initial land cost. This will not affect your equity. Your portion would then be one thousand three hundred.' He looked at her expectantly.

Mynta's head was spinning.

Fortunately, her nursemaid stepped forward to speak. 'We would need to see the land title transfer, as well as proof of the mine. I assume contracts have been drawn up between you all. My lady will need to see them, to ensure she is entering into an equitable partnership and not undertaking the lion's share of the investment.'

'Of course, dear mother,' Duris said respectfully. 'We have the papers here, and we are happy to accompany any servant of the household to the mine. But I must again urge expediency, as we have already lost much time. If my lady is satisfied with what she has heard and seen today, we can immediately lodge the mining request at the palace this afternoon. I would only ask for an initial investment of five hundred drachmae as a deposit into the partnership. If my lady is amenable to such a proposition?'

Mynta kept her face carefully composed, but her heart was pounding. She did not have five hundred drachmae. She doubted she had a hundred. But she did have jewels …

'If you would excuse me for a moment, good merchants,' she said as she rose from the lounge. 'I wish to think upon the offer. Please avail yourselves to food and drink, and I will return shortly.' She nodded to Duris and took her nursemaid's arm as they strolled into the centre garden, letting the small creek disguise any whispers that may drift back to the group.

'I am tempted,' Mynta said softly, as they paused under a small orange tree, its petite white flowers perfuming the air with citrus.

'But, my lady, it is so much money,' her nursemaid said with a worried frown that further creased her face. 'Would it not be more prudent to find a smaller investment with less risk and build from there? Every building, whether it be a hut or a palace, begins with a single stone.'

'Wisdom and boldness rarely walk together,' Mynta countered. She had spent so much of her life being meek, letting decisions be made for her. Since witnessing Desma's strength during her trial by Tinia, a fire had been lit in her own belly. It was shining a light on a dream so ethereal she was afraid to speak it aloud, even to herself. But this opportunity was a chance for her to step away fully from her father. To be independent. To be Amynta of Trilos only.

'How much gold do we have in the house?' she asked.

Her nursemaid remained silent.

'You have conveyed your reservations, Anesidora,' Mynta said with a hint of iron. 'But this is what I wish to do, and our chances for success are greater if you are with me.'

Her nursemaid sighed. 'We have around thirty gold drachmae and seventy silver. The Temple of Februus holds another two hundred and forty-seven gold, four hundred and eighty-one silver, and several small chests of gems. I am not sure of their exact current value, but it would be roughly eight hundred gold drachmae. We would be left destitute.'

'Are you sure you were not a scribe in a past life, dear friend?' Mynta asked with a smile, but her heart had dropped. She could not empty her home of money. Her father's stipend was enough to cover food and a few luxuries for her relatively small household. And she refused to go to him to seek an advance or a loan. 'And the value of my jewellery here?'

Anesidora drew a sharp breath. 'No, my lady. You cannot stoop to selling your adornments like a widow bereft, wandering the streets exchanging rubies for bread to feed her starving children.'

'Do not be so dramatic,' Mynta answered. 'Every foundling enterprise needs capital. What is the difference if my father had given me chests of gold instead of necklaces and earrings?'

'You cannot go back to those men with jewellery to cover your deposit,' her nursemaid said. 'It makes you look like you have no money.'

'But I do not.'

'They do not need to know that! They shouldn't know that. You need to come from a position of strength, not desperation. They need *you*. They need your father's name to ensure the permits from the king and Sabate are granted with expediency. They need your family as much as they need your money, sweet child.'

Her nursemaid's words made sense. Mynta caught a glimpse of the merchants through the branches, all stood together talking while her maids circled them with trays of wine and bowls of food.

All except Duris. He stood apart, watching her through the trees, a pear in one hand, from which he absently took bites and chewed slowly. She felt her cheeks heat again, and she tore her eyes away from him. *Absolutely not.* By all the powers of Artimi, this would not become a sordid love story where she fell passionately for the handsome merchant who spoke to her like she was her own woman, who shared a kind smile and silver words. Her face heated further, but this time she could not tell if it was shyness or anger.

She had to make a decision and start somewhere. She could not drink the wine if she did not first crush the grapes.

'We will agree to take part in the venture,' Mynta said, moving back beside her nursemaid. 'Let us return to them.'

The merchants broke apart from their huddle when they saw the women emerging from the garden. Duris joined the others, hands clasped behind his back, watching her curiously.

She forwent resuming her position on the lounge and instead stood on the last step that led up to the garden. It put her at eye height with the merchants, but she felt taller.

'I thank you all for taking the time to speak with me today, and wish Tinia's and Sethlans' blessings on you all,' Mynta said with a slight nod of her head.

The men murmured kind replies and returned the nod, Duris going so far to offer a very shallow bow.

'I am pleased to inform you that I will be happy to take part in your venture,' she announced. The merchants exchange excited smiles and words with each other. 'However, I do not currently have five hundred gold drachmae at my disposal.' This brought the group to a sudden silence. 'As you would all agree, it would not be wise for a lady to keep such vast amounts in her home for her own safety. This is not to incite worry among you, as I am easily able to retrieve the amount by no later than tomorrow.' Worried whispers rose. 'What I would offer in the interim,' she said in a louder voice, 'and I understand the unorthodox nature of such a measure, is the equivalent in jewellery that I would give to you in trust. Once I have retrieved the money, we shall exchange the gold and gems for the jewellery, along with the remaining portion of my investment. Is this acceptable to you?'

Four of the merchants started speaking at once. Mynta kept her eyes on Duris and Ancus, letting the others' voices fade into a hum while she waited. They held her stare.

Eventually, Duris gave Ancus a slight nod. The younger merchant stepped forward and waved the others to silence. 'I believe it would be an acceptable exchange, my lady,' he said.

'I will ready it for you now, so you may be on your way to see the fifth advisor. In the meantime, please produce the contracts between you all and the one for me to sign. Anesidora will read through them.'

Even Duris looked taken aback when her nursemaid approached them with a hand held out for the papers. Mynta hid her smile, departing for the room where her maids had readied several chests for her.

'Leave me, please,' she said to them.

Once they were gone, she took a moment to walk around the room, hands brushing the open chests, eyes sliding over their contents but not pausing to rest on any one item.

Most of them were gifts from her parents. A few were from Cela and Desma. And some were gifts from diplomatic visits with her father. These were the ones she sorted through first.

Her mother had trained her from when she was a young girl to know the value of jewellery. They had visited many of the finest gold and silver smiths in the city, patronised the most famous artists and jewellers in Trilos and Apasa. Her mother always said it was important to know how much a gift cost in order to judge the suitability of a man.

Piece by piece, she dropped items into an empty chest set with a heavy iron lock. A necklace of coral and topaz that a young suitor had given her when she was fifteen at a sporting feast. A silver ring carved with sage flowers. A necklace of raw emeralds that the Hero-King in Apasa had presented. A comb of gold-streaked marble. Glass earrings from the Empire. A bronze bracelet that gave the sweetest chime when tapped with silver – a gift from one of Sethlans' priests.

She found no hesitation in giving these items away, and before she knew it, they had all been transferred across. But still, she calculated there was only three hundred of the drachmae needed.

She would not give away gifts from her friends, firmly closing that chest. She moved over to the largest chests from her parents. So much money had been spent to make her beautiful, desirable, worthy. Trappings designed to sell her off to the most influential man, to help her father gain more power within the Council. She remembered them all.

An opal necklace on a string of silver shaped like a laurel wreath. Given to her when they had dinner at Councilman Davos' house, where she met his son, who had slurped his food from his fingers. It went into the chest.

A gold tiara with small triremes stamped into the metal that she was made to wear when they met with General Perdikkas for lunch, a greying man who ruled Trilos' navy. He was kind but showed little interest, which her parents considered her own failing. Into the chest.

One after the other, each representing another man, another failed suitor. Another time she disappointed her mother and angered her father.

But perhaps her supposed disgrace was preordained. So many nights had she prayed silently to Ethausva, Goddess of the Home, to protect her against marrying someone she did not care for. So many days had she left offerings at Uni's altar for a husband who wanted her for who she was and not who her father happened to be.

Had the goddesses answered her prayers? Had they filled her with the strength to cast her father from his own home, a strength that continued to drive her now to venture out beyond its walls into the world?

She dropped the last piece into the chest and closed its heavy lid. It was as near to five hundred drachmae worth of jewellery she could estimate without bringing in an expert appraiser.

She signalled two guards, who carried the chest out behind her. In the welcoming hall, her nursemaid snapped at a scribe who was frantically writing, while several merchants looked both indignant and chastised.

'Is everything well?' she asked, her question open to the room.

'Quite well, my lady,' Duris stepped in smoothly. 'Your advisor found several differences between the numerous contracts and is amending yours to ensure utmost protection and benefit.'

'No more protection and benefit than what anyone else has been afforded,' her nursemaid countered with a scowl. 'My lady is not of such carelessness that she can shrug off losing a few thousand gold here and a few thousand gold there. Brashness is the sign of a young man making his way in the world. Common sense is the way of a young woman. And you would do well to remember that through your life, master merchant.' She wagged a finger at him before rounding back on the scribe who had made a mistake.

'Indeed, lady advisor,' Duris said with a laugh. 'I appreciate the advice.'

'Here are the jewels,' Mynta said, gesturing the chest to be set on the ground before flicking open the lid.

The merchants, besides Duris, all moved forward to begin poking and pawing the contents. Mynta tried to remain calm as she answered questions, such as what metal an item was made of, what gemstone it held, where it had come from, and whether there was a maker's mark.

Eventually, the merchants agreed on the appraised value and stepped away, except for one older merchant who remained poised over the chest, frown firmly fixed to his face.

'A problem, master merchant?' Mynta asked.

'It is customary, my lady,' he said slowly, eyes darting from Mynta to Duris and back, 'that when collateral in this form is provided, the depositor would provide additional items – jewellery, in this case – to offset any time spent and potential market fluctuations. As insurance, should the pieces need to be sold in the event of forfeit. It is only good business.'

Anesidora looked ready to pick up a nearby tray and smack him over the head.

Mynta smiled uncertainly. 'If that is the consensus among you all …'

'I believe we can dispense with that condition,' Duris stated, stepping forward to firmly shut the lid of the chest. 'I am happy to accept the collateral and collect the full investment tomorrow. Agreed?'

'Agreed,' the merchants responded as one, except for the older merchant who hesitated before giving his consent.

'Wonderful,' Mynta said, relief rolling through her. 'Then I shall let you continue on to the palace, and we shall meet again tomorrow noon.'

The last of the paperwork was amended and signed. Duris rolled it up and advised he would take it to the Temple of Turms to be sealed. One of the merchants' men came in from the outer courtyard to collect the chest, and the group left with many praises for her entrepreneurial spirit and business acumen. Mynta smiled politely and thanked them all for the opportunity.

Once the final gates were shut, Mynta returned to the shade of the garden and asked for a small plate of food and fruit juice. Her nursemaid joined her, groaning as she slid her feet from her sandals and into the cool water.

'Why is it, when you get old, your body doesn't know if it is on fire or frozen to the core?' she said as she slowly swirled her ankles. 'By the grace of Nethuns, this feels wonderful.'

Mynta was silent as she gazed at nothing, her mind turning over the events of the last hour. A heaviness was settling on her chest, a sense of dread. What if this was a mistake? Could this bankrupt her? Would she have to go to her father, explain her failure, and beg for more money? What if …

'Duris is a handsome young man,' her nursemaid said unexpectedly.

'What?' Mynta said, bringing herself back, stepping away from whatever edge she had been walking.

'He is a handsome man, good family, rich prospects,' she continued to muse. 'Obviously quite fascinated by the daughter of a powerful man living alone.'

'I did not escape from one mother's desire to see me wed for another,' Mynta said sharply.

'I do not wish to see you wed for the sake of being wed, sweet daughter of my heart,' her nursemaid said, lifting one foot from the water to massage it gently. 'I am simply wanting to point out when I believe a man has paid attention to *you*.'

'He seems a kind man, I will grant you that,' Mynta said with a small smile. 'But I am not sure I am who he wants.'

'Not all men want a quiet flower. Some want a bold mistress to be the earth to their sky.'

'And I am not sure if he is who I want.'

Her nursemaid nodded. 'It would be good to find out what it is you do want, my lady.'

CHAPTER FIVE

Salt and cold were her only companions.

Darkness and water her waking nightmares.

The cramped cell was completely enclosed, secluded in the furthest bowel of the ship, built right against the hull. Nothing kept her out of the knee-deep water that sloshed in the blackness, no bench or bed or chair. When her legs gave out, Desma slumped into the water, shivering as she lost feeling in her extremities. When she could stand it no longer, she'd drive herself up to brace her back against one wall, her feet against the other, hanging there, dripping and shuddering, wiggling her toes until painful warmth returned, only for cramps to force her back to the floor. There she would stand with one foot clear of the seawater at a time, until her legs gave out. Then she would slide, defeated, into the water, where she barely managed to keep her head high enough not to drown.

An endless cycle.

Twice there had been a thump followed by a splash as hard bread fell from an unseen chute into the water. She would grabble frantically on her knees until she found it, lifting it clear and squeezing as much water out as she could. She would gnaw on it slowly, brine puckering her lips, the bread threatening to crack her teeth under the thin layer of sogginess.

Other times, there would be a rattle of metal followed by a rushing sound. From one corner, a small fount of water would cascade from a pipe in fits and spurts. She would slam into the wall of the cell hard enough to bruise, eager to catch as much of the precious, clean water in her mouth, letting it wash her eyes and lips clear of the crystallised salt.

Once, her captors were feeling particularly cruel, and instead of fresh water, they poured seawater down the pipe. It burned her already stinging eyes and felt like glass down her throat. She gagged and vomited, her sick mixing with the water in the darkness, acid and brine filling her world.

Time was meaningless in the darkness.

No light had reached her since she was carried below deck and thrown into the cell. No greying that would hint at noon; no deepening that would tell of night. Only total and complete absence of light. How she craved Thesan's welcome of the golden dawn. How she prayed for a glimpse of Usil pulling the sun behind him. How she dreamt of Tiur as she sailed the moon. Anything to drive back her dark world that consumed her.

There were times when it was tempting to stop holding her head above the water. To let herself slip away in the wet cold, to flow to the Beneath and let the blue-skinned Charuns fly her across the blood rivers into the Vale, to be with her mother and father.

But every time she found the strength, as deep as bone and mountain root, to climb back up again. She had a dozen, a hundred, a thousand reasons to keep going.

But one blazed more brightly than all the others combined.

She was going to burn Camillus and Aventinus to ash.

Desma was not yet finished with the world.

CHAPTER SIX

The next day, as the sun was a handsbreadth from sinking beneath the horizon, the doors slammed open.

Cela leapt to her feet while the crew gathered their makeshift weapons of fruit knives and chair legs and curtain rods.

It was Actor.

The general shut the doors behind him, ignoring the guards who tried to follow. His youthful face was haggard, his soft yellow hair swept upwards as though run through many times with his hand. He was well-muscled, though on the slim side, with skin the colour of new-spring honey. Cela took in his broad, shovel-like face, his cut chin, his wide brown eyes. He was dressed in a cream sleeveless tunic, bronze greaves covering his shins, hard leather sandals strapped tight. A plain sword swung from his hip. He looked more than a decade older than Cela, and yet already held the title of war leader, commander of Koriithos' army and navy. The third most powerful man after the king and first astronomer. To rise to such heights at so young an age ... Cela could feel nothing but respect for him.

'Do you know what happened to Desma?' she asked, dropping her knife back onto the table, concern making her words breathless.

His eyes darted from the crew to their weapons. 'I will not speak while you bear arms,' he said flatly.

'Drop them,' Khufu ordered.

After they were empty-handed once more, Actor turned to her. 'Two nights ago, Desma was kidnapped by Empyreans. We do not know any names, but I can confirm that the quinquereme bore the sigil of the Empire, the bronze double-headed axe behind a snarling she-wolf. And beneath it was a blush swan bearing a crown of roses.'

Cela swore viciously.

The swan and rose was the symbol of Turan in the Empire. The Goddess of Love left Apasa nearly five hundred years ago for Aventinus and, according to Desma, was the reason behind the sacking of the temple. As well as the death of her parents.

'Why would they want her?' Khufu asked. 'She has nothing more they could want.'

Actor shook his head. 'I do not know. But I have been speaking with the king, and he has agreed to allow you to pursue.'

The crew raised a small cheer. Delphinus began to drum the table wildly, his hands missing his instruments after so many days.

Actor waved them to silence. 'There are conditions. You will have fourteen days to rescue Desma and return her to Koriithos. And ... I will be your captain.' The general kept his eyes on Khufu.

'Why?' Delphinus interjected. 'Khufu is our captain. We need no other.'

'Because,' Khufu said, cutting over the murmurs of assent from the group, 'I will be kept here as guarantor of your return.'

Actor nodded.

'That is not all,' Arete said, stepping forward, eyes narrow and dangerous. 'Tell us.'

Cela had to praise the general's bravery. Few could withstand Arete's honed stare, trained on them like a hound scenting blood. But he met her with shoulders squared. This was a man who knew his duty.

'If you have not returned by the fifteenth day, you will be declared enemies of the city-state. All citizens of Koriithos will know your names and spit upon your feet. If you enter the kingdom, you will be slain on sight.'

Arete was still as stone. 'What else?' she hissed.

'If you are not back by dawn on the last day, Khufu will be sacrificed to honour the god of our city, Nethuns. Thus speaks the king.'

Cela heard the words but could scarcely comprehend them. She heard the outrage of her companions, but she could not speak. Khufu stood as still as stone, an immovable sentinel. Gylippus would kill him because the Empire kidnapped Desma. She wanted Khufu to strike out. Fist or word, it didn't matter. This could not be so. The trickery of fate would deal him death. He did not deserve that.

But all he said was, 'Very well.'

'Khufu.' Delphinus grasped his arm. 'We cannot let this happen. We must take another path.'

'Such as?' he snapped back. 'Try to fight our way out of the palace? How many of us would survive, if any? Then we still have to get across the city and on a ship. No, this is our best chance.'

Bion was crestfallen. 'Captain ...'

'Why do you think you will fail?' Khufu asked. 'That is the only reason you would fear my death. We are the darklings. You will save Desma and be back with plenty of time to spare. I do not doubt it for one moment.' He spoke to them all. 'Bring back our friend.'

He turned to Actor. 'When do you sail?'

'As soon as we get to the harbour.'

Cela went to speak, but Khufu held up a hand. 'I do not want to hear anything from any of you. Go.' The men and Arete clasped his forearm as they left. Kassandra hugged him tightly.

Cela could not help but embrace him, wrapping her arms around his shoulders and pressing a kiss to his cheek. 'We will return.'

'When you see Desma again, tell her something for me,' he said. 'Tell her "Akbahri". She will know what it means.'

She did not understand the term but nodded, sealing the promise.

Cosmas was the last to leave. Khufu stopped him for a moment, whispering too softly for her or Actor, lingering by the door, to hear them. It was only for a moment, but she swore Cosmas' eyes flashed with a feral light before he turned away. He said nothing as he passed, but Cela felt his chill brush against her. Even Actor stepped away.

Khufu placed a fist against his chest and bowed low, his forehead nearly touching his knees. A profound sadness settled heavily on her shoulders that she was too scared to fully acknowledge. She turned and hurried after the crew, her eyes glimmering salt as she left her captain behind.

The Darkling swept out of Koriithos, the harbour's white stone made opalescent by the twilight, its red tiles softened and green marble darkened. The harbour was spotted with large rocks that held carved statues of Nethuns and his dozen children, who claimed the wind and tide as their domains. Small islands, each a score of paces wide, held shrines and altars. Offerings were left and incense burned for a god who no longer swam in its waters.

Cela stood with Actor at the prow. The wind whipped her hair out of its braid, and she let it flow free, allowing the salt and spray to cleanse her. She breathed in the brine and felt her skin pebble under the coolness. The soft darkness wrapped itself around the ship, a comforting balm for the past few days.

Upon boarding, their rowers were replaced with strange men at the oars who ignored her and looked to Actor.

Cela's peplos, the colour of olive leaves with a leather belt tooled with silver, caught disapproving looks from the rowers when she emerged back on deck. They eyed her bracelets, pulled from the chest Mynta had given her, but she ignored them, head held high. Her apple and jasmine perfume wafted down the ship as the breeze blew past.

Actor stared down the horizon as the ship pulled further away from the harbour. She had wanted to hug him when he defied the king's expectations and told the truth about Desma and the monster. He had bound his honour to hers, steadfast in his pledge that she had slain the beast. Cela did not forget the kindness he had shown them both while they hunted through the forests. But he was here now to fulfil his duty to his king. She did not delude herself in believing otherwise. He would do everything in his power to rescue Desma, whatever his reasons. In that, Cela trusted him wholeheartedly.

'Tell me why,' she said to Actor. Hands clasped behind him, back straight, bronze breastplate gleaming under new starlight, and green-plumed helm by his sandalled feet: the image of a war leader.

'Why what?' he asked, eyes still on the fast approaching night.

She said nothing.

After a moment, he gave a sigh. 'There is a prophecy. It told of the monster and how the one who killed it would be our next ruler. That person would be the monarch Koriithos would need in the days to come. A gift from Nethuns to protect his city and people. As with most prophecies, it was silent on what exactly was to be expected. Imagine our surprise when that person was Desma, despised daughter of Apasa, blood-polluted.'

'Father-Killer,' Cela whispered.

Actor nodded.

'And she is to marry the prince? Are you sure he will not try to kill her first?'

He chuckled grimly. 'You must try to see it from his perspective. The prophecy all but says outright that he is not the king his city needs. He will not be the one to save or protect his own people. And the person who does fulfil the prophecy is a foreigner. His new wife and queen.' He shook his head. 'It is a blow to a man's pride to be told he will be less than his father. For is that not the prized destiny of all children – to be greater than their parents?'

Cela did not answer. Her mother was now High Priestess of the Grand Temple of Turan in Apasa, having taken over the role upon the death of Desma's mother. What higher role was there for Cela? She did not have the depth of faith her mother had for Turan. Their own goddess, She Who is Love Itself, had betrayed her people. How could Cela serve in a temple that Turan herself burned?

And Desma was to be queen, her sister in heart if not in blood. What was her destiny to be?

'What happens if Desma does not wish to follow the prophecy?' she asked.

She felt Actor harden beside her. 'She will be queen.'

The air grew colder. The night darker.

They had turned south, racing through the water, accompanied by the sounds of the steady drumming to keep the rowers in time, the creak of rope and groan of wood.

Behind them, two triremes followed. Four hundred Koriithosan men.

Arete had whispered that, between the six of them, they could take *The Darkling* back from the ten rowers, two officers, and Actor. She had seemed certain they could evade the larger ships. Cela had vetoed the option. It would waste valuable time as they tried to escape the triremes, and there was little chance they could take a quinquereme crewed by four hundred men while they were taking turns rowing themselves.

Their best chance of saving Desma was with the Koriithosans.

She had not said to the shipwright that she did not want to see harm come to Actor.

'Sir,' one of the officers said behind them. 'One of the Apasans is gone.'

Actor raised his brows at Cela, who tried to keep the smile from her lips. 'Who?'

'The quartermaster, sir. Cosmas.'

'How?' Actor said, this time addressing Cela. 'I watched you all board the ship. I counted you again myself once we set sail.'

'He is a good swimmer,' she shrugged.

'We are five miles from land.'

'An *excellent* swimmer.'

Actor stood in front of her, face a hand-length away. 'Where is he going?'

'To save Desma.'

'So are we.'

'There can be more than two paths to the same destination.'

Actor gritted his teeth. 'If we return without him, I do not know what the king will do. He might kill Khufu out of spite.'

Cela stepped forward until their noses almost touched. 'We will all be returning to Koriithos, War Leader,' she said. 'Trust us.'

'You have no idea the trust I have placed in you,' he said softly, his breath hot against her face.

She had not noticed the slight stubble on his chin before. Or the warmth emanating from his skin. She considered touching his face, gently, tracing her fingers from his temple to his mouth. Realising just how close their lips were to each other, Cela moved back, her heart pounding.

'Good night, Actor.' She turned, making her way below deck before adding over her shoulder. 'Oh, and Cosmas is not Apasan. Most of the crew aren't.'

'Where is he from, then?' Actor asked.

'Only the gods know,' she replied.

Groaning and the thump of steps. Desma dragged herself to her feet, legs spasming in pain, gasping. She hobbled the few tiny steps towards the door, waiting to hear if it would be bread or water coming her way.

The door to the cell was thrown open. Torchlight flooded the room and she cried out, her already stinging eyes blazed with pain. She fell back into the water, banging her head against the hull, splashing filth.

One of the men, who was nothing but a silhouette, gagged. 'Disgusting. Get her out of there and throw a bucket of soap water over her. I'm not putting her near the bishop reeking like a sewer rat.'

Desma froze. One word rang out in her mind like an iron bell. Bishop. *Camillus.*

She let the men drag her from the cell and throw her to the deck. After a few minutes shivering on her hands and knees, her face towards the floor, someone approached and hurled a bucket of water over her. It was freezing cold and softly perfumed with orange. Another bucket was placed near her with a brush.

'Clean yourself,' the man growled, stomping over to his companions.

Desma raised her head. The men were watching her. She turned away and inched towards the bucket, her arms and legs protesting. She gathered her hair, slowly lowering it into the water, bobbing gently as she pulled her fingers through the strands.

When her scalp felt marginally cleaner, aware the men were watching her, she dipped the brush into the bucket and began scrubbing herself. Her face and arms, pulling her dress up to clean from her knees down. Desma knew what the men wanted, but she would give them no satisfaction.

When she was done, she straightened and turned to her captors.

The man who had delivered the bucket nodded to the side. She turned her stiff neck and saw a dress folded on a stool. They wanted her to change in front of them. She did not dare ask for privacy. Instead, she collected the dress and turned her back to them, letting the soiled dress she was wearing slip from her shoulders to the floor. One of them whistled behind her, while another made a lewd comment.

Fire flared inside her, warming her frozen bones as she secured the new dress firmly on her shoulders with knots. Her dripping hair had already drenched the fabric through by the time she faced her onlookers once more. She let their eyes travel up and down her body, the dress clinging to her wet skin. Her hands clenched into fists, but she bore their stares. They were taking her to Camillus.

Eventually, one of them jerked his head. 'Let's go.'

They climbed onto the upper deck, the wind cutting but cleansing in its coldness. Desma tilted her head back and stared up into the sky. Stars glittered like tossed gems in the night. Wisps of grey and purple clouds floated under the waning moon. She was outside.

'Move,' the man grunted, pushing her forward.

Desma stumbled but kept her feet. She did not even consider escape. The quinquereme was one of the largest ships in the Middle Sea, a hundred and fifty feet in length and sixteen feet in width, with at least three hundred rowers and over a hundred soldiers. Twin masted, with the larger set further to the stern, it was a mighty warship. Desma had heard that the Empire had even larger ships, with six or seven hundred rowers. She could scarcely imagine the size.

Torches lined the rails on either side, bright enough to light the smaller mast that bore the Empire's sigil of wolf and axe, the swan and crown beneath.

Bile, hot and acrid, filled her throat.

How she wished she had Cisra's pendant, the gift for saving her sons. A strange stone that felt like glass, carved to look like a frond of calamint flowers, purple and green. But it would have been no use. To summon the sorceress, she had to smash it on stone, and she was on a wooden ship in the middle of the sea. Not to mention her necklace was lying on a table back in her room in Koriithos.

Camillus sat on a chair that had been tied to the main mast to keep it steady. She was shoved to the deck before his feet, her knees barking against the wood. Her limbs seized, and she stayed on her hands and knees, breathing through the waves of pain. Once it had eased, she looked up at the bishop.

He sat upon the wooden chair as though it were a throne, clothed in his red and white robes, a circlet of gold rose thorns on his brow. His eyes gleamed darkly in the torchlight, gazing down on her with a sly smile. How she wished her nails would turn to claws and slash the grin from his face.

'Good evening,' he said with a nod.

Desma remained on the deck, her eyes never wavering from his face.

'Wine,' he ordered. A servant stepped from the darkness. Camillus drank deeply, draining the cup. 'Another,' he said. This time he took only a sip. 'Thirsty?'

Her lips cracked as she parted them. 'Very,' she croaked.

'Hungry?'

'Very.'

'Rested?'

'Not very.'

'Good.' He took another sip. 'I was not at the Temple when Turan's wrath brought low the Apasan traitors—'

Desma hurled herself at him. Warriors blocked her path, and one slammed the butt of his spear into her stomach, sending her crashing back down. 'Please do not interrupt.' He continued calmly. 'I heard the beginnings of the battle, but did not wish to dwell among the muck and mess.'

'Murder,' Desma whispered.

'Speak up, child.'

'It wasn't a battle. It was murder,' Desma snarled. 'You attacked before dawn after a festival and slaughtered my people as they slept.'

'Slaughtered my people as they slept …?' Camillus cocked his head, waiting.

She gritted her teeth, bracing for the blow.

The kick sent her rolling across the deck, her ribs aching but thankfully unbroken. Someone dragged her back in front of Camillus.

'Try again.'

Desma spat at his feet with what little moisture there was in her mouth.

She shrieked when something whipped across her shoulders, arching in pain, and glimpsed another guard with a switch step back.

'Can't risk breaking anything serious,' Camillus explained. 'A switch is such a useful tool. Now, try again.'

'You slaughtered my people as they slept, *Bishop*.' The word was poison in her mouth.

Camillus clapped loudly, banging his ringed hand against the cup. 'Well done. You can be trained. Now tell me – where is the Belt?'

She looked at him with a stupid expression. 'The Belt? What are you talking about?'

The bishop gestured and she was switched again. Twice. Thrice. Her breath hissed through her teeth as she forced herself to swallow any sound.

'The Belt of Turan,' Camillus said softly, all pretence of civility gone. His words were feral and predatory. 'You will tell me who has it and where it is.'

Understanding slowly birthed in her mind. 'You didn't find it.' It was not a question.

'But you know where it is.'

Desma shook her head. 'I don't. I swear by the Holy Twelve. We thought you took it when you looted the temple.' She was switched again.

'It is not looting when we take the property of the Goddess to her true home,' he corrected. 'The Belt was not among the treasures and in no room within the temple. Your mother hid it. And you must know where.'

Desma's mind whirred. The last time she saw the Belt was the night before the celebration. Her mother had been wearing it in her room. She had not been herself. The sound of her keening and prayers through the night still haunted her. Desma had believed her mother would unveil it alongside the treasure from Urruc, but when it wasn't, she assumed it was because of the Empyrean presence. Cela's mother had said nothing of the Belt after the attack.

Camillus, seated like a dark godling, studied her at his feet in the dancing torchlight. Her mind flew back to Koriithos and her friends. She had no inkling how long they had been sailing for, but it could not have been more than a few days at most. They would still be sailing around the peninsula. She doubted it would have been more than an hour before it was discovered she was missing. Were ships in pursuit? The rowers were pulling at a steady gait, no double-time beat played on the drum. Had Gylippus even given chase? Or was he perhaps glad to have her taken off his hands? He could claim it was now an argument between his god and Turan over whose destiny she was meant to be following: a game piece in the hands of deities.

Were her friends safe? Would Gylippus release them or hold them as examples? Bile rose in her throat again. Surely he would not have them executed. He must know she was taken by force and would never voluntarily leave her crew behind.

The bishop sipped his wine. She did not have the answer he wanted, had no idea where the Belt of Turan was or what her mother had done with it. But nothing she said would have him believe her. It would be at least two weeks of sailing to reach Aventinus – for she had no doubt that was their destination – and she had no plan. She was stranded in the middle of the sea, on a ship with hundreds of Empyreans who would gut her with a sword given half a chance.

She was alone.

Bracing herself as the guard raised the switch again at her silence, Desma found herself wishing for the darkness of her cell.

CHAPTER SEVEN

Three days out from Koriithos, and Cela was pacing a hole in the deck of *The Darkling*, its wine-dark sails rippling in the breeze. They had scarcely covered over a hundred miles, and each night she got into a screaming match with Actor when he ordered the ships beached.

All she could think was what Desma would be going through in the hands of the Empyreans.

Before she slept and when she woke, she would make an offering to Ethausva, Goddess of the Hearth and Family. Desma was her sister in everything but blood, and she prayed to be reunited. On the second morning, Kassandra had joined her, the overseer carrying a young rabbit that they sacrificed with a silver blade.

The day was overcast, the sea turned to flashing sheets of metal that blinded the unwary eye. At least the wind stayed strong and consistent, but so it would for the Empyreans too.

Cela had dressed as the warrior she needed to be. Binding her hair in coiled braids, a simple piece of leather threaded through, she wore a chiton of soft brown, pinned at her shoulders with copper discs and girded around the waist with a bronze belt, from which hung her sword, its tooled silver scabbard glinting in the dull sunlight. A classic League short sword, though slightly thinner than normal to lessen the weight, it had been a gift from Theokritos, the gnarled commander of the temple guard in Apasa. He had presented it to her once he felt she would be unlikely to stab herself with a real sword, though she knew he had been joking. There were not many in Apasa who could best her in a fight, thanks to Theokritos. He had trained her hard and refused to treat her any gentler than one of his men. She had the scars to prove it.

Though her sword had drawn many disapproving and shocked looks from the Koriithosans, Cela ignored them, and even went so far as to have a sparring session with Bion to pass some of the time. When they had finished up, her hair slick from sweat and her breath ragged, she caught Actor watching her from the stern, his eyes guarded.

Cela stopped her pacing and approached the prow, letting the sea spray cool her heated skin, the bitter salt stinging her lips and eyes as she searched the horizon, desperate for a glimpse of sail.

Arete joined her, dressed in her characteristic short grey chiton, her brown hair tied in a single braid. Her hazel eyes stared off into the waves, but Cela could see they were not idle. Arete's mind was like an adze that was kept perpetually sharp, for it was ever at work.

'We are being slowed,' she said.

'What do you mean?' Cela asked.

Arete pointed at the two triremes trailing them. 'They are holding us back. We could be miles further ahead, sailing faster than a gull. But instead, we are being shackled to these lumbering logs!' the shipwright hissed.

Cela did not doubt her assessment. Arete had built The Darkling. Crafted of pine, fir, and cedar, stained a deep bronze with a single mast, it was a quarter the size of a trireme, needing only ten rowers. 'What do you want me to do?'

Arete turned to her, face set like stone. 'Talk to the war leader. He is standing over there, watching you.'

Cela glanced over her shoulder. Actor stood by the mast, back straight and arms behind his back, his eyes moving over the entire ship. They fell on her and Arete, then moved on without pausing. 'He is not watching me,' she said.

'Yet he is always standing in a place where he can see you.'

'That is not hard – it's a small ship.'

'Mhmm,' was all Arete said as she walked away.

Cela shook her head, but the shipwright was correct. *The Darkling* could move much faster. But how was she to convince Actor to leave their escorts and risk attempting to rescue Desma from a ship that held more than twenty times their number?

'This is madness,' she whispered to no one in particular, sending a prayer to Menrva for wisdom as she crossed the ship to Actor.

His young age still surprised her sometimes when she watched him giving orders to men over ten years his senior. But they treated him with respect, and she could see why. He was pleasant to be around, chatting to those who were off-duty, taking turns occasionally on the oars himself, and eating meals with his men. Yet, he was not afraid to dispense justice or knock heads together when tempers flared.

She remembered the night when they were in the woods hunting for the monster and Kassandra had slapped him. The overseer had been shamelessly teasing him, even going so far as to pinch his buttocks. When he returned the favour, she had smacked him and moved away. The memory made Cela smile – the shocked look on his face, the innocence of it.

Here was a man who led armies.

'Nethuns' blessings,' Actor greeted her, his smile reminding her of freshly baked bread – warm, soft, and comforting. She reprimanded herself silently. He was Koriithosan, and his duty was to bring Desma back to the city to marry his prince. While she prayed to all the Holy Twelve they would succeed, it still meant he was their captor.

'Tinia's light,' she replied. Before the sacking of the temple, she would have responded by calling upon Serene Turan.

'We've got a fair wind with us today,' the general said, looking up at the sky. 'We are making good headway.'

'But not fast enough.'

Actor cocked his head. 'What do you mean?'

Cela rapped her knuckles against the mast. 'This ship was built by Arete, daughter of a master shipwright, and she surpasses his skill. The ship might as well have wings it can sail so swiftly, but we have two giant anchors attached to its stern.' She pointed at the triremes behind them.

'What do you want me to do?' he asked, unknowingly echoing her question to Arete.

'Cut the ropes and let us fly. Give us an actual chance to catch up with Desma.'

He shook his head. 'That would be foolish. My king ordered us escorted, and we would have no chance in the Halls Beneath to fight against a quinquereme filled with the Empire's soldiers.'

'And what would it matter if we had a thousand warriors with us, if we never caught up to them?' Cela countered. 'Trust us. I don't know exactly what we will do when we catch them, but I know we will not catch them as we are now. Please, Actor.'

His wide brown eyes held hers before he scrubbed his face with his hands. 'Gods, you keep asking me to trust you, and *I do*. But when we return to Koriithos, I will have to explain my actions to the king.' He looked out over the water.

'He will see it was the right decision when you are presenting Desma to him, to be married off to his son like chattel.' She bit her tongue sharply.

Actor turned slowly back to her, his face set, eyes cold. 'Do not confuse my admiration for friendship. Koriithos is my city, my mother, my kingdom. I will do all in my power to protect her and my people. Desma is destined to save us. From what, I do not know. But I will drag her to the temple myself if the day calls for it.'

A shiver ran jagged down her spine.

He crossed to the stern, to look back at the other ships. Several minutes passed. Cela did not dare to break the silence, but she wondered if he had dismissed her.

With a sigh, she turned to leave when he spoke again.

'Very well,' he said. 'But assurances must be given.'

'Anything.'

Angry glares still pierced Cela's back, despite the fact *The Darkling* had disappeared beyond the horizon hours ago.

Actor had only permitted them to outsail the triremes if they left a member of their crew behind with them, and Cela had volunteered Kassandra. While the overseer had seen the necessity of the deal, it did not dampen her displeasure.

But it was worth it.

Unburdened by their escorts, the ship soared across the waves, the rowers roaring in time with the drums, sails full and fleet, as rich as wine. At times, it seemed they were barely touching the water, but rather gliding above its surface.

Actor could only shout enthusiastically at the speed and pound Arete on the back for her fine craftsmanship. Though the shipwright grimaced at the good-natured contact, Cela caught the gleam of pride in her eyes as she called out orders that somehow coaxed *The Darkling* to greater speed.

As the last lance of sun disappeared into the waves off their starboard, Actor called for the ship to head for land. They turned west and beached the ship in a cosy cove, a small stand of pine trees and a stream winding to the north offering shelter and fresh water.

Within a short time, they had fires burning, meat roasting, and wine pouring. Sentries were posted, and a few tents had been set up, though it was a nice enough evening that most opted to sleep under the wheeling stars. The moon sailed serenely by, her surface marred by a few wisps of cloud.

Cela gratefully accepted the roasted goat and fresh apples Actor brought her as she stretched her legs towards the flames, her toes digging into the cool sand. She tore the greasy meat into small pieces and popped them into her mouth, accompanied by the crisp crunch of apple. They shared a flask of wine between them and watched in silence as Delphinus tuned his turtle-shell lyre, the men gathering as he sang a few notes.

Already the piper had earned an appreciation from the Koriithosan sailors for his stories and song. His green eyes flashed, and his usually dull copper hair was set alight by the fires. He struck his lyre, voice ringing out like a bell that summoned all to hear.

'Friends, companions, travellers, rescuers. Come and rest. Drink, eat, be joyful. Night has fallen, the stars have been lit, and the sea is quiet. Let us all breathe in the darkness, and let our souls be comforted. Tonight belongs to Fufluns, God of Wine and Story, may his revels dance among us. I will tell you a tale this eve. A song of god-maiden, fair and delightful. A song of betrayal and foolish mistakes, of a mother's wrath and a love advantaged. Destruction untold. A people lost. Listen! And let tear and sob flow.'

Cela's food was forgotten as she listened. She had rarely heard a bard better than Delphinus, in court or temple across the League. And he was in fine form tonight.

The assembled crew listened with rapt attention as he told the tale of Phersipnai being taken captive by the people of an island kingdom, their greed driving them to unspeakable acts. Everyone was pale at the wrath of the goddess' mother, Horta, and the destruction she wrought upon them all.

When the lyre's final notes faded into the night and a deep hush laid on the assembled crew, Delphinus got to his feet slowly, dusted the dirt from his cloak, and walked out of the firelight.

Cela wiped the tears from her cheeks that had fallen unbidden. Actor's face was pensive, but she noticed his throat bob as he swallowed several times.

There was no applause or cheering. It was not that kind of tale. Her crew and the Koriithosans folded the story into themselves, spending the rest of the evening in quiet contemplation as the words seemed to linger, swirling amongst them with the smoke from the fires.

Cela bade Actor goodnight and laid on top of her bedroll, eyes fixed on the stars above as she thought of her own mother. Leonita was a beautiful woman, with wheat-gold hair and sparkling brown eyes, her skin a slightly darker shade than Cela's own honey-mixed milk. She was gentle and powerful, able to command a room and soothe wounded hearts. She had allowed Cela to be who she wanted, with no pressure to follow one path or the other. And while she treasured her daughter's close bond with Desma, she always reminded Cela never to lose herself in her friend. Her words rang in Cela's mind now. *Each have their own path. Ofttimes, portions of it will share the road with others, but the destination is never the same. Remember your own footsteps.*

Cela let her thoughts drift back to Apasa, with its cream and brown stone glistening by the lapping sea, scented with rosemary and roses, apples and myrtle. Her mother, standing proud in a rebuilt temple – though the reality would be years, if not decades from fruition – dressed in the holy garb of the high priestess. Cela's mouth soured; Leonita required a staff now to keep herself upright, her leg having been lost in the destruction of the temple. But her mother's faith in Turan was strong – stronger than her own. Cela could not pray to the Goddess of Love without seeing the smoke and blood, hearing the screams and ring of bronze in a place that had been her home. How could she go back to worshipping Turan after all she had taken from her? From Desma?

She rolled onto her side and imagined her mother wrapping her warm arms around her. Her scent of apple and jasmine soothing away Cela's worries, and letting her drift into a trouble-free sleep.

TALE OF THE DROWNING OF STOLEN SPRING

Far to the west, beyond the Mouth of Cel, lay an island kingdom renowned for its bountiful food. Trees and crops and herds flourished and prospered, for they were blessed by Horta, Mother of Farmers. Though many navies had been sent to conquer the island, Nethuns, Father of the Deep and lover to Horta, protected his love's jewel and its people fiercely.

But the island people grew greedy. Though they had food enough to feed themselves and half the Middle Sea lands, they craved more. They besought Horta to pour forth her blessings, to give and give of her bounty and power, until trees groaned with fruit, crops grew through all seasons, and lambs were born without pause. They plied their goddess with excess sacrifices, a hundred pure white cattle and a hundred emerald snakes. But Horta, wise in all things earth and plants, knew the importance of cycle and rest, so she refrained from granting their short-sighted wishes.

Soon, their requests turned to demands. Sacrifices made at her temples dwindled. Even her priests and priestesses grew bitter at her restraint and let some of her festivals fall from the calendar, her mysteries no longer renewed.

But Horta is patient above any other goddess. She let the island people throw their tantrum and continued to nurture the land so it prospered, giving them time to come back to her.

The island kingdom did not have a change of heart, however. Greed, deep and festering, had turned to wilful spite. Blasphemies slithered like rot towards her silent effigies, spoiled food left at her altars. They conjured a plan, foul and cruel.

Once a year, when the season of growth and spring returned to the world, Phersipnai – daughter of Horta, born of her union with Summanus, God of Night Storms – rose from her throne in the Halls Beneath; she left her husband Aita, Under-God and Keeper of Souls, and ascended to the upper world. Barefoot, she would emerge from a cleft in the earth on the island kingdom to step upon a field of purple and yellow wildflowers, bearing chests of precious metals and gems, gifts she would scatter across the lands. Always, her mother and the island people would greet her with dances and offerings and sweet wine. Maidens and youths would wait upon her, covering her body in flowers and spiced perfumes.

But this year, Horta was away in her city of Artas. Saddened at the passing of her favourite high priest, she entrusted the island kingdom with welcoming her daughter.

However, Phersipnai stepped into silence. A field stripped of flowers. The ground blackened and salted. Her feet burned and stung against the barren earth – a goddess of new growth confronted by death before its time.

She called, but none answered. Passed orchards, empty. Fields, abandoned. She entered the main city of the island, beautifully built of grey stone and festooned with bay trees. Stepped into her mother's temple, the largest in the world.

There, they sprang their wicked trap.

Dark spells and ancient herbs bound the goddess to the altar. Quick-witted, Phersipnai kept her mind about her and went to cast a counter spell, but smoke from a vile concoction wreathed her face and stoppered her mouth. Orichalcum chains, a celestial metal like molten gold suspended in flame, coiled about her limbs. The island kingdom had accomplished a task no other mortal in history had achieved ... they had kidnapped a goddess.

Only Horta's ancient secrets, gifted in love, had enabled this betrayal. The high priests, once stewards of her rites, had twisted her teachings into a snare.

The island kingdom bled Phersipnai's divinity into the soil. Their crops burst with abundance, richer and sweeter than ever before. Apples like rubies, peaches like orbs of setting suns, grapes that caused men to fall on the ground in ecstasy. Meat melted like butter, milk tasted of honey, and bread made from their wheat could keep a man marching for a day without falter.

Time passed, and Horta, still in Artas, grew concerned that her daughter had not yet visited her. She cast her mind across the lands and seas, but found her nowhere. Worry, like a bitter seed in her stomach, drove her to leave the city, walk across the League and beyond, heading westwards. Her voice crossed hill and mountain and vale, stirred lake and river, cracked the sleep of all who heard her, woke babes and sent beasts into fits.

Still, Horta searched, the seed growing into a weed inside her. The blessings her daughter brought for spring, new life and fresh growth, were missing in the lands she walked. Opening the earth beneath her feet, she lit a stone torch so it flared with blue light, and descended Beneath. She continued to call her daughter's name, her distress causing spirits and demons to flee from her presence. In his deep house, Aita heard the voice of his wed-mother and rushed to her side.

'Mother Horta, what is wrong? Why have you entered my kingdom and caused such distress among my denizens?' Aita asked, white robes falling into smoke at his feet.

'Where is my daughter?' Horta cried, hair wild. Her robes were dirty from her journey, her eyes laden with dark rings.

'She left weeks ago to ascend, as she does every year,' Aita answered, alarm rising in his voice. 'I saw her step onto the world above and closed the path after her.'

'Then something has happened,' Horta said, hands clutching his robes. 'I cannot feel her, and the earth is not renewing. What could have befallen her?'

'I do not know. You must find her. You know the laws. I cannot leave my kingdom except by decree of the Holy Twelve,' Aita said. 'Please, Horta. Find my wife, your daughter.'

Horta left his beseeching, returning to the upper world and found waiting She Who is Goddess No Longer, whose covens Artimi adopted under oath to protect. The Old One had heard Horta's calls and had felt strange magicks in the wind. For spells were her domain, be they mortal or divine, and she sensed such spells that made her blood curdle and hair twist. Spells wicked enough to hold fast a goddess.

'Where?' Horta demanded.

'The island kingdom in the far ocean,' the Old One replied.

Clarity struck the goddess with the force of one of Tinia's bolts. Knowledge she had imparted in good faith to a people beloved, now turned against her kin. It was a betrayal that would never be repeated.

Darkness spread a blight in her soul, the stain of rotting fruit and curdled milk, of golden stalks diseased, and tilled soil washed away by storms. Power, great and terrible, wreathed her limbs and raised her hair in a furious crown. She crossed the land and sea to the shore of the island kingdom. The people ran to safety, her footsteps creating great cracks in the ground as she approached the city. But at its gates, she found herself barred by magic flavoured with her daughter's blood.

Screams ripped from her throat as she cast her own spells. She wrenched hair from her head and threw it at the walls. She gathered gravel from the ground, grinding the stones against her skin until they were drenched in golden blood, then scattered them viscously against the gates. But to no avail. For none could undo the magic of a goddess, not even another god. Not even a mother.

'People of the island,' Horta raged, her words reaching every corner of the city like glass shattering against metal, 'I know you have my daughter, Phersipnai, trapped in my temple. Release her, and pray I find mercy in my heart. Keep her, and I will break you until your very name is lost upon the waves. Do you hear me?'

Silence was her answer.

Horta threw back her head and screamed again. Her cries reached the heavens, and the Holy Twelve looked down.

Tinia gazed upon the island, saw the pain of Horta and the trials of his niece. But if he were to come to the rescue of every one of his family who got themselves into trouble, he would never have time to govern the world. He turned away.

The other gods shrugged off the issue. Horta was a powerful goddess. It was better to stay out of her path while she dealt with the annoyance.

Driven wild with grief, Horta turned to her magic. Curses writhed from her like the serpents that pulled her chariot. Orchards groaned and cracked, sheaves of wheat fell like waves crashing on the shore. Fruit withered on the branch, in the hand, in the mouth. Lambs and calves wasted away in front of their parents. Grain became ash, wine turned to vinegar, honey bitter on the tongue. All the island people cared for was ruined before them, poisoned beyond consumption.

They turned to the temple and begged the high priests to release Phersipnai. Fearing a revolt, the priests cast off the goddess' chains and led her, exhausted and sallow, to the city gates. When the doors opened and they beheld Horta in all her terrible glory, they grew frightened and pushed Phersipnai from the city, tripping her into the stone and dust, before slamming shut the gates.

Their fear sealed their fate.

Horta flew to her daughter's side and drew her far away from the island, back to Artas, where her true people rushed to care for her. They washed away the dirt and bruises, wrapped Phersipnai in the softest wools, burned holy incense, and anointed her with oil of pomegranate and narcissus.

Once her daughter was safe and rested, Horta let the hate flow in her heart once more.

She returned to the island kingdom to find the people still hiding in the city. The farms and food they were once so proud of lay soiled and rotting. But it was not enough. She waded into the sea, letting the dark waves wash across her feet, her calves, her thighs, as her voice rang out across the waters and into the unknown depths, calling for her lover.

The waves roiled at his approach, and from the sea emerged Nethuns, God of the Deep and Father of Monsters, for it was his kin that delighted in terrorising citizens and gave heroes a chance to earn their fame.

'Nethuns, my love, holder of my heart, I ask a favour of you,' Horta said as he clasped her in his arms.

'You have but to ask,' he said into her hair. He had felt her pain during her search, but could not step onto land to help her.

'I wish you to break this island.'

Her lover reared in surprise, but her eyes flashed resolute. He saw that no salve he could give her, no consolation he could offer, would calm the hurt she had suffered. Nothing but destruction.

So he raised his four-pronged fishing spear and struck it upon the shore.

The earth split asunder before him, spreading across the island. Mountains cleaved, trees fell, and houses crumpled.

But it was not enough to satiate her wrath.

Horta called for more, demanding the god to wreak her revenge upon them.

Nethuns obliged.

He scooped up the sea in his hand and flung it across the island. Springs and streams turned from sweet to salt, rivers of poison flowing through the heart of the land.

But rage flowed unstemmed in Horta's mind and heart. 'Drown them.'

Nethuns hesitated, but the goddess grabbed him in a fierce embrace, kissing him with a passion that crossed into pain. 'Drown them all,' she said again as they broke apart.

And so the god did.

Nethuns retreated into the sea and called upon his powers over the tide. A hundred waves rose from the endless western ocean, taller than the mightiest mountains, rushing with inexorable speed towards the island.

The people watched as the sun darkened behind the waves, clutching to each other as death, birthed from a mother enraged, hurled itself upon them.

When the sea receded, there was no island. No temple. No name. Only empty waves.

CHAPTER EIGHT

The door wrenched open, lamp light scorching her eyes. Desma turned her head as rough hands grabbed her arms and pulled her out of the black cell.

Another bucket of soapy water was cast over her, and again the men leered as she changed quickly into a dry peplos that hung too loose on her frame. Her slick hair dripped down her back, and her feet left wet prints behind her as she was escorted from the lower deck.

The quinquereme moved swiftly through the waves as the three hundred rowers heaved in perfect harmony. Sunlight, clear and pleasing, struck her face and Desma threw back her head, a smile spreading her lips. It had felt like an age since she had seen the sun.

Perched on his seat by the mast, Camillus was clothed in a simple chiton of cream and a sage himation, a bright ruby clasp pinned to his shoulder, his sandals adorned with gold. But his hair was ruffled by the wind, and his usually trimmed beard had grown longer during the voyage. He plucked a peach from a bowl in his lap, using his thumbs to tear it in half.

'Sit with me, Desma,' the bishop said, waving a juice-soaked hand to the deck by his feet.

The guards pushed her down, swiftly tying her hands and feet with rope. She could move her arms but could not stand.

A waterskin and plate of food were placed next to her. Bread, dried goat, figs, and hard cheese. The food made her stomach twist, but she said nothing as she carefully broke off a piece of cheese and tore a corner off the loaf. She forced herself to chew slowly, her eyes gazing out to the sea. She refused to let the bishop see how starved she truly felt.

Camillus watched her with knowing eyes as he chucked a peach half into his own mouth and chewed.

Minutes passed in silence between them. Desma turned from the sea and watched the crew move about the deck, attending to the hundred and one things that ensured the ship ran smoothly. It was a beautifully crafted vessel, sleek and dangerous. Made from cedar and pine, the hull was painted a vibrant red, with bronze shields lining the side, and at the bow, just below the waterline, Desma knew there would be a bronze battering ram, designed for breaking other ships apart.

She kept her eyes away from the sail and the sigil of Turan.

'How many days has it been?' she asked, still observing the Empyrean crew at work.

'Since?'

She bit her lip to silence a flippant response. 'Since Koriithos.'

He took another bite of peach. 'Several.'

That could mean two days or ten. It was roughly fifteen days to sail from Koriithos to Aventinus, but it would not be difficult for a vessel this large to shorten the time.

What awaited her in the Empire, Desma did not know, but she knew none of it would be pleasant. Camillus sought the Belt of Turan, one of their most holy relics, for it was part of the Goddess herself.

She remembered when she first held the Belt in her hands. It appeared simple when first looked upon – a plainly woven, green belt. But it was so much more. Flowing bands of green, fresh sea foam threaded with flashes of starlit dew. To hold it was to feel the scent of the first rose, the smoke of applewood, the sigh of lover and loved. It was beyond the world and wholly of it. Creation and power. Divinity.

All knew the story of Turan's birth. When Tinia slew the Being known as Firmament and cast Its body into the sea, the Being's dying power and blood mixed with the waters of the Being that would become the Ocean – birthing a goddess so powerful that the Holy Eleven made her the Twelfth, if only to assuage her vengeance.

Waves and coral carried Turan from the depths to step upon Apasa's beach. Goddesses descended to craft her clothes from Turan's own newborn power, and Nature itself circled her waist with the Belt. The same Belt she gave to her first mortal lover, a youth called Atunis. The only mortal to ever betray and reject her. To break the Goddess of Love's heart.

Stories told that she had given him the Belt as a gift, and when he left her, he took the Belt and hid it from the world. Yet Desma had found it in the cursed city of Urruc, in the tomb of the Sand-King, a man who lived hundreds of years before Atunis was born, before even Turan's birth.

But then the Grand Temple was sacked, and now Desma did not know where the Belt was. Nor did she care. She hoped never to see again. But Camillus – and Aventinus – obviously did not believe her. They risked political war to infiltrate yet another kingdom and steal her away.

The Empire's cruelty was well-known throughout the League. Desma had witnessed firsthand their disregard for lives lost when the object of their desire was within reach. A cold hand clamped over her heart. Her next steps would have to be carefully chosen.

She opened her mouth.

'Tell me of Urruc,' Camillus said suddenly, turning his calculating eyes on her.

This was not what she expected him to ask, but she should not have been surprised. All the League and Empire knew of her triumph in bringing the treasures of Urruc to Apasa – the same treasures he had looted from her temple. He knew the Belt had been found in the city. 'What do you want to know?'

'Keep eating,' he urged. 'We will be here for a while, I hope.'

She picked up a fig and took a small bite before drinking from the flask.

He nodded encouragingly. 'I have never set foot in the city myself. I have met men who claim to have gone there, but there are a thousand tall tales for every one of truth. Tell me of the treasure's discovery.'

Desma took a moment to collect her memories. So much had happened, it felt like years ago, when only a few months had passed.

'It took us three weeks to sail across the Middle Sea,' she began, eyes moving from Camillus back to the water. 'We had to avoid Konosoan pirates in the Icarii Sea, and stopped in the town of Ithosin in the Kingdom of Pallan to resupply. From there, we dodged Empyrean ships, though it was not difficult.' The bishop ignored the barb, tossing a pit over the side. 'The sea was deserted within twenty leagues of Urruc. No fisherman or pirate or trader. The land was unlike anything I've ever seen in my life.'

'What did you see?' Camillus leaned forward, peaches forgotten.

She told it slowly, picturing it in her mind.

'Urruc's gulf is thirty miles wide, enclosed by cliffs. They rise out of the waves like giant walls.' Atop the cliffs, Desma thought she'd spied enormous tree trunks at first – thick shapes rising from the stone, weathered by wind and sea spray. But as they had drawn nearer, the truth had revealed itself. 'But it wasn't just cliffs. There were legs, two on each cliff point, carved from stone.' One pair had snapped off at the knees, while the other remained intact up to the waist. No one aboard could say what they had once depicted. Gods? Kings? Some forgotten heroes of a drowned age? 'They must have stood at least two hundred feet tall,' she added. 'Taller than anything in the League or the Empire – or even the Great Lands. I think ... I think they were the once-great gateway to the city.' The crumbling guardians of Urruc.

'I care little for the city's geography,' Camillus said, cutting her off. 'Speak of the tomb.'

Unsure what exactly the priest was after, Desma saw no harm in telling the tale and continued. Most of Apasa knew it, as they made no secret of their adventures once they had returned. Except for what happened when they opened the tomb itself. That, she only told her mother.

The tomb was located in a magnificent ziggurat near the centre of the city. Rising up four stepped terraces, it had miraculously survived the Fundament's destruction. Desma recalled her feelings of exhilaration as they climbed the long staircase to the gated entrance of the first terrace. After weeks of searching and dodging death hidden in the sands, she had reached the final path. Though doubt still tainted the surety she fought to hold tight, she knew Turan guided them, even though she could not enter the cursed land herself. How Desma now rued the goddess' attention.

There was little adornment until they reached the first terrace. They were greeted at the gate by a large tower, open on four sides, and covered in crowned, robed figures who gazed down on them. The men had beards wrapped in coils, and the women wore veils across the lower half of their faces. Lifelike lions, leopards, and hounds surrounded them, snarling fiercely with claws bared.

They stepped through the western doorway and followed a dry creek bed that would once have nourished an abundant garden. Now it was barren, with only a few skeletal trees that crumbled when touched. Cracked stone benches, statues with missing limbs, and empty vases kept silent vigil as they passed.

The entrance to the tomb was once hidden behind thick vines, according to the scroll that Desma had translated with the help of the elderly librarian from the oracular temple in Delphon. But it now stood open to the elements. Carved on its face was the Moon, the Being who once wielded the Light in the Night but was slain by Uni and consumed by her peacocks. Tiur had claimed its dominion and sailed each night, waxing and waning in accordance with her peace treaty with Nethuns, who held her son captive in his underwater palace.

It took the combined strength of Bion and Khufu to force it open, after hacking at its hinges with axes that chipped against the stone. Eventually, they could squeeze Bion's bulk through, and the rest followed. Inside was cool after being under the blazing sun that sapped their strength. Lighting torches, they moved through the corridor, gasps following their steps as the torches illuminated beautiful murals on the walls. Legends and battles long forgotten melded into hunting scenes into coronations. They could have spent weeks alone admiring the artwork, but Desma kept them on track. Columns carved in intricate patterns and the angular script of Urruc supported the ceiling above. She caught a phrase here and there as they passed: *Nammur walked through fire to save the child ... Ikshtir blessed the trees to give forth swords ... Ru-Hat fell into the sky and cried ... Mesanetep wrestled with Balulir and broke ...*

Busts of kings and priests wearing wise expressions jutted out of the walls. Stone weapons angled outwards, sometimes forming arches they ducked under.

As they had moved deeper into the ziggurat, Desma consulted the list of instructions painstakingly decoded months earlier at great cost to the temple coffers. At the rear, Kassandra left guides to find their way back, marks on the wall and a trail of red sand as insurance. Desma doubted they would be able to find their way out without them should she somehow lose her map.

Eventually, they came to a steep ramp that descended sharply. Tying a length of rope around each of their waists to form a connected line, they drove an iron stake deep into the floor to anchor them if they were to lose their footing before beginning the descent. Desma went first, leaning back with her hand on the wall, as she carefully placed one foot in front of the other. She remembered her eagerness, knowing she was minutes away from finding a treasure that would not only exalt her temple, but ensure her name was enshrined in the annals of the League for generations.

The air was dry and old at the bottom, the walls painted in broad strips of red, filled with smaller lines of black and grey with white stripes. They passed several empty rooms with old tools and stone slabs, whose purpose they could not guess. Soon enough, they found a doorway with a strange rune carved at the top, swirls of carved fire lacing down the archway.

Inside, they found a blank wall with the same rune, but this time with the symbol of the Moon Being behind it, a crown and sword on either side. The tomb of the Sand-King.

There was no door or way to unseal the stones. Bion, Khufu, and Delphinus drew out the packed hammers and began to beat upon the wall. Cracks appeared, and soon the carvings were smashed beyond recognition. Desma had felt a pang at the loss. Those symbols had stood for over ten thousand years untouched, and now they were gone. Her home, Apasa, was only two thousand years old, a youngling compared to Urruc.

After an hour of sweaty exertion, the men paused, panting. The wall was dented, but they had no idea how thick it might be. Arete, Kassandra, and Desma took up a turn. Cosmas merely leaned against the doorway, silent; he had been strangely withdrawn since they landed. He barely spoke, cooking meals in the morning and evening, and helping them search – often venturing out on his own. Though, when he thought no one was observing him, his face took on an expression of wonder.

They had replaced the torches three times by the time Bion's hammer broke through. With an exhilarated yelp, the Konosoan attacked the wall with renewed vigour, his arms rippling as they swung again and again until, with a mighty crack, the stone shattered like glass, falling to the ground in a hundred small pieces.

Tomb dust and debris billowed into the chamber as a scream pierced the air, raking its fingers down their spines. They whirled about, weapons drawn, shrill cries and ululating tumbling down the dark corridor towards them.

'Demons,' one of the Empyrean sailors nearby whispered, causing the bishop to shoot him an irritated glare.

Desma nodded. 'That is what we thought as well. But from the darkness ...'

Men, garbed in tightly fitted robes of white and grey and tan, had leapt from the darkness. Wielding blades that widened at the point with a vicious gleam, the assailants continuing to shriek as they descended upon them. Desma met one of the strange blades with her own, twisting to the side and elbowing her opponent sharply in the gut. The man grunted but fell to Arete's sword before he could straighten.

Desma ducked a blow and kicked out with her foot, hitting an ankle, the man tumbling into her sword. She pushed him away and continued to fight.

Dozens of men seemed to be piling into the too-small antechamber. Shouts and howls filled the small space until her ears were ringing.

Cela dodged a sword gracefully, flicking her own blade to slice off the offending arm, before driving it into the attacker's heart.

Khufu bashed weapons away with his winged axe, calling out challenges in his own language, a fierce sight.

Delphinus had lost all semblance of composure as his sword whirled about him, singing an old battle hymn. At times, he seemed to forget he held a weapon and would throw himself bodily at an attacker, bearing them to the ground, teeth and nails in play as much as sword.

Arete moved like a predator in the flickering shadows, sword striking without hesitation.

A blade scored across Arete's upper arm, and Desma dispatched the man quickly. Though they were outnumbered, her crew did not falter. Their attackers were wild but untrained. Eventually, their dead piling around them, the strange men fell back and melted into the darkness.

Desma had stood, panting, sword held ready in case they returned. After a few minutes, Cosmas disappeared after them. They waited, no one relaxing until he heralded his return. There was no sign of the tomb warriors.

Camillus was captivated.

'We weren't sure what to do next when—'

'Sails behind. To arms!' the lookout crowed.

Desma's heart lurched. *What colour are they?* she wanted to shout, but Camillus gave her no chance.

'Take her below,' he ordered, standing and striding past her. A peach rolled from his lap, and Desma managed to snatch it up before she was untied and lifted roughly to her feet. She strained to see beyond the ropes and men, to see the ship, but was shoved below before she could.

Within moments, she was back in the darkness, her legs in the icy water, the peach clutched to her chest. Was it *The Darkling*? Had they come to rescue her? Were they alone? How could her crew hope to take on the might of the quinquereme? She sent a prayer to Menrva, begging the goddess to protect her friends if it was them.

CHAPTER NINE

It was the seventh day of their pursuit, and Cela was practically chewing the mast in her anxiety.

The lookout thought he had seen a ship ahead of them, but a sudden storm appeared, and by the time it dissipated, there was no sign of the other vessel.

They had left behind the peninsula that held the kingdoms of Pallan and Phoroniaa and were halfway across the Aril Sea, only three days' sailing from the southernmost island of the Empire.

Actor's nerves were also getting the better of him. He asked three times a day what they had planned for when they caught up with the quinquereme. Cela would just smile and say all was in hand.

But the gods knew the truth. Arete spent most of the day muttering to herself as she paced the ship, and half the night scribbling in the sand with a stick. Each time Cela approached her, the shipwright would snarl and stalk away.

It was a seemingly impossible task. The Empyrean ship was easily six times the size of *The Darkling*, and they only had a crew of twenty-two, including the four additional men Actor brought on board when they left Kassandra behind.

Twenty-two versus at least four hundred.

And what would they do when they dragged Desma to the railing and threatened to slit her throat if they did not give up pursuit?

She felt like tearing her hair out.

But they were *so* close to Desma. They could not give up now.

Cosmas was also out there ... somewhere. Though it was hard to deny that Cosmas had proved his usefulness many times over, it was still difficult to trust the quartermaster given the history of how he joined the crew. But Desma had made her decision, and did not care to explain further to either Cela or Khufu. Desma was the commander, but Cela had never felt unequal to Desma before then; she remembered the fights they had the few days following Comas' acceptance.

It was the first secret between them, but not the last, as Cela had once hoped. There was what happened in Urruc, only told to her afterwards. Desma had not even consulted her. Then the forest with the monster – did Desma think Cela would not notice how she miraculously had a bag for the beast's head? And that whispered exchange with Cosmas outside the megaron. If Desma felt she could not trust her own second-in command, her sister ... what would happen if she did become a princess? A queen?

And then there was Khufu's message. *Akbahri*. What did it mean? It was obviously a code that only Desma would be able to decipher. Why would Khufu not give her the message plainly? Did he not trust her either?

Actor appeared by her side. 'If that was indeed the quinquereme, then we should catch up to them by evenfall.'

Cela looked at the general, his squarish face serious yet youthful, her eyes gliding across his profile, the muscles of his bare arm. She wondered if he had a wife or a woman back in the city. Or a man.

She frowned. Her sister was in danger, and here she was lusting after the man charged with her rescue. She huffed, ignoring his bemused expression and deliberately looking away to glance over the crew – it wasn't a rescue, it was a recapture.

Delphinus was absently strumming his lyre, humming softly, his mind never strayed far from Khufu, she knew. Bion sat beside him, spinning his great axe in his hands as he hummed along to the tune. Arete paced in front of them, speaking her thoughts out loud, with the occasional grunt from Bion.

'The prophecy about Desma becoming queen,' Cela said, switching subjects in her head abruptly. 'Is it from Nethuns or Aplu?'

He cocked his head to the side. 'Aplu. Though a priest of Nethuns travelled to Delphon to confirm directly with the Young Oracle. Once he returned, the prophecy was shared with the astronomers, and they searched for answers in the stars.'

'And yet none of you could figure out why Koriithos needs Desma to be queen.'

'Correct. The Young Oracle said, "The one who ends the monster's reign will be the monarch Koriithos needs to see it through the days to come."'

'As helpful as ever.'

Actor laughed. Oracles were known to obfuscate their foretellings until they were as clear as fog. Yet, once the event came to pass, their meaning became crystal. The Young Oracle, who resided within the Maze, was said to hear the future directly from Aplu himself. And her words were the most twisted of all.

The sun was setting before them, a great orb of white with rings of yellow that expanded into smudges of orange and red. The sea was turning a brilliant blue-black, the sky now clear of clouds. She looked into the sun, letting tears rise in the corners of her eyes. The white was marred by a wavering dot that looked a lot like ...

'Sails!' The lookout shouted from his perch. 'Sails ahead.'

Actor burst into action. 'Rowers, triple time. Dig deep, men. Row!'

The ten men, shirtless and already slick with sweat, let out a roar as they dug into their reserves. The ship jumped forward.

The crew roused themselves and stood along the bow, hands on weapons, as the dot turned to a blur, then a smudge, and at last an outline.

'Is it them?' Cela asked the lookout, bouncing on her heels, straining to see what he could, to no avail.

'I can't spy a sigil yet,' he replied. If there was no swan and crown, they were doomed. It would take them seven days to return to Koriithos in time to save Khufu. If they did not find Desma tonight, then they risked their captain being killed by the king.

The minutes stretched painfully, no one daring to speak. The ship crept closer, and all waited for the lookout to tell them if this was their quarry or not.

Gods, let it be, Cela pleaded.

'Again?' Desma asked when the door opened. This time, they gave her no chance to wash or change but bound her hands behind her. They dragged her so quickly up to the deck her feet barely touched the planks.

The sky was black, as the moon had not yet risen to any height. Camillus was again by the mast, but no chair was in sight. He held something behind his back.

What tactic would he take this time? Beating? Food? Storytelling? Was it his turn to share a tale from his childhood? If he thought for one moment she would ever forget who he was, then he was a fool.

Thrown with force onto the deck, her face smacked into the wood and split open her lip. She was pulled up to her knees, but doubled over again as a fist slammed into her stomach. Struggling for air, spit falling from her mouth, she had her answer: violence.

'No offer of hospitality tonight?' Desma managed to gasp out. 'Tinia would be disappointed at your treatment of a guest.'

A boot slammed onto her ankle from behind, and she cried out as bone broke. She fell onto her side, sobs choking her as pain splintered up her body. The guard who hurt her bent down and roughly grabbed her foot, wrenching it cruelly. Her back arched as another scream tore from her throat. She wanted to beg them to stop, but she shattered the words as they came to her mouth, so nothing but cries burst from her lips.

She refused to plead.

The guard grabbed her hair and pulled her upright, pushing her to sit back on her ankle. She forced herself to calm down, breathing heavily through the pain, and looked up at Camillus with a snarl twisting her lips.

The bishop's face was impassive. He wore his robes with a cerulean stole. His golden thorn circlet crowned his head, and his eyes had a hard, cold sheen to them. 'Tell me where the Belt can be found.'

She held his gaze and took several steadying breaths. When his hand motioned to the guard, she spoke. 'Trilos.'

He froze. 'What?'

Desma tossed back her hair, deep red in the torchlight. 'My mother spoke of sending it to Trilos. She was great friends with Castur, High Priest to Sethlans. She wanted him to guard it, though she did not confide in me her worries. I assumed it was because of you – and my suspicions proved true.' Her words were steadfast, despite the lies.

Camillus hesitated. He clearly had not expected her to give an answer. 'How do I know you speak truth?' he finally asked.

She shrugged. 'Why would I lie again? You have proven you are more than willing to hurt me, and I thought you had it all this time anyway. It serves me naught to keep the Belt from you. Retrieve it, with my blessings.'

The bishop frowned deeply, folding his hand behind his back. The guards shuffled behind her, unsure what to do. She kept her eyes on him, face smoothed over, as though patiently waiting.

'You know it would take me but days once we are in Aventinus to confirm whether you are lying to me or not,' he warned.

'Yet another point as to why I would not lie to you,' she countered. 'I am sure that Turan would be more than eager to check with her husband whether his devoted have her Belt.'

'Keep her name off your tongue,' Camillus snapped, nodding to the guard, who struck her a blow to the side of the head.

Dazed, Desma groaned as she righted herself, her ankle throbbing angrily. 'So now what?'

'What do you mean?' he growled. This conversation was not transpiring as he had intended.

'I've told you what you wanted to know. Once you've confirmed where the Belt is and retrieved it, what is to become of me? I've done nothing to you, despite the crimes you have committed. Would I be free to go?' She was stalling, hoping that once they were on land she might have a chance of escaping.

'Free?' Camillus laughed. 'Why would I free such a valuable possession?'

Dread washed through her. *Possession.*

'I am no one's belonging,' she said softly.

'Last week that was true,' he said, revealing what he had been holding behind him. 'Last week you were a queen-to-be. Today, you are my slave.'

She froze at the sight of the item cradled in his gloved hands.

It was a long piece of flexible wire, but every inch along its length had a shard of metal woven through. It ended in a leather handle, which he held as he gave it a snap to loosen its coil.

'What is that?' she hissed, instinctively shying away from the twang it made as he whipped it back and forth.

'We call it thorned wire,' the bishop said with a cruel smile. 'We use it to subdue the more rebellious slaves. It is most effective when used against their families.'

Vomit rose in her mouth. She knew the Empire could be cruel to its slaves, but if this was a glimpse into those poor souls' lives, she cursed whatever god gave them such misfortune.

'Turn her around,' he ordered.

'No, no, no, no, no,' she begged, not caring about her earlier promise to herself. Desma could already see the wire glinting in the torchlight as it flicked towards her. Could already feel the sting as it hit her back, the stabbing pain as the shards dug into her skin, the tearing as it ripped her flesh open when it withdrew to strike again.

She thrashed as the guards tried to twist her around, yelping in pain as she flailed about. They bound her legs together from knee to broken ankle and held up her arms wide and far like a lamb trussed for slaughter.

'Don't, please, don't do this,' she whispered, fear clenching her throat as Camillus passed the whip to a guard, before stepping forward to tear open the back of her dress with his own hands. He grabbed a fistful of her hair brutally and buried his face in her coils.

'So beautiful,' he murmured wetly into her ear. 'I was sad when I heard my men had cut off your mother's hair. Such a shame.' He pulled out a small knife and viciously cut a thick lock from her head. 'But yours I will enjoy for many years to come.'

She screamed.

Then her world turned as the ship lurched violently to the side.

Desma fell to the deck, rolling several times before she came to a stop. Camillus kept his feet but dropped the knife, desperately holding to both the mast and Desma's hair. Her guards had fallen and were trying to get to their feet as the ship rocked back.

There was a shout from the bow lookout, and the ship slammed violently backwards. Desma braced for it but still rolled, gasping as her ankle flopped about.

Rowers shouted, heads twisting around as they searched the dark sea.

More screams and the groan of broken wood. *Had they hit a reef?* she thought dazedly, pain clouding her mind as adrenaline faded from her veins. At least she had a short respite from her torture. But then hooks were tossed over the railing from the sea, clattering against the wood and shields as they caught and were pulled tight.

'Pirates!' someone shouted, and the deck exploded with activity. Half the rowers abandoned their oars as they lurched to their feet, running to the quartermaster, who tossed spears and swords to them from the storeroom.

Finally, Desma understood. Ships must have hit them, cloaked in darkness, battering into the sides. But who would dare take on an Empyrean quinquereme bearing the sigil of a goddess?

Giant men leapt onto the deck, clothed in loose tunics with wide belts, bearing great axes and bellowing war cries. *Konosoans!*

Despite being taken by surprise, the Empyreans responded quickly, and soon two hundred men fought with sword, spear, and arrow against the invaders. The Konosoans established a foothold on deck and fought recklessly to gain ground, allowing more men to follow them. And women, Desma noted, clad in loose tunics as well, legs and forearms covered in bronze armour.

Camillus had vanished.

Desma dragged herself across the deck, her legs still bound, until she came to a bench abandoned by two of the three rowers. The third ignored her as he strained against his oar in a futile effort to free the quinquereme from the pirate ships that held it fast.

She could not believe her fortune. Konosoans did not traffic in slaves. If she could only get the attention of one of the pirates, she could plead for them to save her. Once on their ship, she could tell her story and only hope they pitied her enough to take her to Koriithos, or at the very least to the closest port.

That plan fell away as a figure vaulted onto the ship with the second wave of pirates. Desma's mouth dropped open.

'Cosmas,' she cried out, waving her arms frantically. 'Over here.'

Cosmas immediately spun towards her voice, despite the din of clashing blades and yelling. Daggers flashing, he cut down any Empyrean in his path once he caught sight of her. Ruthless as an undercurrent, he coldly dispatched anyone foolish to believe they could cross blades with him and live. His eyes, as blue as a thick sheet of ice, glowed in the fire and shadows. They were empty of compassion as he disembowelled an Empyrean, leaving the young man gasping on the deck, sidestepped a sweeping sword and slipped his knife beneath the assailant's arm, shredding through tendon and artery, before seizing another warrior's wrist as he slid past a blade, spinning the man in a ghoulish dance until the Empyrean faced him once more. Then Cosmas, with a dark smile, drove the dagger up through his chin.

The four pirates following him were almost unneeded, simply ensuring the deaths of the quartermaster's victims as they passed.

'I can't believe it's you,' Desma said when he dropped by her side, throwing her arms around his slim shoulders, ignoring the blood splatter. 'You don't know how handsome you look to me right now.'

He allowed the embrace for a moment before pushing her gently away. 'You will need to curb your desire for the moment,' he said with a ghost of a smile on his face. 'At least until we're off this ship.'

'This is your woman, eh, Potimes?' one of the pirates asked. He had an immense, scruffy beard. 'She is beautiful. I can see why you had a bee in your robes to get her back.'

'Potimes?' she asked, looking at the quartermaster.

'Long story,' he said quietly. He scooped her up effortlessly in his arms. 'Let's get her back to your ship.'

The bearded pirate put a hand on his shoulder. 'Our deal?'

'Will be honoured the moment she is safe,' he said, eyes turning hard.

'Very well,' the Konosoan laughed. 'Let's get your woman aboard.'

The pirates surrounded them in a protective circle, and they moved across the deck, cutting down Empyreans as they approached. When they reached the side, Desma saw a trireme below, the front of it embedded in the side of the larger ship.

'Ready?' the pirate asked. Cosmas nodded.

'How are we going to get down ...' Her question turned into a shout as the giant man picked them up and hurled them overboard. She heard laughter before the wind whipped it from her ears. They plunged through the air, and Desma buried her face in Cosmas' flat chest as he twisted at the last second before they slammed into the side of the Konosoan ship, her broken bones grating with the impact. Cosmas clung one-handed to a net that hung over the side and flashed her a grin as they were hauled swiftly upwards and onto the deck.

Women clustered around them. 'Care for her,' Cosmas said, before spinning and grabbing a rope that was pulled taut between the ships, scurrying up with speed to disappear back onto the quinquereme.

One of the women, with beautiful green eyes and curly brown hair framing a kind face, knelt beside her. 'Where are you hurt?'

'My ankle is broken. Some bruises. And I could do with a bath.'

The women laughed. 'You could at that,' the kind woman said. 'Tell me, child, did any of them touch you?'

It took Desma a moment to understand her words. 'No, thank Artimi.'

'Rest, my dear. You are safe. The others will return soon once they secure their prize.'

She wanted to ask further questions but she was so tired, and for the first time in gods know how long, she could let down her guard.

She let her mind drift as they stripped and cleaned her, giving her a sweet, hot drink that dulled the pain before setting her ankle. All the time, sounds of battle raged above. She wasn't sure how long passed before there was a great explosion and the night sky filled with fire. The pirates leapt from the Empyrean ship back to their triremes and took up the oars, pulling away from the flaming quinquereme. Quicker than she thought possible, they turned eastward and were sailing swiftly away.

Away from her prison and Camillus.

CHAPTER TEN

Desma blinked her eyes open, grogginess making the simple action difficult. The sky was a deep red, with the sun a circle of blood. Her throat constricted in fear for a moment before the sky moved and she realised she was looking up at sails.

Red sails.

'Cela?' she croaked, her throat dry.

Her friend's face appeared above her, eyes creased in concern, her golden hair a halo about her. 'You're awake,' she exclaimed.

'Barely.' She struggled to get her elbows beneath her. 'Help me sit up.' Cela assisted her, piling pillows behind her back until she was upright.

She was sitting beneath the mast on a bedroll, dressed in a brown peplos and her hair was loosely braided. Her broken ankle was propped up on a low stool, splinted and bandaged.

Spying a jug nearby, she asked, 'Drink, please.'

Cela fetched her a cup. Desma's arms shook a little as she lifted it to her lips, but most of the water fell into her mouth. She had not realised how weak she had become.

As she looked at her friend's face, hot tears slid down her cheeks. 'Hug me?'

Cela threw herself on Desma, arms crushing her in the most comforting way. Desma buried her face in Cela's shoulder and let sobs wrack her body, crying silently. She did not know how long she had been with the Empyreans, but it felt like an age. Darkness and fear, finding strength in a deep well, only for it to putter out like a candle ... the image of the thorned wire.

'Thank you,' she whispered to Cela. She had wished they would not follow her or risk their lives, but the relief at being surrounded by her friends, to be safe again, was overwhelming.

Feet shuffled nearby and when she looked up, her crew surrounded her, except for Kassandra and Khufu. 'Thank you,' she repeated.

'As though anything short of Tinia himself descending from the heavens could have stopped us,' Bion said gruffly, eyes blinking suspiciously fast.

'And what a tale this will make,' Delphinus said with sparkling laughter. 'The Race to Save the Queen of Koriithos!'

Arete swatted at him.

Cosmas leant against the mast beside her. Desma gave him a grateful smile, and he nodded his head once, arms folded.

'Tell me everything,' she said, turning back to the rest of the crew.

Arete stepped forward to relay the events since they were violently separated in the throne room after Desma's purification.

When she got to the rescue, Delphinus finally cut her off. 'Please! You have butchered the story to this point. Allow me to at least give the climax the respect it deserves.'

'Go on then.' The shipwright threw her hands in the air. 'Poets!'

The piper gave a wide grin. 'Let me grab my lyre.'

'No,' Bion ordered. 'Just tell Desma. We don't need to be here until twilight with your flowery speeches and epic choruses.'

'Spoilsport,' Delphinus groaned, sticking his tongue at the helmsmen, who blew him a kiss.

'I think it would be best for Cosmas to speak with Desma,' Cela said. 'Give her some peace.'

After some mild protest, the crew departed, Bion throwing his arms around a sullen Delphinus.

Soon it was only Desma, Cela, and Cosmas by the mast. The quartermaster raised an eyebrow at Cela, who met him with a frown. The moment stretched until Desma poked her in the ribs. 'Give us a few minutes, please?'

Her friend nodded and got to her feet, giving Cosmas a final stern look before heading slowly to the bow, glancing back several times.

'Sit beside me,' Desma said, and Cosmas slid down to the deck gracefully, long limbs folding under him. His pale blue eyes held a curious light. 'Tell me how you came to be on a Konosoan pirate ship.'

The Konosoans held a large island to the south of the League, the ancestral home of Tinia before he took his holy court to Quirinale in the Empire. Though the First Spear and King of Konoso both swore the pirates who plagued the lesser waters within the Middle Sea were outlaws, they did nothing to stop them. In fact, the pirates were often very well-equipped, and traders reported their ships docked on the island being repaired.

'Khufu told me to do what I must to get you back,' he said, speaking softly. 'So I did. I stole a team of horses and rode across the peninsula from Koriithos to Phoroniaa, and then to a seaside town called Kybris. From there, I chartered a ship to take me to a small island to the west. It is not much more than a permanent sandbar, but it is known to be a stopping place for pirates waiting to catch ships crossing the Aril Sea. Fortunately, there were two ships beached on the island when I rowed up in a small boat. The Konosoans were curious at the sight of a lone man approaching them. They listened to my proposition and agreed to sail at my direction.'

'Which was?'

'My direction?'

'Your proposition.' She scowled playfully.

'To be honest, they were eager at the chance of spilling Empyrean blood. They have still not forgiven them for what they did to First Spear Demetria in the Battle of Palachiro. And I promised them any and all loot aboard the quinquereme.'

She waited. 'And?'

'And a thousand gold drachmae and a hundredweight in gems upon our return to Koriithos,' he shrugged.

Desma was shocked. It was an incredible fortune, but then she remembered that she was soon-to-be royalty. 'Let us just hope Gylippus is not as tight-fisted as he looks.'

Cosmas jerked his head towards the stern. 'War Leader Actor did not seem concerned when I advised him of the promise.'

Desma glanced behind her. Cela and Actor stood close together. Her friend threw back her head as she laughed, letting the noonday sun glitter in her locks. 'They've gotten close.'

'He is a good man,' Cosmas said simply.

She raised a brow. High praise coming from him. 'What happened to the Empyreans?' To Camillus.

'We slew many of them, looted the ship, and set flame to sail. We crippled it well. They will probably be able to limp the rest of the journey to Akren on the east coast of the southern island.'

'But how did you get across the island so quickly? How did you find the ship when you had all the Aril Sea to search?' She did not understand.

'Sleep was not necessary when you have a dozen horses. And pirates are excellent at finding their prey.' He reached out and took her hand, his skin smooth and cool against hers. 'I saw the cell they held you in,' he said gently.

She turned away, wishing her hair was free to hide her face. 'How long?'

'Seven days.'

Seven days. It only took seven days to nearly break her. It would have been sooner if Camillus had brought out the thorned wire earlier. She was wise enough to know that she would not have been able to stay strong under such torture.

'Did you see the bishop?' she forced herself to ask.

He shook his head. 'I discovered he was on board when I found his crook.'

She looked at him, puzzled.

'The golden staff he carried in Apasa. It is a head taller than he is and curved at the top, similar to what shepherds carry in the mountains. But this one ended in a rose, and the length was studded with gold thorns.'

Recollection hit her. He had carried it during the celebration held at the Grand Temple. It had looked vicious, despite its holy function.

'But I saw no sight of him,' Cosmas continued. 'I was not able to search the whole ship before we had to return to the triremes. Otherwise, I swear under whatever god you wish, I would have taken his heart with my bare hands.'

She clasped his hand back tightly. 'So are we being followed by pirates back to Koriithos?'

Cosmas gave a small laugh. 'No, they would prefer to avoid the royal navy. Once we return, I will arrange for payment to be delivered.'

'They are very trusting for pirates.'

'They know of me. I will keep to my word.'

Another story for another time.

'So back to Koriithos to save Khufu we sail.'

Cosmas beckoned Cela over. 'I think Cela better speak to you again,' he said, before sliding to his feet and walking away.

Confused, she waited for Cela to return, noting the tightness around her friend's eyes. 'What is it?' she asked before Cela could take a seat.

'Khufu told me to give you a message when we found you,' Cela said slowly. 'I do not understand it, but he said you will. He told me to tell you, "Akbahri".'

Akbahri. Her brow furrowed. Was it a word in his home language? Or a place? No – it was a story. One he had told her in Urruc while they had been sitting around the fire.

'It's a tale about an ancient king from a country that was conquered in the Great Lands,' Desma said. 'His name was Akbahri. He told his people to flee the city, remaining alone to negotiate with the invaders. He promised he would find them in three days' time, by the river's curve. So they waited. On the morning of the fourth day, a farmer volunteered to go back to the city. When he arrived, he saw the invaders had made camp within their homes and their sigils adorned the palace. He asked a passing soldier what had happened to the king. The soldier told him how the king had sent his people away to find new homes, and then asked the warlord to take him in lieu of his people. The warlord honoured his request and cut the king's head from his shoulders himself. The farmer returned to his people and told them what had occurred. Weeping, they walked from their home and into the desert, searching for a new land to call their own.'

'I don't understand,' Cela said.

Desma did. 'He is telling me to run.'

Cela clutched her arm tight. 'We cannot do that,' she said fiercely.

Desma was silent for a moment. Khufu was opening the door for them to turn the ship and run from Koriithos, from the prophecy, from her crown. They would be free as long as they never returned to that kingdom. She could disappear. Never to be bothered again by the machinations of crown or temple, hidden from both Koriithos and Aventinus. She could finally find a little hut on some mountainside and disappear into obscurity, surrounded by wine and goats. Khufu would die for her to have such a life. A life unremembered, but hers. A history that would fade as quickly as smoke from a campfire. She would have peace. But he would have death.

'Desma,' Cela pleaded.

Meeting her friend's wide eyes, she said, 'All speed to Koriithos.'

Khufu sat in his cell, watching drops of water fall from the corner of the ceiling into the puddle. It made satisfying *plonks* as each drip rejoined its brethren below. They had moved him from the opulent apartments that originally housed the crew. Now he was truly a prisoner, awaiting his sentence.

Though the cell was not uncomfortable.

It was wide and clean, except for the constant puddle. He had a slim window where he could see the canal cutting through the isthmus and watch the ships sail up and down. He could not really complain, as he had slept in worse. There was a cot on the far corner from the puddle, heaped with blankets, a stool that he currently sat on, and a bucket for his ablutions that was emptied morn and night.

The food was regular and plain, but there was plenty of it.

Seven days since *The Darkling* had sailed from harbour, seven nights he had spent in the cell.

The star-seer, Hyllos, came to visit him a few times. He was trying to be kind, but Khufu had no desire to strike a friendship. He answered the astronomer's questions simply and let the conversations die off.

A wisp of breeze made it through the window, carrying the scent of salt and the sweet decay of flowers. The blooms that had wreathed the city ahead of Desma's marriage to the prince had begun to die, and workers scurried about collecting them in heaps.

Seven more days for the crew to return Desma to Koriithos. Seven days between him and death. But he had made his peace.

Desma deserved her life, for she had given him the chance to find a home, a family, and a purpose. What greater goals could there be? Simple memories and immeasurable joys. She had given him a world he could claim as his own with pride. And it was with that same pride he would give her a chance to find her own.

Though this was not the city where he thought he would meet the final friend.

His home in Opuni was far to the south of the Middle Sea, deep within the Great Lands. Built from the clay of the same earth it stood upon, Opuni stretched as far as the eye could see on a clear day, blending with the land, pocketed by small farms and orchards and fields for grazing.

But what made Opuni famous were its spires. How he wished to have been able to show them to his crew!

Some were as thin as a man and others as broad as an elephant. Crafted from solid gold or silver or marble or clay studded with a thousand gems, they soared into the sky. Most buildings in Opuni were only two or three stories tall. The spires reached as many as ten. They were scattered throughout the city with little apparent rhyme or reason. Many visitors would remark when they saw one spire in the middle of a street, another in a park, and one in the middle of a stream.

The reason was because it looked beautiful and brought joy to that spot.

They were the wealth of Opuni. What materials the city did not need at the time were constructed into a spire the people could all enjoy. When gold or marble was required, a spire was melted or broken down. It was a clear sign to the people of the richness of their city. To try to steal any part of a spire was a crime none of his fellow citizens could fathom even contemplating. But people from other lands would always try. The first offence meant losing the right hand and left foot. A second offence meant death. No leniency was given.

That was why he bore no ill will towards King Gylippus. He had a city of thousands to rule; Khufu had only ever held the lives of a couple hundred in his hands, and his actions did not dictate the course of a kingdom. Many thought mercy was weakness, and that strength was ruthlessness. But the act of allowing the sword to fall, and knowing when it had to be swung, was a wisdom only won by wearing a crown. Or being a captain.

Though the king's actions were fuelled by anger, even betrayal, they were not rash or cruel. There was a strength in making the dark choices, to spill blood when needed, to cause pain if it meant preservation. Desma knew some of this, but she still had so much to learn. It was a hero's duty to walk the paths cast in shadow – but they had to do so by keeping the light in their heart.

All his youth, Khufu had been fascinated by descriptions of a body of water so large you could sail for days and never see land. Water that tasted bitter and salty. Water with animals larger than elephants that swam in the sea and could crush ships. So he had left Opuni as a young man and travelled north. He crossed grasslands and desert and jungle, until he reached a city where the people had skin the colour of dry earth and great cats roamed the streets and were treated as spirits.

It was there he first saw the sea and realised he would never return home.

For he had found it. His heart's song. In tide and sail and brine.

There were many who never found the peace and purpose of their life.

He wondered who would come to collect his soul: Vanth, the fierce winged demon-goddess who brought souls down to the Beneath, or the guide of his own people, Eowu. A gentle spirit wreathed in green smoke, Eowu would come to the people of Opuni and carry them into the eternal grasslands, filled with endless rivers and spotted with singing trees.

In seven days he might have his answer.

CHAPTER ELEVEN

Curse the vile harridan, Camillus swore bitterly in his mind. He prayed her soul would be torn to shreds on the bank of the blood rivers so she may never know the blessed peace of the Crocus Vales.

A great groan sounded behind him, and he turned in time to watch the main mast of the ship tilt sideways as its base split apart. It fell slowly, as though loathed to be parted from the ship, smashing the railing before flipping into the sea. The sigil of the blush swan bearing a crown of roses slid into the water, vanishing into the depths.

'Captain,' Camillus screamed.

Several soldiers nearby shuffled about before one of them was pushed forward. 'Your Holiness,' the young man stuttered. He had a bandage wrapped around his head and blood trickled down his temple. 'The captain was slain last night.'

He gritted his teeth. 'Then who is in charge?'

The man was shaking. 'I think it would be Atrus, Bishop. He is below at the moment.'

Camillus grabbed him viciously by the ear. 'Get him,' he hissed, shoving the man away.

The whole mission was a disaster.

He'd had Desma in his hands, the Belt all but in his grasp. The girl had said the high priest had it in Trilos. He would know soon enough if that was truth. But if it wasn't …

He would need to face the Holy Mother when they eventually made it back to Aventinus. At this rate, he would need to secure horses in Akren and ride across the island. He had several days to consider how he would explain the events to her.

He did not understand what had happened.

His Goddess, Golden and Serene Turan, had smiled upon his sacred mission. He had whisked the girl out of the very palace of Koriithos. She had been aboard his quinquereme, surrounded by four hundred men.

How the Koriithosans had recruited the help of pirates was beyond him. The two ships had quenched every torch and sailed in complete darkness to ram into the bow and starboard. The ship was now taking on water and half the rowers had been killed.

That thin man with the white hair and blue eyes – he had been a demon in the night. Dozens fell to his blade, as graceful as water as he flowed between sword and spear. Though he was ashamed to admit it, it was from that strange man Camillus had fled. He had hidden in a barrel half-filled with mushy vegetables, staying there until he heard his men looking for him, knowing then it was safe to emerge.

If only he had taken the wire to the girl the moment they were on the ship! He would have had her singing the glories of Turan within hours.

If only they had not been slowed by avoiding League ships in the Aril Sea, cautious about being stopped and searched, as was common since the attack on Apasa.

If only.

He fell to his knees, fingernails scoring his cheeks as he cried out to his Goddess. 'Turan, Love of the World, Your greatness and beauty are unmatched among mortal and divine. I beg of You to show me the path. My life is a tool in Your hands. I am devoted to restoring Your Belt back into Your holy presence. Goddess, Heart of my heart, I am on my knees before Your power. Guide me as I fulfil my mission. Hear me, O Goddess.'

He fell forward, hands landing on the deck as he breathed heavily.

The sound of splintering. He grunted as two sharp pains lanced through his hands. Slowly, he raised them, staring at the green tips of thorns that pierced through. He turned them over to find a pink rose thorn impaling both palms, blood collecting in pools in his cupped hands. His Goddess had answered him, but Her message was unclear.

Was this a blessing or a curse? Was this guidance or wrath?

Only time would tell.

But in his hands he beheld the power of his Goddess, divinity in blood.

Thesan, Goddess of the Morn, had flung open the doors to her palace, and a rosy dawn shepherded the last vestiges of night away.

The sky was filled with a soft blue and gold light, mist clinging to the horizon but dissipating swiftly before the rising sun. A chill wind blew from the north, raising pimples on Desma's arms as she stood at the ship's stern, staring at the wake of their passing in a froth of white and deep blue.

It was dawn of the seventh day since her rescue. They had to return to Koriithos tomorrow, yet many leagues stretched before them. Time was not just running out – it was being swept away by a typhoon. And she was helpless to increase their chance of making it back in time. There was only so much strength in a muscle, so much wind in the sky, so much prayer she could utter.

She leant on a crutch Cosmas had procured for her, keeping weight off her broken ankle that throbbed persistently, reminding her of its existence despite her best efforts.

The Konosoan healer had told Cosmas that it was a clean break and should heal in six or so weeks, dependent on her not running around on it. In the week they had been sailing back to Koriithos, Cosmas had watched her like a mother hawk, appearing at her shoulder when he felt she had been moving about too much to guide her back to her cushions. She had begun to curse loudly whenever he approached. He only ever responded with a slight smile, otherwise ignoring her completely. The crew were no better. They had started to report to Cosmas throughout the day on her movements. She would like to know who decided that the quartermaster was suddenly her carer.

Fortunately, she still had time, as he had not yet come to nag her. She felt as though she would snap the head off whoever dared approach her next.

On cue, there was a stamp of sandals and a polite cough behind her. She turned to find Actor waiting. She sighed.

Cela had told her all of what Actor had done to help them. He convinced Gylippus to let her crew set sail. He had left the triremes behind to ensure they caught up to her. He had put his own honour in danger when he vouched for her word in the king's court, standing by her story of how she killed the monster plaguing the kingdom, unknowing that he had bound his honour to her lies.

But for six days, she had avoided speaking with him. He had approached several times, but after a word from Cela, he had kept his distance.

War Leader of Koriithos, general to the king. A role that usually went to haggard and hoared men, weary from battle but eager to relive the glory through younger men and women. But he was young – about thirty or so years. Only ten years older than her, though she felt like she had lived enough in the last few months to satisfy the lives of several people. Perhaps they had more in common than she thought. She was avoiding him because of who he represented, what her return to Koriithos meant. But he had stood up for her once before ... maybe he would stand by her again.

'I must thank you for everything you have done for me,' she said quietly, turning back to face the sea.

He remained silent as he stepped forward to her side. He wore a simple tunic with a red belt, sword strapped to his side, and bronze greaves gleaming. She remembered his boyishness while they hunted through the woods for the monster that turned out to be one of Cisra's sons. A witch from legend, centuries old and powerful beyond measure. It was because of her Desma learned she herself possessed a magic that had never existed in the world before. She had the power to unravel spells, whether the caster was human or divine.

There was a single rule, unbreakable by all, even Tinia himself: no one can undo the magic of a god, not even another god. And yet, she had cast off the curse laid over Cisra's sons by Turan, restoring them from their grotesque beast-forms back to that of young men, giving them back their humanity.

Through Cisra's enchantments, she had managed to fool everyone into thinking she had slain the monster. Her crew, the king, Hyllos, Actor ... all except Cosmas.

Actor had nearly sacrificed everything he had earned in life to support her lie. If the king had continued to call out her falsehoods, Actor would have lost all honour and standing, disgraced. But it was necessary. Those two young men – mere boys when they were first cursed by Turan, who twisted Cisra's magic as she tried to save them – had been trapped in bodies not their own. They did not deserve to die because of the machinations of a goddess.

'You are to be my queen,' Actor eventually replied. 'I would lay down my own life for yours.'

'You have known me for scarce weeks,' she pointed out. 'How can you offer such loyalty so readily?' Devotion was not unfamiliar to her, for that was how both the guards and the community at the temple felt towards her mother. She was their beating heart and, before the very end, their binding cord to their goddess. Desma, too, would have done whatever her mother had bidden. But to have the general of armies say such a thing to her ... what had she done to deserve that power?

'I think, of all Koriithosans, I may know you the best. I spent days with you, saw how you commanded your crew, how you treated the farmer and his family we came across on the road. But when we saw those people that brigand Stolos had put in a cage ... you didn't hesitate. There was no other option except to rescue them. This is a queen I can serve with honour.'

She did not know how to respond. She was to be a queen. Khufu had given her a chance to run, to escape the destiny she was pushed towards. But after all the crew had risked saving her, how then could she abandon one of them in turn?

Once they returned to the city, she would speak with Gylippus and Hyllos again. Perhaps other options existed. Maybe they could delay the marriage. Anything.

She could already feel the weight of the crown on her head.

'I am going to go check on the crew.' Desma turned awkwardly with her crutch and hobbled away, feeling Actor's eyes on her back as she crossed the deck.

She found Arete further down the port side, absently weaving strips of fabric together. The shipwright nodded as she approached. 'How's the ankle?'

'I've had hangovers worse,' Desma joked, leaning her shoulder against the shipwright.

Arete's brow was furrowed, and she missed a plait before swearing and angrily undoing her work.

'What is wrong?' Desma asked.

Arete's shoulders slumped. 'I am still trying to figure out how to rescue you.'

Desma looked up and down the ship. 'I am rescued ... aren't I?'

'Yes, but only because of Cosmas,' Arete growled. 'I had days to draft a plan on how we could have extracted you from the ship, and I came up with nothing!'

Desma kissed her friend's head. 'I am safe. Because of all of you. You have never let me down, and Menrva has always blessed your talents.'

'Maybe if I had another statue from Urruc to offer,' Arete quipped, a smile tugging her lips.

Desma jostled her shoulder with a laugh, before almost losing her balance. Arete steadied her, but not before Cosmas appeared out of the air like a wind god, his face pinched with concern.

'I know, I know,' Desma said, resigned. 'Time to sit.'

He guided her to a pile of cushions and gently helped her lower herself.

'How can one broken bone make life so difficult?' she cursed.

'Next time, have them stomp on a toe,' Cosmas suggested.

'Go away.'

'As the princess commands.' He bowed as he strode away.

'Bastard,' she called after him, waving at Cela as she came over with a bemused expression.

'Not very queenly language,' she chided.

'Not you too, please gods,' Desma moaned. 'How far are we from Koriithos?'

'We are drawing level with Pallan, but time is not on our side,' Cela said. 'We are over thirty leagues from Koriithos. *The Darkling* is swift, but we will be hard pushed. The wind is also not on our side, despite our offerings to Asra of the North Wind to abate and Sera of the South Wind to rise.'

Desma nodded. They had passed the two triremes that had set off with the ship. They had stopped long enough for Actor to communicate with their captains. Kassandra had waved enthusiastically from the rails at Desma. But they again could not be slowed by the bigger ships, and Actor refused to allow the overseer back onboard *The Darkling*. He said they could be reunited back in the city. Desma had relented. 'We will row through the night,' she said.

I will not let you die for me, Khufu.

CHAPTER TWELVE

It was still dark when footsteps approached Khufu's cell. He had not gone to sleep but knelt by the thin window, gazing at the stars and the black sea.

The door opened, and six guards in full armour with plumed helms waited outside. The star-seer, Hyllos, stepped inside, bearing a bundle under one arm.

'Khufu,' he said sadly. 'It is time.'

He nodded. 'My request?'

'Granted by the high priest,' Hyllos said, passing over the bundle.

Khufu released a pent-up breath, opening the bundle to find his clothes from his homeland, ready to carry him from the world as they had carried him through it. He stripped out of his Koriithosan garb, unashamed by his audience, and pulled on loose trousers of fine wool, dyed a forest green with yellow thread. Next was a sleeveless tunic of red and cream. His gold torc had also been returned and he clasped it about his throat, the familiar cold a balm to his mind.

His weapons were not included, though the astronomer promised his sword and axe would be kept safe. He wondered how long it would be so – at the least, until it was clear his crew were not returning.

He had no doubt they would rescue Desma. He just prayed she understood his message. And, more importantly, listened to it.

It would not be safe for them to remain in the League for a while, and they would not go to the Empire. Maybe they would go south to the Great Lands and visit Opuni as they always promised. The thought of them exploring his city brought a smile to his face. Maybe the ancestors would let him become a guiding spirit, so he might be able to see them on their travels.

He squared his shoulders, towering above the men in front of him. 'I am ready.'

The six surrounded him, with Hyllos leading. They left the cell and entered a corridor lined with similar rooms, heading towards a metal door. They emerged in the palace proper and met with a squad of an additional twenty warriors. Khufu smiled to himself. Six men he could defeat. Twenty-six was a little beyond his prowess.

Two priests of Nethuns also waited in robes of brown and green, a strip of rare cerulean cloth tied around their brows. They each bore a staff of driftwood with silver shells rattling musically as they led the procession. What a strange god to worship. A father of beasts and monsters that were blights on civilisation, yet the peoples of the League rejoiced at the chance for their heroes to earn their names. Perhaps it would be better for Eowu to collect him. He loved the people he had met in the kingdoms, but he did not love the League itself. And it would be good to see his mother and aunts in the grasslands.

They walked through the palace, exiting through the rear gates and joining the paved road of green-streaked marble that led up the cliff to the temple.

A circular building, it was constructed of the same verdant and white marble as much of the city, rimmed with columns carved with seaweed and coral. Three steps led up to the temple entrances, except for the main door, that had a ramp guarded by Regorus the Black Serpent and the Many-Armed Kreban, monstrous children of the Sea God, who guarded their father jealously. The roof was slated with red tiles, and at its pinnacle was a twenty-foot-tall, four-prong fishing spear of weathered stone.

Citizens lined the path to the temple, men and women in dour clothing. Men flashed with jewellery and muttered darkly; women looked on, half in spite and half in fear. Warriors were spaced to keep the crowds back, but no one pushed forward. They watched in a fitful silence.

His heart began to race as the weight of their eyes settled on him. They had come to witness his death, but they shared no emotion. There was no final gift of their cheers or sorrow or songs. They would watch him as they watched the sun set, a spectacle but not a memory.

And thus would end Khufu, captain of Apasa, born of Opuni. Alone in this sadly angry city. A bead of sweat stroked down his temple, collecting in the corner of his lip so he tasted salt. He had never craved a warrior's death, though he did not fear it. He would be proud to die protecting his friends, his commanders. But he had always seen himself falling peacefully from life in his own bed, by himself, but in the knowledge he was part of a community. Here, he was simply alone.

One of the priests prodded his side with a staff, and Khufu proceeded down the ramp.

As he walked past the lines of unfamiliar faces, he began to picture those whose images were as second nature to him as his own.

He remembered the games he played with his sisters in Opuni, the delights in seeing men as pale as goat milk visit the city with strange clothes.

He remembered setting foot on a ship for the first time, suspended over water that was fathoms deep.

He remembered standing before his first crew as their captain, pride swelling his chest as he shouted orders.

He remembered winning his first games, crowned by a golden laurel at the hands of the Queen of Pallan.

His breath steadied and his heart settled. His bare feet let the cool marble usher away the sweat from his brow.

He remembered fighting outlaws in the hills of Tethalia with Desma and Cela, retrieving gold stolen from a temple.

He remembered dancing on the perfumed beaches of Anama, lost in revelry and petals, and spending several glorious days with a woman whose name he never knew.

He remembered watching Desma standing proud on her ship as they sailed from Urruc, the treasure of legends in their hold, her face both serene and troubled, her hair like wine in the wind.

His heart became a feather, his body a seed of grass, his mind smoke to the breeze.

The doors to the temple stood open, two giant slabs of white stone painted with the likeness of Nethuns on each side. The god was portrayed as a large man, his scarred chest left bare, with a grey beard down to his waist. He had wide eyes like a deep-sea fish, rows of shark teeth, and a striking nose. Upon his brow was a crown of flashing scales and sea froth.

The left door showed the god as a benevolent but resolute ruler, his face stern yet wise, with arms held wide to welcome petitioners. The right showed the god prepared for war, fishing spear in hand, a whirlwind of water surrounding him as he faced down his foes with terrible righteousness.

The temple was filled with the scent of pine and brine. The floor was covered in pristine white sand. Tall vases were filled with coralline and sea anemones, carved in intricate detail from coloured stones.

He was led swiftly through and out the back to the edge of the high cliff. A paved terrace extended past the tip of the cliff, a path to the sky framed by two tall stone torches. Koriithosan lords watched on, an audience to his death. Gylippus stood next to a man, heavily robed and covered in blue ribbons, who must be the high priest. To the side was the young prince, his face pinched, though Khufu could not tell from what emotion.

Looking out beyond the men and the cliff was a beautiful vista. An unparalleled view of the harbour ringed by the wet cliffs. To the left was the mighty canal, its bright blue waters funnelled into the darker Aril Sea. The sky had brightened in his short journey from the cell, the pre-dawn light growing as the sun journeyed to breach the horizon. The few stars left in the sky glinted weakly as they bid farewell for another day.

He wondered if the astronomers had seen this moment when they read the future in the cosmos.

Pausing at the top of the stairs to take a deep breath, he inhaled the brine sharp and sour, a scent that was as home to him as the sun-heated sands and grass of Opuni. Closed his eyes. Listened to the sounds of seabirds crying and the creak of wood from the ships below, the rhythm of the tide moving. His body began to sway, caught in the memory of moving with the sea, and he released the last worries binding him to the steps. One final moment of peace in this realm.

He opened his eyes and continued his journey.

'Faster,' Desma shouted, ignoring the barking pain in her ankle as she clung to a rope at the bow of the ship, spray dashing against her face. The wind had finally blessed them an hour ago and blew strongly north-west, filling out the wine-dark sail.

They were so close. Koriithos was a growing smudge on the horizon.

They had rowed continuously since yesterday, her own crew taking turns when the rowers slumped exhausted.

The sky was greying at an alarming rate, Thesan not pausing in her duties to herald the dawn. Desma sent prayers to her as well as to Artume, Goddess of the Night, to linger as long as they could.

The Darkling glided upon the waves, flying like a sea eagle, every plank and cord tight with speed. Arete could have built no finer ship in the Middle Sea.

'Faster,' she called again, though she knew they could give no more speed. They would have won gold at every race within the League at this rate. They were well within the gulf that Koriithos shared with Athanai. The lookout had shouted moments earlier that he could spy the isthmus, but he was blessed with far sight. It was still miles away.

The sea behind them was starting to sparkle, catching a few glimmers of the light Thesan was casting forth.

They were so close.

Silence fell among the assembled lords and priests as Khufu walked forward. He came to a stop a few steps from the king and high priest. Hyllos placed a hand on his arm and Khufu looked down on him.

'I ...' The astronomer cleared his throat. 'I am sorry.' He stepped away before Khufu could reply and disappeared into the crowd of men.

Khufu turned back to the king, who had a scowl marring his weathered face. He was clothed in a dark grey chiton and matching himation, trimmed in white thread. His sapphire crown sat atop his grey-streaked, black hair. He held an ancient spear in his hand, its shaft made of black driftwood and tipped with a smoky-grey metal. Khufu was glad that Desma would no longer be a plaything in this king's clutches.

Beside him was the high priest, the many blue ribbons a walking reminder of the temple's wealth. He was not much younger than the old king, his face scoured by salt and wind until a thousand tracks covered his skin. His eyes were shadowed by heavy brows, his head was bald.

He raised a hand, though there was no need to quieten this crowd.

'By word of our king, Gylippus son of Morsimus, we are this dawn to sacrifice this man to our Father of the Deeps, Nethuns, Lord of Waters Salt.' The priest's voice was strong and carried far. 'An agreement struck has been broken, and thus recompense is required by laws both common and divine. This has been sanctioned by the temple. Bring him forth.'

The warriors prodded him forward and pushed him to his knees at the very edge of the cliff, capped in marble to avoid crumbling. The sea below was churned by large boulders to the side of the canal. By instinct, his body wanted to throw himself backwards, away from the danger, the sinking feeling of plunging. A fall from here was certain death.

Yet chains weighted with rocks were still wrapped about him, strapping his arms to his side and his legs together to ensure he sank to the bottom. His breath quickened as the metal rubbed roughly against his skin. He had walked, unaided, to the very edge, and yet still they had to bind him, cage him, place their mark upon his body.

His heart began to beat faster as he pictured slamming into the rocks below. Plunging into the freezing water. Gasping as the sea flooded his mouth, throat, lungs, drowning him until darkness swept him away.

He took a steadying breath. And another. Another.

Calm settled about him like a mantle. He wondered if it was the League's Goddess of Peace, Esia. She would be a goddess to show kindness even to a stranger. Though the League had been his home for over twenty-five years, he had never felt comfortable taking up the worship of their gods.

Part of him hoped that he would be taken to Aita's Beneath, to be judged by the Three-Who-Speak-Doom, and be sent to the Crocus Vales. Because that meant one day he would get to see Desma, Cela, Arete, Delphinus, and the others again. He had not been able to say the goodbyes he desired, but he could not have given any of them an inkling that he hoped they would not return. And he would not trade that decision for any amount of years or gold.

'I am ready,' he said to the assemblage, though no one had asked him.

The sun burst from the horizon like a daffodil blooming, sudden and beautiful.

Fear was a vice strangling her heart, tears mixing with the sea, as Desma strained forward over the bow, willing the ship to greater speeds.

'Give it everything we've got, for Tinia's sake,' she yelled, watching the wave of light roll over the ship, racing them towards the city.

'Move!' Bion roared, hurling an exhausted rower from his seat, taking his place, bulging muscles rippling across his shoulders, chest, and back as he heaved mightily on the oar. Delphinus also took the place of another weary man, grim determination set in his face.

She heard Arete and Cela's voices rise up in a keening song as they called upon all the gods of the Holy Twelve, a plea that cut deep inside Desma, begging them to intervene in any manner.

Actor joined her at the bow, his face set in stone as he raised his arm high and slashed a knife downwards, scoring his flesh from palm to elbow. Blood, brilliant and bright, sparkled in the wind, drops landing on her face and in her hair. He thrust his arm over the ship so it flowed into the sea.

'Nethuns, god of my city,' he prayed, voice full of sorrow. 'I pray you hear me in far off Viminalis. Listen to a son of your first city. Listen to a warrior who has honoured and fought for you his entire life. Turn your attention to our plight. Send us swift waves and strong winds. Give our men strength to row like heroes. Please, Nethuns, God of the Deeps and Lord of All Seas … help us.'

Desma remembered when Arete had promised a statue of Urruc to Nethuns, when they had seen the Empyreans first arrive in Apasa. A groan had emerged from deep below, and their ship had lurched forward in a pool of froth and foam to speed them to the harbour.

But there was no answer to Actor's prayer.

They were alone in this race, ship versus the dawn, life or death the prize.

'Gods be damned,' she swore. 'We're coming, Khufu.' Fresh tears started to fall. 'We're coming.'

Dawn had risen, the sun cloaked in all his blue and gold glory, crowned in faint blushes, and adorned in the scattering of light upon the waves.

The light touched Khufu's face, warm and gentle, welcoming all to the day's embrace.

Farewelling him to the Beneath.

A priest went to bind a cloth over his eyes. 'Please,' he said gently. 'Let me go into the next world with the sight of this one in my eyes.'

The priest looked towards the king, who nodded assent.

The high priest rattled a driftwood wand covered in coral and gold starfish. 'We give this man, his blood and flesh, to the realms of our god, Nethuns of the Holy Twelve, Dweller within the Sea. May his soul find just judgement in the Halls Beneath.'

A sturdy hand fell on his shoulder and another in the small of his back.

He whispered in the tongue of his home. *May the mothers of my line embrace me with open hearts and welcoming songs.*

He looked past the harbour, filled with ships and small island temples and statues of gods on rocks thrusting from the water. He looked out at the open sea and let the water soothe him before it claimed him.

He looked out and saw the outline of a ship cutting towards the city, emerging from the dancing lines of sunlight, sailing faster than Khufu had ever seen in all his days of racing.

Saw the wine-dark sails.

'Desma,' he said softly, a release of breath from his mouth that dissipated into the air.

'It is time,' the king rumbled.

'Desma,' he said again, louder this time, as his chest swelled at the sight of the crew racing to his salvation.

'What?' the man holding him asked.

'Praise Nethuns,' the high priest declared.

Khufu opened his mouth when he was shoved.

For a moment, he disconnected from his body, watching as it tipped forward, eyes wide with surprise. Bound in chains, he could not move, and the stones tied to him were kicked over the edge, pulling him faster.

He slammed back into his body as he fell from the cliff, falling like lightning towards the swirling blue and white waters.

He let the sea take him.

CHAPTER THIRTEEN

Mynta crumpled the parchment, her eyes burning from the words she had read.

Strewn all around her were dozens of papers and scrolls, a detailed story of her father's business deals and trades. A glimpse of the lives crushed, dreams shredded, businesses obliterated in Linos' rise. Mynta supposed he had not taken them with him. They contained nothing truly illegal, only distasteful. Though perhaps her father didn't find it so.

She read about a shopkeeper in the northern quarter who refused to supply wine to their household. Her father purchased the vineyard that supplied him and set up a rival business opposite, undercutting his prices at a loss until the shopkeeper went out of business as he struggled to find stock. Another showed the thugs he hired to stand outside another business, scaring away any customers until the owner agreed to Linos' terms.

She had found two receipts written in simple terms that made her shiver at the dark behind the words. *The problem won't return.*

Her father was currently the emissary to Apasa, spokesman for his kingdom to its closest neighbour. Once a trader of some renown, he'd added to the empire built by his father and grandfather before him, until wealth had as much influence in their home as the gods. But theirs was not an idle god. Linos did not just want gold and secured trade routes – he wanted power. And so he began to charm councillors, using his influence and promises of friendship to buy the votes to join Trilos' Council. Within a year, he was emissary. A lifetime of work to be among the most powerful in the shifting tides of politics, rarely bested and often only overruled by the Prime.

This she knew from snatches of conversation she had overheard all her life. Her father bragging to his friends late into the night as they drank wine and mead; musing with his wife during the afternoon heat as they strolled the courtyard garden; jealous whispers of lesser men at functions, when Mynta had been all but forgotten to the shadows clinging to corners.

But now she saw those moments in a different light. Her father joking about the backs he broke on his climb to the Council. Her mother's gentle words offering solutions and helping her husband figure his next move, her fingers sparkling with the riches of those who could not outmanoeuvre Linos. The bitterness of his rivals that coveted what he obtained.

She remembered the dozens of times she watched her parents dance at parties, laughing as they shone and glimmered in their silks and gold, safe in their nobility, sure of their place in this world. Mynta had been proud of her family's standing in Trilos, of their influence and significance. Now it left her mouth filled with ashes.

But what had they stepped on to get where they are now? *Who* had they stepped on?

She got up from her father's old desk and left the room, unable to stand reading another word. She had been so oblivious. She knew her father was not the kindest man. The way he spoke to her, belittled her, used her as a bargaining chip. But to see the things he had done ... was her mother aware? Or did she turn a blind eye as well, caring more for her bright riches than the nature of the shadows that sourced them?

And Mynta had cast him down, thrown him out. Had he thought, even once, of taking revenge on her, his own daughter?

Her chest chilled, and she rushed into the outer courtyard, desperate to feel the warmth of the sun on her skin. She closed her eyes, face turned upwards, letting her breath settle at its own pace.

Her nursemaid's shuffling steps hastened towards her.

'I am fine, Anesidora. I just needed the light.'

'If you could refrain from worrying an old lady into the hands of a Charun early, that would be appreciated,' her nursemaid grumbled. 'What troubles you?'

Mynta waved back towards the house. 'I was reviewing my father's business practices. Some of them are ... unsavoury.'

'As tightly as men cling to gold, they are willing to spill blood for its sake. But such is the world, and who are we to change things?'

Mynta opened her eyes, troubled, when someone called from the other side of the gate. She waited while one of her guards opened it, poking his head outside, before pulling the door fully open. 'A messenger, my lady.'

'Enter, please,' she said, folding her hands in front of her as the youth approached with a bow.

'Lady Amynta. My master, Duris, wishes to extend an invitation to dine this evening at his home. He has news of your venture and would like to return the hospitality of his previous visit. What answer may I convey?'

It had been two weeks since the gold was exchanged, her household running on enough drachmae to barely fill two pouches. She had seen her mother spend more on her dresses in one afternoon. But this was what investment was all about – risk and reward. She could only give offerings each morning to Turms for success.

But now the master merchant was asking her to dinner. Mynta did not know how to answer. Her father or mother should accompany her. She could not go to an unmarried man's home alone.

It was different when the merchants had come to her. They had come in number during the middle of the day when her full household was present.

But to dine at night ... with Duris.

'I will see him at sunset,' she said in a rush, heat creeping up her cheeks. 'Please provide directions to my guard.'

She spun on her heel and headed into the house. What was she doing?

Mynta waited until the litter was lowered to the ground, accepting a maid's hand to get to her feet. The sun to the west was a darkening pool of peach and blues, a hand outstretched to clasp the nightfall.

Duris' home was smaller than her own but still grand, the garden sprawling around a welcoming courtyard, where small lanterns were strung through tree branches. Small chimes and bells sang softly when caressed by the wind, adding their music to the singers who stood half in gloom, their voices gentle and full of breath, fading pleasantly in the ear.

Two lounges had been set up in the middle of the garden, mounds of pillows for comfort, with deftly woven rugs padding the paved circle. Stood to one side, a fountain featuring the Wine God, Fufluns, frozen in marble about to cast a stem of grapes towards them. His youthful face was dashing, with a wicked smile that spoke of delights too wild for polite conversation.

Around them was the bustle of servants, far outnumbering her own household. Two maids came to lead her forward, while Anesidora glared at a handsome man who offered his arm to her.

Duris emerged from within the house, a smile already warming his face when he faltered.

She could see the moment. The moment he realised he had to endure an evening with her. He was a well-cut man. A loose chiton that bared most of his chest to the evening, muscles softened by good living and sprinkled with downy hair. His hair was freshly oiled, and his calves turned nicely in the torchlight. He should be in the palace or the grand hall, dancing with noblemen's daughters who had not disgraced their fathers, who were not a bad purchase away from destitution. He should be with someone beautiful.

She watched him recover, the smile returning slowly as he walked towards her. 'Lady Amynta,' he said quietly. 'How truly you are blessed by Serene Turan.' He embraced her, keeping their bodies the appropriate distance apart, and kissed her cheeks.

'I'm sorry?'

'Have you not seen yourself this evening? I can have a mirror brought out for you. Though perhaps I should instead fetch a sculptor to capture the vision that graces my home this night.'

A wave of warmth fell upon her. She felt the sun of his gaze trace every inch of fabric, every careful decision. She had clad herself in a peplos the colour of aged terracotta, a white belt loosely circling her hips. Her hair was layered down her back, flecked with dim amethysts, curls artfully looped about her temples. Cassia oil had been brushed through her locks until they gleamed brighter than the gemstones. Her face was smoothed and crafted by creams and blushes and kohl. She had been impressed when she had gazed upon herself, but still, her eye was drawn to the length of belt – double what she had worn a year ago. Her upper arms wobbled when she moved, and she had begun to chafe between her legs from the long summer days. Were these not the things he saw when he looked at her?

Before she could speak, her nursemaid pushed herself between them. 'Pretty words from a pretty man,' she said. 'I see only two couches here. Am I to sit on the floor to eat?'

Duris blinked. 'Apologies, advisor. I did not realise you were joining *us*.' He stressed the last word, glancing at Mynta for confirmation.

'It would not be right for an unwed maiden to dine with a man without a companion,' Mynta said smoothly. 'As my family is unable to be represented tonight, Anesidora will stand in their place. If another couch could be brought?'

'Of course.' Duris clapped his hands. 'Bring my own from the main hall. Hurry now.'

There was a flurry of activity as servants rearranged the garden while others brought in a large couch carved from walnut wood and inlaid with gold.

'Would there be any objection if Lady Amynta and I took a walk about the garden before we ate?' His question was to Anesidora, but his eyes did not leave Mynta.

Her nursemaid groaned as she lowered herself onto the seat. 'As long as my eyes remain upon you, young master. But some wine would be – oh, thank you,' she finished to the maid who appeared next to her with a cup.

Duris' smile grew. 'This way.'

Mynta stepped away with him, her slippered feet stirring a faint hush from the grass. It would take enormous effort to maintain such verdancy, but he did not lack the money or manpower.

'I must confess that I feared you would not come this evening,' Duris said softly, his hands clasped behind his back as they strolled beneath potted fruit trees.

'A few hours' notice was particularly rushed,' Mynta said. 'But I will not deny how glad I was to receive your invitation.'

'I have some wonderful news and was eager to share it with you. But I thought an evening celebration would be more fitting than simply relaying through a messenger's mouth.'

She paused. 'We have received the permits.'

'Indeed. We have workers on the road to secure the site as we speak. They should begin producing ore within the fortnight. The smelters will be casting ingots shortly thereafter and transporting to The Forge. Profits should start flowing in as little as a month.'

She could not contain the thrill that shot through her. She threw her arms around him with a delighted laugh, her hair wrapping about his shoulders. It took her a moment to realise what she had done, but before she could step away, his arms folded around her, holding her loosely but enough that she knew he did not want to let go.

He smelled of fresh water and myrtle and a warmth that moved beyond temperature to scent, like sun-heated stone. He smelled *golden*.

Would she be mad to kiss him?

The startled squawk from her nursemaid brought her crashing back to where she was, who she was clinging to, and she leapt away.

'Apologies, master merchant. I was caught up in the excitement that our endeavour is progressing. Perhaps once the work is underway, we may plan a visit to Sabate to see the mine for ourselves.'

Duris bowed. 'I would greatly enjoy that, my lady. Shall we eat?'

They returned to the dining area where Anesidora was sitting upright, her eyes like a hawk's as she watched them settle on their couches. The food arrived and Mynta momentarily forgot her lapse in composure. Plump mussels poached in rosemary and wine. Leg of goat slow roasted and basted in honey with clove. Slices of apples folded into roses and sprinkled with crumbled cheese. Light-coloured wine sweetened with pomegranate and warmed by cinnamon. As each new delight was brought out, Duris gave her first choice, telling her how each dish was prepared, and which were his favourites. He ate with her, and for once she did not feel ashamed for what she put in her mouth.

The evening passed with idle chatter. Duris told her how he and his sister were raised by his grandfather. She told him of Cela and Desma, their exploits in Apasa, their adventures in the Middle Sea.

Anesidora eventually began to nod off, her chin falling on her chest as the darkened sky blazoned with stars. Tiur had not yet risen over the city but Artume was reigning above them all.

Mynta felt content, suffused by the gentle torchlight, the music, the wine, and the food. She laid back on the couch and gazed up at the sky, both her and Duris falling into a comfortable silence.

'I am glad that you met with us,' he said.

'As am I.'

'Perhaps Turms was watching over our meeting that day. He guided our paths so that we could meet instead of your father.'

'I wonder, though, if there is anything else I should be doing,' she said.

Duris rolled over so he could look at her. 'What do you mean?'

'I assume you and the other merchants are busy organising everything: the workers, equipment, the permits. Surely there must be something I could manage for you.'

'Hmm,' he said thoughtfully. 'There is much to do, but unfortunately you know little of metallurgy and mining. And we have much riding on this investment – we cannot risk a blunder by someone who, despite their great heart, is inexperienced.'

Mynta bristled at his words, though she could not deny them. 'There must be something.'

He was silent for a while before snapping his fingers. 'Surveyors!'

Mynta sat up. 'What about them?'

'It would be good to have proper surveyors to help us locate the veins as well as test their purity. It is important, but also something that a gifted novice should be able to handle. Would that be something of interest to you, my lady?'

Mynta thought for a moment. She did not know any surveyors offhand, but they were in Trilos, where a thousand forges burned daily. It would not be hard. 'Yes, that is something I could handle.'

'Wonderful. I will let the others know and will keep you abreast of any meetings or updates you need to be made aware of. In the meantime, I have been appointed chief coordinator, so you may send anything to me for final approval and payment.'

Anesidora woke with a snort, dropping her cup onto the floor.

Mynta smiled gently at the old woman. 'I think it is high time we return home.' Duris leapt to his feet to offer his arm. Mynta rose from the couch and pressed a kiss on his cheek. 'Thank you for a wonderful evening, master merchant. I look forward to our next business meeting.'

'If only all my partners were as enticing as you, Lady Amynta.'

'And may Uni grant us all some sense amid the wine and garden strolls,' her nursemaid chided, all but pushing Mynta towards the gate.

Duris laughed as he bid them farewell.

Mynta climbed onto her litter, making room for Anesidora to join her. As her bearers carried them out of the house, she looked back to see Duris leaning against a lemon tree, a hand pressed against his chest.

She looked away and touched her own chest, feeling her heart beneath her fingertips.

Turan help her and Turms guide her. Was she being clever or a fool? Maybe both.

CHAPTER FOURTEEN

'Sethlans' blessings on you, fair daughter of Trilos.' The high priest's voice boomed in the welcome hall, his arms flung wide as he crossed the distance between them.

Mynta could not keep the smile from her face.

She had been surprised at how swiftly her petition for an audience had been granted, let alone the accompanying response that Castur would visit her the very next day. She'd expected to attend The Forge and get a few minutes of his attention.

But here he was, embracing her and placing a blessing on her brow, the smell of coal and oil effused into his red and gold robes.

'Welcome to my home, High Priest,' she said with a bow. 'May Sethlans and Tinia bless our meeting and give us good fortune for all our days to come. Wine?'

'If I ever say no to good Thevan wine, then skewer my eye as Culsans must be near,' he laughed, referring to the Two-Faced God who delighted in creating twins of people to wreak havoc in their lives.

Castur was nearing fifty, though his body remained well-muscled from his time at the forge and hammer. Hazel eyes with gold flecks glimmered over his bushy beard, and his voice was pleasant like honeyed bread.

They moved into the central garden, where a generous repast had been laid out on small tables. As they settled in, Mynta could see her nursemaid by a pillar, her face set in a frown. She ignored her.

Mynta helped herself to figs stuffed with sweetened walnut paste, grapes so fresh their crunch sparkled like crystal when bitten, and earthy thyme cakes studded with dried apple.

'What a lovely meal,' Castur said as he piled his plate high. 'Usually when I come to a petitioner's house, they think I want to eat meat. I swear to Laran, if I am served boar one more time, I will set my beard on fire.'

Mynta snorted, shooting crumbs onto her dress that she brushed off, embarrassed.

'Forgive me, but it is good to not always be weighed down by the temple's mantle,' he said with a flashing grin. 'And I was quite eager to visit you, as your friend is the daughter of one who was very dear to my heart. And as you are a woman who outmanoeuvred one of the most cunning councilmen I've seen.'

Mynta blushed, both at the praise but also at the mention of her father. Cunning was not the half of it. The priest had not read her father's business papers. Would the priest's assessment be as generous if he knew what her father had done in the name of drachmae, of power?

His eyes rested heavily on her. 'I find myself begging forgiveness a second time already. I am not used to being entertained by such a beautiful maiden. And to bring up two points of pain to you ... I am sorry.'

'No.' Mynta shook her head. 'I will not make such an honoured guest feel contrition because they know my story. Though I am surprised you know something of what occurred between me and my father.'

Castur shrugged. 'Though I avoid getting entangled in the politics of this kingdom, that does not mean I don't have a finger on a strand or two of the webs that bind us all. And there are always those who seek to curry my favour, little of it that I have to give. I am only sorry that such a gamble did not succeed in granting Desma's petition. And I am sorry for the part I had to play.' Mynta looked at him, puzzled, but he shook his head. 'I have said enough,' he said.

'I hope that she had better luck in Koriithos,' she said, moving the conversation along.

His brows shot high. 'Have you not heard? She was cleansed! King Gylippus acquiesced after she slayed the monster.'

Mynta's face went slack in shock.

Castur picked up the wine jug. 'Seems as though we may need to extend our appointment.'

Mynta could not believe the story the high priest told her, but she did not doubt a word of it. Who else but Desma would think that the easiest solution would be to kill the monster dozens had died trying to slay – and succeed.

Now she was to become a princess, and, one day, would be Queen of Koriithos. Mynta did not know what god or goddess was paving this road Desma trod, one filled with blood and wine and grief and triumph. She only prayed it would not end in a hero's tragedy.

'I hope she will be happy,' she said more to herself.

'As do I,' Castur said. 'But something tells me that she has many trials ahead of her. Koriithos is very different to Trilos or Apasa. I fear that either the city will break her ... or she will break the city.'

A shadow seemed to fall on them.

Castur shook himself, as though flinging the dark thoughts away, and smiled. 'While I am glad to have been able to give you an update on your friend, I need to get back to The Forge soon to add melting salt to an experiment. Otherwise, I will need to replace yet another worktable. What had you hoped to discuss?'

'Yes.' Mynta smoothed her dress, taking a moment to gather her thoughts. 'I have entered into a business venture with some merchants within the city. We have acquired a tin mine in Sabate, with all relevant permits, and begun setting up the operation. But we need surveyors to help find the extent of the veins as well as verify their quality. And I have been made aware the temple has the finest in the kingdom, if not the League.'

Castur nodded. 'We are able to offer surveyors, but they will be expensive. I hope all parties involved have deep pockets.'

'Well, I understand that The Forge is in need of tin.'

The high priest frowned. 'There is a call for supply.'

'Perhaps we could come to an agreement.' Mynta was proud that she was keeping her breathing calm. She had sat before her enraged father and survived. She would make it through a friendly chat with the high priest.

Castur gave her a kind smile. 'Dear one, I can appreciate the game you are trying to play, but it is not going to work with the temple. Try these tricks on merchants – not me.'

She faltered but persevered. 'You need tin and we want gold.'

'You also want my surveyors.'

'How about we pay for the services with a certain amount of tin sold at a reduced amount?'

'At what rate? What happens if there is not as much as you think? What if the quality is poor – will we be able to demand gold instead, or greater quantities at further reductions in cost? Will we need to pay additional for smelting and transportation? Do you have the authority to negotiate this on behalf of your partnership?'

Mynta blinked. This was not how she thought the conversation would go. She did not think it would be easy, but she did not expect Castur to be so dismissive of the suggestion.

He must have seen something in her face. 'It is not your fault. You are unaware of the temple. We do not bargain. We set our price and merchants flock to our doors. Why? Because we are the greatest demander in the League. If we need tin or copper or iron or emeralds – miners across the kingdoms fall over themselves to sell to us. We pay a good price, and they know we need amounts that no other single buyer could match. And we do not have to worry about drachmae. Come, stand with me.'

He offered his hand, which she took. His palm was strong, but his fingers were delicate, used to tinkering with the finest materials and devices.

He led her away from the garden, through the outer court and out into the street. 'What is the biggest ingot of gold you have ever seen?' he asked.

She thought for a moment. It was not often she would come across ingots of metal. She and her mother had once visited a jeweller, browsing his wares as he received a late supply of gold and silver. Slim bricks stacked high, to be melted down into necklaces and bracelets and pendants.

'It was probably the breadth of my hand and twice its length.'

Castur nodded. 'Do you see your home? How high its walls, how wide across, how far back it goes? Far beneath the temple, we store our treasure. Deeper still, we keep our reserves. In vast caverns are our large ingots of gold.'

Mynta's eyes widened. 'You mean you have caverns the size of my home filled with gold?'

He laughed. 'No. I am saying inside those caverns, we have gold ingots the size of your home.'

'Blasted Depths,' Mynta swore. She had chests filled with beautiful jewellery stored in a small safe room that would be worth several thousand drachmae. And across the city, the temple was sitting on gold that could be turned into hundreds upon hundreds of thousands of coin. More than. She didn't even know a number high enough to calculate the wealth.

And she was trying to haggle.

She hung her head. 'Now it is my turn to beg your forgiveness, High Priest.'

He placed a hand on her head. 'Never say sorry because you learnt a lesson. That is the duty of the wiser – to teach the younger so their paths may walk further than our own.'

They returned to the outer courtyard. Castur folded his arms, his muscles bulging through his robes. 'I am happy to provide three surveyors. I feel that number would be sufficient given the size of the area described. It would be at a cost of three hundred gold drachmae for one week, then fifty more coin for every two days beyond that is required of them. If it takes them less than one week, it is still three hundred. If you require additional surveyors, it is at a cost of an additional two hundred gold for the first week, followed by twenty-five every two days. Those are the temple terms.'

Mynta made to negotiate, but he held up a hand. 'I have already shaved some of the cost down, which I will cover myself. I will not deprive my god of the wealth he is owed. I do this because of the love I bore for Timothea and the sadness I bear for Desma. Do not seek to ask further of me.'

Mynta bowed. Three hundred was astronomical. The standard costing for any other surveyor was a hundred gold drachmae for two weeks, including room and board.

But none could outperform Sethlans' priests when it came to the earth and its minerals. They could discover veins missed by another, and could do the work at a fraction of the time. The benefits would outweigh the initial cost. It was the better deal ... wasn't it?

'I accept your terms, High Priest.'

He smiled. 'Very good. I will let my scribes know and to expect papers from you shortly. You may coordinate the details with them. Thank you for your hospitality, Amynta.' He paused as he turned to leave. 'There is change coming, daughter of Trilos. I cannot say what form it will take, but it is something I feel deep in my bones. Secure your future and brace for what is to come.'

Before she could say a word, he turned and left, disappearing into the crowded street, returning to the orichalcum-bound walls of his temple.

Anesidora appeared by her side. 'May Tinia shine on this household,' she said reverently. 'Those are dark words to farewell on.'

Mynta was silent, looking at the now closed gates, struggling with a cold sense of foreboding that was spreading from her stomach. She was only just stepping into a venture where she hoped the riches reaped would secure her for years to come. Is that what he meant? Would it be sufficient for what was coming? She did not know what else she would need to do.

'A lot of gold for some dirt-diggers,' her nursemaid mused.

Mynta felt a flash of annoyance. 'Yes, but it will be worth it.'

'And when will you be going to Duris for the money?'

'We are set to meet later this week. I will have the papers readied with the temple by then.'

'Let us hope he agrees with you.'

Mynta turned on her nursemaid. 'I know you advise caution with every step and word and thought I take, but when you have earned the title of master merchant yourself, then I will consider your opinions. Until then, I beg of you to keep quiet, unless it is support that falls from your lips and not sarcasm.'

Anesidora looked taken aback. Rarely had Mynta ever spoken to her nursemaid as such. But she was mistress of the household. Despite all that

Anesidora had done for her, it was on Mynta's shoulders alone that the house would rise or fall. She was a noblewoman, daughter of a Councilman and Emissary, investor. She had to trust herself or she would bring about her own failure.

She could not afford anything less than success.

CHAPTER FIFTEEN

A thousand doves laid dead at her feet, tiny hearts ripped from their bodies while their wings still flapped weakly, pumping out drops of bright blood on the silver floor.

Turan ignored the offerings and stepped over them, the crunch of soft bones and the tickling of feathers on her bare feet.

She walked onto the balcony, turning a section of stone railing to dust with a wave of her hands, before falling gracefully onto a couch that appeared underneath her. Laying on her side, one arm stretched out to rest her head upon, wings tucked close to her body, feet drifting just above the floor.

Looking out over the city, her gaze pierced cloud and tile and stone as she watched the citizens of Aventinus go about their day, ignorant of their goddess' eyes upon them, aware of their every throb and moan and ache.

The city was a connection of lacework bridges and slender spires, filled with golden statues and pink quartz domes. Streets paved with white and grey marble, walls of silver and sea glass, tiers of balconies and open-air courts worshipping the elegant skyline, all filled with her sacred plants: apple trees and rosemary bushes, myrtle trees and sweet roses, riots of spring flowers and sea jasmine. The ocean shimmered around the arrowhead of land that the city rose from.

Turan watched a shy sailor being urged by his friends to approach a maiden who stacked apples on a table, her brown hair loose down her bare shoulders. The breeze caught her locks, stirring them in its grasp, as she hummed under her breath. The sailor pushed back against his friends, too afraid to seek what his heart desired.

'Follow love,' she whispered, cupping her hand and blowing gently. Myrtle leaves flew from her palm and floated down to the city, brushing unseen against the sailor.

The young man stopped fighting his friends, a smile growing on his face, heart bounding wildly in his chest. He crossed the short distance between him and the maiden and took up her hand, causing her to drop an apple in shock.

She laughed as he spoke to her, words of love pouring from his heart, until she embraced him in a hug. He spun her around, uncaring when he knocked over the rest of the apples, fruit scattering across cobblestones and into the sea.

Turan smiled, twirling a strand of hair the colour of wine in her finger.

A whisper of her name. The other side of the city, where an elderly woman sat on a bench overlooking a rivulet filled with swans. Within a moment, Turan descried her pain: her husband had passed several years before, and she ached for comfort to fill the expanding hole. Turan knew this woman, for she had been a loyal worshipper, always leaving offerings, even in times of hardship, and celebrating every holy day.

Turan felt sympathy in her heart and wrapped her presence around her, though the woman could not perceive her. Peace flowed into the grandmother's heart and soothed away some of her pain. Turan could tell it was not amorous love the woman wanted but friendship, someone to take wine with and speak of days passed and days never to be seen. She would find that someone and send them to cross her path. Perhaps that woman who had recently lost a child to ague ...

Pain rippled across Turan's body and she gasped, shattering stone around her in spiderwebbing cracks while she clutched the couch, breathing harshly.

It was over within moments.

Closing her eyes, she waited for the final lingering threads of pain to disappear. Sweat beaded on her brow. She opened her eyes and let them move slowly down her body, past her curved breasts, under her sheer, green dress to her rounded stomach.

She had been pregnant before. Each of her Lovers had been delivered by Uni herself from between her legs. Six children to six gods. One child to … she wrenched the name from her mind, casting it away.

She did not bother to count her children with mortals, who often died from the savages of love.

But no child had she borne for Sethlans.

Until this one.

And she hated it. Hated the pain and the growth and the thousand maladies that afflicted every mother, mortal or divine. But she was bound by her oath to the hideous imp: bear his child, and in exchange, he would stop his king and priests in Trilos from offering the rite of purification to the spawn of the traitorous Timothea.

A thought occurred to her. This was the first child to a god she would bear since she lost her Belt. Her heart clenched as she acknowledged – just for a moment – the bleeding void at her midriff, an abyss that echoed her pain into her chest.

The Belt had been found. After so many centuries, ever since Atunis had betrayed her, ran from her. But the daughter of Timothea did not have it, nor did she possess the knowledge of its whereabouts. This Turan knew for certain, for why would she hide this information?

The Belt was back in the world. She had felt it. Waited for Camillus to bring it back to her, for Valeriana to host a celebration that would outshine the greatest feasts held by even the gods themselves. She would have been reborn, risen again to the heights of her power that once had the rest of the Twelve turn their eyes in fear. But where had it gone? If she had to empty Aventinus and send her people scouring the Middle Sea, then so be it. If one of the other Twelve found it first …

She closed her eyes again, fingers stroking the surface of her tight stomach. Feeling the alien shape as life grew inside her. Pressing sharply, nails digging into her skin. One problem at a time.

CHAPTER SIXTEEN

Koriithos was decked out like a bride before her wedding once more.

Orange and almond blossoms festooned the palace, perfuming the air with their sweet scents. Pine branches burned in temples and shrines across the city, adding their clean fragrance to the sea air.

Bright pennants and garlands decorated squares and theatres. Uni's temple was inundated with offerings and sacrifices, the columns ringing with citizens calling upon the Goddess of Marriage to bless the union of their prince and new princess.

It had been over a week since the darklings arrived back in the city.

An entire battalion of warriors met them in the harbour and escorted them directly to the palace. This time, they were not separated but put together, in the same rooms the rest of the crew had been given before, Cela told her. A small gesture they were meant to be grateful for, Desma supposed.

They were all numb.

Even when Kassandra arrived two days later with the triremes, there was no celebration. Silence and grief wrapped them all like a too-heavy cloak, unapologetic in its suffocation.

Khufu was gone.

They had watched him fall from the cliff, sacrificed as promised by the king. Desma did not know what god was so cruel as to let them arrive on the stroke of doom.

She could not recall the ship arriving by the pier. Actor must have ordered the rowers and officers. She remembered Bion shouting, his voice hoarse from urging the rowers on in the final sprint. Delphinus had lost all control and had been beaten unconscious to stop him attacking the Koriithosans, the iron sting of blood coating the salt in the air.

Arete had demanded Actor retrieve Khufu's body, but it had been lost in the waves and rocks.

He was dead. Desma repeated it to herself each night and morn; a reminder to herself before and after each nightmare. She dreamt of a red sea, thick like honey, waves crashing over her head again and again. Water, tasting of spice and salt, forced itself down her throat as she drowned, her body hurled against undersea rocks sharp as glass. Khufu, held to the bottom of the ocean floor by golden chains, blind and deaf to her.

She would awake covered in sweat, shivering, her hair a wild mess around her. Cela, who had not left her side, would jerk awake as well. Together, they would lie as the dawn approached, soft and grey.

The astronomers, Kalchas and Hyllos, had visited the day after their return. Kalchas was a small, hunched man with deep lines in his face, peppery hair, and eyes as sharp as flint. He questioned her for over an hour. Who kidnapped her? Why would Camillus risk it? Was he acting under orders from the emperors or the holy mother? Did she know where Turan's Belt was? Did they hurt her? Why did she choose to come back?

The last question cut through the numbness like a nettle sting. Her hands curled into fists, and she took a threatening step towards the astronomers. Hyllos, who had remained silent for most of the interrogation, pulled Kalchas away, and they both left the room quickly. They had later sent a priest of the Healing God to mend her ankle until the pain was nothing but memory.

It was the seventh day when the door opened and Actor came inside. Every bit the general now he had returned home, he wore a polished breastplate over his white chiton, greaves on his finely moulded calves, and hardened sandals. 'My lady,' he said formally, bowing to Desma. 'King Gylippus calls you to attend him. You may bring one companion.'

'At once, War Leader,' she responded in kind. 'Cela?' Desma knew he was acting as he must. She was betrothed to his prince and would one day be his queen. But she still felt sad at the distance stretching between them.

They moved swiftly through the corridors. Enclosed in a block of soldiers three-deep, the tramping of their steps heralded their approach to servants, who quickly vanished from sight.

She thought they would be going to the megaron, the great hall, but they passed it – crossing the courtyard lined with almond trees in large pots – and headed down a flight of stairs that occasionally broke out into the side of the cliff, their faces assaulted by the hard wind blowing off the harbour.

They came to a set of copper doors guarded by four men who saluted Actor before pushing open the doors. The general bade their escort to wait without and went inside, Desma and Cela close on his heels.

They were in one of the king's meeting rooms. Roughly hewn from the cliffside itself, the rock was still scarred from the tools that carved it, yet the floor was smooth with white marble and green sea glass mosaic. The room was roughly circular and widows lined one side that faced the harbour and the mouth of the canal.

The only people besides them in the room were the king ... and the prince.

Gylippus had forgone his royal robes and wore a plain chiton of deep green, a gold chain around his neck. He was sitting at a large table, in the room's only chair.

But Desma's eyes went straight to the prince, Lycon. Her husband-to-be.

This was only the third time she had seen him; the first two times, she had been frightened by the intense hatred in his eyes. Now was no different. Dressed to match his father, he was a handsome youth with black hair, copper skin, and strong shoulders. He leaned against the wall and stared at her.

'King Gylippus,' she said, bowing low with Cela. He was the reason Khufu was dead. Her hands clenched into fists around her dress, anger rousing itself in her chest, but she pushed it down. He had only kept his word as king, a bargain Khufu had willingly entered into with him. To save her.

The king studied her, his face carved deeply by weather and time. After several long moments, he finally spoke. 'Though it is not in my nature to do so, and in this particular case there is no reason for me to say these words, I want to offer my apologies for the loss of a man I take to have been a great captain and friend.'

Desma's eyes widened. Surely he had not called her before him to apologise for Khufu. Her heart hardened. Most likely, someone had advised him not to begin a relationship with his wed-daughter while her friend's blood still dried upon his hands.

Cela elbowed her side.

'Your words are a kindness, King,' she said as courteously as she could manage. 'If you have no objections, I would like to arrange a sacrifice in Tinia's temple to honour his life.'

He bowed his head, acquiescing to her request. 'I am also grieved that this whole affair began because of an attack on my palace,' he continued, his voice growing rough with anger. 'I have already sent a messenger to the Celestial Empire demanding blood price for the murder of my people, as well as tribute to Nethuns' temple for your kidnapping. But the Empire is vast and my navy is small. My kingdom exists because we control a vital piece of the League. I am under no illusion that any other kingdom would come to our aid. Just look at Apasa.'

The king was right. After the Empyreans had sacked the temple at Apasa, no kingdom had stepped forth to offer arms or men or gold to help her kingdom rebuild or seek retribution. They certainly wouldn't rally for a kidnapping – not on behalf of a woman who had been a father-killer only weeks ago.

'Now, for the reason I have summoned you,' the king said. 'As you know, for the last ten years, my city was besieged by that vile monster. Many of my soldiers were killed hunting it down. It was only after we offered gold a hundred times my weight to the first priest to give us a solution that one of Aplu's followers stepped forward. The Singing God is no friend to Nethuns, and his prophecies are more slippery than eels. Many kingdoms have ceased to exist because they trusted their foresight.'

Desma nodded. The League's history was rife with tales of kings and heroes listening to oracles and finding their demise sooner rather than later because of it.

'This priest said to me, "A monster will ravage your kingdom until it stands at the brink of history. The one who ends the monster's reign will be the monarch Koriithos needs to see it through the days to come." And that monarch, by the cruelty of Aplu's jests, is you.'

'I did not choose this,' Desma said. 'I had no knowledge of this prophecy when we came to Koriithos. I only wanted to be purified and leave the city.'

Gylippus sighed. 'I know. And the fact that you do not even want the crown angers me. A woman, a foreigner, is to save us. And she doesn't even want to be here.'

She could say nothing. It was true. The thought of being trapped in this kingdom, being queen to a people who hated her for not being Koriithosan, made her nauseous. But she could not run. She could tell a dozen tales herself about men and women who had tried to run from the path fate had chosen for them. It always led right back to where they should have been ... oftentimes with disastrous consequences.

Neither Hyllos nor Actor knew the nature of the danger she was supposedly meant to save the kingdom from, but she would do her best. As much as she hated Gylippus for forcing a marriage onto her, for killing Khufu, she could not doom a kingdom for a chance at freedom.

'What do you want me to do?'

'I cannot ask for love between you two,' Gylippus said, gesturing to Desma and the prince. 'I can only hope Turan will bless you with friendship in time. But the wedding is in two days. I think it would be good for the two of you to spend time together beforehand, so that you do not appear to be total strangers when you stand in front of the city and lift the veil.' He nodded to the general. 'Actor will take you to the sea gardens for a walk, and I will see you at noon for lunch.'

He waved them away in dismissal. Desma and Cela went out first, followed by Actor, with the prince trailing behind. Their guards formed around the four of them. They moved through the palace in silence, the prince glowering behind them. Cela reached out and took her hand.

They came to a gate set in the northern wall of the palace, opening onto a wide street that allowed people to reach the Temple of Nethuns without going through the palace itself. They crossed the street and came to a set of stairs, its ornate stone railing cut directly into the side of the canal that split the isthmus. Desma's head swam at the two hundred foot drop into the ice-blue waters, for a moment picturing what Khufu would have seen as he plummeted. She shook the image from her head. She would grieve for him, but Gylippus had done what he had to do. It was no different when Hero-King Sophocles had cast her out of Apasa. Crowns do not rest easy upon the mortal brow.

Partway down, they came to a large cave carved into the canal's cliff face. Over a hundred feet wide and thirty feet high, it was a beautiful garden found nowhere else in the League. There was little dry ground in the sea gardens, as most of it was submerged in a few inches of salt water, pumped from the harbour below by an intricate system built by Trilosii from the Thinkery. Rock pools spotted the gardens filled with colourful starfish and sponges, little crabs and seahorses, shy octopuses and oysters. Larger pools contained small sharks and bright fish, their depths obscured by tall, red seaweed that waved. Small bunches of sea lavender and juniper bushes spotted the cave.

But it was the coral that made the gardens renowned. They sprouted from the pools and towered ten, twenty, thirty feet into the air, ranging in colour from blush and orange, gentle purple and teal, spotted brown and red, bone-white, and vivid green. Some were thin like blades of grass. Others like thick fingers reaching for the sky. There were ones that looked like walnuts, filled with whorls and whirls, and others like veins spidering upwards. At first glance, one would think they were beautiful stone carvings, perhaps crafted at the hands of a god. But then one could see the stones *moved*. The coral waved as though completely underwater, moving to the rhythms of currents, pulsating as they breathed, throbbing with life.

Desma let out a gasp that was echoed by Cela. They had heard of the sea gardens. All the kingdoms in the League had wonders that were found nowhere else in the world, gifts from their gods to their favoured children. But it made the cave no less beautiful. The ceiling was left rough-hewn but scattered with crushed glass so it sparkled like dew. Fragrances of clean brine, juniper, and hints of lavender met them, guided them forward. Towards the rear of the gardens was a statue of Nethuns, carved from a solid trunk of an old pine tree, covered in algae and molluscs.

'We will wait here,' Actor said, grabbing Cela's arm to bring her to a halt. She opened her mouth to argue, but subsided when Desma nodded.

She was going to have to grasp the spear eventually.

The prince drew next to her, and they began a slow stroll across the loose pebble and wet sand path that wound its way through the gardens.

They walked in silence, both unwilling to speak first. The garden seemed to breathe, like a vast creature long slumbering. The wind sighed as it finished crashing along the canal, falling into the cavern to settle among the coral that creaked and softly groaned. Beneath their feet was a hum that bordered on silence, deep and wide as it encompassed them – the great pipes that summoned the water from far below. It was strangely comforting.

Desma glanced over to the prince. He was as taut as a bowstring, back ramrod straight, arms tense, hands clutched by his side as he stared directly ahead.

Where did they begin? Two people thrown together by the fates, neither of them wanting to be a part of this marriage. But he was the son of the king, destined to be the ruler of Koriithos. None but the most selfish would abandon their duty to city and kingdom.

And what about her? She had just freed herself from the bonds of Tinia's punishment, only to be trapped by Aplu's prophecy. And to add to it all, Turan's bishop was under the mistaken idea that she knew where the Belt was hidden. She had wracked her brain ever since she was rescued. What had her mother done with the Belt? Perhaps it was buried in the rubble of the Grand Temple. It was possible they recovered it later. Maybe Cela's mother, the new high priestess, hid it rather than proclaim its discovery. Though, if she wanted to avoid what happened to Timothea, she would be wise to just send it to Aventinus.

Desma could only hope that Camillus would turn his search away from her. She had no desire to see the bishop again. Although some part of her wondered whether their paths would cross once more – and the next time, she may be a queen.

She lifted the hem of her dress as they stepped over a large puddle, but her foot slipped on a loose stone that rolled beneath her, and she stumbled into the prince. He caught her about the hips by reflex, absorbing her impact. His body was hard under his fine clothes, she noticed, before she pushed herself off him. 'Thank you,' she said quietly.

He grunted in response.

She stopped, planting her feet firm, forcing him to turn to face her. 'Look, Prince. I don't like this any more than you. So how about we use our words and come to some sort of agreement so we can make the next few decades of our lives slightly easier?'

He blinked. 'Fine.'

'An improvement,' she sighed. They resumed walking. 'So ... what's your favourite colour?'

'What?'

'Colour,' she repeated. 'Mine is orange, like the skin of a ripe peach.'

He frowned. 'Why is this something you need to know?'

'We need to start somewhere,' she said. 'Just answer the damn question, Prince.'

She had pushed too far. He stared down at her, a finger raised warningly. 'I *am* a prince,' he said. 'We are not yet wed, Desma, daughter of a potter. One day, we will be king and queen, but never forget that I was *born* to be king. Koriithos runs through *my* blood, Apasan.'

She rankled. She was also the daughter of a high priestess, but she bit down her pride. If one of them did not back down occasionally, then they would spend their days tearing each other to pieces. 'Forgive me, Prince. It has been a trying time for me.'

They rounded a bend and came across an emerald-green coral, ten feet high, with shimmering red tips that spun in lazy circles as though tracing the air. A man and a woman sat on a marble bench talking quietly. When they saw Desma and Lycon, they both jumped to their feet, bowed to the prince, and moved briskly down the other path.

'Green,' he suddenly said. 'Like a field of grass.'

'I like that colour, too,' she said. 'Now you ask a question.'

He thought for a moment. 'Favourite holy day?'

A few months ago, that would have been an easy question. Turan's Festival of Doves. Held every two years, people would dress in costumes made from dove feathers collected throughout the period. But now ... 'Probably Artimi's Run,' she said quickly. It was a popular festival where young maidens chased men through a forest. The men carried a copper or gold arrow and had to give it to whichever maiden caught him. They also had to wait on her for the three days the moon was full. 'Yours?'

'The Breaking of the Horses,' he answered immediately.

It was back to her. 'Favourite food to steal from the kitchens? Lemon and fig cakes for me. You better pray the palace cooks don't bake them, otherwise there may be trouble soon.' She laughed.

He tilted his head as he thought. 'You know ... I don't think I have even been into the kitchens,' he said. 'I just order what I want, and it comes to me. Why would I steal it?'

She gaped at him in disbelief. 'For fun!'

He frowned. 'But is that not mean to the cooks? They make the food, serving hundreds in the palace, never knowing what order might come down to them. They need to keep track of supplies, place orders, manage budgets. But you would cause them undue trouble and stress by taking food? What if someone is blamed for theft and loses their position? What if unnecessary expenditure was undertaken because they thought they had rats and sent for a catcher? Or did you not think past your stomach?'

His words slammed into her. She had never thought of the consequences. One of the cooks, Lykos, had always snuck her honeyed figs when she was a child. He had been slain during the sacking of the temple. Had anyone got in trouble when she and Cela plundered the kitchens in the small hours of the night? Neither had ever checked.

The prince was watching her, waiting for an answer. Damn him for being so responsible and considerate. 'Never mind,' she grumbled.

They passed another pair, this time two lords who scurried away as soon as they saw Desma. They looked familiar ...

'Is there anything about the wedding ceremony I should know?' she asked. If she had to go through with it, she did not want to make a fool of herself at the hand of some peculiar Koriithosan custom.

His mouth twisted. 'I am aware of no distinction in the ceremony to that of Apasa,' he said. 'Obviously, the vows themselves will take place in the Temple of Nethuns instead of Turan. Ah, yes, the only difference is that we will also be wed to Nethuns.'

She came to a stop. 'Excuse me?'

He paused. His eyes were a soft green ringed with brown. When not alight with rage towards her, they were quite beautiful. 'It is our law. Every member of the royal family also takes a vow of marriage to the Sea God. This is to renew the tie between our family and him, to honour our worship of Nethuns. Do not worry – he has not come to consummate a marriage in several centuries.'

She had to sit down.

They moved to a bench overlooking a large pool that contained several sharks, black stripes down their backs and large eyes that stared up at them as they glided by.

They both looked around the cave; the tension that had begun to thaw was returning.

Desma took a steadying breath. She was going to be a wife. Of course, she knew that was what marriage meant, but she had been too focused on becoming queen one day. But she would be his wife, and he would be her husband. Gods, she felt trapped.

'Do you know the story of Demeas and Nikaia?' she asked him.

'Not well,' he admitted.

Desma told him quickly of the two royals who had vowed to never marry, but were forced to when Menrva and Artimi lost a wager with Turms. Nikaia had fled far to the east but could not escape her fate, and was eventually forced to wed Demeas. But that did not save her from her goddess' wrath for disobeying a command, and within a year, she had gone to the Halls Beneath.

The prince huffed. 'That was a pleasant story.'

She ignored his sarcasm. 'Just one of a hundred about two people the gods wanted married. Few escaped their fates, and it was usually only because they died or Tinia himself intervened. I hope death is far off in our futures, and I somehow doubt the King of Gods will take much interest in what we are doing.' She sighed. 'I don't want to upset whatever god has ordained this wedding, be it Nethuns, or Aplu, or someone else.' She reached down and picked up his hands.

Though he seemed surprised by the contact, he didn't pull away. Desma studied where their hands met. His hands were strong, used to bearing sword and spear, but not near as tough as a true warrior. She turned so she could look him in the eye. 'I am sorry that this is happening to you. I wish you could marry whoever you wanted. But I want to make this work the best we can. Please give me a chance before condemning me to a lifetime of being hated by this kingdom.'

The familiar anger in his eyes was dormant, less directed. The anger of a man trapped with no way out. He squeezed her hands. 'Perhaps we can start by you calling me Lycon.'

TALE OF DEMEAS AND NIKAIA

Demeas was the third son of King Macar of Athanai in the days before the archons, and Nikaia was a princess of Dramaki. Both had sworn themselves to Menrva and Artimi respectively, and taken oaths never to speak marriage vows.

But one day, in the hidden skies above, the gods were gathering for a feast. Turms, God of Tricksters, had a mischievous glint in his eye. He had already tricked Uni into sleeping with Turan, who would later give birth to the Lover Heran, God of Weddings.

When he came upon the Triple Virgin Goddesses speaking together, he decided to have fun with them and ask a riddle. Ethausva declined and left to tend the holy hearth fires that keep the unseen palaces floating above. But Atrimi and Menrva were intrigued. Turms made them promise upon their thrones, as members of the Holy Twelve, that if they could not answer the riddle, they must obey a single command he gave them. And if they guessed it, he would give them gifts of his own making.

While Artimi hesitated, Menrva agreed immediately, for she is the Goddess of Wisdom and Cunning, and none among the gods could outthink her. With the goddess on her side, Artimi agreed.

So Turms asked his riddle. 'What does a woman have two of that a cow has four of?' The two goddesses whispered to each other, thinking of answers. Turms was proud of his filthy mind, often coming up with songs and poems that caused blushes and laughter in equal bounties.

Menrva knew that he was mocking them for rising above the messiness of sex and love, thinking they would not speak of such bestial matters. But guess they did.

'Teats,' they cried, proud of calling his bluff.

But it was Turms who blushed, feigning shock at their crudeness. 'How could you guess such a thing, here in our heavenly halls?' he asked them. 'The answer is legs!'

The goddesses were angered by his trickery, but could do nothing. They had made a vow and would obey a single command. And so Turms, for he loves trouble in all its forms, commanded that Demeas of Athanai and Nikaia of Dramaki would be wed.

How they hated their fellow god! But so commanded, they obeyed. Each goddess approached her devotee separately in their dreams and told them what they must do. While Demeas was dismayed by the order, he would not disobey Menrva's command. So he sent off Dramaki immediately.

But poor Nikaia felt betrayed by her goddess, she who would kill those who broke their vow of virginity. So she fled the city, running east to Trilos and then beyond, past the boundaries of the League. To strange kingdoms she wandered, her gold and jewels ensuring her safe passage until they ran out. She thought she had escaped the bounds of the goddess, for she now dwelt in lands where they worshipped strange gods.

How wrong she was! For Demeas had followed her footsteps, hunting her over the course of years. He eventually came to serve in the court of an easterling king, where he provided sound and faithful advice in many affairs. As a reward, the king wished to gift him a wife, and brought forth a woman he had recently found in a small oasis city and brought back to his kingdom. The woman was Nikaia. And so they were wed in the faraway city in a strange temple, but Artimi and Menrva stood witness.

Artimi was outraged by Nikaia's betrayal and caused her to die during childbirth, though only after she had given birth to a girl that the goddess stole away. But Menrva returned the faithful Demeas to Athanai, where his elder brothers had perished in a war with Koriithos. He became king, married a great lady of the city and saved the kingdom from ruin, having a great many sons and grandsons. To this day, one of his descendants is an archon of the city.

CHAPTER SEVENTEEN

They watched Desma and the prince disappear among the dancing coral, both walking stiff as statues.

Cela prayed that her friend would be happy. Most royal marriages were arranged by parents or gods. If they were lucky, and the gods smiled on them, the couple could learn to love each other.

But Desma had never spoken of marriage. She did not seem to want a husband or wife or children, though she had always been supportive of Cela's dreams when she talked about marrying one man or another. Cela had always seen a family in her future, but now she wondered just how far that dream might be.

She sighed.

Actor shifted on his feet next to her, and she peeked at him.

He was quite handsome, very talented to have achieved his current station so early. And he was kind. He was someone she would have pursued back in Apasa, another bedroom delight, when she felt closest to her goddess, Turan. But she had not been able to lie with a man since the temple burned. Since she left her mother, with a festering leg wound, to chase after Desma. How swiftly and enduring destruction falls when the gods are involved!

He caught her looking at him and smiled, warm and bright. His yellow hair a dull gold by the cave's dimness, his eyes brown forest pools.

'What is in that mind of yours?' he asked.

She shrugged, throwing her hair back over her shoulders to expose them to the cool air, banishing her dark thoughts. 'Marriage. Theirs,' she said, gesturing towards where Desma and the prince had gone, 'and mine.'

His eyes widened. 'Are you betrothed back in Apasa?'

She shook her head. 'No. I am still looking for the spark to my tinder.' She stepped closer to him. 'What about you? Any young Koriithosan maidens catch the eye of the great war leader?'

He stiffened. 'I am promised to someone.'

It felt like a vase shattered inside her. He was already pledged. She had been throwing herself at him like a fool, and *he* said nothing all this time ...

She drew back from him. 'I see.'

'Please, Cela,' he bit his lips. 'I am bound by oaths, and cannot explain as my heart is crying to do so. I am promised to someone for another year. If they do not find a suitable husband in that time, then we will be wed.'

She was shocked. It was not uncommon to string along several suitors until the most favourable was selected. But to bind a potential suitor with oaths so he was unable to seek a wife elsewhere was vile. It was a slap to Uni's face.

An uncomfortable silence grew.

Eventually, Actor spoke. 'What do you plan to do now?'

'How do you mean?' she asked, still picking up the broken pieces inside her.

'As I understand it, you left Apasa to aid Desma on her journey to purify herself. You've done that. Then she was kidnapped and you raced to save her. Now she is here, preparing to become Princess of Koriithos. What will you do?'

She did not know. They always spoke lightly of what they would do once they found a king, priest, or oracle to purify Desma from her blood crime. Return to Apasa, sail the Middle Sea, go to Opuni to visit Khufu's homeland. Desma had mentioned finding a small house by the coast and raising goats. Cela wrinkled her nose at the thought. But they had never decided on anything. All their plans had always been together. Would she stay in Koriithos with Desma? And become what – a handmaiden?

Or was it time to go home, to see her mother again, to help them rebuild? She did not know if she could serve the temple again, not after knowing what Turan had done to Desma and her family. But maybe she could find service with the king.

What would the rest of the crew do? She did not have an answer. They needed to have an uncomfortable conversation. Was this the end of the darklings? How life twisted suddenly like a serpent, changing course and striking without warning.

'I don't know,' she said honestly. 'I haven't had the time to think about it after all that has happened.'

'I understand. I do not know what I would do if I suddenly found myself at the shore of the sea, a thousand possibilities in front of me but no clear course to take. I thank Nethuns that I have known my steps since I was a boy and have served with honour. I pray you find the same thing one day.'

They fell silent, waiting for the future queen and king to return from their walk.

Cela shared her rooms with Arete and Kassandra, the crew being given multiple quarters after Desma was moved to her own rooms ahead of her wedding. She unpinned her himation from her shoulder and draped it on a couch by the window.

The late afternoon sun streamed through the open windows and balcony doors. Her room faced the city that swept down the hills before flattening out into grassland, rippling a few miles out with small hills and dales. The scent of the city spiced with the pine trees drifted through, a touch of salt always lingering.

Actor was betrothed. She must be a woman of noble birth to have the War Leader of Koriithos standing by to be her husband, should her first prospect fail. But why would such a promise have been wrought from Actor? Was the woman unseemly? Mad? Different? Blood and money must not be the issue.

Her cheeks warmed at the thought of her behaviour in his presence. She was not ashamed of her sexuality, and flirted with many men. But with only a handful had she wanted the flirting to go beyond a pleasurable night. She had seen the goodness in him. He did not care for the trappings of power, his title. He saw the oaths he swore, the honour he represented, the people he protected.

Whatever ease they'd once shared had slipped beyond reach. Before it had been so comfortable, their stories and thoughts flowing freely like two brooks coming together into a stream. But now she was afraid it had changed, and she was too scared to find out with certainty.

She was thinking about calling a maid for a bath when there was a knock at the door.

'Come,' she called, thinking it was a servant. She was surprised to see Delphinus slip into the room, his face harrowed and shoulders slumped under his brown cloak. 'What brings you to my chamber?' She hurried to pour them both wine.

The piper collapsed into a chair and took the proffered cup, taking a large gulp before resting it in his lap, his eyes shadowed. 'I miss Khufu,' he said quietly.

Cela's heart cracked.

The piper and the captain had been close companions, in wine and battle, with Khufu often being the only one to draw Delphinus back to sanity when his blood rode wild.

Though she was not aware of their friendship ever falling into bed, she now wondered if perhaps their love was deeper than she knew.

'I miss him too,' she said, slipping to the floor to rest her head against his knee. She could smell he had not bathed for some time. Where had he been spending his nights? Bion said he had not been sleeping in the chambers they shared.

'I cannot stay in this city,' he said, his voice like ringing bronze, even in plain speech. His copper hair had been roughly shorn, cut in mourning for their captain. 'It is draining the song from my soul. These people ...' he gestured weakly towards the windows, towards the city, 'keep their music as dull as their clothes. Half the stories I tell get me driven from halls because they do not praise Koriithos in all things. And no stories of Phoroniaa can be spoken without having me arrested. I am suffocated in this mausoleum.'

'It has been hard on all of us,' she said. Desma most of all.

Delphinus spoke again. 'I want to leave.' His voice was woollen thunder in the dimming light.

Her chest filled with a deep pain, an echo of the piper's hurt. None of them felt comfortable in Koriithos. The people were cold towards outsiders. They had no need to be hospitable, as they controlled the canal and isthmus that connected the southern League to the rest of the world. Trade came to them.

Since returning from rescuing Desma, they had been allowed out of the palace to explore the city. Kassandra had been accosted by men for wearing bright clothes – it was only because Bion had been down the street and stepped in that she was not injured. And Delphinus had been jailed for singing a song about a battle won by Phoroniaa, Koriithos' most bitter rival.

And every day, Cela walked down to the beach closest to the cliff beneath the temple. She knew it was futile, but she still went to the sea to search the waves, hoping for a sign of his body. He had told her once that it was Opuni custom to be buried wearing nothing but one's torc, to be consumed by the earth so the spirit could be truly free. She had hoped to be able to grant him one last honour.

But the sea remained empty of her friend.

'We love you.' She spoke softly, sincerely. She took Delphinus' hands, hands that crafted music that made trees weep and stars shine. She kissed his fingers. 'We are here for you.'

His darkened eyes found her and a chill swept down her body. They were red and smudged, marred by nights of tears that washed his brightness away. Guilt rippled through her for not seeing the desolation breaking her friend, for leaving him to fight the storm by himself.

She threw her arms around him, wanting her love, her warmth, to flow into his wracked body.

'Would you leave?' he asked quietly.

The question struck her heart like lightning. Would she leave her sister in everything but blood? Could she? They had been friends since birth, twenty years of struggles and adventure together. How could she leave Desma for a moment, alone in a kingdom that detested her? With a king that killed their friend, a prince who barely tolerated her, and a general that ... she swallowed sharply.

But to see her mother again. It had been months. She had sent a message from Trilos, but they had left before a reply could make its way back. If it did, she hoped Mynta would send it on to Koriithos and it would somehow find her.

How far did bonds go? She and Desma had always been sisters, partners in everything. But now she was to become a princess, and one day would be a queen. What would be said of Cela, daughter of Leontia?

'I don't think I can,' she replied, voice hoarse with honesty.

Delphinus pulled away to hold her gaze, a glimmer deep within his eyes. 'I don't think I can either,' he said. 'Though I would follow you if you asked me.'

Cela brushed a tear that was forming at the corner of his eye. 'I could ask for no better companion. But you need to sing, Delphinus. Khufu would not want your voice to fall silent because of him.'

The piper's face grew weary. 'Grief is like the sea, able to take many forms,' he replied. 'And none can tell another when it is time to surface.'

CHAPTER EIGHTEEN

It was the first of the two days of her wedding.

Desma had taken part in dozens of marriage ceremonies in Apasa. Couples travelled from across the League to be wed in the Grand Temple of the Goddess of Love. Farmers, soldiers, shopkeepers, priests, sailors, nobles.

But never could she have seen herself preparing for her own wedding – let alone in a foreign city and to a royal.

Desma was woken early in the morning in the private chambers she had been given for the next three days. Thankfully, they were not the same rooms where she had been kidnapped. Cela, Arete, and Kassandra had been permitted to stay with her, as it was traditional for the bride to spend her last days with the female members of her family.

The first day was the Farewell, when she said goodbye to her childhood, her family, and, in most cases, her virginity. Apasa was not as prudish as the Koriithosans, and that experience had gone to a fumbling weaver's daughter when she was fifteen.

She had been allowed to splash water across her face but forbidden to bathe, for that was reserved for the second day. She was dressed in a modest peplos of grey, belted with warm leather, with white ribbons tied through her braided hair.

Desma and her friends were escorted outside the palace, where three women waited. Their faces were covered in black and gold veils, symbolising the Diviners, daughters of Nurtia who was Goddess of Fate: Athrpa, Enie, and Pemphetru. One held the leash to a large boar, its tusks wicked and body bristling with hair and muscle. But its eyes were glazed and its tongue lolled out of its mouth. It must have been heavily sedated to be led so placidly.

Another woman held the leash to a large white swan, its beak and wings tied shut with golden wire, hissing angrily.

The last woman led a beautiful heifer of richest cream, eyes large and knowing, horns curling away from her face.

A crowd had gathered behind the women, for it was not every day they saw a foreigner become a princess in their city.

A crier went before them, calling for citizens to make way as they undertook a sacred duty. Musicians followed them; pipes and drums and bells rang out in praise to the goddesses they were visiting. Several carts brought up the rear, guarded by warriors, cradling tributes to the gods: wide, golden bowls, silver spears, amphoras of wine and oil, precious stones, and fine statuettes.

They wended their way through the city and exited by the Canal Gate. The Temple of Artimi was set outside the walls, for one could not contain the Wild Goddess.

A path barely larger than a game trail led through a grove of pine trees. They came to a clearing that held a clear pool ringed with reeds. A grey marble temple stood, festooned with asphodel and amaranth. It was simple in comparison with other temples in the city. A circular building only a score of paces wide, its domed roof held up by twelve slim pillars.

In the centre of the temple was a block of stone, carved with images of the goddess hunting deer, boar, lions, and bears, surrounded by her hounds and huntresses. Firelight bathed each corner, a stone snake wreathed around the stem of blackened torches: a symbol of the Old One, whose covens Artimi accepted when they became lost.

A priestess stepped forward, her hair long enough to reach her ankles, twisted into a thick braid. Her leather dress, dyed a grey-black, had a diamond cut from her chest, exposing her heart. A large knife was tied to her waist and a quiver of arrows was on her back, though there was no sign of a bow. She beckoned Desma towards her.

The woman with the boar passed the lead to Desma, who pulled the placid animal after her as she approached.

Artimi was the protector of children, keeping them under her hand until it was time for them to step into marriage and abandon her. For she was the Virgin Goddess who objected most against the contract of marriage. The offering was to thank the goddess for her protection and subdue her anger at losing another girl to Uni.

Desma led the boar up to the low stone block. It took some pushing and tempting, but she and the priestess cajoled the animal up onto the altar. It laid down on its own accord, as though accepting what was to come.

The priestess reached out and grabbed her arm tightly.

'It is not too late,' she whispered freely. 'One last gift from Artimi: choose her. Flee into her fields, and she will stay the hand of any man who would raise it in anger. Choose freedom.'

Though she knew the offer was coming, Desma's heart skipped a beat. She could accept. She could swear to serve the Huntress as her mother had bidden her, when she lay dying in the wreckage of the temple. None, not even the king, could come after her.

She gently pried the priestess' hand off her. 'I thank Artimi for her offer, but I must choose another path. I thank her for protecting my girlhood until it was my choice to give it away. She will forever be honoured in my heart, and I will never pass her sacred groves without leaving an offering to her glory.'

The priestess looked sad, but said nothing further. She drew her bronze blade and handed it, hilt first, to Desma. It was cool in her hand. They moved over to the boar's exposed neck, his breath deep and slow, eyes half-closed as it stared into the trees.

Desma took a steadying breath, whispering a prayer of thanks, before swiftly bringing the knife down to slice its neck. Hot, thick, reeking blood poured forth, splattering her face and dress. The priestess moved forward with a deep clay bowl to catch the blood, and would use it for practices secret to her goddess.

The boar kicked once, twice feebly before growing still, eyes glazing, as the last of its life dripped onto the stone.

'The goddess accepts your thanks and your offering,' the priestess said. She held out her hand for the knife. Desma passed it over, noting a slight tremor in her own hand.

'How much?' the priestess asked.

Desma swallowed. 'A lock.'

The priestess took a thick handful of Desma's hair and, with a sharp movement, sliced it away. Desma looked at the lock of her hair, red like her mother's, in the priestess' hand and felt a pang. But the memory of Camillus pressed behind her, breathing wetly in her ear, sawing at her hair, caused her throat to stopper in fear.

'May you pass from her protection and into another's,' the priestess said.

Desma knelt and kissed the floor between the priestess' bare feet before returning to join the others, her bloodied footprints trailing in the grass.

Without a word, the procession turned and led the way back to the city.

Cela grabbed her hand, not caring of the blood that squelched between their fingers. 'We are here with you,' she whispered.

Desma's heart warmed despite her growing dread.

All too soon, they arrived at a temple with doors of solid rose quartz, its columns fluted and white, its gardens filled with roses in a riot of colour.

The second woman gave her the cord connected to the bound swan. It lunged at Desma, jamming its beak hard into her hip. Desma jerked the lead, pulling the swan off its feet, dragging it honking in distress up the stairs.

Apple and myrtle incense choked her and burned her eyes as the doors opened. Two priestesses waited inside, dressed in blush and apricot robes. The image reminded her so strongly of home it felt like a blow to her stomach; her mother stood with arms held open for her, draped in the finery of her goddess, love in all its forms. Tears stung her eyes. She wanted to run, but instead she forced her feet forward, swan at her heels, as she entered Turan's temple.

Inside was luscious and beautiful, but held none of the magnificence of the Grand Temple. Mosaics chronicling the birth and life of Turan filled the floor. A gold statue of the goddess waited behind the altar. Desma couldn't meet her ancient gaze. She remembered how the statue back home had changed, its usual smile turning cold and cruel, letting the battle rage when the Empyreans attacked them. Hate curdled inside her, drowning out sound. She did not hear what the priestess was saying until she pointed at the altar.

Desma reached down and grabbed the swan roughly, hurling it up on the altar. It thrashed mightily until both priestesses held it down, one at its neck and the other its feet.

Desma picked up the gold knife that waited on a nearby table. The bird fought against its captors. The gold wire around its beak snapped, and it let out a scream that was eerily human. Desma brought the knife down swiftly, almost severing its head from its body.

The blood was so hot it almost stung. The priestess at its neck lunged for the bowl, but the swan's body was caught in death throes, and most of its blood was spent on the floor. Desma's legs were drenched.

The priestesses glared at her. 'The goddess is displeased with your offering,' one said, her words cold. 'Love will be hard fought in your marriage. You would do well to bring great offerings to Turan, if you have hopes of finding affection with your husband.'

Desma threw the knife on the floor, the gold ringing out brightly. 'Do not hold your breath.' She turned on her heel and left, eyes burning into her back. She did not breathe easy until she was back on the street and in her friends' arms.

Her shoulders began to shake as she tried to steady herself. The procession tried to resume, but Arete halted them with a sharp word. The three women surrounded her, giving her a moment of peace and privacy as she fought to control the flood of emotions inside her. The street held its breath. Passersby paused, the breeze tugged gently at wedding ribbons. A child's laughter faltered into silence.

Arete took her cheeks in both hands, hazel eyes so close that they were everything Desma could see. 'Strength,' her friend said. 'Find the strength that has brought you this far. Find it to go even further. Strength, Desma.'

This was the closest she had come to Turan since leaving Apasa. To stand in her temple, before her shrine, and make a sacrifice – it had terrified her. And clearly the goddess had not forgotten her, for she had rejected her offering. Not that Desma had held much hope for finding love with Lycon. But maybe she would not need his affection. Her friends offered all the love she could ever want. All the love she had left in the world.

'I am ready,' she said, squeezing her friends' hands, giving them a brave smile. Forming a line, Kassandra to her right and Cela and Arete on her left, they continued through the city.

As they approached their last stop, the Temple of Uni, she heard a disturbance off one of the side streets. The crowd kept its source hidden, but there was shouting and some clattering. Guards moved swiftly to investigate.

Before they had gone much further, a woman burst from the sidelines, her face red with anger. 'Outsider,' she cried, pointing at Desma. She flung something that splatted on the stones in front of them. A rotten apple.

While a warrior pulled the woman away, another two women appeared from the other side.

'Foreigner.'

'Barbarian.'

Desma ducked her head low, arm shielding her, as she was pelted with apples and oranges.

Guards closed ranks, grunting as the more overripe fruit thudded against their armour.

'Get back,' the captain shouted, brandishing his spear at the women. 'You stand between this woman and the gods! Do not think your judgement is greater than theirs.'

Desma was crushed in the tight circle, her friends pressed against her. She glimpsed between the warriors' shoulders. Men and women pushed forward, their stoic faces marred with scowls, shouting at the men blocking them from reaching her. The veiled women and the crier had stepped aside, waiting quietly for whatever the outcome. The cow watched on with doleful eyes.

Arete drew a knife beside her. 'Stay in the circle,' she said, before slipping out between the guards.

'Wait—' Desma grunted as one of the guards accidentally elbowed her.

'Watch it, you oaf,' Cela shouted. 'Give us some space, please.'

They stepped forward, loosening the circle.

Most of the crowd had dissipated, fleeing whatever trouble had begun, but an alarming amount remained. Most were women. Desma was surprised. Koriithosan women were sombre, plainly dressed, and seemed almost without fire. They were quiet and let their men take charge. Yet here they had abandoned their placid demeanours and shoved against the king's men, ferocious in their need to get to her.

'Outsider!'

'Stranger!'

'Witch!'

Her attention snapped to the final voice, but the caller was nowhere to be seen. What did they mean? There was no way anyone beyond Cisra knew her secret. Not even Cosmas, though he was aware she had hidden some of the truth about the monster from them. The crew believed she had slain the beast terrorising the city. No one questioned the disappearance of the monster's body deep in the forest. Its head had been cast into the sea, sinking swiftly – it had been, in truth, an enchanted stone.

A man yelled shrilly as a guard slashed his arm with a spear, blood soaking through the fabric of his chiton. The sight of blood seemed to quench the fire in the crowd, and they backed away.

The tramp of feet announced the arrival of reinforcements, and soon the Koriithosans had scattered, leaving only a handful of onlookers at shopfronts and houses.

'What,' Kassandra said slowly, 'the blasted Beneath was that?'

'Are you alright, my lady?' the captain asked, his face strained.

She nodded. 'I am okay, captain. Were any of your men hurt?'

'No, thank Laran,' he said. 'I am dishonoured that this occurred on my watch. Once we are back at the palace, I will seek out Actor for an appropriate reprimand. My apologies, Lady Desma.'

Without thinking it through, she reached out and gripped his upper arm. He looked at her in shock. 'You have *nothing* to apologise for,' she said. 'You protected us. I will not have you trouble the war leader with nonsense.

Do you understand me? I will be *very* displeased if I hear you have done otherwise.'

He nodded slowly. 'Yes, my lady.'

'Good.' She let go of his arm. 'Where did Arete go?'

Another guard approached, his breastplate covered in cabbage. 'She asked me to give you a message. She said continue to the temple, and she will meet you back at the palace. She said not to be concerned, for Cosmas is with her.'

Cosmas – where did he come from? Was he following them this whole time? She should not be surprised. He went where he pleased.

She turned back to the captain. 'Shall we continue?'

'If you do not wish to return to the palace instead?'

'I am going to finish what has started, captain.'

He bowed before calling out orders. Their procession formed up again, this time reinforced with an additional fifty warriors. Though the crier continued to herald their approach, there was little need as the streets were almost empty.

The Temple of Uni was narrow but no less breathtaking. Three wide steps led up to thick columns of gold and ivory that wrapped the temple, holding up the angled ceiling. Frescoes around the top of the columns depicted the Queen of the Gods, majestic and powerful, rivalling Tinia in regality.

Desma took the lead of the cream heifer from the last of the veiled women. As Goddess of Marriage, Uni held sway over all spouses. She enforced the bonds and vows, and it was her fury that fell on those who broke them.

As she climbed the steps, the cow moved to keep pace with her so they ascended together. A priestess waited for them by the open doorway, clad in cream robes with gold bracelets. She nodded to Desma in greeting before giving a low bow to the heifer, who seemed to blink in acknowledgment.

'Come,' the priestess said, moving inside.

The cow tugged on the rope as it moved forward, taking the lead. Desma followed.

The temple walls were covered in carvings of the goddess, superbly painted. There she gave birth to Ilithiia, Goddess of Childbirth and Midwives. Another portrayed Uni fighting the giant Celsclan, son of the Being called Fundament, who had slaughtered a dozen gods until she brought him low with her flashing purple sword. Another wall showed her shrouding a village of women from brigands who sought to ravish them while their husbands were off fighting a war.

One wall depicted her blessing Atmite, first King of Phoroniaa, who later tried to seduce the goddess. Outraged that he would tempt her from her marriage to Tinia, she had cursed his family. All their children would be dumb, unable to speak silver words, to beguile or trick. The throne had passed to his brother, who made it law that the punishment for adultery was death by boiling.

The gold and ivory altar's front panel was carved to show Uni seated on an amethyst throne, a peacock at her side, a sceptre in hand. Her statue reared a dozen feet tall behind, carved from red Phoroniaan marble, her face stern but soft. She was not a harsh goddess, as long as people followed her rules. She had laid many of the laws that governed the League, for social order was also in her remit.

The cow stopped at the altar, peering up at Uni's statue, as though turning to stone herself. Desma gave her a prod, and she swung her great head, large eyes sharper than Desma thought a cow's could be. Desma did not move, unsure of what to do. It was several long moments before the cow gave a deep low. The sound grew, doubling back on itself, reverberating through the temple. Desma dropped the lead and covered her ears, but it did no good. It felt like her skull was shaking. The priestess also had her ears covered, falling to her knees as she stared wide-eyed at the cow.

Eventually, the sound faded. The cow gave her one last look before turning to walk away, back through the temple and out the doors.

Desma's brow furrowed. 'What does that mean?'

'I honestly don't know,' the priestess stuttered. She rose to her feet. 'I will need to consult with the high priestess in Phoroniaa.'

Desma glanced up at Uni's statue. 'Is the wedding blessed?'

'That I could not say,' she said. 'But I do not believe it has been rejected. The wedding may proceed.'

'I wonder where she will go,' Desma mused.

'I will order the temple guard to follow her. She is sacred to Uni.' The priestess stepped in front of her. 'I cannot tell you what your future may hold, but may the Queen of Heaven share your steps.'

Desma did not know if that boded good or ill for her.

CHAPTER NINETEEN

They returned to the palace without incident. Twin buckets of warm water waited for her in her rooms. Maids helped her remove her dress, sticky with blood, taking it away to be burned. She paused, naked, in front of the polished bronze mirror.

Her face, neck, forearms, and legs from the thigh down were covered in streaks of blood. Her hair, red as deep as sweet summer strawberries, rich like rose petals, blended with the blood on her body. Tangled locks matted. Barbarian, indeed.

Her eyes roved her body, noting her small but firm breasts, the smooth plane of her stomach and back, her strong thighs and slim calves. She was beautiful. But she never understood using these gifts like a weapon or tool to get what she wanted. This was the last night she could call her body her own. For tomorrow, she would be wed to Lycon and become a princess of Koriithos. Her body would be shared with the prince as her husband and with the kingdom as a vessel to be filled. She tried to imagine the prince's hands upon her body, squeezing her, touching her more sensitive vales. She wanted to feel overwhelmed, a slow-burning passion that erupted in a shower of sparks and heat. But she felt nothing. Sex was never an interest to her. She had lovers in the past – mostly due to Cela's urging – but none of them, men or women, brought her pleasure. It was an activity she endured until she could get dressed and leave. But she would not be able to leave this time. Lycon would come to bed night after night, expectations high for an heir.

She shivered.

Scrubbing her skin vigorously with a cloth, the water soon turned to rust. She was given no soap or oils, and had to make do with a single bucket to rinse her hair and body.

Once dried, she stood in front of the mirror again. Skin of burnished copper. Slanted eyes, as was usual among the kingdoms on the eastern coast, a warm brown with thick lashes. Her eyebrows, a darker red to almost be black, were bushier than Cela's.

She touched her reflection's fingertips, the bronze cool to her skin. Was she a witch? Cisra had told her she was not, that she was something different, not seen in the world before. But how? She knew of no ancient power in her family. Her mother's family had served the temple for generations. Her father's kin had been mostly farmers, and only in recent generations taken to arts such as pottery.

She thought about her father's workshop, always filled with dust and the scent of clay. His wares displayed on rickety shelves. His bent figure at his wheel, apron covered in muck. Hands coated in clay, shaping beauty from the earth. How her heart ached to be held by him again! And her mother. To fall into her arms, smelling of applewood and myrtle, to come together like wine into amphora, melding into each other.

She had used magic to undo the curse on Cisra's sons, Alexon and Ector. Turan's magic had twisted Cisra's spell. How could she have unravelled a goddess' power?

She had thought about telling Cela a dozen times, but she could never bring the sound to her lips. If Cela knew, she could be placed in danger. From whom, Desma did not know, but it was a power that had not existed in the world before. Nothing good would come of it becoming public knowledge.

Perhaps it best be forgotten, even by her own mind. She would not use it again. It would be a secret she took to her pyre ...

There was a slight swish behind her.

She spun around, hands looking for the closest weapon. But it was only Arete and Cosmas slipping through the door.

'There you are,' she said, relieved.

'How nice to see you, too,' Cosmas said with a sparkle in his eyes.

She was naked.

Desma shrieked as she ran to her bed and pulled off the blanket. Arete punched Cosmas in the arm, hard, while he tried to contain his amusement.

'You should have your eyes poked out,' Desma growled. 'I will be a royal soon. Maybe I'll order it so.'

He gave an exaggerated bow. 'Whatever your desire may be, Princess Desma.'

'Punch him again, Arete.'

The shipwright obliged.

'Stop that,' he said, swaying away. He took a seat at the table and began to shred the peeled figs into bits, popping morsels into his mouth.

'Where did you go?' Desma asked Arete, blanket wrapped securely about her.

'I followed the first woman to throw something at you,' she said. 'I wanted to see where she would go afterwards. As I was following her, lo and behold, there was Cosmas. He was also trailing her.'

'And what were you even doing with us?' Desma asked him.

He shrugged. 'The palace was getting dull. I thought I would go for a stroll with you. It turned out to be a prudent choice.' His muted blue eyes were bright in the soft gloom, night falling swiftly that afternoon. He smoothed back his sun-whitened hair. 'We discovered something rather interesting.'

'It appears,' Arete said, 'that there is a group of people in the city who have not taken kindly to you becoming their future queen. They appear to have formed a group of some kind, but we need time to learn more. Koriithosans are not particularly amenable to answering our questions.'

'They could be,' Cosmas said with a hint of threat.

'I would prefer we did not harm anyone,' Desma said. 'They threw some fruit at me. Let us be cautious in our approach. It will take people time to adjust.'

Cosmas nodded.

Desma pulled them both into a hug, making sure her blankets did not slip. 'Thank you both,' she said. 'I am blessed by the gods to have you as my friends.'

They bid each other good night. As Arete and Cosmas left the room, the quartermaster paused for a moment, his eyes burning a soft blue. 'Tomorrow, you become a princess,' he said quietly. 'But do not forget your promise to me, Desma, daughter of priestess and potter.'

He slipped out, the door closing with a soft *thunk*.

Desma sat on the bed, letting the blanket fall away. The bargain they had struck years ago, when she had found the strange man on their docked ship in Pallan, poison in hand as he stood over their food supplies. Both had been surprised to find the other standing there.

She had promised to find a solution to his problem, and he had served on her crew faithfully ever since. The only trouble now, was that she might have found the answer ...

Cela wandered the palace aimlessly, her mind as lost and drifting as her body. She paid no heed to where her steps took her, ignoring the servants who asked if she needed assistance, only turning about when she reached a dead end.

Desma was to be married on the morrow and would become a royal, her name forever inscribed in the history of the League. And Cela would be ...

Part of her heart was ever turned towards Apasa, but her feet faltered at the prospect of returning home. She was not yet ready. Once she went home, her destiny would be sealed to the temple. Before her and Desma's world had been overturned, that would have been her fate, and she had been content. But Desma's ambition to find the tomb of the Sand-King had driven them to Urruc, and their misfortune had been spelled out.

Though she herself was not blameless. She remembered the night Desma had awoken her, eyes bright, as she told Cela her plan. How their names would echo in the annals of the League's history. Cela had said yes. She was at Desma's side every step of the journey, through all the planning, studying in the Library of Kelus, bringing the ancient scholar from Delphon. Sailing across the Middle Sea, confronting the terror of the cursed land, the attack from strange men ... what followed.

Had that door been there when she first passed? Beyond, she found a narrow hallway that wended its way inwards. Intrigued, she slipped inside, noting the thin layer of dust that gathered on the edge of the hall. The corridor was used, but not often. And the servants did not care to clean well here.

Maybe she could travel to Opuni, find Khufu's family, tell them of his bravery and sacrifice. The thought made her heart thump with sadness. Perhaps could bring Delphinus with her.

Or she could visit Mynta, stay with her for a while.

She had never been further north than Dramaki, or sailed the Cold Sea. Whole lands existed and thrived beyond the League and Empire. Maybe her destiny was out there. Maybe the gods had forgotten to write her story.

They had certainly not forgotten Desma's.

She frowned at her own petulance. Did she want to have the attention of the gods? Turan had destroyed Desma's family and their home. Tinia's laws drove her from city to city, searching for salvation. Aplu would make her a princess.

The gods were kind in drops and cruel in waves.

She came across a set of rooms with worn furniture also covered in dust. It might have been receiving rooms at some time, though not used for many years. The clean track continued through a door and she followed. Another hall, with no windows and sparsely spaced torches, led to a set of steep steps that spiralled down. She checked her dagger strapped to her belt and thought briefly how foolish it would be to continue before descending.

The air grew colder the further down she went, one hand on the rough-hewn wall. Slight vibrations grew within the wall. Putting her cheek against it and closing her eyes, the rhythm revealed itself: waves. She must be close to the cliff walls that either faced the harbour or the canal. Cela had not realised the palace went so deep into the cliffside.

The strains of singing drifted up the stairs. Drawing her blade and keeping it close to her side, she crept forward, silent beyond the occasional rustle of her peplos on stone.

The stairs ended in a large circular room that had three doors, lit with a mixture of torches and large rocks that glowed with a warm, golden light. Forge-stones, creations of the Thinkery in Trilos. They were immensely expensive, and there were six in this room alone, at home amongst the richly furnished chairs, couches, rugs, and tables covered with a dozen pastimes: sewing, weaving, painting, scrolls.

Several statues of women lined the walls, which Cela found unnerving. One was blindfolded and held her hands behind her ears, as though listening to the world. Another had her arms outstretched, reaching for someone, her mouth open like she was shouting. The one closest to Cela had no eyes or ears, just smooth marble, its face turned towards the ceiling.

The singing emanated from the only door left ajar. Whimsical humming with snatches of words, it often drifted off-key before falling back into the melody.

Cela was wondering if she should slip away when the door flew open and a woman pranced out with a graceless twirl, stumbling slightly at Cela's presence. She froze and dropped the blankets she was carrying, mouth agape and eyes wide.

Cela did not move, simply stared at the person in front of her. She was older than Cela by a dozen years, black hair enriched with earthy tones, tightly braided with green ribbons. Her skin was dark umber, eyes brown, and lips the pink of old roses. She wore a purple peplos girdled by a belt of chestnut horsehair, pinned with copper, and her feet were bare.

'You have not been here before,' the woman said, her voice deeper than expected.

Cela shook her head, quietly sheathing her dagger. 'I have not. My name is Cela.'

The woman cocked her head to the side, her eyes intense. 'Celadine. Shadow in sunshine.'

Cela inhaled sharply. She knew her name? 'I do not know you.'

'I am also in shadows,' she said. 'Have you come to collect my blankets? They are too itchy to allow dreams to come.'

Cela shook her head.

The woman sighed. 'Well, it was pleasant to see you. Goodbye.' She turned to head back into the other room, blankets left piled on the floor.

'Wait,' Cela said, taking a step forward. 'What is your name?'

The maiden looked over her shoulder. 'My name holds power in these walls, Celadine, though I do not wield it myself. Would you take this power?'

Who was this woman? Why was she in these rooms, so far from sun and wind? 'Are you a prisoner?'

'Did you find any doors barred on your way?'

No. 'Are you alone down here?'

'You are here.'

Cela bit her tongue to keep from snapping. Was she purposefully being difficult? Or was something not right with her? 'Are you happy here?'

The woman tensed, arms rigid and eyes wide, spearing Cela to the spot. She approached, feet silent on the rugs and stone, until she gripped Cela's arms tightly. 'Bounded by stone, tied by rules, held by blood. Duty bears the weight of a mountain. Happiness is the leaf caught in a breeze. You have recently learned of this difference, Celadine.' She released Cela's arms and skipped away, shutting the door behind her, leaving Cela alone in the strange room.

CHAPTER TWENTY

Morning came all too swiftly, the sky bleeding from black to grey to rosy.

Maids entered an hour after dawn, but Desma was already awake. Artume, Goddess of Night, had not blessed her with sleep. Her lids were heavy while her mind raced.

It was the day of her wedding.

Traditionally, the mother of the bride would help her bathe and dress. She had resigned herself to doing it with the help of her maids when the door opened.

The queen.

Desma blushed as she bowed. She still did not know the queen's name. No one, not Actor or Lycon or Hyllos, had ever told her. 'My queen,' she said in greeting.

'Rise, child,' she said. Younger than the king but well into middle age, her hair was swept elegantly upwards, its black sheen frosted with grey. Her face was still smooth, a lifetime of passivity keeping it free of lines. Her eyes were narrow, a deep shade of brown, with thick lashes. Her body had gone from maidenly to matronly, thickening her limbs and midriff. She bore herself regally, standing tall in a peplos of dull green, a small necklace of emeralds strung along her pale neck, hands clasped before her. 'I know I can never replace your mother, but I was hoping you would allow me to be your companion during the bathing ritual.'

Still shocked by her appearance, Desma nodded, for there was little else she could do.

'Come, let us begin,' the queen said.

She helped Desma disrobe from her sleeping dress, running a critical eye over her body. Desma wanted to cover herself, but forced her arms to remain by her side, her skin pebbling in the cool morning air.

'You are tense,' the queen said crisply. 'And cold. Step into the bath.'

A great copper tub had replaced her small one for the morning, its surface carved with motifs of fertility and happiness. Pomegranates, apples, and figs. Lyres, garlands, and bonfires.

The water was just under scalding, and she eased in gently, sucking air between her teeth.

Soon enough, she was submerged completely, her hair a pool of red around her. The water was scented with lily and orchids, petals floating on the surface. The queen picked up a soft cloth and began to wipe her arms, humming softly.

When it came to her hair, the queen used a small bowl to gently pour water over her head, combing her fingers through so every strand was wet. She was gentle, her hands as warm as the water, and Desma's muscles loosened. Next came oils. The queen opened one bottle, and the room was filled with the scent of roses.

Desma reached out to stay her hand. 'No, please ... a different oil.' Her voice quivered with suppressed emotion.

The queen was puzzled for a moment before realisation dawned. She gave a sad smile and put the rose oil away. 'Here,' she said, opening two other bottles. 'Cassia and peach?'

Desma smiled gratefully. The queen poured the oil over her hair, massaging it into her locks. Fingers moved to her temples and then her shoulders, loosening knots until her body felt light yet settled. The water became slick and opalescent. The warmth of cassia and the sweetly fresh peach were pleasing scents. Desma closed her eyes, letting herself be swept away, just for a moment, so she was no longer in Koriithos at the hands of a strange woman, but back home.

Eventually, Desma asked the question she was ashamed to put into words. 'I am sorry that I never asked someone before this, but what is your name?'

The hands on her scalp paused for a moment before resuming. 'I am not surprised no one told you, Desma,' she said softly. 'I fulfilled my task of giving my husband an heir, though I am shamed to have only been blessed once. My purpose in life was completed twenty-five years ago. My name is Pinaria.'

'It's lovely,' Desma said.

The queen moved back to her side. 'I am going to be honest with you, Desma. You are not the wife I envisioned for my son. I cannot say I am pleased ... but nor can I say I am displeased. I am waiting. All I can say to you is be the wife Lycon needs, and the queen Koriithos wants.'

And stop being who I want to be, Desma thought bitterly.

'Did you hear what happened yesterday?' she asked.

Pinaria pursed her lips. 'I did. It is an affront to the goddesses to have interrupted your passage.'

'I did not think the people would be so against me,' Desma said honestly. She knew it was not a popular decision, but to have it almost cause a riot in the street ...

Pinaria squeezed her arm. 'It is not the whole city. There have been rumblings from a small group of dissidents since your wedding to my son was announced. Women who hold tightly to the old ways. They call themselves the Dirciade.'

Desma frowned in confusion.

'Princess Dirce was slain by Cisra when the sorceress learnt her husband had betrayed her love in favour of royalty,' the queen explained.

'Why would they call themselves ...' Understanding bloomed like nightshade in her stomach.

'Exactly,' the queen said. 'A powerful foreign woman almost destroyed the city. Their fear is that you will walk in the witch's footsteps.'

'But the prophecy says that Koriithos needs me.'

'Fear is the great distorter in this world. Things that were clear become fractured. Our beliefs twisted. Our actions corrupted.' The queen held her gaze. 'We do not know what Aplu's words mean for you. That is what we are all waiting to see. But I will say one thing that you will not hear from the king or my son.' She lifted Desma's hand to her lips. 'Thank you for staying.'

Desma could not bring any words to form, but felt tears glisten in her eyes.

She rose from the bath and stepped out before kneeling on the stone floor. A large vessel waited by the queen. Used only for weddings, it was half Desma's height, with elongated handles on either side, blazoned in orange and black. It depicted Uni and Heran, God of Weddings and one of the Lovers, blessing a bride and groom kneeling before them. She remembered her father had made several in his shop, always spending more time on them than on other commissions, to make them as perfect as possible.

'This is filled with water from the Nethuns' Spring,' the queen said. 'May it bless you on this day.' A maid had to help her lift the vessel. Desma gasped, the cold and slightly salty water a shock after the hot bath.

After getting to her feet and being dried, the queen circled her naked body, anointing her with oils. Her hair was brushed until it shone. Maids came in to intricately braid it, keeping most of it loose down her back. They formed loops across her brow and a circlet around her head, fastened with gold pins.

Her dress was lavender and fell beautifully on her body. A belt of pale grey leather girdled her hips. Her sandals were soft and stitched with purple thread. A small chest was brought and placed before the queen.

'I know you have your own jewellery, but I thought maybe you could wear some of mine,' she said, opening the lid. 'They have been collected and passed down by Koriithosan queens since Gylippus' grandfather's grandfather was king.'

Desma lifted out a bracelet of orichalcum sculpted to look like a ring of ivy. It shimmered red, gold, and orange as she twisted it in her hands. 'Thank you,' she whispered. 'But I thought ...'

'Women can wear whatever they wish on their wedding day,' she said. 'Most of us take advantage of it and clank like a soldier in full armour when we walk.'

Desma let out a laugh, some of the dread lifting from her chest.

Together, they chose another gold bracelet with beaten divots studded with diamonds. Several rings of gold and bronze with opals went on one hand. On the other was a delicate bracelet of whirling gold and silver, tethered by thin chains to rings on her three middle fingers. Each of the rings had a small rose carved on its surface. A necklace with large, uncut diamonds strung on an orichalcum chain graced her neck. Matching earrings followed.

Last was the bridal crown. A headband of pure white metal that rose in the centre and narrowed towards the ends. Large diamonds with smaller topazes studded its surface. Pinaria placed it on Desma's head, securing it by lopping small braids of her hair through hidden hooks. She then lifted the wedding veil from a small box and attached it to the crown. Dyed a brilliant yellow with rare saffron, it was the sheerest gossamer that allowed Desma to see clearly but keep her face hidden from the world. Only the priests of Heran could weave the veil.

Desma moved to the mirror and let a small smile slip onto her face.

She was divine.

She spun in a slow circle, letting her hair and dress twirl slightly, her jewellery flashing in the sunlight.

'You look beautiful,' the queen said. 'Come, we must leave for the temple.'

They moved through the palace, Desma's stomach fluttering like a flock of swallows cartwheeling through the sky, and she was glad she had not eaten anything.

Beyond the rear gate, the marbled path rose to the temple that claimed pride of place on the cliff's edge. As they approached the white, green-streaked temple, Desma nearly stumbled as she suddenly thought of Khufu. He would have taken the same path as her, leading from the temple to the cliff edge. Killed because he had stayed, so the rest of the crew could save her.

Up saltworn steps and past the columns carved with seaweed. Statues of Regorus and Kreban stood at the doors, frightening and fierce as they protected their father's temple.

The scent of pine and salt washed over her as she stepped inside. The floor was covered in fine white sand that squeaked under foot. Tall vases filled with still-living coral lined the walls. In the centre of the temple was a large altar, carved from a solid block of sun-bleached, weathered pine. Standing around it were the king, Lycon, Kalchas, Actor, and the high priest.

No one from her crew was there.

Her mother and father should have accompanied her to the temple, her family surrounding her.

She was alone on her wedding day.

She took a deep breath and continued to the altar.

Lycon was handsome in his deep green tunic, a gold belt studded with topaz, and a small crown of white sea foam on his bright black hair. He gave her a tight smile as she approached, but she could see every muscle was tense.

Gylippus wore his usual robes with his sapphire crown, and looked ready to have the whole event over with as quickly as possible.

Kalchas stood in the shadows, face obscured.

Actor's full bronze armour was polished to a shine, a man of gilded war with a green plumed helmet, tall spear and a large shield. He did not look at her, staring straight ahead.

The priest wore white and green robes, a driftwood staff in hand with shells and dried starfish tied to it. He frowned as she approached.

Desma stopped. Pinaria held her with a concerned look.

'I'm sorry,' Desma stammered, her heart beating wildly. 'I don't think ...'

She was steps away from becoming someone else. This was the last time she would be Desma, daughter of Timothea and Palamaon. After today, she would be Desma, wife of Lycon. Trapped in a palace, feared by her people, unloved by her husband and his family.

Why? Because of a prophecy that left out all the details? To stay for a city that did not want her?

Her back was wet with sweat. 'Pinaria, please.'

The queen's face hardened. 'I am the queen,' she corrected. 'Keep walking, Desma.'

Her heart thundered in her ears. It was too much. Too fast.

'I will have you dragged to the altar if needed,' the queen whispered sharply. 'Do not mistake my earlier kindness for love. Now, *move.*'

Shouting arose from outside the temple. Was it another riot? Had the people of the city decided to rise up against her? She did not have magic like Cisra. No flying scorpions would come to wing her to safety.

One of the doors was pushed open, and a familiar voice strung through, yelling at the guards. 'If you think you are going to touch me with those dirty hands, you better think again! Now get out of my way, or I will shove that spear so far up your ...'

'Cela?' Desma shouted, hiking up her dress and running back to the temple entry, ignoring the queen's command to stay.

Cela poked her head in, hair dishevelled from struggling with the men outside. 'Desma! Tell this oaf that he better pray he already has children, because I am about to rip—'

'Let her in,' Desma commanded, blinking in surprise when the guards stepped away.

Cela straightened her dress with a huff and gave them an evil glare. 'Come on, Arete. Next time, remind me to invite Bion, because you were as helpful as a lump of coal.'

Arete appeared behind her, dressed in a fine charcoal dress, a red leather belt, and ruby earrings. Cela wore a lemon yellow peplos with a brown belt, and an intricate sage ribbon necklace that matched the fabric woven through her golden hair.

'Can you believe that no one came to get us for the vowing?' Cela continued to complain as she looped her arms through Desma's. Arete mirrored her on the other side. 'I mean, we are your family. It is quite outrageous. We didn't miss anything yet, did we?'

Desma could not keep the tears from her cheeks. Her arms tightened around theirs, a rope in the storm that kept her safe on deck. 'No, my dear, dear friends. Impeccable timing, as always.' Her heart began to cease its racing, the iron band around her chest becoming silken, still tight but no longer crushing,

Cela leaned forward to kiss her cheek. 'Let's go make you a princess.'

They approached the altar and the gathered royals. Gylippus and Kalchas were furious. The queen had resumed her docile demeanour, but Desma could see the sharpness in her eyes.

She thought she saw a quirk of Actor's lips, but it was gone in a flash.

Lycon looked more bemused than anything else.

'It is customary,' the high priest said with a glower, 'that the bride's *family* witness the vowing.'

'And we are her family,' Cela snapped back. 'Chosen by each other. By blood or by spirit, family is family.'

'Family is family,' Arete echoed, planting her feet firmly in the sand, daring anyone to try and shift her.

'Just get on with it,' the king growled. 'I am hungry.'

'Yes, my king,' the priest said with a bow. 'If the groom and bride will step forward and stand at either end of the altar.'

Her friends gave her hands one last squeeze before they stepped aside. Lycon waited with a solemn expression, face impassive and body taut. Desma smiled at him, but realised he could not see her face through the veil.

The priest began to speak. 'We stand here together to ask Nethuns, God of Koriithos and All Seas, to witness and bless this union. Prophecy has brought you together, and together you will bring Koriithos to greatness. Thus has ever been the will of Nethuns to his kings. Do you vow, here before our god and your families, that you willingly bind yourself to each other as husband and wife, to stand as king and queen one day, to fulfil all duties of your roles before the eyes of Tinia and Uni?'

'I vow,' Lycon said firmly.

'I vow,' Desma said in a rush.

The priest turned and bowed to the statue of Nethuns behind him, carved from a solid block of marble, as though the god had been trapped within. Veins throbbed from his stone arms. Muscles bulged in his shoulders and stomach. His face was weathered and scarred, eyes wide like a deep-sea fish, his mouth open to bear his shark teeth. Hair fell down his back like a wave, and atop his head was his scales and sea-froth crown. His legs were hidden in a maelstrom of water, nets, and snarling creatures that looked up at him adoringly – his monstrous children. The god clung to his four-prong fishing spear that contained all the power of a tidal wave and earthquake.

The high priest lifted a finely crafted amphora and poured two cups to the brim with water, gifting them to the betrothed. Desma sniffed and wrinkled her nose. Seawater.

'As is customary when a Koriithosan royal weds, Nethuns forms the third point in the marriage: husband, wife, and god. I bid you now to seal the act by drinking a cup of the sea, taking Nethuns into yourself. Drink!'

Lycon did not hesitate, taking long draughts, trying to empty the cup as quickly as possible.

Desma slid the cup under her veil and took the first sip. Salt and bitterness puckered her lips and she nearly spat. But everyone watched her. She could not fail at this task. She took a swallow, and another. And then one more. She gagged, almost throwing it back up. But she forced the water down. It reminded her of when the beachmaster at Trilos had forced her to eat sand. Her body was trying to reject the seawater, as it had the gritty sand, but she overruled it.

Lycon finished before her, but she was not far behind, tipping her head back to make sure the last drops fell onto her tongue.

They placed the cups, upside down, on the altar.

A moment of still breath, the space between inhale and exhale, as the congregation waited.

Though her throat was raw from salt, she felt fine.

Then Lycon promptly threw up.

He had also skipped breakfast that morning, for it was mostly water and bile that splattered the surface of the altar.

Everyone gasped, stepping back to avoid the mess.

And then Desma coughed, her throat feeling full, her stomach constricting as she clapped a hand over her mouth.

'Oh no,' she heard Cela murmur.

She turned from the altar in time, lifting her veil above her mouth as she began to spew. The salt burned her raw throat, and when she tried to breathe through the pain, she choked. Brine bubbled over her lips and down her front before she managed to spit it forward. Onto the high priest's feet.

Lycon wiped his mouth in horror.

The priest was apoplectic. 'This wedding has been rejected by Nethuns. He has refused to be part of this union and withdrawn his blessing. This marriage has been declared void by the heavens!'

Gylippus slammed his fist on a clean section of the altar. 'Can't you do one thing right?' he shouted at Lycon before turning to the priest. 'This wedding is happening. Do you understand me, Timonax?'

The high priest's eyes went wide. 'My king! Nethuns could not have made his thoughts any clearer on the matter. I cannot sanctify this marriage. It must be called off and cursed in front of the entire city.'

The king gestured to Actor. In a flash, the general had his spear against the priest's throat.

'No,' Cela cried. 'Don't, Actor.' He ignored her.

Gylippus' face was inches from Timonax. 'Listen to me. I am king. The wedding between my son and the barbarian is going to happen today. You will attend the feast and say all is well. If you do not, I will have you killed and your corpse carried far inland so you can never find peace in the sea. And if you still think to be foolish, then know that I will find that daughter you had with the whore down by the docks, and I will sell them both to the Empire. After that, I will hunt down your sons like foxes. Everything you are and have will perish. *Am I clear?*'

The priest nodded, his face as white as the sand beneath him. Actor withdrew, and the priest caught himself on the altar. 'The vowing is complete,' Timonax whispered harshly. 'The temple stands behind the marriage.'

The king nodded before turning to the rest of them. 'My warning covers all of you. None is to speak of what happened here. The marriage has been blessed by Nethuns, as all royal weddings have been since my father's father's father.' His eyes narrowed on Desma, Arete, and Cela. 'You already know I am willing to kill your crew. Do not test my mettle.'

Cela stared at Actor, mouth agape, and Arete looked ready to draw a blade on the king. Desma grabbed their arms and forced them to join her bow. 'Yes, King,' she said, for all three of them.

'Very good,' he said, clapping his hands loudly. 'Let us have you both cleaned up. You have a feast to attend.'

CHAPTER TWENTY-ONE

At midday, they gathered in the great feasting hall of the palace.

Over three hundred people sat at long tables to celebrate the newlywed couple, though the ceremony would not be complete until the unveiling.

Cela sat at a table with the rest of the crew; Actor had been kind enough to arrange their invitation. She was still shaken by his actions in the temple. There was no doubt in her mind that he would have killed the high priest if ordered by his king. To slay a priest in his own temple was the height of sacrilege. Did they not fear Nethuns' retribution? And to do it in order to keep a secret …

The general had entered with the king after most of the room had filled. He had glanced towards their table, but Cela was unable to meet his eye. She scolded herself. What was he meant to have done? He could not disobey his king. She was a fool to think that he would ever put Desma – or herself – before his duty. And would she ever want to place him in such a position? She flicked a glance over the high table. He spoke quietly with Kalchas, but his eyes found hers like arrows across the hall, piercing. She blushed, but forced herself to not jerk away. Which emotion could he glean from the cacophony within herself: reproach, sweetness, hurt, warmth?

Eventually, she had to turn away and instead focus on the hall. Nobles from across the kingdom had gathered. The men, lords, and great heroes of the nation were dressed in fine clothes flashing with jewels. The women wore dour dresses of dim greens and greys despite the celebration.

Cela had made sure the crew stood out among the pigeons.

Vibrant yellow and crimson and purple, with enough gold and gems to make a pirate's eye gleam. They were an explosion of colour that outshone the richest lord, thanks to the chests provided by Mynta back in Trilos in addition to what they brought with them from Apasa.

There was a suppressed ripple in the crowd, barely noticeable among the stiff Koriithosans. Unease spilled like oil on water. Cela looked about, but none of the guests noted the source of the disturbance. No one appeared frightened and no guards readied their weapons, so danger was absent.

Finally, she glimpsed a flash of gold. A woman wove her way out of the hall, her braided hair fluttering with gold ribbons. It was the Great Lands woman! As she glided by, the nobles fastidiously ignored her, falling silent and only resuming conversation once she was out of earshot. A strange phenomenon – it seemed she had the power to stop time with her presence alone.

What was she doing at the feast? What title did she hold, or what husband did she have, to earn her place at a royal wedding?

The herald announced the approach of the newlyweds and, in that moment of distraction, the woman disappeared.

Desma and Lycon entered to great fanfare, lyres and drums playing loudly as a choir sang hymns to Uni and Fufluns and Heran. Desma had changed into a soft sage dress that brought out the flames in her hair. Lycon's rich black and red chiton with matching himation was clasped with a green starfish pin. They walked arm in arm, Desma's face still veiled, until they reached the royal table.

Desma paused for a moment, searching one of the tables, but Cela could not determine what she was looking towards. Lycon tugged her arm gently and they resumed moving.

Once they were seated, Gylippus rose to his feet, cup of wine in hand. 'Good citizens of Koriithos,' he said loudly, his voice full of gravel. 'I am pleased to announce that the mighty Nethuns has blessed my son's marriage to the slayer of the monster.' The lie rolled smoothly off his tongue. 'My ancient blood, that traces back to our first king, Meleagros, son of Nethuns himself, continues through my son. And will only grow stronger with the blood of the woman who killed the beast that terrorised our city for the past decade. I am first to say that this woman was not my first choice of wife for my son, but who among us can defy the gods when they speak to us? Many of our queens have heralded from other kingdoms: Amarhyllis of Athanai, Canace from Konoso, Males from Dramaki, even Brygos from Phoroniaa.' Several of the crowd booed. He raised a hand for silence. 'I empathise with your concerns, but all these queens served well, becoming true Koriithosan women at heart. I do not see differently in this woman who will one day be your queen. Together, we will guide and teach her. The eyes of a kingdom will be upon her.' Cela felt like getting out of her chair and slapping him. Desma was not a dog to be trained, to roll over and speak when commanded. 'But for now, let us raise our cups and toast the bride and groom, Lycon and his wife!'

'Lycon and his wife!' The room echoed.

'Desma and Lycon,' Cela shouted as loud as she could, wine splashing from her cup as she thrust it high.

'Desma and Lycon!' The rest of the crew roared, Bion's voice bellowing over them all.

The king cast them an angry glance, but drank deeply from his cup.

Desma and the prince rose to their feet. They turned to face each other. Lycon gently took the bottom corners of the veil in his hands and revealed her face. She looked nervous, but managed a smile. He seemed just as uneasy as he embraced her, burying his face in her hair rather than kiss her.

With that action, they were wed, and nothing short of a god could sunder the union.

Cela prayed that her friend would find something in common with the prince. Turan had made it clear she would allow no love between them.

The palace cooks had outdone themselves with the wedding feast. Roast boar and beef; chickens stuffed with figs; giant fish roasted wrapped in seaweed; lamb basted in honey and thyme. Celery and fennel braised with cinnamon; octopus wrapped in vine leaves. Spiced, herbal wine filled every cup. Sumac and lemon water helped clear the head before indulging in yet more wine.

Musicians played throughout the day, stopping only for poets to recite epics of valiant Koriithosan heroes, cunning astronomers, and brave kings.

Dancers and tumblers performed between tables, often slipping away with guests to more private rooms or corners.

As the sun set, washing the room with soft oranges and pinks, the king rose to his feet again. 'And now to bed,' he shouted, swaying slightly, wine cup in hand.

The crowd roared its approval as Desma and Lycon rose to their feet. Their faces were blank. They left the hall to cheers and many pieces of lewd advice. For a people so outwardly prudish, they had wild imaginations. Some of their advice did not sound physically possible to Cela, and she was quite limber.

'Let's go,' she whispered to Arete, who had sipped only on water. They followed after the married couple as they were escorted through the halls by warriors until they reached what must have been Lycon's rooms. The door shut behind them, the sound of the lock clear.

'You are both on door duty as well,' a voice said behind them. Hyllos, dressed in green and black robes with a necklace of gold strung with small flecks of different coloured gems.

'We did not want her to be alone,' she said.

'She needs all the friends she can around her,' the astronomer said. 'Come, we are supposed to sit right outside the door.'

There was a single stool, but he called a servant to fetch two more. A choir of youths stationed themselves a little down the hall. They began to sing softly, hymns and paeans to the gods and goddesses of fertility.

Cela watched the choir, thinking about what was supposed to be happening in the room behind her. Desma had never found the pleasures of the flesh as enticing as she did. Most of Turan's festivals usually ended in people coupling, involving anywhere between two to a dozen people at once. She only ever knew Desma to indulge once or twice. And she had always been quiet the next day, despite Cela needling her for details.

Now she was married, spending her first night with her husband. Cela had tried to find out what kind of man Lycon was, but the servants were quiet on the subject. A small seed of fear nestled inside her that he might not be kind in bed. Some men did not care for a woman's pleasure, grunting like a pig and hardening further at the discomfort their fumbling and rutting inspired. 'Can you hear anything?' she whispered to Arete after the first hour had passed.

She shook her head. 'How? The walls and door are thick, and with the squawking over there, it is impossible.'

'I think they have lovely voices,' Hyllos said, nodding along to the current song about Fufluns, God of Celebrations, getting six women pregnant during an evening of primal ecstasy in one of his hidden woodland parties.

Cela thought for a moment before asking, 'Do you know what kind of lover the prince is?'

Hyllos blushed deeply. 'That is not something I have made a priority to know,' he said. 'But he is not someone prone to violence or cruelty, if that helps to assuage any worries.'

It did not, but she said nothing.

'Did Kalchas say anything of the temple blessing?' Arete asked.

He stiffened. Clearly the first astronomer had told him. 'We are not to speak of it,' he whispered harshly, eyes darting, though no one was near enough to hear them.

'Then tell us if you have seen anything in the stars,' the shipwright said. 'Has anything further been revealed about what Desma's life in this palace will be like? What will happen when she becomes queen?'

Hyllos weighed his words. 'There has been nothing new. We still see the same thing we have ever seen. An axe cutting down a wave. Crowns emerging from the earth. An arm made of marble. A serpent river. From these images, we all have the same feeling – that they mean the end of our kingdom. And Desma stands in the way of that path. She *must* be our queen, or we will fall. This I can say with certainty.'

'The axe forms part of the sigil of the Empire,' Cela said. 'I don't know what it means to cut down a wave – how is such a thing possible? A marble arm ... gods know. Arete?'

Arete shrugged. 'I would guess nothing more than what you have. But prophecies and oracles have a way of only becoming clear after the event. I doubt staring at the sky would be any different.'

'Your confidence in my profession is flattering,' Hyllos said.

'Get a more practical job, then. Sweeping all these halls would keep you busy.'

'Oh, stop that,' Cela interjected as the astronomer opened his mouth to retort.

They were silent for a few minutes, the choir moving on to a tale about Tinia making love disguised as a rabbit.

'Do you think you could see my future in the stars?' Arete asked.

'Not if you paid me your weight in gold,' Hyllos replied.

'Oh, Menrva save me,' Cela moaned.

Desma blinked blearily in the soft gloom, her eyelids heavy and her head dull. She groaned as she forced herself to sit up. Fufluns above, she shouldn't have drunk so much. She had only planned on sipping from her drink, but there were dozens of toasts throughout the feast, and she was expected to empty her cup each time. The food had been delicious, though.

Her surroundings were unfamiliar, then she realised they were not her chambers but Lycon's. She tensed as she frantically tried to recall the evening and slumped in relief. Nothing had occurred. Indeed, she had slept on the couch across the room from the bed.

The prince – her husband – sprawled across the mattress, partially covered by the blanket, breathing deeply in sleep. She crept over to him, a cloak wrapped around her though she had kept her dress on, pausing when she reached the bedside.

He lay on his stomach, his head turned to face her. Asleep, he looked softer, tension eased from his face and limbs. Her eyes wandered the lines of his body. A handsome man – broad and well-sculpted shoulders, a strong back, arms lithe yet defined. The blanket covered him from the waist down, but a bronzed leg had slipped free. He was not as pale as many other Koriithosans.

Messed from sleep, his hair swept about his head like waves. The thought of touching it lingered at her fingertips.

She moved away, finding a wardrobe filled with her clothes, choosing a long chiton and a green himation before leaving the bedroom. In the outer room, she filled a clay basin with water and washed her face vigorously, trying to scrub the woolliness from last night away. She rinsed her mouth before plucking a small bundle of parsley and mint from the table to chew on. Even she was offended by her breath.

When they had retired last night, her heart beating like a fistful of thunder in her chest, Desma had been terrified of what was about to come. Only a part of her was calm, resigned to the fact that it was happening and would be over soon.

She had spotted Cela and Arete outside as Lycon closed the door, and it had given her courage. They were only a piece of wood away from her.

She had stood, arms clutched around her as he went to the bathing room, returning naked. Her throat constricted at the sight of him; her eyes darted down to his manhood, but it had remained asleep.

He looked her over, standing with her back against the wall, fully clothed, eyes wide. 'I am tired,' he announced. 'If you wish to join me in the bed, that will be your choice. Otherwise, the couch is quite comfortable.'

He went into the bedroom and she followed. The bed was large, stone pillars at the corners connecting it from floor to ceiling.

She lingered in the doorway.

He climbed into bed and blew out the lantern next to him. A small light spilled through the doorway from the outer room. 'Sleep well, Desma.'

And that was their first night as husband and wife.

It was expected they consummate the marriage, though not essential. All legal requirements had been fulfilled by the lifting of her veil before witnesses.

But why had he not pushed the issue? He had every right to expect her to come to bed with him, to meld together in a tangle of limbs and grunts, to try to conceive an heir.

But he had left her alone.

There was no reason to expect the same treatment tonight, or any other night to follow.

She crept to the hallway door and creaked it open. Something thumped against it.

'Tinia's blasted beard,' Cela swore, rubbing the back of her head where it had struck the wood.

'What are you doing sleeping against the door?' Desma whispered, waiting until her friend moved before opening it wide.

Arete jerked awake at the noise. 'Oh good,' she said with a yawn, 'breakfast.'

'There's food?' Hyllos mumbled, sitting up from where he had stretched out. 'Count me in for a plate.'

'You've been here all night?' Desma asked the three of them.

'That is tradition,' the astronomer replied. 'To make sure neither of you ran away. Luckily, you had three very attentive guards on hand.'

'Very attentive,' she said with a smile. 'Lycon is still asleep so we will need to get food elsewhere, or we'll wake him ...'

'Lycon was awoken by someone swearing,' the prince said behind her.

She spun, but did not realise how close he was to her, slamming her face in his bare chest. 'Ow,' she said ruefully. 'Sorry – that was Cela.' His hair was still a mess, and he wore a short chiton wrapped around his waist, held in place by a silver clasp.

'Tattletale,' her friend accused, finally getting to her feet. 'Prince,' she said by way of greeting.

'Celadine,' he said. 'I guess my wife has already extended an invitation for you to break your fast with us.' He called for a servant, who appeared from around the corner and sent him off for food, then opened the door wider. 'Please, come in.'

Arete smiled apologetically at Desma, and Cela patted the prince on the shoulder as they entered. Hyllos looked like he would rather jump into the sea than be in the room.

Lycon dressed as the platters of food arrived, alongside a clay pot of warmed wine to ward off the morning chill.

They ate in silence for a short while, and Desma was hit with the surreal feeling that she was eating breakfast with her husband. The idea was going to take some time to become the norm.

'So, Prince Lycon,' Arete said pleasantly. 'The first couple times we saw you, you looked ready to bite Desma's head off. What has changed?'

Desma let the cheese drop from her fingers. Hyllos looked ready to faint, and Cela just grinned.

'For a master strategist,' Desma hissed, 'you have all the subtlety of a blind ox.'

Arete shrugged and waited for Lycon to answer.

The prince wiped the crumbs from his hands before answering. 'You are very impudent, but I will answer. I admit, I was angry. When I first saw you, a ragtag group of trouble, I knew that you would be the ones to kill the monster. Don't ask me how – I just knew it in my heart. Perhaps a god whispered it in my ear. And there you were, Desma, the Despised Beloved as we had come to know of you, standing there before the king, asking for his help with all the arrogance of a godling. It was a sight to behold, and my father did not have kind words to speak about you after.' He looked down at his plate. 'You have to understand, I was not allowed to hunt the monster, for fear I would be killed and the throne pass from my family. I had hoped it would leave one day, sating whatever desire drove it to our city, and bypass the prophecy altogether. But alas, here you are – a foreigner with a disturbing past.' He looked straight at her. 'Think how you appear to us. A pirate in all but name that sailed the Middle Sea, hunting for treasure with Turan's power behind you. Then your temple is sacked by Empyreans, it seems, at the behest of the goddess. Then you kill your own father and become tainted. You did not come to us with pristine credentials. It will take time to build you up in the eyes of our lords and the people.' His eyes flicked to the astronomer. 'And Hyllos spent every evening lecturing and berating me into understanding that you did not come seeking glory. And, for that alone, I should give you a chance.'

'It would be better for the kingdom if there was an alliance instead of animosity between you,' Hyllos said. 'Better also for you both.'

'Sage advice indeed, Second Astronomer,' Desma said. 'Perhaps I will name you my tutor.'

'Princess?'

That was a title she would also have to get used to. 'I know only the basics of my adopted kingdom and people,' she said. 'I will need wise counsel in the days to come. If my husband has no objections?'

Lycon shrugged. 'As long as it does not interfere with your duties to the king, Hyllos, then I have no issues. You will need people you can trust moving forward, Desma. You have entered the realm of political intrigue, and I have not yet mastered the dangerous tides we now sail together.' He reached forward and placed his hand on hers. 'And it would be good to know that we are not trying to sink each other.'

She smiled at him, placing her other hand on his.

'Artimi preserve us, they're lovesick with each other already,' Cela elbowed Hyllos.

'Oh, shut up,' Desma laughed, throwing a fig at her friend.

Hunched on the rose quartz tiles, ragged remnants of white and red clinging to his shoulders, Camillus knelt alone in the nave of the Aventinus church – dwarfed by its vast magnificence, swallowed by the hush and splendour of sacred stone.

He had failed Her. He had lost Desma, and swiftly learnt that the Belt did not reside with Sethlans' high priest in Trilos.

He had been punished. He deserved it. To fail one's goddess was the worst disgrace.

Tears stung the cuts on his cheeks as they fell, bloodied, onto the floor.

His ship, damaged as it was after the attack from Konosoan pirates, had limped to the port in Akren, where he commandeered horses and galloped them to death to get to Aventinus within a day and a night.

He went straight to the Holy Mother. Told her all that had happened.

Her rage, bright as a bonfire, had scorched him with righteous anger.

But only after he had been thrown into a cell deep beneath the church – dark and rank, the floor rough and walls wet – did he come to know true sacred anger.

He had fallen into a fitful sleep when She had come.

Turan. Goddess of All Love. Holiest of the Holy Twelve.

She had visited his dream, filled with smashing wood, roaring flames, the sea drinking all that fell into its maw, Desma being carried away from him.

Turan had vanished the turbulent scene, changing it to clouds that drifted away, and left him on a soft sanded beach, surrounded by a hundred rose bushes. Their sweet scent calmed him.

'Camillus.' His name was on Her tongue. Her voice was beautiful, like a mural layered with lustrous paints. Hushed, but clear as finest crystal. Sweet, but deep with huskiness, midnight kisses falling from every syllable. Ecstasy.

'My Goddess,' he breathed, looking upon Turan. Her beauty was a maelstrom. It struck him and tore his soul apart, and he cried at the passion that engulfed him. She was everything. She was the world. He was Hers.

'Camillus,' She said again, bending as She towered over him, sea green wings flaring open to eclipse the sun. Her hair, dark as the deepest wine, bright like the oldest ruby, shining like fresh-spilled blood. Her eyes, flecks of sea foam. Her lips, plump and rosy. Her body drove him mad, blood pumping and throbbing.

He fell back from Her, waves of passion rolling over him until blackness crept into the edges of his vision. It was too much. She was too much. He needed more.

'You have failed me, Camillus,' She said, Her voice rose petals and whips, spearing his heart. Tears flowed fresh.

'I am sorry, my Goddess,' he whimpered. 'I can do more. I can still serve. Let me serve!'

She drew back to stand tall, Her face looming dozens of feet above. He was a worm, a maggot, a clump of dirt before Her. 'Twice you have been given a chance to serve me. I would have raised your name to the stars. You would have been exalted throughout the Empire. But now you will be cursed. Your story will be taught to children and disciples as a warning for when I am disappointed.'

He screamed. His world was on fire. 'Mercy, Golden Turan. Please. Let me love You. Mercy!'

She turned Her back on him, Her footsteps shaking the earth as She walked, mist cloaking Her naked body from his sight. Before She disappeared, Her words reached back, poison to his ears. 'I cast you out, Camillus.'

His world was ended.

And so he huddled before the white throne of the Holy Mother. It was carved of purest white marble from the quarries outside Caelius, forming two swan wings intertwined. Its arms were inlaid with rose quartz and the seat cast in gold. Valeriana sat, enthroned in her power, ready to cast his doom into the world. She wore shining raiment – robes of gold and blush with wide sleeves of spectacular cerulean – and a tall diadem of orichalcum with beaten roses across its surface. She was terribly beautiful.

Grown plumper with age, she was still lovely to look upon. Grey-streaked hair smooth and oiled, eyes a cutting green, bright as glass and sharp as iron. Her face bore the lines of a life lived by a hard woman, whose pleasure came from advancing herself and tearing down her rivals. A fierce lioness. And now, he was her prey.

'Bishop Camillus,' she said, her voice bearing a lyrical note. 'For thirty years, you have served Turan's Church well. You have risen through our holy ranks to serve at the pleasure of the head of our Church. But twice now you have failed. Twice you have lost the Belt of Turan, the holiest artefact upon this earth. This cannot be tolerated. Golden Turan herself has come to you to pass judgement. And she has spoken: you are cast from this Church. You are stripped of all rank and are devested of your right to speak for Turan. In rags you came to us, and in rags you will leave.'

Her words were hammer blows, his life shattering about him in pieces. This was not what he had envisioned. The path to his destiny had been clear – leading straight to the very throne before which he knelt, Holy Father of the Church of Turan. But now ... a groan rent itself from his throat, low and guttural, pained beyond his ability to form words. He held up his hands to her, his palms bearing the holes from being pierced by Turan's thorns, beseeching her wordlessly.

But there was no mercy in Valeriana's face. 'In the old days of the Church, you would have been castrated and branded. But Golden Turan is merciful.' She pulled forth a long cloth of brilliant blue. His stole of office. With a vicious twist, she ripped the expensive fabric in two, letting the pieces flutter from her hands to the floor. 'Begone.'

He could not speak. Guards grabbed him roughly under his arms and dragged him across the mosaic floor. A giant stained-glass window above portrayed Turan surrounded by a thousand birds, beautiful and seductive, hands clasped over Her womanhood, eyes coy but knowing. She had left him. Ever since the old priest had arrived in his village – robes dusty from the road, incense clinging to his every step – he had served and loved Turan. The Goddess' name had settled in his chest like fire, and he had carried it with reverence ever since. But now he felt truly alone, the warmth of his Goddess a painful absence in his chest. Though his body had been punished to the limits of his endurance, skin torn open, bones cracked, toes burned ... it was his soul that caused his tears.

He was thrown down the steps leading up to the main doors of the church. People stopped and stared at the tatters of a bishop landing in the mud on the street.

Pulling himself to his feet, every part of him cried out in pain. He looked up at the tall spires of the church, a monument to Love in all its forms, and felt his devotion transform. Once a raging fire in his chest, now it was crystal, sparkling and honed.

The sun shone through the stained glass set high above the church's doors, soaking the square in colour. The image of a rose, adrift in a sea the colour of Turan's hair, turned the ground vermilion. Camillus climbed to his feet, his shadow stretching long before him, dark and tinged with red – as if his very spirit, his rage, had broken free to wreak itself upon the world.

For there was only one path left to him while he resided above the Halls Beneath. A path dripping in blood – whether his or Desma's, only the Diviners could tell.

CHAPTER TWENTY-TWO

'Let me through before I put you into the bloody ground,' a voice shouted, anger rending the clear evening sky.

Mynta jumped, spilling her plate as Anesidora stood shakily to her feet, stepping in front of her.

One of her guards came running into the room, hand clasped on his sword hilt. 'My lady, master merchant Duris is without.'

'What? Let him in.'

The guard hesitated. 'My lady, he is quite angry. I will remain in the room, with your permission.'

She waved her hand. 'Fine, fine, but let him in.'

The guard gestured to someone down the hall. A door slammed open, followed by the slap of sandals. Mynta looked nervously at her nursemaid, who had stationed herself a little ahead of her.

Duris' cold rage was condensed into a fine point, all the more dangerous that it had been distilled.

'Duris, what is wrong? Is there trouble at the mine?'

The day after her meeting with the high priest, Duris had sent her a message saying he had to travel to Sabate unexpectedly. That was ten days ago.

'The mine is fine. However, your surveyors arrived two days after I did. Your *temple* surveyors.'

Mynta froze. In his message, Duris had asked her to send the surveyor as soon as organised. With Duris out of the city, she was not able to access the funds, as they required his signature as well. So she had gone to the temple to include in the contracts that the surveyors would be paid upon arrival at the mine. She had given them a letter for Duris to explain the situation. 'And?'

His eyes bulged. His chiton was covered in dust, his face red from the sun as well as anger, and the smell finally reached her nose. He must have travelled three days straight to her.

'Three hundred gold drachmae? Has Fufluns taken your wits!' He stepped towards her, and her guard rattled his sword on his belt in warning.

Duris pierced him with a glare, but turned his eyes back on her. Gone was the charming man who had walked with her under torchlight and laughed at her stories. Mynta rose to her feet. 'I am aware they are expensive. But I felt that we needed to ensure we maximised our profits from the mine and—'

'We know there is tin there.' He cut her off. 'We can bring back surveyors as we progress. We do not need to map the entire vein network immediately. Once we have made back our investment and start to see a profit, then we can invest further. No wonder Castur came himself to negotiate. A novice is the easiest to squeeze coin from.'

His words stung, but the thought that the high priest had used her stung even more. Why would he waste his time to manipulate her out of coin that was a drop in the temple's wealth? Or ... was all of that a lie? Her eyes flicked to her father's study down the hall. Were there papers in there about a business deal with Castur that had left the priest high and dry? Was this some kind of revenge?

'I am sorry,' she stammered. 'I was only trying to do what I thought best.'

Duris shook his head. 'I gave you this task because it was one of the simplest. Find a reputable surveyor in a city that is filled with them. It is as though I sent you to the market to buy a saddle and you came back with a herd of stallions. Foolish girl.'

'That is enough,' Anesidora snapped. 'You will not speak to my mistress in her own house like this.'

'Be quiet, old woman,' Duris growled. 'You should have been turned out of this house long ago.'

Mynta smacked her hand on the table, pain shooting up her fingers, but she ignored it. 'Watch your tongue, master merchant.' Her voice was cold and steady. 'I may have made a business decision you did not agree with, but it was mine to make. I am an equal partner in this venture, and I demand the same respect that is shown to any other. If you are unhappy with me, then tell me so in a reasonable manner. You call me a girl? Well, then you are acting like a thug.'

Duris' hands clenched by his side, but he took several deep breaths. 'You are right. I let my emotions, carried on the back of three days' hard ride, colour my words. Misjudgments happen in business. Turms knows I have made several in my career. And I, too, have been shouted at by masters and partners, which was never pleasant. Forgive me. Let us move on, for we cannot break this contract, so we must pray that your gamble will pay off.'

'Stay and refresh yourself,' Mynta offered. 'After, we can dine and drink, and you can let me know how is Sabate.'

Duris nodded and allowed a servant to take him to the bathing room. Mynta sent a maid to her father's room to find clothing, and sent word to the kitchen to prepare something hearty.

Once they were alone again, Mynta rubbed her face. Her heart had started to slow again, though she felt like she had run a sprint. She had witnessed her father or one of his associates many times fly into a rage over some Council issue or business deal. She just had never expected it from Duris – let alone her being the cause of the trouble.

'He is a man passionate about success,' Anesidora said beside her. 'He holds himself to such standards that sometimes he forgets that others do not, or cannot yet, do the same.'

'It is not your place to defend him,' Mynta said quietly.

'I am only trying to take the sting out of his words, my lady.'

They waited in silence for about twenty minutes before a maid appeared to take them to the small dining room.

Duris entered in a green chiton and softened leather sandals, his hair slick from oils. He helped himself to the roast lamb, honey-baked bread, and a large cup of wine, draining more than half in a few gulps before finally acknowledging her.

'We will need to await word from Sabate on the surveyors report,' he said, his voice holding a slight chill. 'And I must warn you, Lady Amynta, that the others are also not happy. There may be a vote.'

'Of what?'

'Not to terminate you from the contract, let me assure you. However, I feel it is only right to prepare you. The partners may vote that you must bear the cost of the temple surveyors, minus the fee that would have been shared if a more prudent choice had been made.'

Mynta was shocked. They would make her cover the entire fee? Hundreds of drachmae in addition to what she had already contributed. 'And which way would you vote, Duris, if such a call was made?'

The merchant at least looked mildly chagrined, though perhaps only because he was the sole focus of her attention. 'At this moment, I would vote with the majority.'

Her nursemaid grumbled something under her breath, but Mynta ignored it. 'That is ... disappointing. I will wait until such a vote eventuates and defend my case.'

'A trick of the trade is to not take personally what is only business,' Duris said, softening his words. 'It can take many years to grow skin thick enough to weather any blow, whether it be from partner or fortune.'

'I understand,' she said slowly. 'Though I must say how surprised I am at your reaction to this overstep. I understand money is tight but the situation is far from dire.' She caught the tightening of his mouth. 'Duris, if something has occurred then I have a right to know.'

He sighed. 'It is not yet confirmed, so I did not want to say anything. However, there is a farmer a few miles away from where we have begun to mine. It seems that he discovered a small vein of tin on his land a decade ago and has slowly been extracting it himself over the years. He had a local surveyor confirm the vein was solely on his land and registered it accordingly in Sabate.'

'Yet?'

'The temple surveyors provided their preliminary report before I left, and it suggests that the farmer's vein is actually connected to our mine.'

Mynta frowned. 'What does this mean?'

Duris rubbed his hands through his hair. 'A bureaucratic nightmare. We secured the rights to the entire mine, as it was undiscovered. However, if it is confirmed that the veins are connected and the farmer can prove his initial discovery, then he has rights over our mine.'

Her jaw dropped. 'You do not mean to say he could take it all?'

'There are three options. We could take him on as a partner, for which he would receive a share of all profits, or he could assert predominance, and we would have to abandon the mine. Though he would need to reimburse us for all costs, as it was not a purposeful trespass.'

'What is the third option?'

'We buy him out. We purchase his land, the vein, as well as fair compensation.'

Mynta's eyes widened. 'But that would be hundreds – no, thousands, possibly – of drachmae.'

Duris nodded. 'More than we have available to commit to this project all at once. If he is amenable to a payment plan, then I think we could offer five thousand gold followed by monthly instalments once the mine is profitable.'

Five thousand more drachmae! That would mean over seven hundred each. She had less than fifty to her name after the initial deposit, and now there was the risk the other investors would make her cover the costs of the surveyors, which would put her a thousand in debt. Her head began to swim.

'I know it is a lot,' Duris said, reaching over to place his hand on her arm. 'I, too, was not prepared for this eventuality, and by now I should know that no sea is ever smooth. But it is not insurmountable.'

'Perhaps for you, master merchant,' Mynta said, annoyed at the tremor in her voice. 'But my income is far more limited than yours. Such an additional cost would place a great burden on me.'

'Oh,' he withdrew his hand. 'I did not realise the House of Linos was in such a state.'

She shook her head. 'It is my house, not my father's, that is not as wealthy as either of us would hope.'

'There must be some way forward,' he said, more to himself than to her. He tapped his chin thoughtfully. 'Some income stream we have not considered.'

Mynta gestured around her, shoulders slumped at the impossibility of the idea. Her gold bracelets jingled.

Duris' eyes widened. 'I think you might have solved the problem at our first meeting.'

'How so?'

Duris reached out again to gently capture her arm, fingers roving over her jewellery. 'You offered your adornments as collateral while you secured the coin for your original investment. Which means you still have such treasures available. You would be able to use them as such again!'

Mynta withdrew her arm. Sell her jewellery? She recalled her earlier words to Anesidora when she raised similar trepidation. Mynta had been bold then because it was a loan – the items were returned to her the following day. But to actually sell them? What would her mother say if she heard her daughter was hawking her belongings like a beggar? These were her possessions, and Duris just expected her to part with them.

Duris must have read her thoughts in her face. 'If what you have suggested is true, Lady Amynta, then I do not think you have another option. You have already come this far and the payout is exceedingly substantial. I foresee you buying back any pieces you sell within the season. Or you could buy new pieces with all the drachmae you will make. Unless ... you could ask your father for a loan, if you do not wish to part with these baubles. I am sure he would be interested in this business deal.'

'Excuse me,' she said, standing abruptly. 'I need a moment.' Anesidora followed her from the room.

Mynta did not know where to go. She approached her father's study but found she did not want to enter. Instead, she found her feet carrying her across the garden and into her mother's room.

It was dark, as no torches were lit. The maids came in once a week to dust, but otherwise it remained empty. Mynta brushed her fingers over the small boxes and jars on the table, only hairpins and makeup and oils, as she had taken all her jewellery with her to the palace. Remnants of her mother's perfume, effused into the wood, drifted upwards, spiced plum and almond flowers. The bed was stripped, the linens packed away, and only a few items hung in the wardrobes. The round rug still softened the floor, its red and cream pattern one she had long memorised as a child as she played while her mother readied herself.

Mynta sunk onto the floor, rubbing her hand against the softened wool. She wondered why her mother had never changed it in twenty-odd-years.

'What am I to do?' she said quietly, the question not directed at anyone.

Anesidora groaned as she lowered herself down with the help of a chair. 'You are worrying over the doors not yet open,' she said. 'It is only a possibility. Do not start counting your wounds before you enter the battle.'

'I have depleted the house,' Mynta said, gesturing around them. 'Our coffers are as empty as this room.'

Anesidora didn't answer.

'You think I made a mistake, don't you?'

'You have asked me to keep quiet unless it is support that falls from my lips,' her nursemaid said gently.

Mynta sighed, defeated. She regretted her harsh words to the woman who had raised her, saved her. Everything had seemed so simple at the beginning. Now there was nothing left to give and more was being asked. She could not let Duris see how fraught her position was. This was her chance to step into Trilos, not as daughter of Linos, but as a merchant. She had not really considered that it might fail – or what failure would mean for her.

'I need your wisdom,' she said, taking her nursemaid's hands. 'Please.'

'You need to withdraw as a partner.' Mynta had been expecting her words, but still they fell on her heavily. 'You cannot take another loss. Withdraw as partner, remain as an investor for a smaller percentage of profit. This frees you from any requirement to continue putting money into the venture, and there is hope of at least making back what you gave. Withdraw, in Turms' name.'

It was the right thing to do. Cut her losses, save herself and her household. But what would she do after? She had no gold to invest further, no means of making more. She had given everything to this one gamble. A foolish mistake. She truly was a novice.

Beyond her mother's balcony and the garden, Mynta could spy the welcoming hall. Not long ago, she had sat there, flanked by Desma and Cela, as her father burst through the door. She had remained poised under his anger, gathered herself when she was thrown to the floor, had found the strength to strike him back. She had defeated the most powerful person in her life in this house. She was Amynta, lady of Trilos. She was Amynta, merchant of Trilos. Her name stood alone, and alone she stood.

She had no one to rely on but herself now.

CHAPTER TWENTY-THREE

There were no further visits from Duris. Or any of the merchants.

Mynta received a message, every fifth day without fail, to provide an update. And each time, she gave a message in return, but never received an earlier reply.

She had not been able to watch when Duris' men carried away several chests from her house, the receipt for payment crumpled in her hand that shook with embarrassment.

The tin veins were connected, and the farmer had chosen to be bought out. In addition, the partners had voted in Sabate, without her knowledge, that she must pay for the surveyors minus a hundred gold drachmae.

Nearly one thousand gold was owed.

And so, once again, she had found herself requesting that it be paid in jewellery, but this time it was not in trust. Duris had sent an appraiser to ensure their worth. He had also added a note that, while they would endeavour to get the best price for the pieces, if they could not reach the amount owed, then they would need to collect the balance.

Mynta's face had burned in shame as the appraiser rifled through her gems and necklaces and bracelets. On several occasions, she had to snatch an item from his hands and place it in another chest. There were some pieces she would not part with.

Anesidora had said nothing more on the subject since Mynta had returned to dinner with Duris and confirmed she would continue to be a partner. She knew her nursemaid disagreed with her, but she had no choice. She had to see this through. Turms would bless her with good fortune. He had to.

On the fourth visit from the messenger, Mynta decided she had enough. True, she had misstepped, but she had paid for her mistake. Her father would not have been so inexperienced. She had uncovered no record in his study of any blunders or waste of resources. But her father had been raised by his father, taught the undercurrents of trade and the perils of business. Linos had never thought to share what he knew with her; Mynta's role as a daughter was to marry and bring him greater power and wealth. Possibly, she represented his only plan to have ever failed.

But she did not deserve to be treated as an outcast. She would force Duris to treat her as an equal, even if she must step on his toes to remind him of such.

'Attend me,' she said to her maids as she moved to the bathing pool. Anesidora had gone out for the afternoon to visit a friend in the market, but Mynta did not need her. This was her fight alone.

Soon, she was scrubbed clean of the day's sweat, her hair brushed until it was silken, gleaming with the last of her oud oil from the Great Lands. Cream and kohl and paste were applied to her face. Fennel and lemon perfume set the room sparkling with its freshness. She chose a peplos of pale grey, but with fine stitching in gold that shimmered when the sun or torchlight set upon it. A belt of yellow leather, patterned with thyme flowers, slid about her hips.

'Jewellery, my lady?' a maid asked as she looked at the empty places her chests once stood.

Mynta hesitated. Would it be better to go without, as strange as that thought was? The idea flashed away in anger. She was not a pauper, walking half naked through the street. What would Duris think if she came to him disarmed of her gold and gems? 'Bring me the most expensive pieces remaining,' she ordered. 'And send a runner boy to prepare my litter. I will not mess up my dress walking in the dust.'

Within a half hour, she was being carried swiftly through the city towards Duris' home. She had not sent word, but knew he was in the city, as the messenger had said as much.

Her hands fidgeted in her lap as she jostled on the cushions. She did not have the funds to keep litter carriers as part of her staff, and the quickest available were apprentices. Two had not yet finished growing, and she fought to keep herself sliding backwards as the litter tilted due to their shorter height. But she did not lose focus.

Duris was the leader of the merchants. She had to regain his trust, prove her worth. He could be a powerful ally among the merchants of Trilos, in a world where reputation was almost as valuable as precious metals.

She had faced her father's rage and succeeded. She could stand before Duris' disappointment and annoyance. One was a bonfire, the other a brazier.

Quicker than she would have preferred, the litter turned down his street. The men had barely stopped before she was climbing down, hopping slightly as the litter tilted unsteadily, but she kept her feet.

She strode to the gate and collapsed her bronze fan, using the handle to rap upon the wood.

A count of five breaths before she rapped again.

Five breaths.

She raised the fan once more.

The gate opened, a guard's surprised face peering down at her.

'My lady?' he said uncertainly, turning to look behind him. As he did so, the gate widened slightly and Mynta pushed her way through, catching him off-guard.

'I am here to see Duris,' she said curtly. 'Resume your post. I will find him.'

'No, wait, my lady—'

The guard scrambled to get ahead of her, but Mynta gave him no headway to halt her progress. His only choice was to match her pace or physically block her with his body.

He made the right choice.

Servants ahead murmured to one another, and the silver brightness of a lute drifted on the air. He must be dining. She started to feel a little foolish at the thought of interrupting him. What if he was busy or meeting with

someone important, and she was about to burst in on him? And for what –
because he wasn't giving her the attention she felt she deserved? This was her
sole endeavour, but he was a businessman with numerous deals and projects
underway. Maybe she should leave now before …

A woman's laugh cut through the music.

She faltered. Was Duris *with* someone? Her face heated, though she
could not decipher why. Perhaps she was the wife of a trader and had
accompanied her husband to dinner. Or maybe she was a merchant herself,
same as when Mynta had dined with Duris and walked through the garden.
Her feet quickened, dress flapping around her legs as she hurried just short
of impropriety.

She passed the welcoming courtyard, following the scent of food and the
sound of instruments to an inner dining hall.

Duris was dancing with a woman who sparkled like fresh cut amethyst,
her laughter weaving effortlessly with the lute. Taller than Mynta and
willowy, her skin perfectly bronzed, her hair gleaming like riverbed earth over
a peplos the dark purple of old wine, a green belt wrapped around her slim
waist. Mynta's hand drifted to her own midriff, aware of the greater length
in her belt to cross the distance of her body. But as Duris spun her, Mynta
felt a pain that had not yet drawn its first breath boil away in anger.

Around the woman's throat was a necklace of raw emeralds. The same
necklace Hero-King Sophocles of Apasa had gifted her during one of her
family's visits. The same necklace she had given to Duris as part of the
payment for the thousand drachmae she owed.

Her anger stilled into a shard of ice, spearing her insides, leeching cold
down her veins. Without thinking, Mynta raised a hand and pushed a vase
off a wooden plinth stood just inside the doorway.

The shatter of clay on stone broke the spellbound evening. The music
screeched to a halt, and all eyes turned on her.

'Lady Amynta,' Duris said, surprise clear in his voice as his eyes darted
between the woman in his arms and her. 'We did not have an appointment.'

'No.' Mynta fixed a smile, false and bleak, across her face. 'But I am here,
and you will see me.'

Duris gestured to a servant, who stepped forward, his arms slightly lifted, as though to bar her from approaching further.

'I have struck men far more powerful than you,' she said to the servant. 'Step aside.'

The man's arms trembled, but he stood his ground.

'I think it is better if you return home, Lady Amynta,' Duris said politely.

'How much did you buy?' she asked over the servant's shoulder.

He raised a brow.

Mynta gestured towards the woman who was watching with a bemused expression at the exchange. 'How much of my jewellery did you buy after I gave it to you? What discount did you treat yourself with?'

'Mynta, I— '

'How many women's pleasure have you paid for with my gold?'

Duris stiffened. 'You do not know how treacherous the ground you stand upon is becoming. This is Aglaia, youngest daughter of Nicander, Prime of the Council.'

The ice within her started to melt. This was the daughter of one of the most powerful men in Trilos, and she had all but called her a whore. The pain returned and finally Mynta knew it by name. Shame. Betrayal. Hurt.

She bowed low. 'My apologies, Lady Aglaia. I hope you enjoy my necklace.'

With that, she swept out of the room, nimbly stepping around the broken vase, holding her dress above her ankles so she could half-run through the house. The guard kept pace, gesturing for the gates to open as they approached. She threw herself into the litter and bade full haste home. Though the night had grown cold, she lifted her fan and let it dance before her face – not to cool, but to scatter the tears before they could fall.

Why was she weeping? Duris had never given any clear indication he had feelings for her, that he wished to pursue her. And he had been harsh in their business dealings – why should she expect anything less in matters of the heart? Memories of his garden haunted her; he had shown her nothing but kindness, attention, praise. She had embraced him, been surrounded by his scent, had wondered, for a moment, what would happen if she kissed him. She was a fool for not noticing the path he led her down, full of pitfalls that she would not see. Her fan shut with a vicious snap, fury burning the tears from her cheeks. She wished that some spiteful goddess would turn her into a siren. Force talons to sprout from her nails, wings to burst from her back, a wicked beak to form from her mouth, and allow her to soar free into the sky and vanish from the minds of men, never again to concern herself with the petty dealings of Amynta of Trilos.

They arrived home and she was exhausted. Mynta shuffled through the gates to find her nursemaid pacing the outer courtyard, her hair in disarray as though from constantly running her fingers through it.

'And finally, she returns home. Praise be to Uni,' Anesidora exclaimed. 'A maiden, unwed, unaccompanied, slinking back into her house for the world to see. Tell me – did you bed him?'

The question was like a blow. Mynta staggered in disbelief, her mouth falling open. 'I did not.'

'Then praise be to Artimi as well,' Anesidora sighed, lifting her hands to the sky in thanks. 'Come inside and let us undress you for bed.' As Mynta drew near, her nursemaid saw her streaked face. 'And tell me what has happened this night to wound you so.'

An hour later, Mynta laid in bed freshly bathed, all efforts from her earlier preparations undone. Her hair still smelt faintly of oud, but now also of lavender. As her nursemaid tended to her, Mynta told her everything. Anesidora grimaced when Mynta mentioned Aglaia. 'She is the nightshade in a field of violets. Let us hope we do not hear of this again.'

All but one candle extinguished, Mynta found her eyes drifting closed as Anesidora hummed, moving about the room slowly and setting things to order.

'Can I ask something farfetched?' Mynta said softly. 'Do you think I could do as Desma and Cela have done and leave? I have been in Trilos all my life. Maybe the gods are trying to give me a message. I rejected the plan my father had for me – maybe the city is rejecting me as well.'

Anesidora sighed before coming to sit on the bed beside her, wrinkled fingers threading through her hair soothingly. 'Do not make romantic the pain your friends have experienced,' she said. 'Desma did not choose to leave, she was banished from her home. Her mother was scarcely cool in the urn, and she never got to witness her father's burial. And Cela was presented a choice that would earn itself a heroic tale. She had to choose between duty to her mother and temple, and the love she holds for her friend, her sister. Just because she made her choice, does not mean it rests easy on her soul. Both of your friends have stony paths ahead, with many gashes and blisters to bear before they find soft grass again.'

'Do you think I will one day have their strength? To stride between kingdoms and wrestle with fate?'

'Who says you are not already? Strength comes in many forms. The bravery of a warrior's heart, the dedication of a mother as she brings forth a child, the hope of a wife as she waits for her husband to return home from sea ... the risk of a merchant as they gamble for riches. You look to Desma and Cela for strength, but you did not see what I witnessed when they were here. They looked to *you*, my lady. They saw your power, your strength, your passion. They witnessed a woman who realised she was a queen, however fleetingly that belief has held.'

Mynta grew tired. She'd had enough of speech for one day, no matter how painful or how true. She laid her hand upon her nursemaid's. 'Let us draw a close on this day, and let Artume take away our problems for a night. Tell me a story.'

Anesidora smiled. 'As you call upon Artume, let me tell you an old favourite of my sister's ...'

TALE OF SETHLANS AND ARTUME

Centuries after the gods had tamed the world, killed or subdued the Beings, and wept for the loss of Urruc, peace reigned.

Tinia and Prumathe grew bored of their endless lovemaking, despite Uni's displeasure, and turned their attention to matchmaking. With Turan's arrival, the two gods had found love in each other that Tinia rarely felt with his queen, and they thought that all their brethren should experience their wonder.

They visited Turan in her palace of roses and oils to request her help, but she laughed at them for thinking they could dabble in her domain.

'If you think the gift of finding two hearts that are the speech and echo of each other is a simple task, then I wish you good fortune.' Her smile and the way she brushed her hair caused them to retire until they were both spent. But they were not deterred.

Tinia had broken the world order and anointed himself King. He had gathered the gods into an army and made the Beings kneel before him. He could perceive the darkest heart and know the brightest mind. Love was just another realm that fell under his crown.

And so they studied the gods together, observing who spent time together, who teased another, whose eyes lingered and whose breath quickened.

What they did not expect was one of the gods to seek them out, least of all that it would be Sethlans.

He approached them, limping, since Tinia had twisted his feet backwards in a rage when the Forge God had defied his order to make weapons. With him, he carried a spear of solid silver that left its own impression in the air as it shifted, moving out of time, able to strike at the future so its blows were impossible to avoid. This he gave to Tinia. Then he produced a diadem wreathed in golden mist, basil leaves beaten into its surface and dotted with drops of orichalcum. This he gifted to Prumathe, for it allowed the wearer to solve any puzzle before them.

'These are kingly gifts, brother mine,' Tinia declared as he skewered a passing nymph, the tree spirit never seeing the blow and turning into a birch forevermore. 'What is the occasion?'

'Or the request?' Prumathe asked, his sparkling eyes discerning more than the king.

Sethlans bowed his head, the embers in his beard sending small plumes of smoke into his eyes. 'I have heard that you are finding husbands and wives for us. I wish to be the first to step forward.'

Tinia and Prumathe exchanged looks. Though none of the gods could be called anything less than beautiful, Sethlans was the least of them. He had crafted weapons that helped them slay the Beings, but he had not taken part in any battles. Since their dominion was established, he had toiled away in his fire mountains and now spent much of his time in his new city. What god or goddess would want him?

'Is there one among us who has already caught the eye of he whose hands capture beauty in metal and stone?' Tinia asked.

Sethlans hesitated. 'I ... I have noticed our sister, Ethausva.'

Tinia struck his hand through the air, lightning crackling around his fingers. 'No. Ethausva has declared herself sacrosanct against marriage. She will remain forever virginal and home keeper for us all. This doom I speak.'

Sethlans bowed again. 'Is there a goddess you would see fit for me?'

They exchanged a look. 'Perhaps Vanth?' Tinia suggested.

Prumathe snorted. 'The Demon-Goddess? Would eat him for her supper. Let us not look Beneath. Munthukh?'

Tinia shook his head, his golden hair, peppered with blinding white, swaying against his broad shoulders. 'No, she has her eye on Aita.'

Prumathe sighed and looked upwards, his far sight watching Usil lead his chariot downwards towards the west. He snapped his fingers. 'What of Artume?'

Tinia smiled. He had once turned himself into a meteor and streaked against the sky to find Artume floating in the darkness, shattering against her in passion. Did she not bear him a child? He must be out there in the world somewhere.

Artume was an ancient goddess, older than some of the Twelve. She had been a maelstrom in the war against the Beings – her darkness smothering lands, her coldness choking creatures, her vastness undefeatable. For what can destroy a power great enough to cloak the earth each night in shadow?

'Agreed,' Tinia said, pleased at the idea and the success of their first coupling. 'Turms!'

The Herald appeared in a streak of multi-hued light, always nearby and ever with an erudite smile on his face. 'King,' he said with a smooth bow, his winged helm fluttering demurely.

'Fetch Artume and summon the court. We are to have a wedding tonight!'

Turms vanished as swiftly as he appeared, and Tinia smiled at the stunned Forge God. There was no use in delaying what he decreed, and a wedding was the perfect excuse for wine, debauchery, and enough ambrosia to flood a river.

The gods gathered, drifting into the glade in small groups or singly, dressed in finery that only a deity could have wrought on such short notice.

Uni stood between Tinia and Sethlans, the Goddess of Marriage ready to weave the sacred bindings that tied immortals together.

Nymphs and dryads filled the gaps, singing hymns of love and fertility. Turan watched on, grinning at each utterance of her name, her blessings called to shower upon the newlyweds-to-be.

A hush fell over the glade as Artume descended from the sky, her twilight cloak – stretching back into the heavens – shearing itself in twain, falling about her and pinning itself with stars, until she was the evening, and midnight, and deepest night made flesh upon the ground. Her hair was black but limned with silver, wreathing her face and shoulders in an ethereal glow. Her arched nose was proud, her lips darkest plum, her eyes galaxies contained in finite orbs. Turms accompanied her, his silver staff blazing bright, making Artume's darkness all the greater.

Sethlans stood as tall as his hunched back allowed, sharing a small smile for the goddess who would be his wife. Who better to match the forces of creation than the Night Sky herself? He could see her cool hands soothing his fevered brow as inspiration burned within him. Her kneeling by his aching feet, tending the warped flesh and calloused scars. The children she would bear him, powerful and mighty, deities that would echo through mortal histories until they brought about their own destruction. With Artume, he could be content.

As she walked towards him, he saw Turan lean towards her and speak loud enough for the assembly to hear. 'Dawn and Day are already wed. I did not think that anyone would be happy to wrap themselves around your cold body, Artume.'

The goddess rounded on Love, her darkness spilling about her feet in an expanding circle. 'And yet here I am, to be wed before even you, Turan. How sad that Love is unable to find it for herself.'

Turan rankled, eyes flashing as the scent of rose and cassia grew stronger. 'Watch your tongue, Night. I am sure Sethlans is not after you for your wit.'

Artume laughed coldly, looking at the assembled gods and goddesses. 'I will be sure to call out your name while we are in bed, thanking you for the pleasures he will give me.'

Tinia, who had grown bored of the exchange, clapped his hands once, producing a burst of thunder that rattled the ears. 'Enough. Let us get on with it so we may get to the feasting. Come along, Artume.'

Sethlans had never glowed brighter. His heart pounded as if the crowd might hear it, the way it did when he looked upon something he had crafted – hard-won, and all the more beautiful because of it.

Artume lifted her arm, her pale, grey skin like alabaster, and held out her hand to him. Sethlans reached out, seeing only the goddess before him. Then, with a blink, she was gone.

Gasps rippled from the assembly as everyone stared down at the Goddess of Night, sprawled on the dewy grass, dirt on her dress and ants beginning to crawl on her leg. 'What ...' Sethlans looked up to see Turan, a vicious sneer on her face directed at the goddess she had just shoved out of her way. 'What are you doing?'

She ignored him. 'Tinia, King Before Us, I ask that I be married, in this moment, to Sethlans, God of Creation. I ask you, as is my right as one of the Holy Twelve, whose desires stand above and beyond all other goddesses. Do you hear me?'

Tinia, amused by the turn of events, could not contain his laughter. 'You are as unpredictable as the sea, Throne-Sister. Fitting, given you were born within water's salt. I would grant your request, but as the other is also of the Twelve, it is within his right to decline. Sethlans,' Tinia turned towards him. 'Which goddess do you choose? Night or Love?'

Turan was devastating in her dress the colour of pomegranate flesh, dripping in rubies and garnets as though the seeds of the fruit themselves. Her hair like molten metal glimmered in its braids. Her eyes were sea foam, her neck bronzed and graceful, her perfume enticing like the first scent of home on a weary road. He looked down at Artume and saw her as Turan described. Cold. Distant. Her vastness would not support him, but smother him. She would quench his creation and wear the glimmers of his inspiration about her throat like she did the stars.

But with Love ... what greater inspiration could there be for him?

'I choose Turan.'

The goddess pressed her lips, soft as river moss, to his cheek. Her triumphant smile bore down upon her defeated opponent.

Artume rose to her feet in a terrible anger. Night swirled around her, as though she was the centre of a great, dark hole from which nothing could escape. 'I do not have the power to curse this union,' she said, voice echoing the terrors that prowled the night. 'But there will come a day when you will step into my domain. And be warned – nothing is as devouring as the night.'

And so Artume fled to the greater heavens, abandoning her wedding party, her heart growing colder than the sky she inhabited. She watched from on high as Turan and Sethlans were wed. And she did not miss how Love's eyes did not stray from Laran all the night ...

CHAPTER TWENTY-FOUR

Another piece of paper fluttered from Mynta's fingers, joining the expanding blanket around her of old records and dizzying sums. She'd had the idea the night before to look through her father's papers for any deals or trades Linos had dismissed as too trivial, but might be of interest to her. Any additional business, however small, would be beneficial.

And she needed something to distract her anxious thoughts.

It had been two weeks since her impromptu visit to Duris' house. The usual messenger had not returned during that time, but she had been too embarrassed to send someone to find out what was happening. It was better to give Duris some time and hope that eventually he would forgive her trespass.

'Open these gates in the name of the Silvered Deity, Herald of the Holy Twelve, God of Merchants and Paths – Turms!'

The words climbed over the walls and flowed through the house. What was it this time? Mynta rushed from her father's study. The guards were already opening the gates as she approached. Only a priest on official temple business would use such an entreaty, and they must be admitted immediately.

The priest swept inside, his multi-hued robe of red, green, brown, and yellow marking which god he served. His long, brown hair was held back by a band of silver with a beaten pattern of wings, and he bore a strawberry tree staff carved with tortoises and hawks, all sacred to Turms.

'The hospitality of my house is yours, great priest,' Mynta said, bowing low. 'I offer you wine and spices and fruit. Shade and hearth and pillows. May you find comfort in this dwelling, under Tinia's peace.'

'Arise, daughter of Sethlans,' the priest spoke, his voice like a sun-warmed lyre. 'I have come at the bidding of master merchants Duris and Ancus, to serve a writ upon you in accordance with your agreement concerning the Sabate tin mine.'

As Mynta straightened in surprise, she finally caught sight of Duris and the younger man who had followed behind the priest. Both of their faces were grim.

Fear gripped her throat. Her mind flashed to the contract. There were clauses to force out a partner, but surely she had not violated any of them. She would pay for the vase she broke, if needed. But that alone could not result in such a drastic response. 'Please, come in and we can get out of the sun.'

The priest raised a hand, stopping her maids before they could move. 'I will decline your offer. I have been tasked only with delivering the requested news.' He drew out a scroll and unrolled it slowly.

Mynta looked to Duris, but he did not meet her eyes, stiff with his arms behind his back. Ancus also avoided her eye, seeming ready to flee at a moment's notice.

'Upon the agreement of the majority of partners in this endeavour,' the priest read, 'it has been decided to end the partnership due to the failure of the mine.'

Mynta gasped. What did he say? 'What do you mean failure?'

'The shallower veins were confirmed and mined of tin. However, as the mine expanded, it was discovered that the supposed tin was, in fact, cursed iron, a substance difficult to differentiate from a host of metals, even with surveyors from the temple.'

Mynta wished there was a chair beneath her. This could not be.

'To lessen the loss among the partners, all land and equipment has been sold to pay off any outstanding expenses. The remaining profits are to be shared equally among you all.' The priest gestured to Ancus.

The younger merchant stepped forward, pulling out two large pouches from his belt. 'My lady,' he whispered, handing them to her. They were heavy and clinked dully inside.

'As witnessed by me, the pouches contain your share of the profits, amounting to one hundred gold drachmae. As witnessed by me, the coins have been delivered into your hands. As witnessed by me, your partnership is hereby dissolved. May Turms bless all your future endeavours and may your hands gleam with silver.' The priest raised his hand in benediction before leaving, the silence astounding at his sudden absence.

Mynta reeled. She looked to the merchants, waiting for a further explanation.

'Come, Ancus,' Duris said. 'Our business is concluded.'

'Do not dare leave this house,' Mynta said, then, softer, 'please.'

Duris paused. Mynta wanted to reach out and take his shoulder, but she found her feet would not move. It was all too much, too fast. How could their entire endeavour be over in the space of one proclamation?

'Please,' she repeated. 'Tell me how this could happen.'

Duris turned his head so she could see his profile. His face was harder than the first day they had met, when he had watched her in the garden, waiting for her answer. Gone was the belief in her, the gentle encouragement, the drive to succeed together. In front of her was a master merchant of Trilos – nothing more. 'Investment is an attempt to predict the future,' he said bluntly, 'and one at which failure is more common than success.'

Mynta said nothing as they both left. The guards closed the gates, muffling the sounds of the city. Closing the wall around her own little world.

A world that was collapsing.

Mynta sat in her garden, her noon meal untouched at her feet, her wine cup knocked over accidentally when she shooed away a bee.

It had been ten days since Duris had come to her home with Turms' priest and shared the news of her maiden voyage into investment and risk.

A risk that had turned around like a serpent and bitten her.

Two thousand and three gold drachmae lost.

Her house was destitute.

She had enough coin to see them through the rest of the year but then she would be faced with a choice: marry or go to her father for help.

Her stomach roiled at the thought of either option.

It had all gone wrong so quickly.

She ought to have known the risk, should have suspected cursed iron knowing the mine was so close to Trilos. During one of their many arguments, Sethlans had accused Turan of sleeping with the God of War, Laran. Furious at her husband, Turan spat on a heap of metal sat by his forge, a lump of iron. The metal became corrupted, turning to dust when exposed to water and spluttering when heated until it produced noxious smoke. All iron throughout Trilos became unusable and had to be shipped in from other kingdoms in the League.

Shame burned in her chest. She had been a fool. Filled with pride and confidence, thinking she had the aptitude to step out into the world because she had defeated her father, the strongest man she knew, in a single argument. Perhaps the truth was he had let her, foreseeing she would indeed never fulfil any useful purpose, and the independence she had thought hard-won was simply the by-product of being discarded at last. Mynta had thought for a moment she could be like Cela and Desma, fierce and fearless, queens of themselves.

'A blasted, stupid fool,' she hissed, kicking the cup into the creek with a splash.

Word would have found its way back to her father. About the failure that was his daughter.

She had sent a messenger to the palace, asking her mother to dine with her. Mynta had not seen her mother since she left with her father for their palace rooms and hoped, at the very least, that she would visit her daughter and Mynta would have someone to talk with about her problems.

But the messenger returned with a curt response from her father's secretary, advising that Emissary Linos and his wife were busy with affairs of state and requested the sender to attempt scheduling a meeting at a later date.

It was a slap to her face equal to when she had actually hit him.

The soft shuffle of her nursemaid's feet neared, and she hunched down on the bench. She just wanted to be left alone, to put off the inevitable return to everyday life. Not that her nursemaid often cared for what Mynta wanted. Anesidora always pushed for what she needed.

Her nursemaid sighed as she settled on the marble bench next to her, straightening her cream peplos, folding her hands in her lap, and letting silence fall again.

Mynta reached out and held her gnarled hand, finding comfort as she always had in her nursemaid. 'I was a fool,' she repeated.

'Yes,' Anesidora agreed. 'But that does not mean it was wrong.'

'How so?'

'We are all fools throughout our lives. Fools with money, fools in love, fools through anger, fools for greed. You do not blame a child for falling over when learning to run.'

Mynta scoffed. 'So I am like a child?'

'Of course! You have spent your youth struggling to survive while your parents moulded you into their form of a perfect daughter, a woman who represented everything you are not. You were not made to marry a rich lord, grow fat with a dozen children, and gossip in the shade with other women,' her nursemaid said. 'You chose to strike a different path. You threw out your father after demanding he help your friend. You seized an opportunity that even the most seasoned trader would have seriously considered. It did not pay off. Life is full of risks, Amynta, and so it should be. For only through the chance of losing can we truly appreciate when we triumph.'

'Such wisdom and passion in a nursemaid,' Mynta joked, leaning her head on the old woman's shoulder. 'Perhaps you should be running this household.'

'Bah, I have lived my life well enough,' Anesidora replied. 'Now is my time to help others find their life's journey.'

They grew quiet again. A couple of maids chattered amiably as they went about their tasks. The cook slapped dough loudly on a table, singing a hearty tune to herself. The guards' leather armour creaked in the hot sun in the outer courtyard. Beyond the walls, the low thrum of life in the city, constant and soothing, occasionally reverberating with the clang of a thousand forges at work.

Men and women going about their lives.

Raising children, opening shops, weaving cloth, carving statues, sailing ships, guarding roads, training new soldiers, making supper, crushing olives, tending sheep, counting money. So many purposes and goals. A multitude of dreams.

'What should I do now?' Mynta asked.

'What do you want to do, child?' her nursemaid asked in return. 'I cannot answer the question for you. And no one should. It is yours alone.'

Mynta searched the kernel of stubbornness inside her, the one her shame was trying vainly to hide from her. 'I want to try again.'

'And do what?'

'I want to become a master merchant.'

'In what?'

Mynta paused. 'I don't know. I don't have a specific trade or item in mind.'

'What do you want to accomplish?'

Again, she hesitated before answering. 'I don't want to just become rich. I was rich before. Still am, by many citizens' standards. I want to be able to prove that I can do it.'

'But why become a merchant? You are a deft hand at weaving. You could learn to craft dresses the envy of women in Trilos. You could open a shop and serve all the noble ladies,' Anesidora said.

Mynta searched inside herself and was surprised by the answer she found. 'I want to become the first Councilwoman of Trilos.'

Her nursemaid clapped her hands loudly as she stood. 'Then let us get on with it. There is much to do. But brace yourself, daughter of Trilos, for there is much hardship ahead. Such is the fortune of those in the vanguard.'

Mynta smiled brightly as she gathered her skirts and left the garden, a dozen ideas already running through her head.

For a moment, she allowed her fantasy to unfold in full before her.

Councilwoman Amynta.

BOOK FOUR:
UNRAVELLING

CHAPTER TWENTY-FIVE

Desma sat quietly while another tutor yelled at her.

She had a dozen teachers, all men, to train her in the ways of Koriithosan court women. Though she had asked for Hyllos to be her tutor, Kalchas kept him too busy to attend to her. It was a ploy by the first astronomer, perhaps even by the king, but Desma could say nothing. She had found a few times to talk to Hyllos, and he always promised that he would come to her as soon as his duties allowed.

This particular tutor, more than most, tested her vow made in Khufu's memory that she would accept the trappings of her new role. He was nearing sixty, head covered in a thick mane of white hair, teeth yellowed by too much mead, dressed in a charcoal chiton and white himation clasped with a gaudy pin. He had arrived at Lycon's rooms – hers now, too – over a month ago to teach her the ways of a demure Koriithosan woman. Desma had dressed in a red peplos with a shimmering gold shawl, dripping in garnets and topaz, hair loose down her back and scattered with ruby pins.

He had taken one look at her and burst a blood vessel in his eye. Thus began their little war. He had called her whore, harlot, foreign mistress raised in depravity. She had sipped her wine and let her shawl fall down her arm, revealing a significant portion of her bosom.

When he grabbed her arm roughly, she broke his nose with her palm.

It had taken four guards to separate them.

Desma had been shocked at his presumption and demanded he be removed from the palace. When he had returned the next day, she seized a knife from her lunch plate and only stopped when Lycon entered the room. He had informed her, in no uncertain terms, that she was a child in the ways of Koriithos, and as such, the tutor was within his rights to discipline her as a child if required.

Desma had been tempted to stab her new husband instead. But rather than react with the same fury as her tutor, Lycon had calmly crossed his arms, brow creased in solemn disapproval as he asked the tutor to step away.

'You continue to act as though you did not choose to return, Desma,' he'd said once they were alone. 'Before you is a man fulfilling the duty required of him by Koriithos'—Desma wasn't sure, looking into her new husband's eyes, whether he meant himself or the surly tutor—'yet you still conduct yourself like a mischief-maker stealing treats from the kitchens, without a thought for the title you hold, the responsibility Koriithos deserves of you.'

Desma had caught herself before she shuffled her feet, as though she were twelve years old again being hauled in front of her mother for tripping Theokritos into the well. Her mother's stern reprimand, the reminders of her duty to temple and goddess. Was this situation any different? She had not wanted this – the path that Khufu tried to spare her from.

But she had married him and become a princess of his kingdom, an outsider that could not leave the palace without a score of warriors, for fear of being attacked by the Dirciade. Though there had not been another riot, the city women would stand on the street watching her, arms folded, sentinels of disapproval. Lycon warned her that enough whispers constituted a roar.

She had made her choice. Though it had not been enough to save her captain's life, she would not taint his honour by turning her back on her word. She would not anger whichever god wanted her in Koriithos. She'd had enough of divine punishment. And though it grated against her bones, she had apologised and asked her husband what she could do to improve the situation.

Lycon suggested she limit visits with her crew, implying that her clear preference for her foreign friends gave the impression she did not respect Koriithosan customs. Though Desma had sensed he would prefer she sent them away altogether, he did not object to their visits outright, as long as they did not interrupt her tutelage. But he had insisted that she abandon her

Apasan way of dressing and keep her promise of adapting to the life of a true Koriithosan wife.

So, Desma had packed away her dresses of lavender, peach, red, yellow. Locked her jewels in boxes. Folded away her cloaks embroidered with gold and silver. Her wardrobe was replaced with clothes the colour of mud, fog, and ash. Her favourite was the deep green, for it set her hair aflame. She was given ribbons of lighter colours to tie in her hair, around her wrists and throat. Her sandals were plain, her belts of simple leather with no embellishments.

Even her perfumes were dour. She found she had to pour half a bottle to find the scent. The women seemed to favour pine and cinnamon, which she found too conflicting to be pleasant. She had Cela bring her favourite scent of apple blossoms and jasmine. While the tutor had frowned, she used it lightly enough that he let it by.

Her maids did not speak to her when they came in the morning to ready her or in the evening to help her bathe. They hurried through their tasks, and often changed, never serving for more than three or four days at a time.

She learned how to embroider and weave and sew. Weaving she quite enjoyed, though she often tangled the shuttle and knotted the weft.

She was taught how to eat – slipping the food between her lips to hide her teeth, chewing as lightly as possible so her jaw did not move, and sipping from her cup every third bite to ensure her throat stayed moist, making her swallowing less noticeable.

She rediscovered how to walk, placing her feet gently so her sandals did not thud or clack. No abrupt movements, so her clothes did not swirl about her. Her hair was bound tightly, so it did not wave in the wind. Her face was to be kept plain with no makeup, except to hide a blemish or mark.

Six weeks.

Six weeks of learning how to be a ghost, an ornament plain enough to not draw notice. Six weeks of changing everything that she knew to be herself.

But she endured it all.

For Khufu.

'Are you listening to me, or do I need to bend you over my knee?' Her tutor's voice broke through her reverie. She had been gazing outside the window over his shoulder. Her eyes focused on him, hardening with the heat of anger towards this petty man who lorded his maleness over her.

'I am listening,' she said flatly, erasing all emotion from her voice. It was uncouth to display her feelings outside the company of women.

The tutor waved his hands. 'You expect to be a proper queen to my people? You sit there like stone, but I can feel the seething beneath your marble exterior. You have crafted a fine veneer, Princess, but it is not enough. You become harder and harder, turning to stone, but that is not what women are. They are clay – to be moulded and sculpted by her father, and then her husband. Only to be placed in the kiln once perfection has been achieved.' He grabbed her chin, pulling her face close to his. His breath reeked of fish. 'Release yourself, and let me remake you.'

'Remove your hand from the princess,' a soft, cutting voice spoke from behind her.

Her tutor blanched. His hand dropped away from her and he stepped back. 'The prince ordered we are not to be disturbed by foreigners while she is being taught.'

Cosmas stood by the door, his pale grey chiton pinned on his shoulders with river stone, a thin dagger strapped to his white leather belt. His sun-white hair curled around the nape of his neck and his temples, pale blue eyes honed on the tutor. He was relaxed, smiling, arms folded loosely. Yet only a fool would not sense the danger he brought into the room.

'He is not my prince,' Cosmas shrugged. 'Lesson is over for the day. And the princess is busy tomorrow. Come back the day after. You are dismissed.'

The older man made to argue, but Cosmas simply raised his brow, as though surprised he was still there.

The tutor left in a huff, making his displeasure clear only once he was through the door and away from Cosmas.

'Thank you,' Desma said, getting up to pour each of them a cup of lemon syrup water. 'It was hard at first, listening to that man, but now it is just the crackle of a fire to my ears.'

He was silent as he sipped, eyes searching her face.

'What brings you here?' she asked, a little disconcerted. Was he going to ask about her promise again? She sent iron down her blood, waiting for him to answer.

'I thought you might like to take a stroll through the city,' he said.

She did not hide her surprise. 'Through the city? But the Dirciade ... '

'Will not bother us,' he said. 'They hold no sway where we are going.'

He refused to say anything further as they left her rooms, warriors trailing. She was surprised they kept their distance, but then noticed they had their eyes trained on Cosmas, not her. 'What did you say to them?' she whispered.

The corner of his lips lifted. 'I told them that I was more than capable of protecting you. It took a few bouts in their training ring to convince them. Don't worry,' he said when he caught her concerned look, 'they will all recover.'

Another four guards joined them at the palace doors, yet Desma still flinched every time a woman in the street sniffed or sneered at her. She could almost ignore the men who stared at her openly – some with lust, a few with curiosity, but most with disgust. The woman who rescued their city and married their prince. The Despised Beloved who was to save their kingdom.

They passed the temple of Tinia.

A few days after the wedding, the crew had gathered there to make a sacrifice for Khufu. Constructed of white marble and grey stone, it was twice as large as Nethuns' temple, and filled with painted statues of the King of Gods. Before his altar, large enough to slay a dozen bulls at once, they had brought their offerings.

Kassandra left a bronze sword with streaks of red running down the blade. Bion left a silver statue of a bull with eight horns. Arete gave a ship made of copper with metal sails that waved if it was moved. Delphinus, who had grown cold and quiet since they returned to the city, his golden voice almost silent, left a set of wooden pipes. Desma tried to touch his arm, to offer some comfort, but he slid away, barely looking at her.

Cela, crying openly, sliced a handful of hair from her head and bound it with gold ribbon, adding it to the pile.

Desma laid a gold torc she had procured from the palace smith, cleverly carved with scenes of Khufu's life – from his journey from Opuni, to winning races, to captaining her ship. A large obsidian surrounded by uncut rubies sat in the centre, a firebird carved into the stone. 'May your gods and mine give you peace,' she whispered, her tears held tightly inside. Her hand lingered on the now-warmed metal, unwilling to make the final release.

Cosmas was the last to step forward. He gave a low bow to Tinia's statue that reared high above them, holding it for several minutes while the crew shuffled behind him. He eventually straightened and pulled a small bottle carved from a dull blue stone. He opened it and poured sparkling water over their offerings before placing the bottle beside it.

When he withdrew, a priest of Tinia appeared from behind a pillar, leading a large white bull with horns dipped in gold. The bull lowed mightily, but followed without complaint as the priest led it up the steps and onto the altar. He pulled its head downward, and the bull laid on its belly. A bronze knife, glinting in its sharpness, rose high before slicing the bull's throat. Its rich blood poured over the altar onto their offerings, bathing them in the animal's life.

The bull lowed again, eyes rolling as it looked at them all, blinking once before glazing over in death.

They left the temple in silence, Desma's guards forming around them, and returned up the hill towards the palace. Before long, Kassandra, Delphinus, and Bion peeled off, headed to a tavern, the Konosoan giving Desma a one-armed hug before departing after the piper.

Desma had longed to go with them, but it would have been inappropriate for the princess to be seen drinking among the commoners. So she returned to the palace and her tutors. She had chosen this life, had returned when Khufu had given his life to let her be free. She had cast aside his sacrifice.

As the temple disappeared from view, Desma reminded herself the only honour she could now give Khufu was to fully accept her new role.

A curved wall ran the length of the city, offering protection from the west and south. Beneath its shadow, they came to the outskirts of a quarter Desma had not entered before.

The buildings were mostly wooden with stone foundations, strange in their design, for they were wider at the top than the bottom, and were tiled in black rather than the common red. Stacks of marble lay in squares or on street corners, waiting to be used.

The people were not Koriithosan. Thick black hair was wild and unbound, coupled with skin a rich, dark brown. Eyes ranged from brown to grey to almost-black. Their garb was also distinctly not Koriithosan. They wore multiple layers of robes with pants; some men wore small turbans, and their feet were wrapped completely in leather.

Cosmas turned to the guards following. 'Wait here.'

'We are instructed to keep the princess in our sight at all times,' one of the warriors said.

A knife clattered off the stones by his feet. Desma had not even seen Cosmas draw the blade. 'She will be safe,' he said softly.

The guard, eyes wide, turned to Desma. 'Princess?'

She admired his bravery. He would follow her if she asked, despite Cosmas' threats. 'It is fine,' she said. 'I will return in … '

'An hour,' Cosmas supplied.

The guards did not look pleased but settled on their heels, spears upright, faces grim, to begin their wait.

As he led her further into the quarter, Desma turned to Cosmas. 'Who are these people?' she asked. 'They are not Koriithosan.'

'Indeed not,' he said. 'They are a poor people with a terrible history in this kingdom. Koriithos has attempted time and again to drive them out, but they are hardy and cunning. Now, they are mostly ignored, barely able to venture from the quarter except to leave the city. But I want you to hear their tale from them.'

'But who are they?' she asked again.

'They are Arydorians.'

She frowned for a moment before memory struck. Arydor.

These were Cisra's people.

Northeast from Apasa was the Cold Sea, joined to the Middle Sea by the Straits of Athamantis. It was beyond the influence of the League and was known to be overrun by barbarous peoples who raided each other and found honour in bloodshed. Few dared to venture towards Trilos, for they were no match against the automatons. Though she had seen no map marking it, she knew that Arydor was on the far eastern side of the Cold Sea, over a thousand miles from Apasa.

She could not help but stare openly as they walked.

The women were as opposite to their Koriithosan counterparts as fire was to water. They wore bright jewellery, though their clothes were still dark, with only flashes of red or yellow or green. They argued loudly with each other and the men, shaking fists and cursing when needed. Food cooked in pots, the smell of cabbage and smoked spices drifting in the air.

The Arydorians stared as they passed by, whispering.

'Princess.'

'Hair like fire.'

'Apasan.'

'Hair like wine.'

'Turan's child.'

'Hair like blood.'

Cosmas stopped outside a house, a strange hooded figure burned into the wooden door. 'Go on. I will wait outside.'

Desma hesitated for a moment. Cosmas would not bring her to harm deliberately. She had always trusted him, and he had given her no reason to cease.

She pushed the door open.

CHAPTER TWENTY-SIX

The house was dim, the windows covered, a low fire burning in the centre of the room with a large metal funnel above, the connecting pipe disappearing into the ceiling. A loom sat in one corner, the other filled with pots and crockery. Several tables held half-made clothes and bundles of herbs hung from beams. Two beds were covered in brightly woven blankets.

A woman sat by the fire, wrapping wool around a small wooden frame. The crackle of the flames accompanied the twang of the threads snapping tight.

Triple Desma's age, her hair was like a midnight sky dampened by clouds and obscured her face. Her fingers were slender and swift as she wove, nicked with a thousand scars. Her robe of red, worn beneath an outer grey cloak, was well-made, though her feet were bare and covered in ash.

'Mistress,' Desma said politely, closing the door behind her and waiting. 'Tinia bless you and your house.'

'Ha, what does the bearded fool care of my house?' The woman chuckled harshly. 'If my gods deigned to turn their gaze towards this part of the world, I doubt your Holy Twelve could do much to stop them.'

Desma had to stop her mouth from falling open. Tinia passed down the laws that governed host and guest. While Ethausva ruled the hearth and home, Tinia ruled the people within it. To insult the King of Gods invited punishment.

'Do not worry, child,' the crone said, her fingers never pausing. 'He cannot see into my home while it is guarded by the Wanderer on my door. He has served my people well in this city, his powers are crafty and deep.'

Desma moved to the proffered chair. 'I am ...'

'Desma, daughter of the slain priestess and murderer of the potter,' the crone said. 'Slayer of foul beasts, princess of a city who hates women with fire in their bellies instead of children. Yes, I know who you are.'

'Did Cosmas speak with you?'

'Cosmas? You mean the ... yes, he did. Strange company you keep, child of love and hate. Strange company.'

'May I know your name and your face, mistress?' Desma said, fear fluttering in her stomach. Who was this woman who spoke of gods and powers like food and wine?

The crone raised her head and her hair fell away.

Desma let out a small cry.

Twin scars, white with age, began under each eye and swirled upwards, to meet again on her brow in an intricate knot. Her eyes were shards of flint, brows bushy, mouth a deep blush, chin sharp. Her neck bore further marks, angry burns of dull purple, streaking down to disappear under her clothes.

'It is alright, child,' she said. 'My appearance leaves much to be desired, but they are scars I bear proudly of the life I have survived. As for my name, it is Eidia.'

'Why have I come here?' Desma asked. 'Did you ask for me or is this a design of Cosmas?'

Eidia laughed. 'There are designs within designs within designs, Desma. Have you not learnt that already? Yours, mine, the gods, the world itself. We dance and trip and stumble around ourselves. Some are graceful, others fools. I saw Cosmas wandering the quarter and stopped him for a talk, told him that you are welcome here if you ever felt the need to sit with someone who knows what it means to not be Koriithosan.'

'How are you here?' she asked.

'Pour us some mead, Desma, and I will tell you my tale,' Eidia said, gesturing to the table. 'And bring that plate of meat in case we feel hungry.'

Once Desma had brought over the food and drink, Eidia put down her threading and sipped from her cup, sighing in appreciation. Desma found the mead sweet but smoky, a touch of bitterness at the end. It was heavenly.

'We brought a hive of bees from Arydor when we travelled here,' Eidia said. 'They are different from the bees native to the League. They are black and red instead of yellow and build their hives in the trunks of recently burned trees, which gives the honey its unique taste and thus the mead we make from it.'

'It is like nothing I have tasted before,' Desma said honestly.

Eidia smiled over her cup. 'Our story. You have heard the tale of Vikare and Cisra?'

Desma nodded. Two hundred years ago, Vikare had travelled to Arydor to obtain the Golden Bough that shed silver leaves to bring back to the king of Koriithos in exchange for an army to take the throne of Thevai back from his sister. As the story went, Cisra fell in love with Vikare and helped him through the trials of her father, Chief Evas. When the chief decided to kill Vikare, Cisra stole the Bough and fled with Vikare back to Koriithos. There, Vikare fell in love with the king's daughter. In a jealous rage, the story claimed Cisra had killed the king's daughter, her own sons, and destroyed half the city. A twisted tale, for Cisra had been pierced by Love's spear and forced to serve a man she had no feelings for in her heart.

'Cisra knew she would be leaving with Vikare, though the circumstances had not yet revealed themselves,' Eidia said. 'So she began to sneak some of her people onto the ship. Maids, friends, their families. They brought our bees and weaving and objects dear to us. One night, while they waited on the ship, hidden from the chief, they heard a great commotion – men fighting, buildings set alight – before Vikare and Cisra boarded the ship with the Golden Bough in a great hurry.

'And so, Cisra brought several dozen of her people to this city, where women are shadows and men flames. For a while, we dwelt peacefully, though it was full of unease. Once Cisra fled, we were almost driven from the city.' She fell silent for a moment, watching the fire. 'For two hundred years, we have been separated from our people. Some have left, to travel the distance and brave the dangers, though I doubt many found home again. It was only because your gods guided Vikare that he found Arydor. Two hundred years we have been hated and spat upon, our men killed and women assaulted. But we have endured.' The crone plucked a slice of smoked meat from the plate and tore it in half with her teeth.

Desma had only been in the city for a couple of months, and already she was tired of feeling unwelcome. She could not imagine two hundred years of such treatment, to know that one's mother and grandmother and great-grandmother had felt the same, treated as less than a citizen.

'Why don't you go to another kingdom?' she asked. 'Dramaki or Athanai?'

Eidia shrugged. 'This is where we were brought. We made this our home. We have done nothing to the people of Koriithos except follow their laws. Our chief's daughter led us here, and we must believe there is a greater reason for that.'

Desma had no reply. She had done the same. She had left her own home and found her path ended in Koriithos.

Eidia took her hand. The Arydorian's palm was rough from a life of work, her calluses and scars telling a hundred tales. 'I asked Cosmas to bring you here to meet me. I want you to know that, no matter what happens in the palace, you will always have a bed in my house. Indeed, in every Arydorian home. We understand what it is to be a foreign princess in this kingdom. Cisra was our kin and our chiefess, and she was cast aside and vilified. All for the crime of not being born in the League. Though that has not stopped them looking at us, born since on Koriithosan soil, as outsiders still.'

Desma pressed a kiss to her palm. 'I thank you, Eidia of Arydor, for your kindness. But I do not wish to bring more trouble to your quarter. If the Dirciade were to hear of me visiting ...'

'Bah,' Eidia spat with disgust. 'Spineless women who are too afraid to stand up for themselves to the men who truly treat them ill, but will grow claws at the first sight of a woman who could offer them freedom. They are girls who would soon learn how a true woman fights if they stepped into our home.'

Desma could not help but smile. Though she was not so foolish to think there was not another reason behind this visit, it would still be pleasant to go someplace other than the palace where she did not feel afraid. 'May we walk through the quarter then?'

Eidia gestured to a dark-wood stick leaning against the wall by the door. 'Retrieve my staff for me, Princess. My bones seem to grow older faster than the rest of me.'

They wandered the streets. Though people still stared, she now saw it was curiosity, not disapproval, that turned their attention to her.

Men and women greeted Eidia as they passed. Some offered food or drink, others bolts of cloth or bright ribbons. She smiled and thanked them all, but took nothing.

They came to a square where a group of young men danced barefoot on the stones, their knees bent low, backs straight, feet somehow flashing quickly despite the awkward position. Without warning, they would suddenly shoot upright, gaining tremendous height as they leapt towards the sky, arms stretched above them with a great shout, before landing back in their bent knee stance.

Spectators stood around, clapping in time with the fiddle and drums, singing in a language that tickled Desma's ear with familiarity, but had enough quirks to keep the meaning hidden from her.

They passed a narrow street that had been boarded over with planks of wood and stone rubble. Through the gaps, Desma could see homes with belongings strewn on the ground.

'Water sickness,' Eidia said quietly, grief ringing in her words.

Desma stepped away. The plague was known to her, as she had been in Athanai when it struck the city three years ago. They had fled by land before the gates were shut, watching ships burn in the harbour and houses sealed. It was a sickness that made the waters of one's body turn thick and grey, robbing them of breath and sight, causing a slickness to the skin that stung when touched.

Only a priest of Esplace could heal water sickness, but they were a small order and rarely helped the poorer quarters when the affliction struck. The most effective method was isolation or death. Nearing a thousand years ago, Dramaki had lost half its population to water sickness. It only remained a kingdom because none of the other cities wanted to risk bringing the disease home if they invaded.

They entered a small market, and Eidia showed her the crafts of her people. Besides the smoky honey and mead, they also made a multitude of sweet nut treats, as well as intricately knotted breads filled with herbs and spices. Desma bought two different loaves to bring back to the palace.

One woman had dozens of different ribbons in front of her and wooden frames no larger than her palm. Desma watched a young girl approach her and ask for a chicken. She watched, amazed, as the woman plucked white, red, yellow, and brown ribbons from the table and began weaving them around the frame, swifter than Desma's eyes could follow. All the time, the purveyor chatted to the girl, telling jokes and asking about her family. Within a few minutes, the woman had crafted a woven chicken in mid-peck. The girl laughed delightedly and handed over a small coin before taking the chicken and running back to her parents.

Desma headed over without delay. 'Good day, mistress weaver,' she said. 'What skill you have!'

The woman bobbed her head politely, her lips trying to hold back a smile. 'Thank you, Princess, but it is a small skill. Something to while the day away and bring some delight to children and tourists.' Her eyes flashed to Eidia, who waited nearby.

Desma did not let her words deter her. 'It is a talent that should be admired by anyone with half a brain to see skill and beauty combined with such elegance.'

The woman tilted her head. 'Is the princess interested in a ribbon creature?'

'I am,' Desma said. 'What are you able to make?'

The woman shrugged. 'If I have seen it, I can make it.'

'A bear? Lion? Falcon? Heron?'

'Since I have seen them all, I can make them,' she replied. 'Which would the princess like?'

Desma thought for a moment. 'A dove?'

The weaver nodded. She plucked white ribbon and began to thread it through a frame, hand darting out to grab a small piece of grey. At the last moment, she also added a touch of blush to its underside. Desma could not move, fixated on the woman's hands, barely blinking as she watched her work. Within a minute, she had a beautiful white dove, grey in its wings and pink at its heart, sitting serenely in her palm.

'How much?' Desma asked, her heart aching at the creation.

'A gift,' the woman said. 'Money should never be made from grief.'

Desma gently took the dove, the ribbons soft, almost believing she could feel a tiny heartbeat in her hands. 'May the Holy Twelve bless you, weaver.'

'And may the Seamstress lay her hand over you, Princess.'

Eidia took her elbow and led her back into the crowd. Desma did not pay much heed to what she saw. Her eyes were far away as she held the dove to her chest. Eventually, the older woman took her to where Cosmas waited with her guards at the edge of the quarter.

'Visit me again soon, Princess,' Eidia said warmly. 'I can teach you how to make our pepper bread.'

Promising to return, Desma placed her dove in her belt pouch, but kept her hand on top, protecting its precious cargo. She remembered the brooch she had taken with her when she left Apasa. It had been one of her mother's – an opalescent, white dove carved from a large pearl, entwined with myrtle carved from green sea glass. It had been the one thing she had been allowed to take. But when she had reached the cliffs above Apasa, just as the storm broke above, she had cast it away. A bolt of lightning the colour of softest blush then struck, shattering it in midair in a display of Turan's power and anger. Since then, Desma had not touched or worn a dove in any form. What made her ask the weaver to make one, she did not know.

She barely spoke to Lycon when he retired for the night. Sat on the edge of the bed, she stared out at the wide and dark sea, the lips of the waves shimmering with starlight, the ribboned dove resting in her lap.

Cela could not stay away.

Ever since she had stumbled across the strange woman, she could not keep her voice from her head. Her words rang like bells in her mind, drawing her back down the stairs into the windowless chambers.

There, she found the young maiden waiting for her, a table set for two with dinner and fruit juice.

The strange statues kept silent vigil as the woman rose, gesturing wordlessly for Cela to sit across from her. A silver bee pinned a pale red chiton over her dark shoulder, her hair brushed and oiled with fennel and clove. Brightness and deep sweetness. The scent suited her.

Cela had not told Desma of the woman, feeling it was not her secret to tell. Yet.

Was that why she had come back? To learn more about this strange woman? She felt a purpose unfolding, but it was like remembering a dream that faded in dawn's greying.

'Your feet are heavy and tangled in choice.' The maiden's voice was strong and silky. 'Come, Celadine, and enjoy a repast with me. The stars sleep this night, and the astronomers stare in vain. A quiet evening.'

Cela took the seat across from her, watching, though the women made no threatening move. She unsettled Cela nonetheless.

The woman poured them both a cup before taking hers, slipping her feet under her as she sipped it daintily, eyes gleaming. 'The charred stone grows again. The lost foundations will be relaid, and the cowl will cover the sword.'

'I do not understand your speech,' Cela said, holding her drink in her lap. 'You speak in riddles as though their meaning should be clear as glass. Tell me, what is your name?'

The woman laughed, hollow and deep. 'Still, you ask for my power,' she said. 'I see much in my darkness, Celadine. I see you trapped between tide and temple. A heart will release you, but another calls from across the sea. Whither shall you go, obedient daughter, faithful friend? What call will you heed? Which heart will you listen to?'

'Stop,' Cela cried. How could she read her soul as though words were printed on her chest? Did her heart sing out its hidden song to her? 'Who are you?'

A grin. 'I am crowned in seaweed and shells. I am born from sand and grass. I am home, yet I am far flung. I am hidden, but walk high. Who am I, Celadine?'

Cela shook her head. None of her words made sense. Hidden but high? She was sequestered from the rest of the palace, but was clearly a noble, having been present at the royal wedding. Her skin was dark as umber – was she Opuni? But her face was of the League. Perhaps one of her parents heralded from the Great Lands and the other from Koriithos. Home, yet far flung. Khufu had told them of his homeland, the sweeping grass plains and deserts larger than islands. Crowned in seaweed – Nethuns was God of the Seas and Koriithos was his chosen people ...

Cela jerked so violently she spilled her drink across her dress, but she took no notice. Her eyes searched the maiden's face. Her eyes, nose, chin, cheek. Glimpses, echoes of her father and brother.

Gylippus and Lycon.

'You are a Princess of Koriithos,' she whispered.

From behind her, the woman swept out a diadem of silver and sapphire, sparkling in the light from the glowing stones, and resting it nobly on her brow. 'I am Alnea, daughter of Obawhenta, Throne-Carer of the White Oasis. I am Alnea, daughter of King Gylippus of Koriithos. I am Alnea, betrothed to Actor son of Sinon, War Leader.'

Clarity struck Cela like a wave. This was who Actor was promised to wed if no other suitable husband was found within the next year. A woman of the League and the Great Lands, illegitimate daughter of the king. Someone who looked at her so clearly and so deeply.

'Actor is bound to you,' was all Cela said, her words stiff and chilled.

Alnea nodded. 'Yet another heart you have tied yourself to. How can you move with so many strings?'

This strange woman, who drew Cela to her like tide to sand, was the reason she could never pursue her feelings for Actor. That brave, insufferable man whose honour was his life and whose duty bound his bones. Was this Turan's punishment for helping Desma? For how else could such cruelty come about?

'How long have you been down here?'

She shrugged. 'Since Gylippus returned from the Twin Kingdoms of Gold with a babe in his arms. He spent a year sailing the coast of the Great Lands, even landing on Urruc's beach, though he did not leave sight of the water. He travelled down the Blue Mother, life-giver to the many kingdoms of my land, until he came to my mother's home. A story repeated a thousand times. They fell in lust, and from their mingling a child was born. But alas, my mother did not survive the harrows of childbirth, dying in battle to bring me life. And so I was brought here, hated by the queen whose heart rages cold, scarcely acknowledged by my younger brother, shunned but royal. My companions have been books and scrolls, learning all the libraries of the League has to offer.'

'Do you ever go outside?' Cela asked, imagining a life in these few rooms.

Alnea laughed. 'Yes! I have seen the sun and moon, felt the wind and swam in water salt and sweet. I am not a prisoner, just unwanted. I have learned that the more I stay away, the more likely Gylippus is inclined to grant my requests.' She rose and hurried into another room. Cela heard rustling and things being moved about before Alnea returned with arms laden with scrolls. Most were written in League-script, though some Empyrean was discernible. Others were written in strange loops and swirls, and one was covered in tiny pictures. One in particular caught her eye. 'That is from Urruc!'

Alnea grinned. 'Yes. I found it particularly difficult to learn, but now the stories of the dying city dance in my mind.'

'You can read it? It took Desma months with the help of a renowned scholar to puzzle it out, and even then their understanding was fragmentary at best.'

Alnea picked up the scroll and began to recite the story. 'And so Nammi, Wreathed-of-Cloud, walked the walls of Urruc unseen by its peoples, bleeding from her wrists and ankles. She shed her divinity upon the mortals and their stones, casting protection with the last of her everlasting breath. And so Nammi ascended into Firmament, dissipating into ethereality, to never again sit by the Dune-King's side and whisper words of wisdom and love.'

'Truly you are blessed by Aplu,' Cela said, citing the God of Learning and patron to all libraries.

Alnea's face turned to thunder. 'He does not give blessings,' she snarled, her voice gravel and iron. 'The Singing God, the Golden God, the God of Freedom. He lies!' Her voice was a shout. She dashed the scrolls to the floor, eyes wild. 'He gives nothing but curses. And he *laughs*. He laughs at us mortals as we crawl through this life. Do not fear Tinia or Aita or even Serene Turan – fear Aplu, for he knows true destruction.'

Cela grabbed her hands. 'I am sorry.' The princess shook with the force of her feelings. 'I did not know the harm of my words. Forgive me.'

Alnea's eyes held hers tightly. 'I am glad you found me, Celadine of Apasa. I sense a kinship in you I have not felt with another, not even my own brother. And so I will tell you my greatest secret. A secret I am forbidden to speak, but there are no chains on my tongue. Part of you already knows this, for it is a fearsome power – one reserved only for the most sacred, the most dangerous.'

Cela's heart pounded as she waited for the princess' next words. Words that resounded with the toll of fate.

'I am a prophetess.'

CHAPTER TWENTY-SEVEN

Cela felt like a newly caught swallow thrust into a cage, beating its paper-light wings against gold, silver, iron bars.

She stalked through the palace halls, ignoring the curled lips and the sharp-eyed judgement of her attire – a yellow peplos and topaz jewellery. A bright flower in the mausoleum. But as much as she tried, each stare was a knife prick on her skin.

She knew how Delphinus felt, trapped in this suffocating city that sought to change them. None of the crew were Koriithosan, and the majority of them had spent the last four years at least in Apasa, a city warm like sun-drenched waves.

Despite their efforts, the city was changing them. Desma most of all. She had dimmed. It was the only way Cela could explain the change in her dearest friend. The bright flame that hunted the world over for the treasures, who challenged kings, priests, and monsters to purify her, who kept her heart in one piece even when her family was torn from life ... had paled since her wedding.

She dressed in darkened clothes, kept her hair bound in ribbons, even ate differently. Desma's heart would not abandon a kingdom to its dark fate without doing all in her power to save them. But what would she be forced to sacrifice?

The weight of Desma's burden pressed heavy on Cela's shoulders. She had urged Desma on *The Darkling* to not abandon Khufu. While her heart had cried out to save their captain, a quieter part of her had acted for Desma's sake – she couldn't bear the thought of Desma living with the knowledge that she'd condemned him. Cela had wanted to spare her that.

And yet, it had all been for naught. Her feet led her from the palace and into the city, past the inn where they had stayed upon first arriving, its doors guarded by Nethuns and Horta. She headed for the public sparring grounds, as sometimes Bion and Delphinus would be there, the Konosoan grappling with soldiers, shirtless and slick with oil, while the piper cheered on the sideline, the few times he regained a glimmer of his bright self. But her steps slowed, fingers tightening in the fabric of her peplos. Her presence would not be welcomed by the citizenry, and she could not bear having yet more eyes on her.

Spinning on her heel, she headed west, down through the city, letting the scent of brine and weathered timber guide her to the harbour.

The sea was a mixture of greys and greens, the sun hidden by a blanket of clouds, though flashes broke through occasionally.

She spied their ship down the way. Arete was on deck, gesturing emphatically to a workman, no doubt explaining in detail what she wanted him to do. She made the fussiest mother look negligent when it came to her craftsmanship.

Arete was the only one who seemed unaffected by the city. She was a storm cloud, indomitable and bold, moving through the palace currents without pause or unease. How Cela yearned for her steadfastness!

She turned away from the harbour.

There had been so many twists and turns in their lives recently. She could not speak to them of her worries, her troubled thoughts ... the choice in front of her that she could not dare face. Desma had been forced to step away, so Cela had to be their tiller, guiding them, keeping them together while they navigated the treacherous waters of the city. And right now, her mind was a maelstrom that she had to sail alone.

There was nowhere in the city that was a comfort. Nowhere that felt like home.

Except ...

The path was the same as weeks ago, but this time she trod it alone, no procession trailing her. Soon she stood before open doors carved from solid rose quartz. Myrtle and apple incense curled in a beckoning haze, calling to her in a way it had not in a long time.

Inside the temple, her steps carried her toward the golden statue of her goddess, Turan.

The building was not the same as the Grand Temple in Apasa. It was smaller, though more ostentatious. She ignored the peach-blush robed priestess who welcomed her, and they left her to commune with their goddess.

Kneeling before the altar, white marble and studded with diamonds, she kissed her fingertips and circled her heart. The gesture evoked years of memories and, for a moment, settled a mantle of peace across her shoulders.

She let her hand slip into a bowl of rose petals, their silken softness another balm on her troubled thoughts. They fell from her fingers over the small brazier, aroma spiralling towards the heavens to join a thousand other devotions.

She closed her eyes and imagined herself home, within the naos, listening to her mother sing hymns, pretending that her life had not burst apart all those weeks ago.

Cela had sent messages from Trilos and Koriithos back to Apasa, and she had received letters in return from her mother. The remains of the old temple had finally been cleared and salvaged, and the construction had begun on the new building. But many priestesses had abandoned the temple after the attack, claiming Turan had removed her love from the city. The community who supported the temple was broken, with a quarter of the populace killed during the attack and another quarter leaving for the city proper.

Her mother had never written the words, but the request was clear. *Come home. Help me rebuild. Your mother needs you. Your high priestess calls you.*

What was her path? Had Turan rejected her? She knew her jokes sometimes bordered on sacrilege, but never had her faith wavered. She did not have the patience of a priestess, but that did not mean her love for Turan was any less. It was only that her love for Desma was greater ... or it had been.

Their lives, once woven threads in an unbreakable rope, were now a twisted mass of knots – a dozen threads that no longer served a single purpose.

'Turan,' she whispered, her throat tight, words harsh. How long had it been since she prayed? 'I know of the grievance you bear towards my sister's family, though I profess I do not understand it. I don't seek to intercede on Desma's behalf. I just want to know if you have a fate for me?'

The silence, once broken, grew yet deeper. The hush of slippered feet and gentle crackle of flame alone in the temple. The moments stretched, her knees aching against the cold stone, ankles uncomfortably crossed. An itch developed behind her ear, but she fought the urge to scratch.

'Please, Serene Turan,' Cela begged, biting the inside of her cheek to keep her tears in check. 'What am I to do?'

She waited.

She did not know how long she knelt in quietness. At some point, she had begun to hum. An old song, a simple hymn to Love, nearly as ancient as Apasa. Each exhale was another rhythm, an inhale was a pause, letting the note die peacefully. The hum became words, quiet and pleasing, so humble in its asking for the simple joys that it was still sung at every festival. Her mother used to sing it as a lullaby.

Again and again, a chorus of devotion, strained and blackened but still beating beneath the ash and blood. She sang for her mother, struggling to hold her city's faith together, for Apasa, for the strength that resided deep in her bones. She sang for herself, to know where her steps led – to palace, sea, or temple? Cela sang until she could summon her voice no longer, the silence returning like a blanket around her shoulders.

Someone laid a hand on her shoulder and she shifted, groaning as her stiff limbs protested. A different priestess stood beside her, her face matronly and sweet.

'Come, my daughter,' she said softly. 'I do not know what you are asking of our goddess, but I can see that there is no answer for you tonight.'

Tonight? Cela blinked. Lit torches lined the temple walls. Night had fallen. She had been praying for most of the day.

'Do you think she even heard me?' Cela asked.

The priestess shrugged. 'I like to think she has. Though I am sure even a goddess has limits to her patience, listening to so many of her children crying for her attention. But perhaps consider that her silence may be the answer you need, though not what you originally sought.'

Cela climbed to her feet, throwing a final fistful of petals on the fire, and the priestess accompanied her slowly to the doors.

From the top of the temple steps, the palace shone ethereal in the moonlight. Desma was up there, maybe only just finishing another tutoring session. Cela pictured her like a shark, a fierce hunter in the sea, now bound in a net and cast ashore, drowning in the air as men gathered around her with bright knives.

How could she even consider abandoning her friend? How could she break the promise they had made each other times uncounted – to always be there, to guard the other's back, to stand before fire and shadow and death?

How could she tell Desma that she wanted to leave?

There was a knock at her door, and Desma called for them to enter. The servants were finally bringing her lunch.

'Princess,' Hyllos greeted from behind her. 'Good morning to you.'

She spun around, startled. He was one of the last people she expected to see that day. The king and Kalchas were doing their best to keep the second astronomer apart from her.

'What are you doing here?' she asked.

'I was feeling unwell this morning,' he said, a sparkle in his eyes. 'But I began to feel immeasurably better once Kalchas left the palace. Since I had no duties assigned to me today, I thought I would take this blessed opportunity to visit the princess.'

'May Esplace continue to favour your recovery,' Desma said with a grin. 'Come, sit with me.'

They moved to the balcony that overlooked the harbour and settled on marble stools shaded by a potted fig tree. The breeze raised pimples on her arm, but the sun was warm when it slipped from behind the clouds. Sails flapped from the busy harbour, loud enough to be heard atop the cliff, shouts and curses rising above the docks. She even spied a ship from the Great Lands. The people on board had lighter skin than Khufu, though that did not lessen the sharp pain in her chest at the sight of them.

'Tell me,' she said suddenly, 'what is Koriithos' relationship with the Great Lands?'

Hyllos cocked his head, eyes curious. 'Much the same as with most of the League. We trade mostly with the coastal kingdoms and tribes, though more with the easternmost and westernmost points. The centre lands do not have much need for the League.'

'And there is Urruc.'

'Exactly. Throughout history there have been some clashes, but generally we tend to keep to our own side of the Middle Sea. Though as more and more lands are mapped, it seems the world is growing smaller. I sometimes fear that unless peace becomes the world's ultimate goal, war will spread.'

'A dark view,' she said, picturing a battlefield of men like Khufu fighting men like Actor. She shuddered.

'I pray to Esia I am wrong.'

'Has anyone ever travelled throughout all of the Great Lands?' she asked. It stretched hundreds, if not thousands, of miles to the south. Khufu said that Opuni alone was a journey of over a hundred days walking. She could scarcely imagine the distance. To cross the League from the most southern point of the mainland to the north was no more than thirty days. And, according to Khufu, his city was close to the heart of the Great Lands.

Hyllos shook his head. 'No one from the League or Empire. There is much we do not know of the Great Lands. They are not interested in trading in knowledge or history, and keep to themselves. I have not visited any of their cities, but travellers record many wonders that rival our own. There is a great river that splits the land in two, from which all fertility flows. On its bank, amid sand as dazzling as gold and crushed diamonds, there is the greatest library in all the world. It is said that even the Holy Twelve are envious of all it holds. But it is fiercely guarded by god-like creatures from the time of the Beings. Ah, how I would love to see it one day!'

'Have you ever left Koriithos?' She knew so little of Hyllos. Nothing about his family or upbringing, how he came to be second astronomer.

'I've been to Athanai twice, but otherwise I have not left my kingdom.' His eyes searched the clouds limned in white-silver. 'But I travel further than most bound to this earth. I walk among the stars and into the days unborn. For this, I give thanks to Nethuns daily.'

'Though it seems you often travel with both eyes closed,' she said, a note of bitterness in her words.

He smiled. 'I cannot deny the truth in your statement.'

'I wish to ask you something we have been forbidden to speak about,' she said quietly.

She felt him stiffen beside her. He knew what was on her mind.

'Princess—'

'Why did the king blaspheme in Nethuns' temple on my wedding day? The Sea God had made it clear he did not wish us wed, and yet the king would have killed the high priest, shed holy blood on the altar. I do not understand.'

Hyllos was quiet for a long moment. 'We are walking in shadows and shifting tides. Not even the gods know how the future will unfold. They have desires on the outcomes, and use their power to twist the world to achieve their desires, but they are not Nurtia or Aplu. Nethuns knows that you must wed Lycon for the future of Koriithos, but he does not have to approve.' Sorrow marked his face. 'I fear you have stepped from the displeasure of one god into the annoyance of another.'

'I am caught in one device or another, no matter how I turn,' she said, sourness staining her words. 'And so many have been hurt because of it.' Khufu was the latest in a long list of those hurt or killed because she could not seem to escape the attention of the gods. Would another of her friends be next? Arete, or Bion? Cela?

'You are gods-touched, Princess. Rarely is it without pain or blood. Divinity and mortality cannot coincide peacefully. How can it, when the blood of one is gold and the other red?'

They could leave us alone, she thought. If Turan had let her be, then the temple would still be standing and her family alive. If Aplu had kept his prophecy to himself, then Desma would have been free to leave the city after her purification. Khufu would be alive. The crew could set sail on *The Darkling* and ...

What would happen if she threw herself off the balcony, spat in the eyes of all the gods and their sacred plans?

She stood abruptly. 'I would like to go for a ride outside the city. Please inform my guard to ready the horses while I dress.'

Hyllos' mouth dropped before he smoothed his features. He rose to his feet and bowed. 'Yes, Princess,' he murmured, leaving in a soft rustle of robes.

Desma remained, letting the wind wash over her as she breathed slowly. What treacherous sands she walked. Was Hyllos someone she could trust?

A troop of six warriors awaited her once she was ready. Without speaking, she passed them and headed to the stables. Word had flown ahead of her, and she found a dapple mare waiting with a groom brushing her nose.

Her guards were barely atop their own mounts before she set off at a brisk trot. Desma wanted to push the mare into a gallop, but the streets were busy, and she did not want to risk harming a citizen in her haste. But each minute rattled her insides, as though her soul had finally begun to shake, disturbed from its seat at her centre.

They were stopped for two excruciating minutes before the Canal Gate while her guard spoke to the stationed men. Once clear of the gate and the people concentrated nearby, she urged her horse to greater speeds, letting the wind rip her hair from its ribbons. One of her guards shouted at her, but she ignored him.

She did not know where she was heading.

Maybe she could just keep riding. Into the sea, the sun, to the end of the earth. To fall into the abyss, to let something else claim her. It was all too much.

Princess of Koriithos.

Khufu dead.

Despised Beloved.

Her family gone.

Witch.

She recalled the pain once she had unravelled the spells surrounding Cisra's sons. Blood pouring hot and acrid from her mouth, her breath stolen from her throat. The shattering explosions that ripped her apart. Veins, bones, blood, skin – all were fire and ice and glass.

She was not a godling. Her parents were both mortal. As were their mothers and fathers. Yet she wielded a power that could not exist. What would happen when it became known? A thunderbolt clapped through her. What would *the gods* do when they found out? A mortal that could do what none of them were able – undo their spells.

She pushed her mount to a greater speed

Desma had always wanted fame, wanted her name remembered, to be renowned in Apasa. Her mother had seen the sun glowing inside her and given her the chance to shine upon the world with a ship and sword instead of robes and incense. Desma had carved her history into the kingdom's annals by bringing home the greatest trove of Urruc since its destruction. She had endured the horror of the poisoned land, had killed for it, had done ... terrible things.

Blood was blood was blood.

Strangers' blood. Enemies' blood. Father's blood.

It all felt the same on her hands.

Would that the ground might open up and send her plunging down into the Halls. If she prayed to Aita and Phersipnai enough, would they grant her wish?

Is this how her father had felt? Swept into a sea that had no end, grief flooding where love had once flowed, until all that was left was to let himself drown?

She pulled the mare to a halt and dashed the tears from her face, scattering them to the ground, wet spots disappearing in the dust.

Tears are to be caught, to not share any sadness with the earth or water. There is enough pain without us adding to it.

The words fell into her mind like an embrace. She turned to her guard, who had only just caught up to her. 'Which way to Irna?'

Thales stumbled on the stony path, struggling to keep sight of Timo, who dashed ahead. He was older than seventy harvests. Breath came ragged in his chest, and his knees sent lashes of pain up his legs in protest as he tried to keep pace with his oldest grandchild.

His youngest grandson had come running into the field, screaming that warriors had surrounded the house and a princess had kidnapped his granddaughter.

Timo had dropped his hoe, dashing bare foot through the wheat to the worn path that led to their humble house. Thales shouted after the youth to do nothing rash, but he had seen the glint of the bronze knife in Timo's hand – the boy's blade all that remained of his father. Thales bade his other grandson to hide and took off after him.

What could they want with them? They were simple farmers, blessed with a fertile plot of land that grew wheat, a few apple and fig trees, and a small field of vegetables. They had no cattle or goats of value – Timo had grown into a fair hunter, but they dined on game only.

His already hammering heart nearly burst at the sight of the six men standing outside his home, their horses tied to nearby trees. They seemed relaxed, but stiffened at the sight of Timo charging towards them with a blade held high.

'Sheathe your knife, boy,' Thales yelled after him, lungs burning at the lack of air. 'For Tinia's sake, please, don't hurt him,' he pleaded as the men drew their swords.

'Give us back my sister,' Timo roared, reason having fled his mind. He had already lost his parents to the monster that had prowled the countryside. He could not bear to see his siblings harmed.

Thales knew how the scene would unfold. The guards would try to disarm Timo, but he would lash out wildly, anger replacing grace. The guards would be forced to cut him down, his blood feeding the earth. Would they kill him, too? Thales did not care for his own life, but what would happen to the youngest boy? What would they do to his granddaughter?

The door to the house opened and his granddaughter stepped outside, eyes wide but holding a small cake. The woman who followed was dressed in a fine grey peplos, green himation, with bronze bracelets and a river of hair rich as summer wine.

'Desma?' Thales tripped on a root and went sprawling on the ground. He laid there, dazed, the iron taste of blood in his mouth. He heard more shouting but struggled to lift his head. He prayed into the dust that Timo had dropped the knife and surrendered himself to the warriors.

Hands grabbed him under the arms and pulled him to his feet, and he blinked the dirt from his eyes. Timo held his sister tight against him, eyes wary against four warriors who watched him back.

The two men who had helped him up gave him a quick dusting down before stepping away to allow the red-haired woman to approach. Desma. The girl who hunted the monster and succeeded when all else had failed. He remembered the day she rode in his wagon to Irna, with the bard who sang and told tales better than any storyteller he had ever heard.

'Desma,' he said again, unable to wipe the surprise from his face.

'Her title is Princess, farmer,' a warrior growled.

Desma grabbed the man's arm. 'Leave him be.' She stopped a pace from him, a kind smile on her face. But shadows lined her edges, a sadness that wearied with a thousand cuts. 'Hello, Thales.'

'What has happened to you, dear child?'

CHAPTER TWENTY-EIGHT

'I am sorry to have caused you this stress,' Desma said, setting down spiced wine and sliced fruit alongside the cheese and smoked meat arranged on the small table. She had waved Thales to sit down after bringing him a bowl of water and towel to clean his face.

'Do not add this to your worries, Princess,' he said, taking a sip of wine to clear his throat. 'If Timo had not run off hot-headed, he would not have been a breath away from Aita's Halls.'

'He has a brave heart,' she said. 'It is noble.'

'But needs to be tempered by wisdom,' Thales responded. 'He needs to step out in the world, but he would never leave his brother and sister. And I do not think it would be wise for me to raise the young ones alone. My days are numbered by the handful.'

Desma squeezed his arm. But she did not offer any false platitudes. Lies had no place between them.

'Why have you come here, Princess?'

She shook her head. 'Please, in here ... call me Desma.' She did not know why she had come. She needed to speak to someone who was not Cela, or her crew, or someone from the palace. Why the thought of Thales brought her to his door, she did not know. Perhaps some god was guiding her this day.

'I just needed to talk to someone,' she said quietly, glad that Timo had taken the children to Irna and they were alone.

Thales waited. She took the moment to study him. An old, weathered soul that had not lost its grip on life. Grey hair cut under his ears, streaked with the brown of a lifetime past. Wide eyes held hers in sympathy, despite the surrounding wrinkles expanding in spirals. Cracked lips, dried from working in the wind, still upturned in a gentle smile. Though there was a slight tremor in his arms, he still moved with surety.

'Someone who isn't of the palace,' she continued, 'with an agenda that I cannot fathom because I do not know the games they are playing.' She could have turned to Eidia, to commiserate and share in their outcast state, but the Arydorian was as tainted by the city's oppression and politics as any noble. She needed to step out of the shadows and webs, to breathe clean air and feel the warm sun. She needed Thales and the remembrance of a simple home.

'What of your friends? The soldier and piper? And bright Cela?'

How could she explain? Actor was the general of Koriithos' army, with a duty greater than his connection with Desma. She had scarcely seen Delphinus since they returned, and Cela ... the city was a wedge between them. From their scarce glances and stifled conversations, Desma could see a dullness creeping into Cela's light, the same greying she had seen in her father when he had been cast adrift. They didn't share openly with one another anymore. Cela and Actor had been close on the ship back to the city, yet not long afterwards they had become strangely distant. Desma realised with shame that she had not even bothered to ask her friend what had transpired.

But Desma did not offer Thales these truths, and instead told him of all that had happened since she'd last seen him, following the slaying of the monster and her purification.

'Every step my friends take beside me feels like another debt I can't repay,' Desma said. 'They remain with me, but I wonder if perhaps that is right – especially Cela. Her mother needs her.'

'The choice is up to her,' Thales said. 'But perhaps she does not know what she wants. Or she does, and yet has not summoned the courage to pursue it.'

'What can I do?' she asked.

'Keep the door open,' he replied. 'The river knows its journey, though it may take time to wear its path.'

She considered his wisdom, his eyes bright with knowing. 'Have you always been a farmer?'

'Since I was born.'

'Yet your words rival the finest philosophers of Athanai.'

A tired smile. 'Understanding life is not difficult when your path is straightforward. I only speak from my own experience. It is up to the listener to apply it to their own life. My wisdom is knowing which words to speak. Your wisdom is seeking their truth for yourself.'

Desma took a sip of her wine, a gleam in her eye. 'What a tale this will be around Irna! The foreign princess kidnaps a farmer's granddaughter and then sits with him to tell her worries. How I wish I could bring you back to the palace with me.'

Thales shook his head. 'Please do not ask that of me, Desma. I am old, and my only wish is to remain here long enough to see my grandchildren safely married. I know of soil and rain, not crowns and stratagems.'

'I would not burden you in such a way,' she reassured him. 'It is hard to think in the city. So many people, so many plans and double-sided words. I scarcely know what my next step should be.'

'It is people's way to multiply the bad and simplify the good,' Thales said. 'But I find it makes life far easier to think the other way. If you had to sum all your worries and fears into one question, what would it be?'

Desma was silent. A hundred thoughts leapt to her mind. Lycon and how he felt towards her, when he might call her to their bed. Eidia and her strange warmth. Hyllos and his uncertain loyalties. The Dirciade.

They all tied back to one thing – her crown.

Maybe it was a simple question, as Thales suggested. Instead of trying to solve a dozen concerns, she need only concern herself with one.

What kind of queen did she want to be?

The small dining room was reserved only for the royal family.

Desma had invited Cela, Hyllos, and Actor to eat with her.

Cela had been jovial upon arrival but paled when Actor walked through the door in a simple grey chiton.

Hyllos came last, a frown on his face as he sensed the tension in the room.

Servants brought in roast fish with parsley and thyme. Seared octopus with orange slices and vinegar. Bread baked with goat cheese and dates studded throughout. Wine lightly spiced and cut with water. Fresh fruit and honeyed roses. Musicians played in the corner; a drum, lyre, and pipe that whispered of pastoral delights and dappled sunshine.

A meal befitting a livelier occasion, consumed between terse words. Hyllos watched her under his eyelashes, afraid to ask any questions. Cela pretended Actor was not seated next to her, and the general spoke only to Desma and the astronomer.

When the plates had been cleared away and warmed mead brought for them to sip on, Hyllos finally drew the nerve to ask, 'What brought about this lovely dinner, Princess?'

'I wished to advise you both'—she nodded to the astronomer and Actor—'that I am ending my current tutelage.'

They two Koriithosans glanced at each other. 'This might best be a discussion to have with Prince Lycon ...' Hyllos began.

She waved him silent. 'I have learned all I need to know about the women of this kingdom,' she said coldly. 'But it was not one of them who slew the monster – it was I who cut its head from its body and carried it to the palace.' The lie sat uneasily in her stomach.

Hyllos blanched, but Actor gave her a small smile.

Desma continued. 'I am to be queen one day – may Uni grant it is many years in the future – but I need to learn *all* there is about the kingdom. And I will be the one who decides what I learn, and from who.'

Hyllos chose his next words with care. 'I only have your best interest at heart, Princess,' he said slowly. 'I would be happy to ...'

'And while I trust you will do what is best for this kingdom,' she said, words as keen as a knife, 'I cannot always believe you will do what is best for me.' Her eyes were iron, and he could not stand before her will. He bowed his head.

'I am happy to support the princess in any way I can,' Actor said.

'Wonderful. I will begin tomorrow.'

Soon enough, Hyllos and Actor bid them goodnight, the astronomer all but fleeing to speak with Kalchas. Actor left stoically, not once looking back as Cela closed the door behind him.

They were alone in the room.

All that was unsaid between them slithered into the air, choking and intangible.

Desma reached for her wine cup as Cela returned to the table but misjudged the distance, knocking it over and sending dark liquid spilling across the table.

Cela jumped back before it reached her dress, her shout turning into laughter as she grabbed a towel from a side table and mopped up the mess.

Desma shook her head ruefully as she moved plates and knives out of the way. 'I guess I owe you a coin,' she joked. A little custom from a lifetime ago, paying a silver drachma to the other if wine was ever spilled. Cela smiled.

'I noticed that you have not been spending much time with Actor,' Desma broached. 'Has something changed?'

Her friend stiffened, hand clenching the towel until wine ran across the table anew. But she did not look away from Desma. 'He told me that he is pledged to someone else.'

Desma gasped. This was news to her. 'Who?'

'Lycon's sister,' Cela said through gritted teeth. 'Alnea.'

Desma froze. 'His ... sister?' How many secrets did this family have?

Cela nodded and told her Alnea's story, stumbling as she explained Actor's role.

'He is her second choice?' Desma exclaimed. That kind, honourable man deserved far more than to stand to the side, waiting to marry a woman who did not care for him and whom the city kept out of sight.

Cela sighed as she sat back down, wet hands falling by her side. Her eyes were darkened by her hair falling over her brow, but Desma could see the glint of pain. She knelt by her friend, grabbing her hand to her chest, uncaring of the wine.

'I am sorry, Celadine,' she whispered. 'I am sorry for everything you have endured since Apasa.' She placed her head in her friend's lap, breathing in the apple and jasmine perfume, the warmth and familiar softness of her body. How often had they held each other in joy, sadness, fear? Twenty years they had been companions, their lives intertwined until it was hard to tell where love started and blood ended.

Cela placed a hand on Desma's head, holding her in her lap. Small tremors shook Cela's legs and Desma mapped them as they moved up to her midriff, to her chest, her arms, until her entire body quaked. She encircled Cela's waist, holding her as tears fought against her strength, a flood against a dam.

Cela had lost her temple, her home. Her sister had killed the father she had chosen, yet she had still left her wounded mother, refusing to leave her sister to break a murderer's curse alone. She had dared open the door to her heart, however slightly, and had it slammed shut again.

Desma had grieved over and again, shed tears into the ocean and on land. She had screamed and raged in palaces and cages. She had wrought wonders ...

While at her side, Cela had endured like the sun, bright and unceasing. What grief hid beneath that light, not shared with Desma as the cause of her pain?

'Cry, Cela,' she whispered into her friend's dress, wet with wine and her own silent tears. Cela choked back a sob. Her hand formed a fist, pulling Desma's hair by the roots, but Desma did not care. 'Cry, please.'

Cela's heart, a vase of exquisite beauty that could last a thousand years, had cracked from a hundred blows.

'I'm sorry, Cela.'

Finally, it came. A wrench and a gasp, as though tearing itself from her by force. A deep breath. A shudder. A pattering as the first tears fell, sparkling and clear like spring water.

'Desma.' It was more growl than word, raw and biting.

Cela rocked back in her chair, as though hit with a blow that tried to unseat her, but Desma held firm. She buried her face further into her friend's lap, her arms vices to hold Cela together as the hurricane broke within her.

The cries were harsh and gravelled, choking themselves off too early as breath ran out of her body. Deep, heaving gasps as she drew in more air. A keen that drilled into Desma's ears. Cela cried out again as she jerked in the chair, her body freezing into a straight line as she wailed before slumping back down.

The door opened and two guards came through, faces worried. 'Get out,' Desma snarled, flashing them fiery eyes until they slammed the door in their haste to flee.

'I ... I can't ... ' Cela gasped. 'It is too much. Too much.'

'Then let it out,' Desma pleaded. She sat up and held her face. Cela's eyes were puffy and red, streaked with vessels and swimming in falling tears. Her mouth was twisted in a grimace. Her hair wisped around her as though grief was felt in every strand. This was pain Desma had inflicted upon her, the result of her choices and those of her mother. Her family had broken the golden light of her friend. 'Give it to me,' Desma said softly, leaning forward to kiss Cela's cheek. 'Share it with me.' She kissed her other cheek. 'To love's end and back, Celadine.' She pressed her lips against hers, breathing in her soft scent, spiced with salt.

Cela sobbed against her mouth, their breaths mingling and growing warmer. The kiss grew beyond the moment, stretching back into memory and forward into love. It held their friendship like moonlight in a palm, ethereal and real.

Cela's breathing slowed, stilling into calmness as her tears dried, the river emptied.

Finally, Desma withdrew her mouth, face wet, hair clinging to her skin. 'I love you,' she said, brushing Cela's golden hair aside. 'You are my sister.'

A tired laugh slipped past Cela's lips. 'To love's end and back.'

Desma strengthened her heart for her next words. 'I want you to leave Koriithos.'

Cela's eyes widened. 'What?'

'I release you, Cela,' she said. 'You have bound yourself to my path, but it is mine to walk. I am telling you. Be free. Find what the fates have woven for you and you alone.'

Cela threw her arms around her, burying her face into her shoulder. 'Thank you, Desma. I did not know what I wanted.'

'You did,' Desma said. 'But your heart is too kind. Love for others can blind love for yourself.'

They held each other long into the evening, the moon rising high, though it was a sliver of its full glory. They held each other as they had not done for too long.

Lycon stood in their bedroom, a simple cloth about his waist, clothes crumpled on the floor for a servant to pick up. He frowned with concern at the state she was in.

Her hair was messed, wine stains on her lips and in patches across her peplos. Her face was puffy from her own tears, but Desma did not care.

She looked at him as she had feared to do since their wedding.

He was average height and not too broad. But his shoulders were strong, arms muscled nicely. His calves were well-sculpted, lean legs supporting a firm stomach with lightly defined muscle. Complexion darker than most pale Koriithosans, but lighter than her own bronze skin.

A pleasant face, with dark, round eyes, firm nose, pink lips. Cheeks chiselled, though marked with several dark spots. His brows were thick, and he had a small, gold earring with a green stone in his left ear.

'Desma,' he said warily. 'Is all well? How was your dinner?'

She undid the copper clasp that held her peplos, letting it spill down her body to the floor. She wore nothing underneath and instantly felt her face heat, her skin pebbling in the cool night air.

His eyes darkened, lines marring his brow. 'What is this?'

She paused at the heat in his words. Even one as untrained in the bedroom as she could tell it was anger, not passion, that fuelled his tone.

Running her hand through her hair, she tore out the few ribbons until it was cloaked across her shoulders, dark and shimmering in the torchlight.

Despite all that had happened, she was a daughter of Love. She was the breathless hush. She was the lioness of silk and sweat.

She stalked towards him, her sway the threat of entanglement to come. Her breath came fast and shallow, its harshness dancing in the air between them.

'Stop this,' he said, taking a step back from her.

The huntress awoke. She was a woman. The gasping sigh. The bedroom surrender. She was Lover and Want. Her fingers trailed down her cheeks, neck, chest, stomach, thighs.

She was Offering. Sacrifice.

He would have her. She would take him.

She had crossed the space between them. Her hands only grazed the cloth before it fell from his body.

Heat. Hardness. Musk.

His breath matched hers as they stood inches apart, not touching. A thousand possibilities tantalised between them. Pleasures to come, but not yet begun. Cresting and ending and burning.

'Have me,' she whispered, words like candle flame.

'What has happened?' His shoulders shuddered, though his hands remained clenched by his sides, eyes clasped onto hers.

'Have me,' she said again. All the nights they had shared, weeks of sleeping across from one another, and not once had they been husband and wife. A cycle of the moon and no seed had been spilled, blood speckling the sheets.

Something wild was inside her. A creature she did not know existed, one that frightened her. This was not her. She did not want in this way.

Uncertainty flickered in her eyes.

Take me, she mouthed, her voice giving way.

He reached for her, the fire on his skin igniting her own flesh ...

But he did not touch her. Leaning around her, he drew a blanket from the bed, draping it about her shoulders. Her eyes flicked down and she saw him soft, asleep, safe.

'I will spend the night elsewhere,' he said, the anger gentle but still coating his words. 'Sleep well, wife.'

He stepped around her, naked as a newborn, and left the room. The door clicked loudly in the sudden emptiness. Why had she come to him like this? What had she wanted? Because it was not what she had been asking for.

She slid to the floor, buried in the centre of the blanket, a nest. She had no tears left to shed. The fire had gone cold, her skin cooled.

Sleep slipped quietly through the window, wrapping her in its forgetting embrace, and carried her away for a moment's respite.

CHAPTER TWENTY-NINE

Cela returned to the palace after visiting the harbour.

She was free.

Desma had told her to go, all but pushed her from the path she was walking. She found the idea almost disturbing, as though she had been untethered, and the wind was threatening to raise her into the sky, setting her adrift to only the gods knew where.

She met with several ship captains to inquire about their journeys. Most were sailing to the corners of the League. A few to the Empire, but she had no desire to join them. Two were headed south to the Great Lands, and she was tempted. To see the oasis cities, travel the deserts said to be larger than all the League combined, to visit Opuni, see the Twin Kingdoms of Gold …

The morning after the dinner, she awoke angry. Once the flood of emotion drained away and her mind regathered the debris, she found herself wanting to march to Desma's room and slap her friend.

After two decades of companionship that went past sisterhood or marriage, she had cast her aside so she could wear the crown of Koriithos alone? The greatest journey, the most perilous quest, the challenge with the highest stakes – and she chose to do it alone.

But the anger cooled faster than an ember cast into the sea. She did not want to be a handmaiden, even to Desma. That could not be the life destined for her. Celadine of Apasa deserved her own story. She had always thought they would share their tale, but she would not be relegated to being a member of the chorus in Desma's play.

She realised her feet were guiding her to the dusty rooms occupied by Alnea. Princess of Koriithos. Actor's betrothed.

Prophetess.

Oracles were rare amongst the League, only a handful residing outside Delphon, the patron-city of Aplu. They differed from astronomers and auguries, who watched for signs in the sky and nature. Oracles received visions directly from the God of Foresight, speaking his words, riddled with mystery, before they inevitably came about. One must be brave to ask a question of an oracle, for their answers were known to drive many to madness or destruction.

Is that why Alnea was pushed into the shadows? For a kingdom that respected the art of seeing the future, why would Kalchas and Glyippus ignore such a power? Because she was a woman? Or because she wasn't truly Koriithosan?

When the princess had revealed the truth, Cela had fled, afraid to be twisted up in doomful words, as happened in stories unnumbered. But here she was again. Whether she was drawn by some fateful string or by unheard whispers of a god in her ear, she wondered if it would be wise to ignore it. She had prayed for a sign as to what she should do – return home to Apasa or …

'Princess?' Cela called as she stepped for a third time into the round room with its sentinel statues. 'Are you here?'

'I am here, Celadine.' She stepped from behind the statue with no face, black dress glistening with gold waves stitched along its surface. Her eyes were solemn, and she stood expectantly, hands clasped in front of her. Looking for all the world like a supplicant before an altar. 'I see the dam has broken. The strings have been untied. The cup returned.' Her face softened. 'I am glad you came back.'

'I feel as though I had little choice.'

Alnea's eyes flashed with inner fire. 'We always have a choice, daughter of heroes. Yours line the path you have walked, brave and bold. And they advance before you, lighting the way.'

'Do you love him?' she found herself asking, her voice cracking on the last word. She clutched the sides of her peplos.

The princess blinked slowly. 'I do not know what love is. And so I can answer truthfully. No, I do not love Actor, son of Sinon. And he does not love me.'

Cela breathed a sigh of relief, the vice around her heart loosening.

'But he will not marry you,' Alnea continued, her words soft but heavy. 'I do not see him raising your nuptial veil, nor do I see you grow old in each other's arms. Actor's path is one of glory – and he cannot have that if he is with you.' The words were like stones dropped on her body. Alnea continued. 'Actor will obey his king and wed me within the year, as I do not see another candidate appearing for myself. He will bring honour to the shame of my skin. Thus is the Koriithosan way.'

'Is there nothing you can do to stop it?' Cela asked desperately. She could see Actor in the Temple of Nethuns, drinking the saltwater cup, eyes resolute in his duty, face tight with unhappiness. Bound to this strange woman who lived in shadows and who spoke truth like a warrior wielded a sword.

'I see but one path that would free us all,' Alnea said. 'I must leave Koriithos. And you must help me escape.'

Desma sipped nettle tea as Eidia ground herbs in a pestle.

Lycon had been distant. He spent more time out of the city than before, more nights away from their bed than sleeping beside her. Part of her was glad that she did not have to relive the embarrassment of her rejection often. Though a smaller part wondered why he had left her standing in the cold.

He was not there when Cosmas and Arete began to bring in historians and teachers from the city, men and women not of the palace, to teach her of the kingdom. Most were trepidatious at first, and some left after the first lesson. But the few who stayed seemed intrigued by the Apasan princess, who paid rapt attention and questioned the smallest detail.

Desma realised she had stagnated since being purified. She had let the world roll over her, fate pulling her along behind its chariot. But no more.

She had asked Cosmas to accompany her through the city after her session with a trademaster, an expert in imports. Eidia had been surprised to see her on her doorstep but swept her inside, closing the door firmly in Cosmas' face.

After exchanging a few pleasantries and questions of health, they fell into silence. Desma's heart turned to stone in her chest as she struggled to find the words she needed. She knew what she wanted and had considered a hundred ways to get it. But now, sitting in the smoky, wooden home, anxious thoughts pervaded what had once seemed a clear plan.

'Your tongue is heavy, Princess,' Eidia said, her voice rough as though scorched with smoke. 'I will not hasten your words, but know that all spoken inside these walls is guarded by the Wanderer. Speak free, but by your choice only.'

The words fell like rocks down a cliff. 'I need a spell.'

Eidia's hands paused, stone pestle still. 'A spell?' Her voice had dropped to a whisper. 'Magic outside the temple is not well received in Koriithos. The covens of Artimi steer clear of the city and keep their casting in the wilds and hills.' She pointed the herb-covered pestle towards her. 'What is it you wish to possess, Princess?'

Desma's stomach clenched, but she forced the words out in a rush, a faint blush staining her copper cheeks. 'An amulet to pause my womb.'

Eidia continued grinding. 'There are herbs enough that accomplish the same task.'

Desma shook her head. 'I cannot risk this to herb lore or the prince finding them. I need something I can keep on my person at all times that would draw no attention. Please, Eidia of Arydor. Can you find someone with skills in the teachings of the Old One?'

Eidia scooped the green sludge she had pounded into another bowl, crunching dried lavender in her hands, dried petals falling. 'The Old One was matron to both our peoples,' she said quietly. 'We did not have Artimi to gather our lost covens together, to help us through the fog and forest. But there are a few of us who kept to the old paths and survived. I will find one,

Desma, though what you ask carries some risk. This magic goes against many of your gods. And if someone in the palace was to learn of this … '

'I heed your words, Eidia,' Desma said, 'but trust that I know where I step.'

The older woman bowed her head. 'Wait here. I will send the thin one in to keep you company, and be back in an hour.'

It was past midnight, and Desma sat on the edge of her bed alone.

Lycon had travelled to a town on the edge of the isthmus near Phoroniaa with several young lords. She had not thought to ask why they were going, but was glad to have a couple nights' reprieve.

The night was cool through her thin sleeping robe. Once Eidia had returned, Desma had swiftly left for the palace, spending the rest of the day in her rooms. Maids came, different women once again, to bathe her and bring dinner. Desma tried to take a bite of the bread but found herself unable to swallow.

So she sat on the bed, facing the windows, where she could see the sky dying in a bloody display of colours – blue to bright red to bruised purple to silent black.

She cradled in her lap the dove from the Arydorian weaver and the amulet. She had kept the dove on the small table in the bedroom, set atop a silver box. Lycon had noticed its arrival but made no comment. She still did not understand wholly why she had asked for a dove, symbol of Turan and her mother. But where before it had poured grief and anger anew inside her … now, it brought a small sense of peace.

Laying the dove next to her on the pillow, she turned her full attention to the amulet. A triangular piece of obsidian wrapped in grey ribbon, tied through with twine, it had a ruby strung on one side and an emerald on the other. Simple enough that she could wear it every day without drawing the ire of Koriithosans and their prejudice against jewellery. It was cold to the touch, even after being held for the past several hours.

She felt guilty at deceiving Eidia, for she had no intention of wearing it.

She was going to attempt to unravel the spell.

The thought alone made her stomach plummet to the Halls Beneath; she recalled the pain that had turned every vein and bone and organ into shattered iron. Would she have died if Cisra had not been there? Would she die now?

She had unravelled powerful magic four times in Cisra's cave: once to pass through the glamour that hid its entrance; again to reveal the hidden door, as was Cisra's test; and then twice more to remove the curses from her sons, which were corruptions of Cisra's and Turan's power. Perhaps it had been too much for her all at once.

Which is why she had asked for something small. A simple amulet to pause the body's flow of blood and fertility. She prayed to Artimi she was right, for she knew little of magic.

And there was no one she could ask. Her power had never existed before in the world. The power to undo magic, even that of a goddess.

Cisra had cautioned to keep it hidden. Her magic could topple the foundation the League was built upon, and the gods may see it as a challenge to their supremacy. Her mother had warned her to remain hidden from the world, to be forgotten. She was failing miserably.

But she could not bury this aspect of herself any longer. Desma did not know where the power came from or what its purpose was in her fate. But she resolved to learn as much as she could in secrecy.

Knowledge was a weapon, ignorance a blindfold.

Cisra had told her to imagine a web and cut it away. But that was not what she had done. She closed her eyes, trying to feel the magic wrapped around the stone and ribbon. It came quickly. Thin threads twined around and through the amulet. She tugged at the threads, though her hands were still, fingers gripping tightly. The magic grew brighter the more she twisted and unknotted. When she opened her eyes, light the colour of blush, tinged with night-black, shimmered around the amulet and her palms. But she did not allow her concentration to slip.

The magic was fine, newly cast, and simple. Nothing like the great ropes that had bound Cisra's sons. It came apart within moments, with the faintest concussion of air, like a breeze expelling from her hands. The light turned to dust and faded away.

The amulet looked the same, but Desma knew it would do nothing to stop a child being conceived.

She waited.

It had taken some time after unravelling the curse on the boys for the pain to hit. And it had been close to an hour after she pulled down the gully wall's glamour.

How long would it be now?

An hour passed. Then another.

The crescent moon had passed beyond sight of her window when she felt the first cramp.

At first, Desma thought it was from sitting still for so long.

But then it came again, followed by a long, building, stabbing pain that slowly pushed the breath from her lungs.

But the pain did not ebb. It kept going, until her toes were clenched and her hands fisted the sheets, the amulet rolling to the floor.

When she felt she would not be able to bear another second, a blade sliced through her stomach – ice-coated, wreathed in flame. A scream leapt to her tongue, but she clamped down hard. The knife twisted, shattering into shards that lanced through her abdomen and chest, into her thighs and shoulders.

She fell onto the bed, back arching and collapsing as she rode the waves of pain.

But soon the waves were a little shorter, less intense. Though it took an eternity, the pain subsided like a tide going out to sea.

Her breath was ragged and sweat pooled around her.

But she was alive.

She had done it. She had unravelled magic and survived the consequences. Pulling herself upright, every limb weak, she could not keep the triumphant grin from her face.

She did not know if the pain was less because the magic was smaller or because she was growing stronger in her ability, like a muscle toughened by repetition.

Persistence was necessary, but finding a way to obtain spelled objects without arousing suspicion posed a greater challenge. A full cup of wine steadied her hand, and she drank deeply.

Artimi's words drifted back to her from that beach on the road to Trilos. *You have not finished with the world.*

CHAPTER THIRTY

Turan screamed.

The sound ripped the air into pieces. Murals covering the marble walls and ceiling cracked and twisted, the images themselves trying to flee the scene before them.

It was too soon. This day should have been weeks, months away.

She screamed again.

The most ancient of pain. It linked most of creation, mortal and divine.

The next wave came before she had time to draw breath, and it felt as though her throat would snap, her jaw break, as soundlessness spewed out. Her body convulsed, legs flailing before they could be held down, knees up and ankles apart. Her arms lashed out, hands wrenched into claws that drew blood as they found flesh.

Her wings flared, disappearing into the silks and stone beneath her, shimmering between corporeal and ethereal.

'Calm yourself, Turan,' Uni said from between her legs. The Queen of the Gods was drenched in blood and fluids, her purple dress soiled beyond repair; her flashing green eyes were hard, offering no comfort, though this was a celebration. Finally, a child born in wedlock to her rightful husband, Sethlans. 'You must breathe. Focus your powers on the child. This is your body – command it!'

Turan wanted to rip Uni's eyes out, but her arms were held down by spirits of nature: hands of bark, water, stone, and leaves strong against her struggles.

'Get it out of me,' she screamed – her voice, capable of seducing gods and driving mortals to ecstasy, now hoarse and shaking. Never had she felt such pain. Her Lovers had slipped from her like petals from a flower. Even the godlings had been but moments of pain soon forgotten.

But this child, this creature ... it was killing her.

'Ilithiia,' she panted, calling the Goddess of Childbirth to her side. Older than Turan, her grey eyes were full of mercy and strength. 'Help me.'

'You are strong, Daughter of Beings,' Ilithiia replied. 'This task grows greater only with your consent. We are here for you. Munthukh and Esia are by your side. Heavens' Queen embraces your womb to welcome the child. Listen to your body and its rhythms. Push and breathe.'

'Damn you all to the darkness without end,' she cursed, spittle flying from her blush lips. 'May your thrones crack and your light fade. May—' Her words descended into a howl as another contraction rippled from the centre of her body.

Hours had passed since she had collapsed during a feast of the Holy Twelve. Tinia had called them all to gather in song and wine, as he was wont to do when bored with the mortals below. She had donned a new dress the colour of river moss and fresh-cut figs, and sandals made with leather as soft as down to gently protect her feet from the heavenly ground. Her hair, rich as Tuscanai wine, had been brushed with rosemary sprigs then coiled like a great serpent at rest on her shoulder. Golden set amethysts draped her slender neck, sparkled on her ears, and laid heavy on her wrists. She kept her delicate fingers free, but with nails opalescent like pearls and painted green like her wings. Her skin rubbed with rose oil, perfumed with wave-salt, apple leaves, and orange autumn roses.

Now her dress was soaked with sweat, its hem torn to allow her legs to be opened to the assembly. When she fell to the floor, Uni had been by her side immediately, banishing the gods from the hall. Sethlans had tried to stay, but Ethausva sealed the hall against men. Goddesses and spirits had flocked to Turan's side, female energies effusing her with strength.

She had been witness to many divine births, and they had not taken this long or been this difficult. Something was wrong.

Wrenching one arm free, she reached between her knees to grab the Queen's hair, pulling her forward over her distended belly. 'What is inside me?' she snarled, her teeth slicing through her lips at another contraction, blood pouring down her chin, sparkling and gold.

Uni's green eyes were dark with worry. Her face, which had remained in a state of severe perfection for centuries, now showed signs of distress. Her voice, that commanded the stars and set order among mortals, faltered. 'I do not know.'

Turan fell back on pillows that felt like ground glass on her skin. Everything burned.

'Bring me Nurtia,' she said breathlessly, before the next wave of pain washed over her.

The Corded Goddess appeared in mere moments, for she had been waiting outside in the hall, drawn to occasions that sent ripples down lines of destiny. Though she was blind, she walked unaided, moving unerringly to Turan's side. A white dress fell to her heels, and a dozen black cords twisted about her body, arms, and legs. She was bound to fate and saw the splintering paths that laid before mortals and divine. In one hand, she bore a large nail, with which she pierced a person's fate to them when need arose.

'Tell me, niece,' Turan panted. 'What kind of child is this?'

The goddess knelt, placing a hand on Turan's belly, face pointed towards the starry sky lit on the horizon by dawn's glow. Nurtia was still as stone. Another contraction clamped down on Turan. Her mind swirled, dazed. Golden blood pooled around her. A mortal woman would have died long ago.

'He has lost himself,' Nurtia whispered, her voice a chill in the air. The assembled goddesses fell silent, breaths held tight.

'What do you say?' Turan asked, closing her eyes and letting her head loll back.

'A child of Creation and Love, he had the potential to be the Holy Thirteenth. But alas, he has been drowned in his womb with hate. A mother's love turned sour and vile.'

Gasps echoed from the goddesses around her. Nurtia continued. 'He has been poisoned before he has drawn his first breath. Fear him, divinity, for he may wield our destruction. Remember the promise of the Firmament before Its death. From It would come a creature that would have power beyond our imagining and be the end of so many things. I fear this may be what It prophesied.'

Uni withdrew her hands, coated in ichor, and stepped away, her face broken in fear. 'I cannot help bring this monstrosity into the world,' she said.

Turan screamed again. 'He is killing me.'

Uni's face grew cold. 'The world existed before without Love. It will continue without it once again.'

Bitch, Turan swore in her mind, for she had no breath to spare. They have always wanted her to fall, resented her being born from the froth and blood and waves. She had shaken the pillars of the world when she stepped upon Apasa's sand. The gods had wavered in fear at her power, giving her a throne among the Twelve to rule civilisation by their side.

Now, they would abandon her to be torn apart by this foul monster growing inside her. Yes, she hated it. Cursed his father as he grunted on top of her, pleased to have finally wrung the promise he had sought from her for thousands of years. All to keep Timothea's daughter blood-spoiled. And that fool, Gylippus, had cleansed her anyway. All for killing one monster.

Something sheared inside her, an unnatural cleaving, and blood fountained from her. Blackness flickered in her vision. This would not be the end of her. She would not allow it!

'Summon Artimi,' she said, her words stained with bitterness.

Of the three Virgin Goddesses, she despised the Wild One the most, and the feeling was returned. Artimi blessed virginity and abstinence above all else, calling young maidens to her covens in the forests, to avoid men and hunt them when need arose. Sex was forbidden, pleasure of the touch denied. Turan could not walk where Artimi rode.

But it was the domain of the Old One she needed now, She Who Is Goddess No Longer.

Spirits fled the heavens and flew to forests outside the city, where Artimi had withdrawn from the feast, disgusted by the sight of childbirth.

Agonising minutes passed, each filled with depthless pain, as they waited. Only Ilithiia stayed by her side, unable to leave her charge during what she saw as the most sacred moment in life.

Finally, a clear horn sounded from afar, followed by a rattling of hooves on marble. The Goddess of Witches and the Wild burst into the chamber, vaulting off her pale stallion and striding across the floor to stand over Love.

Turan knew how she looked. Her body wracked and torn. Her beauty tattered. Her allure now blood upon the sheets. She fought to keep from sneering at the goddess above her.

Artimi was trim and muscular, her brown skin bearing a silvery glow, like moonlight on copper. Her hair was held back by a strip of leather where it fell flatly to her shoulders. A knife glinted from her belted chiton.

A cold, cheerless smile lit her face. 'Hello, whore.'

Turan blinked the tears from her eyes, angered that her body would betray such weakness in front of Artimi. 'Wildling.' Tremors ran through her limbs. She went to speak again, but her world went black.

When she blinked her eyes open again, Artimi had moved and was kneeling near her ankles, dragging a finger idly through her blood. 'It has been an age since a god has shed such blood,' she said wistfully. 'The World's Love ... defeated by a babe unborn. A child of hate. The irony.'

Turan wanted to summon her power. Wanted to rip the chamber apart stone by stone, star by star. She would chain and torture the goddesses who now refused to help her. She would cut the crown from Uni's head, burn Ethausva in her hearth, lock Munthukh into a nightmare of horrors.

But she was helpless, fading. The only one who could help was her archrival among the divine.

'Artimi, I beg a favour from you,' she said, the words acid in her mouth. 'Save me from this child inside. Call upon the magic gifted to you by the Old One, who you chose to help when all else turned her away.'

Artimi rose to her feet and crossed her arms, black eyes sparkling. 'What will you give me?'

Turan gritted her teeth. She was at her mercy. Nothing could be refused. 'Name your price.'

'I want to be the one to tell your husband what has happened.'

Turan hissed. Spite. Artimi was nothing but spite. But she had no choice. She nodded, sealing the bargain. Witnessed by a roomful of goddesses.

Artimi raised a hand and a stone knife appeared, carved with symbols of the Old One. She knelt over Turan's rippling belly, placing the stone tip against her stomach, piercing the skin gently enough to only draw a trickle of golden ichor. Chanting under her breath, in the secret tongue of witches, she drew upon her strange power like a gleaming mantle about her.

Turan let out another scream as the child, sensing danger, began to move furiously. His claws raked her insides, his horns piercing her, his tail sliding around. *What was inside her?*

'You must stop this,' cried Nurtia. 'Stop this madness! You are laying a new path, but it leads to the same end. Destruction! Destruction is coming and it cannot be stopped. Hear me, sisters – the end is at our door!'

But Artimi did not stop. Her words had grown heavy and dark with magic, her aura flickering with black and grey light. The stone knife was glacier cold against Turan's skin. The babe inside her was slowing, growing weaker. Something was happening.

Artimi released her hands from the knife, but it remained standing on Turan's belly. Artimi snapped her fingers at Ethausva. 'Get me a jar with a silver lid. Hurry!'

The Hearth Goddess gathered her dress above her ankles and ran.

Turan could feel him moving towards her entrance, but he was softer, less sharp. Whatever spell Artimi had cast was working. Her body was relaxing, knowing the fight was over. Ethausva returned with a clay jar just as Turan sighed, an exhale from her womb.

Artimi grabbed the jar and wrenched open the lid, dropping down near Turan's ankles.

Turan had never felt more exhausted in all her long life, but she managed to lift her head to see her child. She gasped.

Fog, thick and grey, flowed from her body. Almost smoke, it roiled angrily and tried to lash away from the Wild Goddess, but her magic was too strong, and it was drawn into the clay jar. When the last wisp had been contained, Artimi closed it with the silver lid. She drew a finger through the congealed blood on the floor and sealed the rim with it, chanting all the while.

'Here,' Artimi said, tossing the jar at Turan so she had to fall back to catch it. 'The jar will not contain him – it – for long. I would suggest not opening it in the city.' She turned to Ethausva. 'Lift the spell against the gods. I will tell Sethlans the joyful news that his wife has had his child.' She picked up her knife from where it had fallen onto the sullied sheets. 'Congratulations, mother.'

Turan was too broken to reply.

Artimi gave her a disgusted sneer before collecting her horse's reins. 'Stop snivelling,' she snapped at Nurtia, who had retreated to the far wall, sobbing into her hands, before leaving to find Turan's husband.

The jar still smelled faintly of olives. It was a beautiful, burnt orange, with an image in black of two men feeding each other. The silver lid must have come from somewhere else; a jewellery box, possibly. Her blood had dried on the seal, hard as metal. The jar vibrated slightly, shaking with the wrath it contained. Inside was her son, turned to fog, warped by hate and magic. What was she to do with it now?

The door to the chamber flew open, and in stomped the Forge God, her husband.

Shaped like a large boulder, Sethlans was imposing and ugly. His skin, though rippling with muscle, was forever stained black with soot and coloured red from fire. His chest, bared from beneath his robes, was wide and hairy, pockmarked with scars from the forge. He would have stood taller, if not for his hunch from thousands of years of toil. And though he usually walked with a cane, it had been discarded in his haste to reach her, a crooked amble hindered by his feet being twisted to point backwards.

His face was splotched crimson with rage that paled slightly as he beheld the scene before him: his wife's blood a great pool around her, her body wracked from her labours, dress torn and stained, the jar in her arms. Tears ran down his face, catching in his beard where they shimmered like pearls.

'Why, wife, why?' he asked, his hoarse voice breaking. 'I did as you asked me. All I wanted was a single child between us. But even this you cannot allow me.'

What could she say? She would not apologise. She had held her part of the bargain. A child she had given him. Never had she promised to be a darling mother, to be part of a caring family, to raise this child in love. She agreed to use her body for breeding, and she had delivered. Then why, oh why, was there shame creeping in the edges of her heart?

Her face remained stoic. Silence only enraged him further, his face purpling.

'I hate you,' he growled. 'I despise you, vile wretch. You never held an ounce of love for me in the thousands of years we have been married. Enough! You have killed my son. Nothing you or Artimi can say will convince me otherwise. Keep the jar.' He ripped from his cloak the pink quartz rose she had given him on their wedding night and ground it in his hands, scattering dust on the floor, on her blood. 'Do not come to Quirinale or Trilos anymore. You are forbidden in my temples and cities.' His eyes blazed like embers, smoke wisping from his limbs as the heat of creation burned under his skin.

She wanted to reach out to him, touch him, cool the heat inside him. The feeling surprised her.

He pointed at the jar. 'I name this child Miasma. May his life be as foul as his mother's heart.' He turned to leave but paused to look back at her. 'Tell your other spawn, the Lovers, to be wary. For if any of my children cross their paths, they will not live to spread this vile corruption you call love.'

And so her husband left her.

Tears threatened to fall, but she hardened herself, slamming iron down her veins and spine. She was Turan, Goddess of Love and Desire. She wanted for nothing, for she was everything. The goddesses around her offered nothing but pity and disgust. In silence, they left the chamber, abandoning her.

Alone, she laid on the cold floor, wretched and wet, weak and tired. A sob broke the quiet; Nurtia walked towards her, face shiny with tears and snot. She knelt beside her, and for a moment, Turan felt a flicker of warmth; here was someone who had not left her side.

She did not see the nail until it was too late. The Corded Goddess drove the iron nail into Turan's thigh, matching her scream at the sudden pain that bloomed like forest fire across her leg. Turan's arm flung out and struck the blind goddess a terrible blow, sprawling Nurtia across the floor to crumple in a heap.

Turan pulled free the nail, letting it fall. It rolled with a metallic ring until it stopped, its path blocked by the prone foot of its mistress.

Nurtia lifted herself and turned cloth-bound eyes on Turan. 'Your fate has been sealed,' she said. 'I warned you. I warned you all.'

'Hush, daughter,' a warm voice said. Turan turned to see Aplu in all his resplendent, golden glory, his light blurring his features. He crossed the hall and crouched by Nurtia, taking her softly by the shoulders and helping her to her feet. 'Let us get you home to Delphon.'

'Yes, Father,' she said gratefully, resting her head on his muscled chest. 'I am so tired.'

As they walked past, they came to a halt.

'Do you have one last thing you wish to say?' he said gently to Nurtia.

The blind goddess turned to Turan. 'Because you have chosen this path, one last word of prophecy I will leave you with. From this choice, a kingdom will rise from the grave and another will die at the birth.'

Her words echoed like a tomb.

Aplu shared a large grin. 'Such exciting times,' he said, his laugh echoing long after his light faded from the chamber.

Turan looked down at the jar in her arms and wondered how she found herself, alone and hated, lying in her own blood, with a child of fog.

'I am the Goddess of Love,' she whispered to herself, lying on her back, too tired to rise. 'Love is me.' Blackness swirled in her eyes. 'I am Beloved.' Sleep laid its cloak over her.

Then why was she so despised?

CHAPTER THIRTY-ONE

Mynta pushed open the rough wooden door to the kitchen, the scent of warm bread, tangy lemon, and fresh parsley hitting her nose.

Her cook, a middle-aged woman with blonde hair plaited in a sensible bun, turned at the noise and quickly bowed, hands covered in sticky dough that she had been kneading. 'My lady,' she said, aghast, 'you are in the kitchen!'

Mynta laughed as she plucked a plum from a bowl and seated herself at a bench where her lunch was being prepared. Fish wrapped in vine leaves with dark olives. Goat cheese soaked in thyme and olive oil. Peaches in sumac syrup. Small rosemary cakes with crushed walnuts. She poured herself a glass of light wine cut with warm spices. 'I just wanted a change of scenery. Please, continue with what you were doing.'

The cook looked from the dough to her and back again.

'Perhaps I can give you a hand ...' Mynta said, going to put her wine down.

'No, my lady,' the cook cried, leaping back to her bench and taking up her dough with a vigorous beating, slapping it wetly on the surface.

Maids bustled into the kitchen, giggling between themselves, and began to plate their lunch. They continued to talk about their children, how their husbands spent more time at the gymnasium than home most evenings, and other everyday banalities.

The cook tried to get their attention surreptitiously, which made it all the more obvious.

Mynta pretended not to notice, nibbling on a rosemary cake as she looked around the kitchen.

One of the maids finally saw her and dropped her wooden plate with a clatter on the stone. The others jumped back, exclaiming, before they also noticed the lady of the house sitting in the kitchen, smiling at them.

They all dropped into low bows, blushes staining their cheeks, apologies tumbling from their mouths.

Before Mynta could speak, the door behind her slammed open to reveal her furious nursemaid, scroll clutched in her wrinkled hand, hair awry. She stormed into the kitchen, ignoring the frozen staff, and smacked the paper on the table in front of her.

'What is this?' she asked, her voice skittering the edge of propriety.

Mynta flicked her eyes at the bound scroll and sniffed. 'Poetry? How am I to know until you unroll it?'

'This is a letter to the Temple of Ethausva to inquire into the selling of this house!' Anesidora's voice rose until it ended with an almost-shriek.

Mynta brushed the crumbs from her hand and slipped from the stool, towering over her nursemaid, though she was barely a half-foot taller. 'Who is the lady of this household, Anesidora? It is I. Remember that before you dare approach me like this again.'

Her nursemaid crumbled before her words, deflating as her anger left her. 'My pardon, lady,' she said, bending until her forehead was nearly level with the table, hands clasped over her heart.

'Stand, mother of my childhood,' she said gently. 'It is not something I ever thought I would consider, but I find myself investigating all avenues open to me. Come, let us take a turn about the garden together.' She took her by the arm, scroll still clutched in the old woman's hand, and left the kitchen. They remained silent until they were under the cover of the trees, the scents of orange and almond and peach perfuming the air.

'Anyone around?' Mynta asked from the corner of her mouth.

Anesidora swung her head from side to side, as though cracking her neck, before replying, 'Not a soul.'

Mynta kissed her gray head. 'Well done,' she said. 'You think they will take the bait?'

'Like buzzards on a battlefield,' her nursemaid laughed quietly.

'Your friend in the palace will help us?'

'Yes, she is well placed among the servants to see all the comings and goings from your father's rooms,' her nursemaid said. 'She will catch who in the household is keeping your father updated on your movements.'

'I don't want them punished,' Mynta said firmly. 'They are simply doing as their lord bid them. Just release them from my service and send them on their way. Though how will we know that we have caught all those loyal to my father?'

Anesidora patted her arm. 'I will sporadically set tests for the other servants, though I do not think there will be others.'

Mynta paused by a rose bush, admiring the orange and white petals. 'And how goes the search for more guards? If my business is to expand, I will need trustworthy men, and many of them.'

'Do not fear, my lady. I know a good man. Sebastos was a captain of the city before leaving the service. He worked in several lords' households, training their guard, before retiring to a fair house out by the river.'

'I trust he is still up to the task?' Mynta asked.

Anesidora gave her a look. 'Age does not immediately make one useless, child. He is as much a man now as he was when I knew him thirty years ago.'

'And you are sure he will come into my service?'

'He is sick of the fresh air and idleness,' Anesidora assured her. 'He will be here, day after tomorrow.'

Sebastos was a tall man, unlike most other Trilosii, who tended to be stocky. His face was weathered and worn, giving his mouth a downward twist that made him look displeased. Slanted, brown eyes sat above a nose that had been broken several times, which did not distract from the chunk of ear he was missing. It was the face of a man who had seen much of life and found it both beautiful and harrowing.

Now, he stood before Mynta in the welcoming hall like a general under inspection. He had arrived a few hours past dawn. Grey threaded through thick, shoulder-length curls, freshly oiled and smelling of anise. A deep red chiton, trimmed in black, fell to his knees, and a copper belt girdled a slim waist. Bare arms showed strength beneath wrinkles, and well-sculpted calves rose from battle-worn sandals.

At his hip hung the plain bronze dagger Mynta had allowed him to keep, for they were bound by their mutual vows to Tinia, swearing protection for and from both host and guest. To break such vows was to spit in the face of the King of Gods.

'You know why I have asked you to attend this audience?' Mynta asked.

'Yes, my lady.' His voice was rough from a lifetime of shouting orders.

'It is a far cry from the esteemed roles you have previously held,' she said. 'I will make many mistakes, and we will have many arguments. I will rely upon you even when I do not know that I am doing so. You will watch where I cannot see, defend what I hold precious, and shed blood for me because of the gold I give you. Is this what you wish to do in the twilight of your days? I will not be offended by your response, be it bitter or sweet, so speak freely.'

Sebastos stood silent, studying her.

She maintained her poise, becoming a statue under his gaze, and waited, mistress of the moment.

Eventually, he turned to her nursemaid. 'It has been an age, Anesidora,' he said, 'since you refused my nuptial veil.'

Mynta's mouth fell open. This was news to her. She fought the urge to turn in disbelief towards her nursemaid who, for the past twenty-two years, had never left her side.

Anesidora scoffed. 'Let us not forget that it was you who refused to even speak about marriage while you were in the army,' she said. 'Another path called me.'

'Ah, but how it meanders until it joins again,' he said.

Anesidora clapped her hands. 'Enough of this lovesick speech. My lady asked you a question, and you are disrespectful in ignoring her. Shame on you.'

He bowed his head in contrition. 'Always one to walk the proper path.' He turned back to Mynta. 'Forgiveness, lady, but my heart had to have its say first, under Turan's blessed eyes. Your words ring of a wisdom far older than your scant score of years. You seek loyalty beyond gold. You wish to tie blood to hearth. That is a noble desire, but not one that is forged in the space of a day. I would join your service, but truth bids me tell you it is because of Anesidora, not you, that I do so.'

Mynta pursed her lips. 'I see.' She understood it was too much to ask for undying loyalty at the first meeting, but she did not know that she trusted his reasons

'I would also say,' he continued, 'loyalty is reciprocal. You would ask of your men a great deal, and we would ask the same of you.'

'How so?' she asked. This was not how she had seen her father or other lords deal with their men. Was he trying to take advantage of her naivety? She knew that her nursemaid would never normally allow someone to do so, but was her judgement perhaps clouded in this situation?

'You take our honour and life's duty into your hands, my lady,' he said. Unashamed, he spoke to her like a novice, lecturing her on how to lead her guard. Indignation flared inside her before she quenched it. She *was* a novice. Yes, she had ordered men to escort her around the city, but that was all. What she had planned required a squad of well-trained, well-armed soldiers. A tiny army in all but name. Was she so foolish to let wisdom fall to the wayside over her own vanity? That was what had led her to her current situation.

'The orders you give to me will reflect on my own soul before the eyes of man and god,' Sebastos continued. 'All men want purpose in life, to feel pride when he goes home to his family each night, to thank the gods for their good fortune rather than pray for it. It is by remembering this in every action that you will inspire loyalty. Be a woman I want to serve, and I *will* serve ... with blood and soul.'

She rose from her seat and crossed the few steps to stand before him, staring up at his weathered face. He seemed faintly surprised at her approach but did not move, staring over her head, a soldier at attention.

She picked up his hands and placed his hands on her chest, folded over her heart. He tried to pull away, but she held firm. 'I swear, before Tinia and Sethlans, before Uni and Laran, before Ethausva, that I will uphold the honour of this household in all my actions. None, be they guard or maid or cook or messenger, will be forgotten or neglected. Honour in every step I take. This I swear upon the gods, calling them to listen and observe, for the destruction of my household is the balance.'

He searched her face, looking for what she could not say, but she was genuine. She had seen the lords of the city, the Council who ruled Trilos, and while there were noble men of good heart, there were double their number who sought only to further themselves.

She would not be one of those men. She would rise alongside the people around her, not over their backs.

Whatever he saw must have satisfied him. He nodded before sinking to his knees, still clasping her hands in his, and said, 'I pledge my services to you, Lady Amynta of Trilos, and seek honour in your name.'

'Rise, Sebastos, and let us talk of the work to be done,' she said with a brilliant smile, embracing him once he was on his feet. The shame of her past failure was a fading shadow on her heart, for the path in front of her was bright.

CHAPTER THIRTY-TWO

Mynta sat straight-backed in the litter, curtains drawn back so all in the street could see who rode in the procession.

She had her silken black hair intricately plaited high upon her head, thin braids falling to frame her face, a net of gold studded with amethyst chips strung throughout. Her eyes were lined with olive oil and charcoal, her lips red with ochre and beeswax, and her neck scented with cinnamon and juniper.

Let them see her beauty and her wealth. She had donned her softest mauve peplos and a white himation hemmed with purple. A belt of fine leather studded with bronze buttons curved over her waist. Her sandals were thin with gold stitching, a necklace of cascading bronze graced her neck, accompanied by several bracelets and rings that flashed with gold and gems.

She had hired an expensive litter with sheer, golden curtains and covered in small bells that rang with each step and jostle. It had taken much of her fast-diminishing gold, but it was a calculated tactic. Four burly men carried her with ease, though their tunics were already soaked through with sweat beneath the hot sun, despite the occasional cool sea breeze that slid over the city walls. Her nursemaid sat on the edge of the litter in front of her, waving a small fan over herself.

Mynta had brought all eight guardsmen from her home, with Sebastos leading them, surrounding her litter and the small wagon behind, burdened with small ironbound chests.

They moved through the streets of Trilos noisily, drawing attention as one of her messenger boys proudly walked in front, calling out for people to make way for the Lady Amynta.

She smiled as his voice often broke shrilly mid-cry. He was still on the cusp of becoming a man, but he never faltered in his duties.

They marched through the city to the western quarter, where the bulk of jewellers and gemstone cutters worked.

At first, Anesidora had balked at her idea, aghast at the scandal it would cause. But Mynta did not care. This was the only way forward, and she would be damned if she played by the rules others had set for her.

They stopped outside one of the more renowned establishments. Mynta waited until the litter was set on the ground, taking the hand a carrier offered to help her up. It was one of the few shops in the district her mother had not taken her to, as the style was not to her liking.

Mynta swept into the store, breathing a sigh of relief at the relative coolness. The shop was built of stone, with high windows in the front to let in natural light. Simply furnished with a few empty shelves and tables, the products were undoubtedly stored safely in the back, only brought out for customers to look upon.

A well-dressed man behind a table looked up at the disturbance and greeted her with a wide smile.

'My lady.' His voice was smooth and courteous. Apollophanes – one of the finest jewellers in Trilos. Pristine in his chiton of fine cotton with a himation of beautiful silk belted with gold, his hair was swept back with oils and his beard glistened. He hurried over and bowed. She noted he wore no jewellery himself. 'How may I be of assistance?'

Her nursemaid stepped forward, snapping open her fan to draw his attention. 'My lady, Amynta, daughter to Councilman Linos, wishes to have several pieces appraised by your esteemed self. She is also interested in selling some items, dependent on the veracity of your appraisals.'

Apollophanes' face tightened at the implication he would undervalue anything, but it slid away like oil on water. 'I would only be too happy to assist. What pieces would you like me to see?'

'Thank you, shopkeeper,' Anesidora said, making him bristle. 'One moment.' She ducked back outside before holding the door open for her carriers to bring in several chests, placing them on the floor before leaving again.

Mynta had to fight to keep the smile from her lips as Apollophanes' jaw dropped. And this was after having to give several chests to Duris to pay the additional costs for the mine. 'You may need to close up shop for the day,' Mynta finally spoke.

'Indeed, my lady,' he said as her nursemaid went from chest to chest, unlocking them and throwing open the lids. Gold, silver, bronze, copper, tin. Rubies, sapphires, emeralds, amethysts, topaz. 'A veritable treasure trove.'

'Do you have a seat?' she asked.

Her question jerked him away from the chests, embarrassment colouring his face at his discourteousness. 'I beg your pardon, my lady. Tellis! Pero! Attend me!'

A young man and woman appeared from the back of the shop, both dressed similarly to Apollophanes, though they wore several pieces of jewellery each. 'My son and daughter,' he said. Tellis was the mirror image of his father. Pero had lighter eyes and sharper cheeks that she must have inherited from her mother. 'Fetch my lady a chair, cool drinks, and some food. Then get all the tools necessary to properly assess a variety of metals and stones. Quick as a whip!'

The children scattered to do their father's bidding.

Once Mynta was seated, a cup of pomegranate wine in hand and a tray of goat cheese with grapes by her side, she watched as the family set about lifting each piece from the chest. They weighed them on an ornate scale, peered at them with strange-looking glasses, rapped tiny hammers against them, even waved them through a white flame.

Mynta remained quiet, sitting reposed as she sipped and nibbled, occasionally murmuring something quietly to her nursemaid who watched the jewellers like a hawk.

Halfway through the collection, Apollophanes stood up straight, cracking his spine with a groan. 'My apologies, lady, but, by Sethlans' beard, my back is not what it used to be.'

'Do not worry, good man,' she said. 'What have you gathered so far?'

'Well, my lady,' he said, casting his eye over the many pieces laid before him, 'I can tell you where many of these pieces come from. Most are from Trilos itself, though some are from other kingdoms. The glassware is from the Empire, naturally, for their skill far outstrips our own with this art. It is a beautiful collection. And though I cannot fathom why you would bring such a valuable array to me instead of calling me to your home, I believe I can present you with a near-perfect estimate given the current economic climate: nine hundred gold drachmae.'

Mynta nodded. She had hoped to surpass a thousand, but she was not surprised she had been overly generous in her estimate. The rest of the chests in the shop contained roughly the same. The others on the wagon were filled with sacks of flour and broken tile. That would mean roughly two thousand in gold. Enough to see her household running for several lean years, but leaving her with only a single small chest left at home, containing her most valuable and sentimental pieces.

But sacrifice was required for the chance of greatness.

'A fair estimate,' she agreed, taking another sip of the tart wine. 'I am happy for you to take a break and continue.'

Apollophanes looked troubled.

'Speak your mind,' she said.

He glanced at his children, who quickly left the room. 'My lady, may I ask what it is you are hoping to achieve today with this assessment?'

'Is it not clear?' she asked, eyes widening with surprise. 'I wish to sell. All of it.'

She picked up a corner of crumbly cheese as Apollophanes spluttered. She popped the tangy morsel into her mouth, giving him time to compose himself.

'But why?'

'How dare you impose yourself into my lady's business,' Anesidora said angrily, stepping forward to wave the folded fan under his nose. 'It is of no business of yours as to my lady's actions.'

He blinked but, to his credit, held his ground. 'I beg to differ, old woman,' he said gently. 'This shop has been held since my great-grandfather disobeyed his father's wish to carry on the farm, sold everything, and bought this building. I grew up at this table, learning the craft and trade. And in all those decades, never has a noble lady walked in to sell her entire collection.' He turned to Mynta. 'I apologise for any disrespect you may feel, my lady, but I do not know you personally. I have, of course, heard of the Councilman, but I cannot verify that you are his daughter. I will need to seek corroboration that you are who you say you are and that these jewels are your property and not stolen.'

Anesidora turned apoplectic. 'Stolen property! By Tinia's throne and all the goddesses, your words are vile to my ears, shopkeeper. You dare stand there and accuse my lady of being a common thief? We have marched through the streets of Trilos under Usil's eyes, in broad view of all citizens. We have not skulked here like vagabonds in the night, whispering in dark corners and hiding the flash of gold being exchanged. By Sethlans' fire and smoke, I will not stand—'

'Enough,' Mynta said, waving her nursemaid silent. She set her cup down and rose to her feet; she was a good foot shorter than Apollophanes, but he shrank at her approach. 'You have every right to be careful,' she said. 'I am happy to wait here while you send your children out to confirm my identity. A priest of Aplu can tell the truth of my words, or a servant from the fourth advisor's office will be able to confirm my identity. In the meantime, I would ask you to continue your work, as I am hoping to achieve my goals before nightfall.'

He gave her a grateful smile at her understanding. He summoned his children and sent one each to Aplu's temple and the palace, and returned to his work. It was slower going with only a third of the workforce, but it was not long before his son returned, accompanied by a tall man, bronzed by the sun with bleached hair more white than gold. His eyes were a vivid green, and he bore the golden tattoo of his god on his brow. His robes were richly embroidered with gold and silver, flashing in the sunlight from the high windows.

'I am Acoetes, priest of the Singing God Aplu,' he said, his voice rich and beautiful. His eyes swept over them all to land on Mynta, closing the distance between them in three steps, ignoring the chests. 'You stand before an acolyte of truth. I have been called upon to verify your words. Do you consent to this?'

'Yes,' she said, fighting to keep her voice calm. Though she had seen the rite performed, she had never been on the receiving end before. Aplu's punishments for those who broke their word were particularly cruel, even amongst the gods.

'I will ask you simple questions. Your answers will be yes or no. If you lie, my god will hear. If you lie, you will be forced to pay a hundred ingots of gold to Aplu's temple. If you lie, you will be stripped naked and walked through the streets to Aplu's temple. If you lie, your hair will be shorn, and you will only wear ashen sacks for the next three months. I ask again, do you consent?' His words were hammer blows.

'Yes.' Calmness.

'Are you Amynta, daughter of Councilman Linos, of Trilos?'

'Yes.'

He nodded, confirming the truth.

'Do these jewels in this room and on the cart outside belong to you?'

'Yes.'

'Did you steal them, or come to their ownership illegally?'

'No.'

'Were they all either purchased by yourself or were gifted to you by others?'

'Yes.'

Acoetes clapped his hands together, the sound filling the room to the brim before fading away. 'Truth has been spoken. Aplu is pleased by your honesty and blesses you, child.' He turned to Apollophanes and held out a hand. The jeweller handed him a pouch tinkling with coins.

'Thank you, priest,' he said with a bow of his head.

'May gold shine in all your endeavours,' Acoetes intoned, holding a hand in benediction over the jeweller's head before departing as swiftly as he arrived.

'Satisfied?' Anesidora asked with a raised brow once the door shut behind the priest.

The jeweller nodded and sent his son to fetch his daughter from the palace. A little over twenty minutes later, they both returned, panting and sweating.

'She hadn't even reached the palace yet,' Tellis said.

Pero swatted his shoulder. 'I got stopped by Chiore in the street. She is one of our biggest clients. I was not going to ignore her.'

'Peace, children,' their father said. 'Refresh yourselves quickly and get back to work.'

The afternoon wore on before Apollophanes finally laid the last necklace back in the chest and shut the lid.

'The second half contained more valuable pieces than the first,' he said, wiping his brow. 'I would put the total value at one thousand three hundred gold drachmae.'

Mynta had to struggle to keep her mouth falling open. That was three hundred more than she had hoped. 'Wonderful. How much would you like to purchase?'

He hesitated. 'My lady?'

'You did not think I would cart my valuables here for appraisal without selling a single piece?' she asked. 'How much would you like? I am not sure you have the capital on hand to purchase it all, but at least a formidable portion of it.'

'My lady is very generous to give me first offer at such a beautiful trove ...'

'You are not the first,' her nursemaid interrupted.

He blinked. 'What?'

'You are the third – or is it fourth now? – we have visited this week. Much of my lady's jewellery has been purchased. And we have the rest on the cart as well. What you don't buy today, we will take to another establishment tomorrow.'

'I am visiting with Lady Creusa tomorrow,' Mynta reminded her, the untruth barely hitching on her tongue. Her nursemaid could have been an actor in another life, her lies rolling smoothly off her tongue.

'Ah, gods help my slow mind, of course,' her nursemaid exclaimed. 'The day after, then.'

'Why would you be taking your jewels from shop to shop, getting different appraisals?' Tellis asked before his father could shush him.

Mynta shrugged. 'It is interesting to see any variation in opinions. And, of course, they could only buy as much as they could afford.'

'You are friends with Lady Creusa?' Apollophanes asked, wariness touching his voice.

'Of course! She is a dear friend of my mother's, but we have grown close as well.' Mytna kept her smile sweet. Creusa's husband owned the richest gold mines in Trilos. It was well known that his wife handled much of the business. She was known to favour certain goldsmiths and jewellers, lavishing business upon them, which drove their rivals wild with jealousy.

She could see Apollophanes' mind ticking over. A young woman appears at his shop with jewellery worth thousands in coin, looking to sell as much as she can, and admitting she had already done this exercise several times. A friend of the richest patron to his guild. A Councilman's daughter ...

'I will give you two and a half thousand for all of it,' he said.

His children stiffened in shock, Pero going so far as to cover her mouth.

Mynta scoffed. 'Do not be a fool, Apollophanes. I will not have you overpay me, by Tinia's throne above. I will not take a coin more than what you have valued them.'

'Then I shall take them all for my appraisal's worth,' he agreed. 'But you must take this small gift as a token of my gratitude for visiting my shop.' He disappeared in the backroom and returned holding a magnificent diadem of beaten gold and copper, sparkling with rubies and topaz, interwoven with foiled olive leaves. It was beautiful.

And worth at least the difference between the appraised value and the amount he had offered.

She accepted graciously.

Soon, the chests were packed up on the cart, and Apollophanes accompanied them to the Temple of Februus, who would oversee the exchange.

Februus was the son of Aita and Phersipnai, the God of Riches. His temples acted as safehouses for the money and treasures of the League. Built of dark stone, it differed from most temples, as it was not open on all sides but had walls linking the tall columns, keeping out thieves. Though only the most foolish attempted to steal from Februus. Outside the city guard, the temple held the most armed men, patrolling the temple and surrounding streets. Anyone caught without a talisman inside had their eyes put out. Anyone caught inside the vaults without a priest were slain on sight.

The only entrance was the front doors cast from obsidian and inlaid with mother-of-pearl, where a dark-stone statue of Februus watched over the stairs. Depicted as a young man, he was sleek of limb with curly beard and hair, in a chiton that was falling off him, exposing his body with its golden veins.

Inside, a priest appeared with a slate tablet to make note of their business before disappearing again. He returned with two acolytes who guided them deep inside, the halls lit only by torches, until they came to a large chamber where the drachmae retrieved from the jeweller's vault awaited. They performed the exchange, watched over and sanctioned by the priests.

Once completed, Mynta embraced Apollophanes, as was tradition, kissing his cheeks and forehead. 'I want you to know that if I ever have need to commission a piece, your shop will be the first I grace.'

'May Sethlans and Turan bless your days, my lady,' he said, returning the kisses.

Mynta departed the temple elated, fighting the urge to keep herself from yelling wildly in joy. Her vault was filled with coin, and she finally felt like she was regaining her feet.

But this was the easiest part of her plan. Next, she had to find something to trade in ...

She had several ideas.

CHAPTER THIRTY-THREE

A week later, Mynta's house was a constant flurry of activity.

Sebastos did not hesitate in his duties and soon had men marching into her hall, youths always accompanied by an older man. They greeted Sebastos as a friend, being warriors he had served with, and brought their sons or nephews or cousin's children to be interviewed. She had provided him a budget for twenty men on a novice's salary and five senior men, with two officers to stand as his lieutenants. It was a significant drain on her newly obtained funds, but it only motivated her more to take the next steps in her plan.

Her household council currently constituted herself, Sebastos, and Anesidora. They met daily in her father's office – though she may as well start calling it her own – to discuss preparations and how she might try again to enter the trade market.

'I do not see how we can begin purchasing property when we do not even know what we are going to trade in,' her nursemaid said for the fifth time.

'We can hardly buy product first and then have nowhere to store it,' Mynta responded yet again. Sebastos sat quietly, arms folded, as he watched the verbal match.

'But will it be wheat? Gold? Textiles? Cattle? Do we need a stronghouse or a barn? You need to consider this first, child.'

'Perhaps we should see the object for the space and not the other way round.'

'Bah, you are as strongheaded as Sethlans' anvil,' her nursemaid said, throwing up her hands. 'And why this warehouse?'

'I have done my research,' Mynta said guardedly. 'This is the one I want.'

'Peace, please,' Sebastos finally said. 'There is no harm in having a look, Anesidora.' She scoffed at him. Turning to Mynta, he said, 'But she does have a point, my lady. We need to figure out what to trade and quickly, or you will not have the capital soon to invest.'

'Do you have any ideas?' she asked.

He shrugged. 'I am a soldier. I can tell you if the spear is strong or the sword sharp, but nothing else.'

Mynta rubbed her face. Bags had begun to appear under her eyes, despite her renewed energy over the past few days. She had continued to search her father's records, to ascertain how he did business or had first begun trading, but he had inherited from his father and had only expanded upon what existed – Mynta was beginning from scratch.

She needed a market that no one else was currently investing in. Something that Trilos wanted but did not know or have yet. It was a risk, as whatever it was may be something Trilosii did not care for – her primary hesitation whenever a decision seemed close to hand. Failure yet again was not possible, for she would be truly destitute. And the idea of crawling to the palace to beg from her father made her hackles rise.

She *could* do this herself.

'Let us go to the district,' she said. 'We will figure out the rest after. Are the men ready, Sebastos?'

He nodded. 'Always, my lady.'

'Then let us depart.'

Clouds obscured the midmorning sun and made the heat heavier than usual in the city centre, but the breeze was constant and helped cool sweat on skin.

Mynta rode in a plain litter that her mother had left behind, no doubt forgotten, as it was mostly used to carry her to market and back. It was carved pine wood with copper tassels and a woven roof that crisscrossed her with shadows.

Six men surrounded her as an honour guard, flashing bright in new armour, feet stamping proudly as they bustled through the streets. Sebastos strode at the litter's side, while Anesidora rode in the litter with her.

The city was simple in design, laid out in a square with straight roads that evenly divided Trilos into various quarters. Carved from warm yellow stone with high towers and snapping pennants, it was surrounded by fertile land that made the kingdom the bread bowl of the eastern lands and much of the League.

Throughout the city, standing sentinel in squares and markets, under bridges and by gates, were the automatons of the king. Constructed to look like dread soldiers from ancient times, some towered many times the height of a man, made from bronze and stone, powered by Sethlans' fire. Tied to the kingdom, they could only move and fight within Trilos' borders and had guarded them for centuries.

In the southern quarter, towards the inland wall, were the poorer sections of the city. Though the streets and fountains were cared for by the king, and sentinels still guarded the citizens, most houses needed maintenance. Parks were overrun or had dried out. People stood on the streets, loitering. Eyes were warier and stomachs hungrier.

She wondered if she should have brought more men.

They eventually came to a square that had a statue of Horta with a crown of wheat, handing out a loaf of bread to stone children.

'You know what some men say about the gods,' Sebastos said quietly.

'What?' she asked.

'One hand holds bread, the other hand holds nothing, and a third hand holds the knife.'

She blinked at his words. They bordered on blasphemy. He offered nothing more, and she turned back to the square, troubled.

Most of the houses were in need of masonry work. Windows had shutters missing and murals were chipped. Yet, the square bustled with enough people to give it an air of busyness. On one side was a foodhouse that seemed to be doing good business, if determined by the enticing smells drifting from it. Across from the foodhouse was their destination – a ramshackle warehouse.

'Halt,' Sebastos barked. The carriers lowered the litter, and he helped her out onto the street.

Mynta had argued with Anesidora that morning as to what she should wear for this meeting. She did not want to be so gaudy as to be perceived as frivolous and, worse, risk the more desperate in the quarter to take their chances despite her guard. Nor did she want to dress so plain that she was not taken seriously.

She opted for a yellow dress of fine wool, a white horsehair belt, and a light himation with copper buckles. Her sandals were well-made but also plain, studded with a single topaz each. A simple string of gold around her neck with bronze pendants, matching earrings, and only one bracelet. Her hair was loose down her shoulders, with a circlet of golden fennel flowers laid on her brow.

Sebastos knocked on the sturdy warehouse door. Several moments passed before he knocked again, pounding his fist, the wood shaking under the impact. Shuffling footsteps approached, growing louder. The door opened to reveal a man of middling age, but upon whom life had consistently ground down.

His hair had gone from thick to wiry, thinning on his crown, but still the colour of granite. His slanted, brown eyes were wary, but Mynta thought she saw a softness to them, a kind man made sharp. His face was shadowed by a beard several days old, which he continually scratched. A slight frame was made more apparent by his clothes that hung loose, speaking of lean times behind him.

'Sethlans' blessings,' he said, his voice slightly high. 'Appointment?'

'Lady Amynta wishes to discuss business with you,' Sebastos said brusquely. 'Is it common practice for you to keep prospective partners outside in the sun, rather than extending Tinia's hospitality?'

The man quailed slightly under the old warrior's presence. He pulled open the door and beckoned them inside, apologising all the while. 'So sorry, swordbearer. My contrition humbles me, my ladies young and old'—he bowed to Mynta and Anesidora—'I am caught surprised by your visit and wholly unprepared for business this day. You see – gods, my apologies again for including you in my woes, and may Artimi shield you all – but my daughter is unwell, and my mind is by her side even as I talk to you.'

Mynta looked about as he shut the door behind them. The warehouse was on the smaller side, no more than a hundred feet by forty feet. Light pierced through the ceiling, and there was water damage on the upper walls. The floor had mildew in several sections and broken stones in others. Most of the shelves were bare, and what goods she could see appeared abandoned, covered in dust.

It was perfect.

'Are you Tros?' she asked.

'Yes, my lady.' He blinked. 'Wine! One moment, I beg you.' He disappeared into a small room. There was a great amount of clattering followed by a small crash before he returned with four cups and a small amphora. He placed it on a rickety crate and poured the wine, passing one each to Mynta, Sebastos, and Anesidora before taking one himself. 'May Turms guide our business to the benefit of all,' he intoned before taking a large, nervous gulp.

Mynta smiled as she took a small sip. The wine bordered on vinegar, but she kept the distaste from her face. 'And may Februus bless our endeavours.'

'How may I—'

There was a sharp squeal from a young boy of about six running through the warehouse followed by an older boy, both wielding wooden swords that they smashed about them. 'Sons,' Tros shouted, running towards them. 'What did I say about playing in here? And with guests as well ...'

Mynta beckoned Anesidora over and whispered to her before passing a small pouch of coins. The nursemaid nodded and went outside to speak to one of the messenger boys.

The warehouse owner soon returned, red-faced and puffing. 'My apologies once again, my lady. Children ...'

'That is quite alright, master merchant,' she said, bestowing the honoured title on him that she doubted he was entitled to claim. 'To cut to the quick, I am here to inspect your premises with the idea to utilise them. Do you have any availability?' The warehouse was all but empty, but kindness was never a currency one could be too free with.

He gaped for a moment before collecting himself. 'Of course, my lady. Please follow me.'

He led them through the warehouse, apologising every second step for its current state, until Mynta wanted to shake him. Contrition was savoury only in small doses.

Tros owned three warehouses in all – one next door and the other directly behind the first, connected by a small alley. The other two were in similar states to the first, though the last held more products waiting to be collected by merchants.

They eventually made their way back to the first warehouse, where a table and chairs had been set up with a simple fare of crusty bread, apples, and hard cheese. Fortunately, water was also on the table, and Mynta declined any further wine.

After they had broken their fast, Tros nervously broached the question that was clearly burning in his mind. 'Does what you have seen please you, my lady?'

Mynta paused, as though still considering her response, before saying 'Yes, master merchant. It is exactly what I require.'

Tros clapped his hands loudly. 'Wonderful. If you would like to send over your trademaster, I can negotiate the terms with him, rather than take up any more of your valuable time.'

Mynta sighed. 'Unfortunately, I do not have a trademaster as yet, but do not fear. I am more than capable of continuing the discussion.'

Tros took it in stride, despite the peculiarity of a lady performing her own business matters. 'Of course. How much space are you wishing to rent and for how long?'

'I am afraid you have grabbed the snake by the tail,' she said, 'for I am not looking to rent. I am looking to buy.'

His face went cold. 'Buy, my lady? My property is not for sale.'

She nodded. 'I understand. But I would still wish to purchase all three warehouses. I think a thousand silver drachmae would be a fair price.'

His face tightened further. It was a lowball price and barely met the minimum the warehouses were worth, even in their current state. 'I am afraid this has been a wasted journey. My property is not for sale.'

She had to harden herself for her next words. 'Come now. It is clear your business is going through hard times. I doubt you have brought in the same amount in the last three years combined. I am offering a chance to get yourself out of your current state. It is fair.' Her words struck him, and she had to swallow her guilt.

'I ...' he hesitated, giving her the opening she needed.

'However, there is a condition I would need to impose upon the sale,' she said. 'I would require you to come into my service as my trademaster.'

Anesidora blinked in surprise. Mynta had not discussed this with her. 'What? My lady, I ...'

'And as this is the founding of my fledgling mercantile empire, I would demand long hours from you as we build my trade. Thus, I think it would be best if you and your family come to live in my house for the foreseeable future.'

He was speechless, staring at her as though she had grown two additional heads like a hydra.

She gave him an abashed look. 'I am also ashamed to say that I cannot pay the cost in a singular lump sum. Instead, I would propose that I pay triple your salary and an additional fifty silver drachmae at the end of each month until the debt is paid to you. Would you find that agreeable?'

Before he could answer, the door opened to show one of her messenger boys poking his head inside. He pushed the door open the rest of the way to reveal a priest of Esplace waiting behind him.

'Ah, please enter,' Mynta said, rising to her feet to greet the priest, a stern older man with a harrowed face. 'A daughter that resides within this man's house is in need of healing by your touch. Did you find payment appropriate?'

The priest nodded and turned expectedly to Tros.

The man looked, bewildered, from the priest to Mynta. 'I don't understand.'

'I have given you much to consider,' Mynta said. 'But it is impossible to properly focus your mind upon business when you are worried about your daughter. We will retire to the foodhouse across the street. Please come and find us once you have made your decision.' She signalled the others to follow as she headed for the open door.

'Wait,' Tros called after.

She turned to him.

'What happens if I say no?' he asked, the priest still waiting by his side.

'I go home, and you can still celebrate the renewed health of your daughter,' she said with a smile before heading towards the wonderful smells that beckoned her.

CHAPTER THIRTY-FOUR

The foodhouse was busy.

No one heeded Sebastos as he pressed open its heavy door, but a hush fell as Mynta entered. She stalled as all eyes turned upon her, but her nursemaid pushed past, heading for the only free table, snapping at the customers closest to stop gawking.

Paved stone lined the floor beneath a high roof. Though the walls were thick, they offered little protection; the poor masonry let wind cut through the gaps. A single window looked out onto the square, while the rest of the light came from torches, giving the room a gloomy aspect. A dozen tables were scattered throughout, each holding two to six people. Most appeared to be labourers – clothes worn and patched, faces tired.

Mynta took a seat on the cleanest stool and waited as the matron approached, apron covered in fresh stains, but hands clean. Her skin was the colour of mature olive oil, her black hair braided loosely, eyes crinkled with laughter lines. 'Lady,' she said with a slight bow. 'We don't get many noblewomen in here. Lost your way?'

Mynta laughed softly, shaking her head. 'No, mistress. I have business in the area and was tempted to take my repast here when I smelled some delightful scents. Is that lamb on the menu?'

The woman nodded. 'Yes, wrapped in vine leaves with roasted figs and fennel.'

'Wonderful! We'll have a plate each with some bread. And wine too, please, but nothing too strong.'

The matron seemed unconvinced but disappeared into the kitchen.

Conversation resumed slowly, but Mynta knew she and her group were the main subject – voices lowered, eyes flicking away whenever she turned.

She ignored them as best she could and waited patiently for their food. Despite the foodhouse's appearance, it smelled delicious. The matron obviously knew her way around the kitchen. A few tense minutes passed before she returned, followed by a serving girl with platters and cups. The table filled with food, and Mynta set to eagerly. The lamb was spiced and tangy, wrapped in lemony vine leaves that helped cool the piping hot meat. The bread was warm and crusty, the figs soft and sweet, caramelised to perfection. The fennel cut through the fat and sugar with its anise and had a delightful crunch. All in all, a splendid lunch.

'Mistress, I have not had lamb this good outside the palace,' Mynta said honestly as the matron collected their plates. 'If I did not already have a cook, I would offer you the job here and now, by Uni's hand.'

The woman blushed, then scowled angrily at a man who guffawed, snapping him with a towel. 'Quiet, you, or I'll kick you to the street.' She turned to Mynta. 'Your praise sings to my heart, my lady. If you think you have room, I have several cakes I think would be to your liking.'

Mynta's eyes lit up. 'That sounds—'

The door to the foodhouse banged open. Sebastos half drew his sword.

Several men entered, trailed by a large man who looked to have Konosoan blood. Broad-shouldered and thick-calved, he wore a short chiton of red cloth with a wide copper belt, a large knife at his side. Curly hair fell to his neck, and fine fur covered his chest and arms. Two earrings adorned his left ear. His eyes – wider than most Trilosii – were a light brown, bordering on hazel; they locked upon Mynta and her table.

He gave a grunt before stalking towards them, surprisingly light on his feet. The matron backed away, her body tensed.

Sebastos slowly rose to his feet, the other two guards following suit. Mynta's neck was strained as she tilted her head back the closer the man got to her. He stopped a few steps away and pointed at her. 'You lost, pretty flower?'

Mynta frowned. 'Why does everyone think I am lost? I have lived in Trilos my entire life. I know where I am.'

He grunted again. 'You have not been around this quarter before, I can guarantee that, pretty flower.'

Sebastos bristled. 'You will speak to Lady Amynta with respect.'

He eyed the old warrior. 'Why? She is not my lady. Because she has money, that makes her my lady? Sethlans' shit, I would be crawling in the dirt every time I left the quarter if that was the case.'

'Beast,' Anesidora said, wrinkling her nose.

'We all shit, old woman,' he shrugged. 'Gods, beasts, and pretty flowers alike.'

'Would you care to join us?' Mynta asked. 'The good matron was about to bring us some cakes, but I do not mind if you wish to eat lamb with us. It is very good.'

Faster than she could move, he reached down and pinched her thigh. 'I can see you haven't missed a meal in a while,' he grinned.

'Stop,' she commanded, halting Sebastos' sword an inch from the large man's throat. 'Stay your blade, Sebastos.' She looked the stranger in the eye, inches from her face. 'I like food. And so do you, for you to have grown to be the size of an ox.' She then hit him in the groin, hard.

He bent double, face purple as his eyes bulged.

The matron burst out laughing. 'Nothing less than what you deserve, Aivas. Now leave the lady alone, or that warrior of hers looks about ready to slice you up finer than my lamb.'

Aivas let out a long breath as he straightened. 'Good blow,' he said begrudgingly. 'I think I might join you, if only because I don't think I can walk to another table.'

He sat gingerly on a stool one of his companions pulled over. The matron returned with lamb and bread for him, and honeyed almond cakes for Mynta's party.

Aivas watched as she broke a small cake in half and popped it in her mouth. It was bliss. Sweet and warmed by the cinnamon. She briefly considered whether she could afford two cooks ...

'If you are not lost, then what brings you to the city south?' Aivas asked, shoving a hunk of lamb in his mouth, grease smearing across his lips.

'We are looking to purchase some property,' she said, making a note of wiping her mouth clean with a napkin.

He laughed, drawing the back of his hand across his lips before tearing a hunk of rosemary bread and dipping it in olive oil. 'Tros' warehouses?'

She blinked, surprised.

He smiled sharply. 'You have no reason to know this, being the pretty flower you are, but I run most of this quarter. If I don't already own it, then I know who does. I know what trade comes through here, be it reputable or not. I know which palms to make heavy with coin and which like a blossom for themselves.'

Mynta stiffened, letting the cake fall from her fingers.

'A thug,' Anesidora said flatly.

'You wound me, old woman.' He did not look offended. 'You would not say the same of any city advisor or councilmen? I perform much of the same responsibilities they do elsewhere in the kingdom. They choose to ignore this quarter and so I have stepped in to help – as is my civic duty.' He almost looked noble as he spoke.

'And how much of people's hard-earned money goes into your pocket?' Mynta asked. 'Do you take a cut everywhere? How much money does this foodhouse generate each month and what is your portion?'

'Easy, flower. I do not discuss the details of my business with pretty women out playing merchant.'

She cocked her head. 'Do I give you cause for concern?' she asked quietly.

His face grew hard, his food forgotten. The muscle of his arms caught her attention – biceps thicker than the thigh he had just pinched. She nearly reached out to squeeze one, just to see how solid it really was, but caught herself in time. Foolish. The thrill of the day had made her giddy. Forcing her gaze back to his face, her cheeks warmed as she met his gleaming eyes.

'Why would you think that?' he asked.

She gestured around her. 'You arrived quickly. We could not have been in the quarter for a half hour or so, and yet you rushed from whatever business you were attending.'

'It is not every day a noble lady deigns to grace us peasants with her presence.'

'So you will not interfere with my business?'

He chuckled. 'Of course I will. I cannot allow you to buy old Tros' warehouses. I have been trying to get him to sell to me for nearly a year now. You have no right to be here, and we will not tolerate it. I think it is time for you to scurry back to your safe little garden, pretty flower.'

She leant forward. 'Well, my heavy-headed ox,' she retorted, 'I am going nowhere. And I am surprised that you could be so short-sighted, a man with such business acumen as yourself.'

He frowned. 'How so?'

'You moan and insult me, assuming you know everything about me because of how I appear,' she said. 'A rich, dainty lady out for a wild adventure in the southern quarter. Attacked by thugs and eating amongst the poor. Fine tales to regale her friends with as they sip wine in the palace surrounded by dancers painted in gold.'

Everyone openly watched their exchange. Mynta had not expected to be confronted by a man who no doubt committed crimes as easily as drinking wine, and she was only being bold because of Sebastos and her guards. It was a risk, but she had come too far to back down. She needed these warehouses, and this Aivas was just another obstacle to overcome. She sent a silent prayer to Menrva for wisdom.

'You are letting a golden opportunity pass you,' she continued. 'I made no secret of my visit here today. I rode through the streets of Trilos in a litter with a company of guards. I sit in this foodhouse, dining on food that would make the king's own kitchens envious. Soon, I will begin trading in this quarter. I will conduct business meetings here, order supplies from local shops, hire local citizens. Wealth will follow. But not if you keep me out.'

He studied her, silent, before draining his wine in a few long swallows. Wiped his mouth and let out a small belch.

She wrinkled her nose.

'If I did allow you to set up shop here,' he said slowly, 'then you would need to pay the same taxes as everyone else.'

This was what she had been waiting for him to say. She could not risk becoming entangled in extortion and bribery. Every deal, every purchase, every action she took – it all had to be pristine. Her future depended on it.

'Again, short-sightedness,' she said, shaking her head. 'You are looking at this chance all wrong. If you try to gouge me of as much money as possible, then I will have no funds to invest in the people of this quarter. If the bribes I am forced to pay are steep, no one will follow in my path to come here. I am an investment. A noble lady building her business in an area of the city most would avoid. Curiosity will lead to fear of losing out on an opportunity. Give me a chance, and money will come.'

A hush settled over the room. Aivas' eyes flicked around at the men and women who were now watching him, waiting for his response. She had caught him in a corner.

But Mynta could see the other thoughts running through his head. If he granted her an exception to his taxes, he set a dangerous precedent among his existing clientele.

'And if you don't deliver on these miraculous promises?' he asked.

'Then I will sell my warehouses to you at half what I paid and leave the south quarter for good,' she said. 'Under Turms' eyes.'

He spat on his hand and held it out to her.

Both Sebastos and her nursemaid bristled.

She looked at the glob in his palm in horror.

He laughed. 'Too delicate to make a commoner's pledge?'

Gritting her teeth, she spat as delicately as possible into her own palm and clasped his hand. He squeezed tightly until it bordered on pain, saliva squelching loudly. 'Under Turms' eyes.'

Mynta and the others returned to the warehouse. It had been well over an hour since Aivas departed, and Tros had yet to fetch them. There was no sign of the merchant inside. Sebastos called out several times.

'Is that music?' Mynta asked, catching faint sounds of a pipe. She followed the music through to the second warehouse and out the rear door to a small courtyard, overlooked by a two-storey house.

She gave a delighted laugh – Tros and his family danced in a circle, singing at the top of their lungs. A young man sat on a crate playing the pipes, tapping his feet in time.

A middle-aged woman she presumed to be Tros' wife held on to the hands of the two boys she had seen earlier. They in turn held the hands of two maidens. They all spun around Tros, who danced in the centre with a young girl, around the age of two, who squealed in his arms.

The priest of Esplace leant against the wall of the house, his face feverish but with a faint smile. Mynta crossed to him and bowed respectfully. 'How is she?'

He nodded towards the young girl. 'She had smelter's fever. Dangerous at such a young age. But my god is merciful and allowed me to draw the sickness from her body and balance her humours. I also found a small growth in the walls of her lung. It would have caused her much grief within a decade or so. Now ... she shall live to find a husband and bear children without fear. Such are the blessings of Esplace!'

Mynta bowed again. 'I cannot thank you enough. May I not offer more in payment to your temple?'

The priest waved her away. 'This is more than enough payment,' he said, gesturing to the family.

Mynta nodded and turned to watch the celebrations. Tros finally noticed her and gave a great shout. The family rushed to her, and she found herself surrounded by laughing smiles and hugs and kisses.

Eventually, Tros shooed them away, passing the girl to his wife with a kiss on both her cheeks that made her giggle and blow a bubble.

Tros appeared ten years younger, worry dripping away from him. 'I cannot thank you enough, my lady, for the blessings you have given us. The priest told me what ailed my daughter and, because of you, she has regained her life twofold. My life is indebted to you.'

'No,' Mynta said. 'I ask for nothing in return for this kindness.'

He eyed her intently. 'Though I may bring shame asking this – was bringing the priest a tactic? A way to guide me to sell my warehouses to you?'

Mynta held his gaze, her eyes bright and clear. 'Never. I did not know of your daughter's health until you told me. And as I said before, you can refuse my offer now, and I will return home. But I go elated in the knowledge that I have left things better than I found them. In Aplu's name, that is the truth.'

Tros took her hands in his and kissed her fingertips. 'Then let us settle the contract. Congratulations on your new property, my lady.'

'And welcome to my household, trademaster,' Mynta said, drawing him into a warm embrace. 'We have much work to do.'

The evening rain had dissipated, a soft blanket that filled the air with the scent of moist earth and cooling stone. The garden glistened wetly, flowers drooping low under their heavy, watery burdens.

Mynta flung the papers away from her, getting to her feet with a groan. Her shoulders were tight and her legs stiff. The candles had burned low, and the moon was hidden behind clouds.

The household slept, aside from the guards who patrolled the gates and walls. Strange how she had never noticed the warriors when her father ran the home. But now, she took notice of every guard, servant, maid, and labourer she employed. Every coin set aside for their salary and the miniscule amount coming into her chests.

She had bid the others to bed hours ago, wanting the quiet to read the reports Tros had written. In the three days since he moved in with his family, Mynta had learnt the man was a blessing from the gods. Cunning and clever, he found money in unlikely places, and tracked the ebb and flow of trade within the city like a spider in a web.

He had begun by giving her tutelage in the art of trading, teaching her mercantile secrets and business rules, obscure tax laws, and a hundred other dealings. She absorbed everything, but her head was always splitting at the end of the day. Rosemary oil and peppermint tea did little to help.

But she kept pushing, often outlasting the candles as she read scroll after scroll. For a business that barely existed, the amount of paperwork was unfathomable.

She needed a break and something to eat. Supper was long past, and she barely had a cup of wine since.

The kitchen was dark but still warm from the ovens; the cook had banked the coals for the morning bread.

On the bench was a bowl of fruit, a plate of leftover fig and walnut cakes, and some hard cheese. She grabbed a plate and piled it high, picking up a small jug of sweet lemon water before heading back to her office. She pushed the scrolls aside and began to eat, her eyes moving mindlessly around the room.

Beautiful weavings her mother had picked out softened the space. Four shields of ancient Trilosii design decorated one wall. The other held shelves filled with scrolls and tablets. It was windowless but had a view of the garden through the door. The floor was plain but cool beneath her feet. Maybe a nice rug ...

There was a timid knock at the door.

One of the messenger boys stood in the doorway, hair a mess, rubbing blearily at one eye. He wore only a cloth bound around his waist for sleep.

'What are you doing up at this time?' she asked softly.

'I had a bad dream,' he said with a quiver in his voice. 'I got up because my mother always said that a good meal keeps the wolves away.'

Mynta laughed. 'You're hungry? Come sit with me. My eyes are bigger than my stomach, and I've got too much on my plate.'

The boy was uncertain but soon shuffled over, sitting on the stool she had pulled beside her. She shared her food onto a plate left on the desk from lunch; she sliced up an apple, cut a cake into quarters, and broke the cheese into several pieces.

He tucked into the meal eagerly, occasionally glancing up at her, but she continued with her own food. After a while, she asked, 'What is your name?' She was a little ashamed she did not know it, nor the name of the other messenger boy.

'Bel, my lady,' he said around a mouthful of cheese.

'And how long have you been in my house?'

'Since I was eight. I am eleven next month during the Feast of Fires.'

Three years and she doubted she had ever spoken to him. 'How did you come into my service?'

He eyed her from the side but answered, albeit cautiously. 'I was orphaned in Fernta when my father did not come back from the mountains. My mother went to find him but she also never came home. So my uncle brought me to Trilos and left me with Master Philor. He taught me how to be a messenger boy, and then one day he brought me here.'

Her heart ached at his words. 'And are you happy here, Bel?'

He nodded emphatically. 'Yes, my lady. It is much nicer than Master Philor's house. We had to all sleep on the floor and there weren't enough pillows. Master Philor was kind to us. I heard that other masters would beat the boys when they didn't train well enough. Master Philor never hit us, although sometimes he wouldn't give us food for the day if we upset him.'

She pursed her lips but said nothing, adding another cake to his plate. 'Well, I want you and the other boy – what's his name? Olus? – to feel like you can come to me about anything. Do you understand? I am always happy to talk to you.'

'Thank you, my lady.' He pushed the scraps of his food around the plate. 'Are you going to make me leave?'

Mynta was shocked. 'No! Why would you ask that?'

Bel's eyes were wide with such concern it made her heart ache. 'I heard people saying you were going to sell the house and we would have to move. And they said that you would probably release many of us from service. Is that true, my lady? Will I have to go to a new house or back to Master Philor?'

Mynta felt a rush of emotion. Sadness, distress, and anger at herself. She had not even considered what her trick with the maids would have meant to the servants. It had simply been a ploy to find out which of the women were reporting to her father. But she had not thought of the worry that would ripple through her household.

She wrapped an arm around the child. 'I am not selling the home, Bel. And even if we had to leave, I would take you, Olus, and whoever wished to continue serving me. You need never fear for employ or a roof over your head.'

'Yes, my lady,' he said, smiling before his mouth opened in a giant yawn.

'I think we've managed to keep the wolves away,' she said gently. 'Come, let us get you back to bed.' She took his hand and let him lead her, as she did not know where he slept. In a small room off the kitchen, she found bags of vegetables to one side and two sleeping pallets opposite. The other boy was fast asleep.

She knelt and kissed Bel on the forehead. 'Sweet dreams,' she whispered. 'I will ask Tiur and Artume to watch over you tonight so you have nothing to fear again.'

He gave her a hug and laid down, eyes closing and breath steadying fast.

She stood at the door, watching them sleep, her heart warmed by the sight. Eventually, she closed the door quietly and returned to her office. Sleep was a good idea – dawn was only a few hours away, and her nursemaid did not believe in sleeping in.

But before she retired ...

She grabbed a scrap of paper and wrote a reminder to request an amulet of Artume to give to Bel. At least one of them deserved a peaceful night's sleep.

CHAPTER THIRTY-FIVE

The Koriithosan sky was heavy with clouds, the sun a dim white orb that struggled to pierce through to the earth. The nights were growing colder, the heart of summer receding day by day. It had rained the day before, a fine mist that lasted most of the afternoon and left everything slick and shining.

Desma journeyed to the palace through the city, returning from Artimi's temple beyond the walls. Over the past two weeks, she had visited temples throughout the city, spending time in quiet devotion and prayer, leaving lavish tributes at the altars. Word spread through Koriithos of her piousness, how she stopped to talk to the poor on the streets, had set up dispensaries of bread, cheese and spiced wine to the beggars and the stricken. She had even held concerts in several small theatres, allowing amateur musicians and poets to play before royalty and win the chance at a patronage.

Desma was working to win the hearts of her new home.

But she had another reason for visiting the temples. They were the only places she could visit, without suspicion, that were filled with the magic of the gods.

Desma had asked Cela and Cosmas separately to find her a similar amulet to the one Eidia had procured. She was confident neither of them would tell the other of her request, ensuring it could not be traced back to the palace. Desma feared what the king would do if he learned she was trying to avoid children, though she and Lycon had yet to lie with each other. When they shared the large bed, they slept in cold silence, a distance between them. He was kind enough, asking about her day, raising no objection to her new tutors. But she could not remember the last time they had even touched each other.

This isolation allowed her, late at night, when her husband was nowhere to be seen, to unravel the magic from her amulets. One from the temple of Menrva and the other from Esplace. Each time, the pain came on with less ferocity and duration. She had been right – her power was like a muscle and needed to be worked to grow stronger.

Desma still did not know where it had come from, nor what purpose it had for her future, but it was a skill she would learn to wield, as she did with her sword and now with her crown.

Visiting the temples helped her test how she sensed magic. When she focused, she could scout out spells and enchanted items from a sizeable distance. The temples hummed with their gods' power. Though her eyes were often confused by the crisscrossing lines of different spells, she was becoming sharper at tracing them to their origin knot. She had even tugged at a few, but was not foolish enough to vandalise a god's property, leaving their magic intact.

In her belt pouch laid the woven ribbon dove and the stone necklace gifted by the sorceress Cisra. She often thought of breaking it on the stone floor to summon the witch, to talk to someone about this power inside her, but refrained. Cisra had understood scarcely more than herself.

Desma bumped into the back of the captain, thudding against his bronze armour. Her guards had stopped.

Her heart seized, then lurched into a frantic rhythm.

They were halfway across a large square. A statue of Tricon, fish-bodied son of Nethuns, lay prostrate across a plinth in the centre, where a hush had fallen.

Women blocked the roads into the square, parting only to allow unwary citizens to stream out, but closing ranks again once Desma and her guards were alone. The warriors tightened formation around her, the five men raising round shields and gleaming spears in warning. Desma turned in a slow circle. There were dozens of women. Most were in the simpler garbs of common citizens and farmers. But there were a few in richer clothes with a sparkle of modest jewellery.

'What should we do, Princess?' her captain asked, spear pointed outwards.

Desma did not know how to answer. They were surrounded, but the women made no move against them. She was loath to order force, but feared it may come down to bloodshed. These women were clearly of the Dirciade. Desma saw them most trips out of the palace, but usually in the form of a small group of women, whispering disapprovingly as she went by.

'Let me speak to them,' she said, keeping calm through the panic growing inside her. More women were joining, becoming a hundred strong. Still, they were silent.

Desma moved out of her protective circle, standing alone before the wrath of the women's eyes. 'You know who I am,' she called out, the silence carrying her voice far. 'And I know who you are – the Dirciade, named in honour of this city's tragic daughter, Dirce.' Silence. 'I know why you hate me, though I cannot claim to understand it.' She turned as she spoke, ensuring she addressed all.

They began to shuffle their feet, angry murmurings rising to a dull drone. She spoke over them. 'I was brought here by the gods, though I do not claim to be a hero, or to have ever sought their divine eyes upon me. But here I am! I am a humble servant before Aplu and Nethuns. I refuse to leave this city, this kingdom, when danger approaches. Just like any one of you would stand in my place to defend your people. I am Apasan – I am proud of my heritage, proud of my family. But now I am equally proud to be of Koriithos! I would give my blood, my tears, my body for you. All I ask is that you give me the chance to be the queen the gods have demanded.'

The creak and chatter of distant streets flowed into the square. Seabirds squawked overhead and wagons rattled by.

'Outsider.'

'Poison.'

'Barbarian.'

'Stranger.'

'Snake.'

The words struck her like hammers, iron nails piercing her chest. What could she do to make them see she was not someone they need fear? That she was not the Cisra from their stories? She dressed like them, ate like them, worked to help the less fortunate.

One woman, tall for a Koriithosan but still pale, with tightly braided brown hair and a muted green chiton, raised a hand; the others grew quiet. She turned deep brown eyes on Desma and raised her voice so all could hear. 'We have suffered before at the hands of a foreign wife,' she said with venom. 'Our princess was killed in the most vile way, with dark and cruel magicks. Our city was broken and burned. Women are powerful, this cannot be denied, but it is a dangerous power. Demureness and quietness are our ways, for the safety of the kingdom. You bring disaster and blood in your wake. This is one of Aplu's tricks, mocking Nethuns and our astronomers with his lies. How can a Father-Killer, an Apasan, be the queen we need? You will poison the mind of Prince Lycon and slowly bring down your curse on the palace. We stand in your way, witch, candlelight in the dark, to shine the truth for all citizens. The darkling princess, the Despised Beloved, has no home in Koriithos!'

Desma's captain of the guard stepped up beside her. His battlefield voice met every ear. 'You dare challenge the right of Princess Desma?' Anger was hot in his words. 'You defy the king and the gods with your madness! Move aside, or I will pronounce treason on everyone here. Choose, women of Koriithos!'

The lead woman stared him down, and the tension was a roiling cauldron of oil, a single spark from violence. Finally, the woman stepped aside, clearing a path out of the square.

Her guard assembled around her once again, and Desma moved forward. The women present, one hundred strong, drew out bundles hidden in the folds of their himations. They seemed to be strips of red cloth ...

Desma's face turned ashen.

Clumps of hair dyed red. They were not quite the colour of her own locks, but they could represent nothing else. Each fistful dripped red onto the stones – dye or blood, she did not know. As they neared the women, her guards used their shields to widen the single-person space, pushing the Koriithosans back.

The women began to wail. Not in pain or outrage at the guards, but a single keen, taken up by a hundred throats, that echoed and smashed across the square and buildings and streets, until it faded away. It began again once new breath was drawn, sending shivers and ice-cold spikes across Desma's skin.

Once through the blockade, Desma and her men began to hurry. The tramp of steps followed behind, the wailing never pausing. Desma's feet grew wings, and the Koriithosans gave chase.

They ran through the city, the captain shouting at nearby patrols to join them, marshalling a force fifty strong by the time they reached the palace gates. Desma was hurried inside while the guard turned gleaming spear tips on the women.

But no battle ensued. The women stopped their pursuit and, with a final cry, dropped their red locks and dispersed, ghosts disappearing into the nooks and crannies of the city.

Desma burst into her room, chest heaving as she tried to force the sobs to stay inside.

'Desma?' Lycon's voice was filled with concern. 'What has happened?'

Her captain explained the situation before the prince dismissed him. Desma clutched the door frame. She had not realised she was shaking, did not understand why the Dirciade made her so afraid. She had fought monsters, survived the horrors of Urruc, killed Empyreans …

But these women hated her so much they would defy god and king, curse her, want her dead or driven from the kingdom. Was their oppression so great that they would fight to protect their own cage?

Warm arms surrounded her, and she stiffened. She looked up into Lycon's face, so close to hers, as he held her in a loose embrace. His wavy dark hair was slightly damp, and his clothes smelled fresh. He must have only just finished bathing.

His soft green eyes, ringed with a warm brown, were kind. She realised how pleasant it was to be held in his strong arms, to feel – even for a moment – that he truly cared for her.

'This can no longer be tolerated,' he said, his voice firm but gentle. 'I will speak to my father. We will hunt down the leaders of this Dirciade and arrest them. They will disband without their leaders, and you will be safe.'

Safe.

Had she felt safe since the night her home was destroyed? Weeks of travel, fighting for her very blood, begging kings and priests. Would this palace ever feel like a home?

'Kiss me,' she whispered.

His eyes widened. 'Desma ... ' he began to say. To refuse her.

'Kiss me, husband. That is all I ask.'

She parted her lips, giving him the final choice, the right to claim her. She waited.

He bent his head, his cassia and pine scent like soft fingers, his breath warmed by wine. His arms tightened around her, drawing their bodies closer. Desma melted against him, her curves filling the gaps and pressing against his legs, abdomen, chest.

His mouth took hers.

The world closed around her.

The palace, the city, the kingdom, the crown – all turned to mist.

The touch of his skin, smooth with pinpricks of new stubble, glided against her own. His hair flicked against her brow and cheeks, rich with oils. His lips burst against hers like rose petals, soft and full of flavour. His tongue was shy but sent a tingle down her spine.

It was a moment she needed. Her worries and fears abated, even if only for the length of a kiss.

It was enough. A kiss to soothe the troubles of her world.

They drew apart. Desma smiled, blushing at how coy she felt for sharing a kiss with her husband.

Lycon let out a soft chuckle, muscles rippled under her hands.

He jerked. Shuddered.

Something was wrong.

His face had gone tight, skin stretching back, mouth open as though he was going to speak, but no sound emerged. Eyes vacant, he stared down at her.

'Lycon!' She tried to break away, but his hands had turned to stone, tightening until bruises bloomed on her arms. 'Lycon, let go.'

Drool leaked from the corners of his mouth and a harsh gurgle began to bubble up from his chest. He swayed on his feet, but his legs remained rigid.

'Let go,' she cried, pushing him away. He fell backwards, still holding her arms, and Desma rode him down, circling her hands behind his head to protect him from the marble floor. Finally, his grip loosened enough for her to wrench free, hurrying to the door to shout for help.

Guards came running.

A few terrifying minutes passed while she knelt by him, unsure of what to do. Lycon was frozen in a moment of pain.

The door slammed open to reveal Kalchas and a company of servants. He immediately began giving orders, sweeping past her to check Lycon's eyes, throat, wrists, and chest. The prince was gently lifted onto a stretcher and carried away, warriors running ahead to clear the corridors.

Desma went to follow but Kalchas stopped her. 'The prince is fine. Go about your day, Princess.'

Desma shoved his hand out of her face. 'I will be with my husband.'

Kalchas slapped her. 'By order of the king, this does not concern you, Apasan,' he growled. 'The prince is fine.'

The door shut after him, leaving Desma alone.

CHAPTER THIRTY-SIX

Desma finally saw Lycon the next day.

She spied him down the corridor, walking back to their rooms, Hyllos by his side.

'Lycon,' she shouted, picking up her hem to hurry towards him.

He turned at her voice. 'Desma, wife, how are you faring?'

She slowed to a halt, confused. Her eyes searched him, but she found nothing from the event yesterday marking him. 'Never mind me. How are you?'

He shrugged. 'Fine, as always. If you will excuse me, Hyllos and I have business to attend as a matter of urgency. I will see you at dinner this evening.'

He continued on his way, Hyllos following a moment later, the astronomer's eyes resting on Desma with a flash of sympathy before cooling into blankness.

'What in the Blasted Beneath was that?' she swore quietly to herself.

After Lycon had been taken away, she had waited the rest of the day and the night in her chamber, desperate for some word either by Kalchas or a servant as to the condition of the prince. But none came.

And she had just spent most of today hunting the palace, asking nobles and astronomers, guards and maids, for news of Lycon. None would speak to her. Desma wondered how quickly Koriithosan tongues would turn loose if they had to face the bishop's thorned wire whip. The thought had stopped her in her tracks. How could she even entertain that dark thought?

She still seethed at the memory of Kalchas hitting her. How dare he? He whisked her husband away after he suffered some form of illness and expected her to do nothing? And when she finally finds Lycon, he acts as though nothing was amiss!

Desma returned to her room, slamming the door as hard as she could.

She had just thrown herself onto the bed when there was a knock. 'Enter.' She rolled over to see Cosmas walking silently across the floor towards her, his muted blue eyes bright upon her. She sighed and rolled back, so her face was buried in a pillow.

'I see the princess is hard at work.' His lips quirked.

'I am in no mood for your dry wit today,' she mumbled.

'Very well.' His voice took on a chilled note. 'It seems you have been busy, Desma. Asking favours of friends, old and new.'

Desma sat up quickly, brow furrowed.

'To ask for three amulets to guard your womb.' He folded his arms. 'One would think your prince was particularly virile. And yet, I have learned that seed has yet to be shared between you. Why then, Princess, do you need *three* amulets?'

Desma cursed inwardly. How had he found out? 'In case Lycon found one,' she said, thinking quickly. 'And this way he would not get suspicious if I wore the same thing day after day.'

'An attentive husband to notice such small details.'

Desma slid off the bed, facing the taller man. 'What is it to you?'

Cosmas unfolded an arm and opened his hand. From it dangled the amulet he had given her, the one procured from the Temple of Esplace. A copper coiled snake with a glittering topaz eye. She did not bother asking how he now possessed it. She waited in silence.

'This is different,' he finally said.

'It is the same one you gave me.'

He shook his head. 'The same metal, yes, but its essence is gone.'

She did not speak.

He dropped it to the floor, the copper ringing dully on the marble. Stepping over it, he closed the gap between them until there was only a foot separating them. 'You have many secrets, Desma. Some I keep for you. But there are some I know of you that you do not. I care not for the games you are playing with crowns and hearts. What I do care about is the promise you made me all those years ago.' His voice was an icy undercurrent. Smooth on the surface but terrifying beneath. 'My patience grows weary. Three years I have helped you, and yet your ledger remains unbalanced. An oath was sworn, Desma, and to the oath I will keep you.'

'I know, Cosmas,' she said. 'But do not think you can spend so many years hunting for the answer and then expect me to accomplish what you could not in less than a handful of years. I have never stopped looking. But if it is your oath to me that is causing you such pain, then I release you. You are free to leave, knowing that I remain bound to you. I will continue the search. And when I find the answer, I will send you word by swiftest messenger. This I vow on the thrones of all the Holy Twelve.'

Cosmas moved like a serpent, grasping her arm and twisting, fingers hard as iron. He turned her arm until the inside faced upwards and exposed a tiny mark just above the crook of her elbow. A mark of two faded, waving lines Cosmas had carved himself the night they met.

'I go nowhere,' he whispered. 'I will be by your side, slaying your enemies, fighting your battles, saving your hide. Do not mistake selfishness for loyalty, Princess. I protect you for myself.'

She pulled away, rubbing her arm, a new bruise joining those from Lycon's hands. Cosmas did not ask about them. 'Get out,' she said softly, her eyes never leaving his face.

Cosmas' smile held no warmth. He stepped back in a graceful bow before departing the room. The copper snake amulet was left lying on the floor.

Desma needed air. She stepped out onto the balcony, enjoying the faint heat of the sun, though the breeze was cool.

Secrets. Promises. Prophecies.

Her life was a tangled mess, of which she struggled to clear a path. She wondered if she should have accepted Artimi's offer from her priestess to join the wild covens and flee this fate.

But it was too late.

From her pouch she drew out the ribbon dove, its white and grey body with a touch of blush on its heart so delicate. She drew strength from it, for in it she saw her mother, untainted by death and betrayal, the woman who was the bedrock from which Desma built her own life. Timothea had never shied from the challenges of life, and Desma refused to do any less. Thales had told her to cut through the noise and chaos and distil a single question to guide her. Gylippus, Kalchas, Lycon, even Cosmas be damned. She would win the city, whether it be through love or strength. She was the darkling princess.

She turned to go in search for her bright dresses and jewels.

It was time to dress as a one-day queen. Not the one Koriithos wanted.

But the queen she wanted to be.

Nearly three weeks had passed, and Cela remained in Koriithos.

Desma, as ever, had been the one strong enough to make the painful choice. She had cut the cord that bound them, tying the wound in silk, and gifted Cela the freedom she did not have the voice to ask for.

Now Alnea held a lamp high in the driftless sea, providing a course to set her sail.

Cela emerged from the sea gardens, having become in the habit of starting each morning with a walk among the quiet coral and watchful fish. The low thrumming of the waves in the canal and the pipes that pumped the water through the cliff was soothing. But now, she headed for Alnea's rooms in the palace.

The ostracised princess wanted to escape the city – a sentiment Cela could wholeheartedly agree with. Even her own crew, Leaguemen all now that Khufu was gone, were treated poorly by the Koriithosans. She could not imagine what Alnea experienced growing up as the bastard daughter of the king, her Great Lands skin richly umber, never loved even by her own family.

So, nearly every day since her plea, Cela had returned to her windowless quarters to plan their departure. There was much to consider. Despite how she was treated, she was still a princess of the city. Neither of them doubted that Actor would be far behind, and Cela did not want her friends to repeat what happened with Khufu.

Cela turned the corner and stumbled to a halt.

Arete was leaning against the doorway that led to Alnea's domain. The shipwright was dressed in her usual grey chiton, a red leather belt girdling her slim hips, and her hazel eyes speared Cela to the spot.

'How long did you think you could keep this a secret?' Arete asked.

'What do you mean?'

'Your mystery lady down below.'

Cela hesitated. 'What do you know?'

Arete pushed off from the wall and opened the door. 'Not much. But you have time to tell me.'

Cela sighed. There was no point in trying to dissuade her from coming. As they descended, she quickly filled her in on who was waiting for them.

Arete's eyes flashed in surprise. 'Lycon's *sister*? Actor's *betrothed*? Next thing you will say is that she is a godling.'

Cela chuckled. 'Not quite.'

Cela was not shocked to find Alnea waiting for them, a table laid for three, and a pile of scrolls at her feet.

'Good morning, Celadine,' Alnea greeted, her dark eyes turning on the shipwright. 'And Menrva's blessing on you, daughter of rope and timber. Sit with me.'

Cela had to nudge Arete to move. Soon they were all seated, eating ricotta-stuffed figs and honeyed walnuts. Alnea poured them all water with a dash of orange. At first, they ate in silence, Cela's gaze moving between the two women who had not taken their eyes off each other.

Eventually, the princess put down her cup and wiped her mouth on a small cloth. 'How fast your mind whirs in your head, Taitale's daughter. So many thoughts, I am surprised you can remember yourself in the maelstrom.'

Arete cocked her head, a hawk trying to discern prey from foe. 'Know yourself,' she said with a smirk. 'One of my first teachings.'

Alnea seemed to stiffen at her words. 'How wise. Perhaps your next learning can be to accept your failures.' Arete's face hardened. 'Or perhaps to own your fear that your name may be forgotten, as have all of your line.'

The shipwright launched to her feet, scattering fruit. 'Only one burdened by Aplu's sight can wield words with such cruelty.'

A laugh burst from Alnea's lips as she clapped delightedly. 'Such astuteness! To descry so quickly what many fear to even consider. Yes, I am a prophetess. Remain in my company if your bravery allows or your pride demands.'

'Enough, please,' Cela interjected. 'There is no reason to harm one who could be a friend. Arete.' She motioned back to the cushion.

The shipwright slowly resumed her seat, though her eyes were full of storms. 'I have only met one other who Aplu has touched. He came to my and my father's home, asking shelter for a night. We gave it. When he left, my father was never the same man, for he had spent the night discoursing with someone who saw the splintering paths of life. Now he is obsessed with the idea of crafting the finest ship the Middle Sea has ever seen. So much so that he has forgotten he has a daughter.'

Cela's mouth dropped. She did not know this. Arete rarely spoke of her father except to relay what he had taught her about ship building. When they were in Apasa, she would visit him but never mention what occurred. Cela had accepted her as a private person – but now she wished she had asked, just once, so Arete knew she was safe to share this pain.

Alnea sat still as stone while Arete spoke. She reached out a hand and laid her fingers, lightly, upon Arete's shoulder. 'I am sorry your father has suffered at the hands of the Singing God. I know the burden of clutching the threads of my own tapestry together, terrified what would happen if I were to let go. May Menrva ever shelter your mind, and I pray Aplu never brighten your door.'

The shipwright nodded in thanks. 'And now tell me why there is such secrecy between you two. It is not a crime for you to spend time together, unless ... you are going to commit one.'

Cela gave a grin. 'Just a small one – Alnea is running away.'

'Right,' Arete said with a slow nod. 'How far in the planning are you?'

She looked sheepish. 'We know the final destination – Delphon.'

Arete waited a moment before she realised Cela had finished. 'That is all? I am disappointed.' She turned to Alnea. 'Can't you just prophetise the best way to escape?'

The princess shot her a sharp look. 'No.'

'Thank the gods you have me, then,' Arete said, cracking her knuckles. Her eyes went distant as she began to ponder. Cela picked up the figs and grapes that had rolled onto the floor. Alnea hummed gently, swaying, also seeming to leave the room while her body remained seated.

It was a few minutes before Arete blinked, a grin splashing across her face. 'The Celerian Games!'

Cela's brows drew together in confusion. The Games were a festival of athletic and musical competitions open to the three cities surrounding the isthmus: Koriithos, Athanai, and Phoroniaa. Though the latter city rarely sent competitors to take part, due to the ongoing tensions between the two kingdoms. It was held every two years, and the next was four weeks away. The city had already begun preparations.

'It's the perfect distraction,' Arete continued. 'Alnea can slip away in the bustle. You will just need to pay a captain a lot of gold to leave the city during the Games. If you aren't adverse to travelling on foot, you could even charter the ship for Trilos or Apasa, but have them drop you off near Athanai to throw Actor off the scent.'

Alnea's face grew sad. 'So sharp and yet still not able to discern important truths.' She rose to her feet. 'I will leave you two,' she said, and left the room.

Arete turned puzzled eyes on Cela, who took a deep breath before letting the words spill out of her. 'I am leaving with Alnea.'

'Oh.' The word was more an exhale, and she seemed to grow smaller. 'I see.'

'I am sorry, Arete,' Cela said. 'I was trying to think how to tell you, and Delphinus, Bion, and Kassandra. But every time I scrounged up the courage, it wilted in the moment. To be honest, I am afraid to tell Delphinus, as he will want to come.' She remembered that night – how defeated he had been, how he said he would follow her if asked. 'Alnea has already said she would tolerate no other to travel with us. And I do not know if this journey is what he needs. But I don't know what he needs.'

'The darklings are falling apart. Khufu is dead. Desma is a princess. You are leaving. There has already been talk among the others of what would become of them.' Arete shook her head ruefully. 'I guess four years is all the gods would bless us with.'

'Do you think I should tell the crew?'

'No. I think you just need to leave. We have all gathered at a crossroad and need to decide upon our own paths. For me, I am still happy to walk behind Desma. For now. The others? They need to come to their own decisions and not be lured to follow you. That is not your fate.'

'I will miss you.'

'And I you.'

'Take care of Desma.'

Arete laughed. 'She seems to be taking care of herself. Kalchas looks as though he is ready to spit teeth when he sees what she's wearing each day.'

Cela smiled. Desma had regained some of her old fire. Her visit to Thales appeared to have been the spark to the tinder. She could only pray that the city did not douse her once again. But perhaps it would be Koriithos' turn to bend. Maybe she did not have to worry about her friend as much as she feared.

'There is still the concern of what the king will do when he discovers Alnea is gone,' Cela said. 'All well and good we make it out of the city, but I do not want any of you to be the target of Gylippus' retribution.'

'I wish there was a way we could convince him that it was my idea to leave,' Alnea said, appearing from her bedroom. 'But obviously I cannot tell him so directly, for he would lock me up. And I cannot trust Pinaria as far as I can spit. And I haven't spoken to Lycon since we were twelve years old.'

'What about Actor?' Arete asked.

Cela shook her head along with Alnea. The general's duty was to the royal family. He would never allow Alnea to leave without the king's leave. 'Hyllos?'

Alnea scrunched her nose. 'The astronomers and I have never liked each other.'

'Would the king actually care if you left?' the shipwright asked. 'No disrespect, but maybe they would prefer it if you just disappeared.'

'I am still of royal blood. They would fear my raising an army and returning to claim the throne. They need assurances that I have no intention to wear a crown.'

'Why *do* you travel to Delphon? I see little love between you and Aplu.'

The shipwright's question seemed to fall like iron on the princess. Alnea's voice turned dark and hollow. 'Where can I go and not be feared? I have spent my life alone, untrained, my visions like broken glass I try to piece together in hands wet with blood. I do not care for Aplu – but his temple is my only chance at salvation.'

'Then let us have Aplu help us,' Arete said.

'How so?' Cela asked.

'None can doubt the words of one of his priests, for truth is their domain. Let us go to Aplu's temple here and have them verify Alnea's desire. Once confirmed, we can request that they attend the palace after your departure is discovered, to relay what has happened. Thus, not only is there a chance they may leave you without pursuit, as you are set on a holy pilgrimage, but the king would know that it is not some plot by Desma. The crew would be safe.'

Alnea grabbed Arete gently by the cheeks. 'Thank you, mistress of ships,' she said quietly. 'And for your help, I will tell you these words, though I profess I do not know their meaning – when the sky turns white, cut the rope.'

'Cut the rope,' Arete repeated.

Alnea released her. 'You may both go now. You have much to arrange before the Games. Do not worry for coin. I have more gold than I could spend in ten years. Farewell.' With that, she vanished into another room.

Arete looked askance at Cela. 'Are you sure you want to travel with her?'

CHAPTER THIRTY-SEVEN

The palace resounded with whispers and hushed conversations. It glimmered with long glances, hovering ears, and faces filled with disapproval.

But Desma sensed something else beneath the righteousness and disdain: fear.

She had become a hurricane, an infection, an unseen current in their halls of power. They believed they had beaten her down, bound her in drab colours, and stolen her power when they took her jewels.

And though she hated Turan, there was no goddess so indomitable as She Who is Love. With a smile, Turan had tamed the mighty beasts of the Halls Beneath. With a sway of her hips, she ruined princes. With a lilting laugh, she caused cities to burn.

And so Desma armed herself for battle.

She retrieved her dresses and jewels that had been hidden deep in the palace storerooms. Desma dismissed her ever-changing maids and brought in women from the countryside, had Kassandra teach them how to bathe and dress her, apply makeup and sculpt her hair. Their designs were simple, but her hair needed no further finery than its blessed colour, gifted to her and her mother by a goddess. Another weapon strapped to her body.

Kalchas had tried to storm her room to take away her clothes but found Desma, armed with a spear, waiting for him. Lycon was the only reason that no blood had been shed; he ordered that she be left alone to dress herself as she liked. It was one of the few times he had spoken to her since his mysterious fall.

Nobles began to fear the sight of her messenger girls, announcing her arrival in sashes of cloth the colour of spilled wine. Desma would meet with lords who ruled towns and villages throughout Koriithos, interrogating them with questions regarding the trade of their domains, number of people, who could bear sword and spear, their debts, local customs and festivals. At first, some had laughed at her attempts to learn from them, and even embellished or lied. Until Desma started to correct them, somehow knowing down to the cupful how much wine was in their cellars or sheep in their fields.

The kingdom reports were open to her, even though she was only a princess, and between her and Arete, they soon came to know more about Koriithos than many of the nobles.

She would sweep into the feast hall at evening, dressed in a peplos of red or sun-yellow or the bright green of mint leaves. She donned great necklaces of amethyst and rubies and gold, bracelets clattering on her arms, gems woven in her hair. She bought perfumes from traders in the harbour, so any room she entered was spiced with clove and cassia and moringa.

The king and queen eyed with distaste, then ignored her all evening – as much as one could ignore a rose in a field of grass.

But it all came to a head when she began to rise early in the morning and attend the army training grounds with her sword. Bion, Cela, and Arete would join her, and together they would spar for an hour. Desma's tightly bound chiton and hardened leather sandals let her move across the sanded yard like a thundercloud, clashing against Cela as they danced. At first, the men would stand far off, whispering of the impropriety of a woman – their princess – fighting with blades and sweating. But eventually, Desma began to hear murmurs of appreciation, especially about Cela as she was flame incarnate, incandescent in her brightness and ruthlessness, a master swordswoman.

On the fifth such day, Desma gave the signal to Cela, who spun away from her mid-strike and tossed a spear from a rack to an unsuspecting youth, his beard still patchy, and called out a challenge. The man was frozen in shock, unsure how to respond under the watching eyes of his brethren. Cela struck out, forcing him to parry the blow.

They fell into a sparring match. The youth did his best to overpower Cela, but he was always a moment too slow, an inch too far, from landing a blow. After a few moments, Desma joined with a shout, the young man now facing two opponents. When he realised one of them was the princess, he let his spear slip in hesitation, and Cela scored a mark across his shoulder, drawing a thin line of red. Another man roared and charged into the battle from the sidelines, forcing Desma to peel away and face him alone. He had no hesitation in fighting her, and Desma grinned at the challenge, meeting his blade with her own.

Every day since, she trained against a new opponent, learning from Bion that the barracks had drawn straws to determine the order they crossed swords with her. She clasped the hands of the losers, bowed her head respectfully to the winners. Daily, the circle around the sparring yard grew wider – and stayed longer. She began to win over the city warriors.

Until Gylippus himself strode onto the field one day, Kalchas following like a storm crow. Hyllos hovered nearby, clenching and unclenching his hands as he watched on.

Desma dropped her sword point into the sand, waiting patiently as the king approached, wiping sweat from her brow as her opponent scurried away.

'My king,' Desma said clearly, bowing low. 'I bid you good morning.'

'Be silent, insolent wench,' he hissed, his charcoal robes shapeless and unadorned. 'Uni has certainly turned her eyes away from Koriithos rather than watch such an unwomanly display. Put that down!' He kicked a barefoot at her blade, which she deftly turned broadside so he did not slice his toes.

'Uni herself slew the giant Celsclan with a sword,' Desma said with a level tone. 'She killed several gods in the fight to claim her throne as Queen of the Heavens.'

The king's eyes bulged at her words.

The first astronomer stepped forward, using the little height he had on her to appear looming. 'How dare you attempt to compare yourself to Uni,' he berated. 'She is Queen of the Heavens and has laid the rules for how women should behave. Koriithos is mighty because both men and women know their place – and it is not on the battlefield or dressed like whore.'

'A sword in my hand was good enough for you when there was a monster to slay,' Desma said as demurely as she could. 'I am the one the prophecy says Koriithos needs. If you needed someone who behaved like a Koriithosan woman, then a Koriithosan woman should have ventured into the forest.'

Gylippus' expression soured. 'You are treading on treacherous ground, daughter of Apasa. I thought my tutors had winnowed this boldness out of you.'

'Man cannot take away what the gods have given.' Desma bowed her head.

The silence stretched before the king gave a begrudging grunt. 'It seems that even the rain cannot dampen this unseemly fire inside you. I will allow you to continue. But this does not spread. Any woman who emulates you in any way will be stripped naked and sent to scrub the palace steps from sunrise to sunset. And you will watch them, dressed in your finery and gems, so all know who is responsible. Understand?'

Desma bowed again. 'You are wise, my king.'

Gylippus left without another word. But Kalchas remained for a moment, his face twisted by hatred. 'Remember this, Desma,' he spoke softly, like a blade in shadow, 'it will be many years before you become queen. Much can change.'

'May Nethluns bless your day, First Astronomer.'

Kalchas stormed away. Hyllos held for a moment longer before following his master.

Desma had thought she had a friend in the second astronomer, but he had made it clear whose camp he had staked his banner in. She could not be angry at his decision; he had chosen his king, prince, and master over the foreign princess. But it still stung.

'Let's call it early, Cela,' Desma said, sheathing her sword and stretching her arms high above her head, easing her sore muscles.

They headed through the few streets to the palace, laughing with Bion, who nursed a black eye from a warrior's lucky blow with a spear butt. Six guards followed behind, eyes wary for the Dirciade who clung to Desma's footsteps like shadows, always watching and following.

Turning a corner, they found their way barred by a line of women. Desma sighed. Why did they not see that she wished them no harm? She had made her decision to help them, as ordained by the gods. Why did they fear her so much?

Perhaps it was time she walked their path.

'Carry on,' she said, continuing in her strides, surefooted and back straight.

Her captain of the guard called to her, clattering to get ahead, but Desma reached the line of women first. The woman in the centre was dressed in a fine black peplos, a dull red ribbon in her hair, and a single copper bracelet. Her brows arched as Desma approached, a familiar distasteful curl to her lip.

Desma smacked her across the face, hard.

She would no longer fear them.

The woman reeled back, clutching her cheek, eyes wide with shock, as her companions stepped away gasping.

'I am here,' Desma said with a hint of a snarl. 'You harry and chase and torment me. You want to get rid of me? Here I am. Strike me.' She drew her sword and threw it at the woman's feet, bronze clanging harshly on the stones.

'Princess!' Her guard captain moved to grab the sword, but Bion blocked his way.

'Leave it, captain,' Desma ordered without looking at him. 'This has gone on far too long. Pick it up, woman of Koriithos. Your princess commands you.'

The woman looked to the others, but they gave no sign of helping. How easily their bonds crumbled when challenged.

'You will regret this, Father-Killer,' the woman hissed. But she stepped away from the blade.

Desma did not hesitate. She struck the woman again. This time with a closed fist. Sprawling to the ground, the woman clutched her stomach from the blow. Desma did not let up. The anger inside her was blinding, a white flame. She kicked her, and again. The women around her were calling for the guards to step in, but they did nothing. Royal justice was being carried out.

Desma slammed her foot onto her ankle and felt bone snap. She was suddenly returned to the quinquereme, to when Camillus' man broke her own ankle. Disgust swallowed her rage, and she finally stepped away.

The woman lay before her, huddled in a ball and crying. Desma knelt and reached out to move her hair from her face. 'I am sorry that it had to be you,' she said gently. 'But you will carry this message to all the Dirciade. I will no longer be threatened. I am a princess of this kingdom and will one day be its queen. You cannot win this fight.'

She rose and stepped over the Koriithosan, leaving her sword on the stones, and carried on to the palace. The other women parted from their group like a wave, coming together again round their fallen comrade.

Desma did not look back.

CHAPTER THIRTY-EIGHT

The ground shook.

Mynta woke up in a daze, the pillow sticking to her face; the night had been humid, the air thick, every surface wet to the touch.

She blinked as her eyes tried to form her vision into shape. The sky was the dimness of pre-dawn, clouds hiding the gold and peach that would normally greet Thesan's welcome to the day.

The ground shook again, rattling a cup off the table to shatter on the ground. She bolted upright. The vibrations grew stronger and more consistent, and there came shouting out in the street. A sudden shriek, like metal tearing metal, followed by a great thudding had her up on her feet.

'Anesidora, Sebastos!' she shouted as she raced through the house.

Servants, awoken by the commotion, began to gather in the courtyard. Guards stood by the gates, spears and swords clutched in steady hands. Sebastos was already there, armoured as though he had slept prepared, his face grim.

'What is happening without?' she asked, skidding to a halt.

'I am not sure, my lady,' he answered. 'Though some cries carry fear in the air, most are of surprise. This is not the sound of a city under attack.'

She did not want to imagine the memories that taught him the difference. 'Then I think we should take a look.'

'My lady ... your garb—'

But she was already out the door.

The streets were filled with people, most still in their sleeping dress, standing in doorways while a few braver souls ventured further into the street. It was not the time of year for the Parade. Something else was happening.

A hulking figure disappeared around the corner, its shadow following it longer than was right.

'It cannot be.'

Mynta took off down the road, Sebastos giving chase, followed by a rattle of armour as men flowed after her. She did not care. Her bare feet throbbed as she ran, the stones threatening to turn her ankle at any moment.

She raced for the city walls.

The crowds grew the closer she got to the main gates. Sebastos and his men caught up with her easily and helped to clear a path. As they rounded a corner, Mynta let out a screech as Sebastos pulled her back, his arm like iron around her waist.

An automaton, twenty feet tall and broader than three men abreast, strode above them. Feet crashed into the ground with a great whirring and grinding as internal works spun. A sword slung across its back, its helmed head stared only forward, unheeding the people scattering around it.

Mynta followed until the gates came into sight. She watched it duck beneath the stonework and join the line of other automatons leaving the city.

'Quickly, this way,' she said. The masses were too large to even attempt pushing through, so she pressed sideways, away from the main thoroughfare. Down a side alley, through an unguarded postern and clambering up a tight spiral stair, they emerged atop the city wall, sprinting along its length, until the gates came back into view.

Mynta froze in awe at the sight before her.

She did not know the number of automatons in Trilos. Some were stationed across the kingdom, at key trading posts or important towns. Occasionally, the king would bestow one of the dread guardians to the house of a noble or councillor who pleased him. Most were within the city itself, but she had never counted them.

Arrayed across the road into the city and lining the golden sands were hundreds of the ancient creations. Crafted by the Clevers and controlled only by the king, they were the main reason why Trilos had never lost an inch of land to another kingdom. Unstoppable wielders of destruction, made of bronze and stone and iron, without blood and without fear; they could stand before any army or eastern horde and not flinch.

Ranked by size, the tallest was greater than the city walls themselves, while the lesser was still twice the height of a man. As the dawn grew old, the sun pierced the clouds and shone upon the army, their armour bright, alighting the orichalcum hammer and tong like flames on their chests.

'What is happening?' she whispered.

Once a year, the Parade would take place – the king would rotate the automatons in the city, moving them to stand guard in new positions for the year ahead. It was a reminder to the Trilosii of his power, but also a warning to visitors of the might of their kingdom.

But they were never gathered outside the city in such a fashion. The only reason would be that Trilos was in danger – or they were taking the danger to someone else.

Horns sounded, and as one, the gathered citizens turned to the main gate. Two huge braziers had been lit further along the wall from Mynta's party. There stood King Hilarion himself, upon a raised platform above the city gate.

Mynta had not seen him since he denied Desma her petition to be cleansed. He had not spoken a single word or allowed them a chance to voice their submission before leaving the hall.

Now, he stood flanked by warriors and priests. She frowned. Where were the councilmen and other nobles? The king went nowhere without them. But standing by his side was the high priest, Castur.

He did not look like the same man who had visited her home. His eyes were hollow, and his skin wane. He stood stiffly apart from the king, as though desperate to step away. What had happened?

'Lady Amynta,' a voice said beside her. 'I am surprised to see you here.'

She turned to find a thin, older man with worried eyes. He was dressed hastily in robes, his hair still mussed from bed. It took her a moment to recall him. Serapion, a member of the Council who had spoken in favour of granting Desma's audience with the king. He shrugged his robe from his shoulders, revealing a long chiton beneath. 'Please.'

Looking down, she realised she was barefoot, unadorned, and dressed only in a thin gown that clung to her, revealing more skin than was modest. Flushing, she took the robe hastily, and Sebastos helped straighten it around her. 'Thank you, Lord Serapion. I must confess that the excitement overtook me.'

'As long as your father does not see you dressed like this on the wall.'

'Have you seen him of late?' The question was out of her mouth before she could stop it.

He shook his head. 'Linos is descending in the Council. Galen rises high, and even the Prime and First Advisor struggle to keep him in check. But now ...'

'What is it?' She could not disguise the eagerness in her voice.

He looked at her hard for a long moment. 'I should not discuss these matters with you. But ...' He sighed. 'I am afraid I am also reaching the final turning of my career.' He nodded towards the king and Castur. 'The high priest has been daily at the palace for many weeks now. Castur was always a reserved man, avoiding politics in favour of working within The Forge, guiding those who sought Sethlans' inspiration. He used to be good friends with Hilarion's father, but even then, he did not come between the king and the Council.'

'So what has changed?' Despite the straightness of his back and the set of his shoulders, Castur looked haggard. He did not speak to anyone around him, but only looked out above the automatons, as though looking far across the sea.

'That is something the Council would very much like to know,' Serapion said. 'There have been rumblings in the city. Trades cut, ships recalled, invitations cancelled. It makes no sense!'

Before Mynta could ask what he meant, drums began to beat slowly, gathering speed until they matched the pace the automatons had set when walking through the city. All at once, they fell silent, and the king began to speak. Heralds near him began to repeat his words, echoed by more heralds further away, so that all those gathered would know the king's words.

'People of Trilos, blessed disciples of Sethlans from whom Creation flows and to him alone belongs mastery of metal and stone. I have been visited by our patron-god himself, and he has issued commandments. From this day, and until the end of mortal-kind, all ties to Apasa have been severed.'

Mynta gasped, and she was echoed a thousandfold over. Apasa was their greatest ally, their closest sister-city, their richest trading partner. This was inconceivable. Serapion's jaw went slack.

'We will no longer trade with Apasa, nor trade for Apasan goods from other kingdoms. Apasans are welcome to continue residing in our city and towns but will now have to pay new taxes and face heavy penalties for any infractions against Trilosii law. Additionally, no Apasan may enter Trilos bearing a weapon on threat of losing their arm. I have created the role of the Tenth Advisor to oversee all Apasan matters and permits.'

Mynta's head was swimming. The repercussions were enormous. Without Apasa, only goods from Dramaki would come over land. The roads south would fall out of use, and the taxes gained by their tolls would dry up. Hundreds of merchants and shopkeepers would go out of business, unable to pivot to the significantly smaller pool of supplies available. Prices for items would shoot skywards.

And the Apasans. Trilos was home to hundreds of people who had moved from their home city, had married Trilosii, borne children. How far back did the new laws reach? Would grandfathers be sent hobbling on the road south? Would children who knew no other place be shipped to a strange port?

And where was the Council in all this? They were the balance upon the king's power for precisely this reason. She turned to the councilman, but he had already anticipated her question.

'Most know that the king is checked by the Council, and the Council cannot act without the king,' Serapion said. 'But there is a third leg to the tripod. If the king and high priest stand as one, then the Council becomes advisory in all matters they claim.'

She had never heard of such a law. When she returned home, she would set Tros the task of gathering all Council laws and regulations.

The king continued. 'Furthermore, a holy decree will be issued both here and throughout the Middle Sea. The marriage between Sethlans and his wife has been dissolved. No longer will they be worshipped as husband and wife, their devotions intermingled, their gifts shared. Trilos will no longer house any shrines or priestesses or temples to Turan, the Loveless One.'

The murmur of the crowd fell away to eerie silence. It was not unusual for the gods to bicker, hold generational grudges, pit favourites against each other, and do whatever else to inflict pain on their brethren.

But Turan was of the Holy Twelve. She deserved to be venerated, respected, worshipped. To cast her out ... it was forsaking Love itself.

'May the gods preserve us,' she prayed.

'I have gathered the might of Trilos' armies before the city as a warning throughout the League.' Hilarion thrust a hand outward, sweeping west to south. 'The Kingdom of Trilos is not to be trifled with, to be played with, to be betrayed and hurt. We rule our portion of this world as Sethlans rules his domain among the gods. And under his hand and hammer, we will show our enemies the bronze in our spine and fire in our hearts. Glory to Sethlans!'

Warriors surrounding the king and down in the city took up the cry. Slowly, the people of Trilos began to echo it, raising their hands high. But others, Apasans and their relatives or friends, begin to slink away in the brightening morning. Their lives had been destroyed in a single speech.

Serapion nudged her. 'I know your heart is bleeding, but you must join,' he whispered quickly. 'Glory to Sethlans!'

Priests were walking along the wall, amongst the crowd, watching. Mynta raised her arm, tears sliding down her cheeks, as she forced the acrid words from her mouth. 'Glory to Sethlans.' What was happening to her city? 'Glory to Sethlans.' What had changed to make the king and Castur choose this path? 'Glory to Sethlans.' What had Turan done?

CHAPTER THIRTY-NINE

Mynta rose with the dawn, leaving a small offering on her eastern window to Thesan in thanks for another day. She left her home in a white peplos strung with small copper pendants from shoulder to hip. Her hair was loosely braided and threaded with a bronze ribbon. Anesidora complained of stiff hips so she left her to rest; Bel and a maid followed behind her, as well as three warriors.

The market was half-filled with stalls selling fresh fruit and vegetables to the nearby homes. She had no pressing purchase she required, Mynta had simply wanted to leave the house. She bought a small bag of roasted nuts covered with spice that she shared with Bel, ignoring the maid's disapproving frown to the boy.

Tros' family had settled in well. His children followed after Anesidora and Sebastos, pestering them with questions, or shadowed the maids and guards until they shared the tricks of their trades. Tros' wife had taken over as housekeeper, and the house ran as tight as a ship. Mynta had half expected her nursemaid to throw a fit, but Anesidora seemed content to let her have her way.

Tros had truly been a boon to her life. Even Anesidora had expressed admiration at the skill he had in growing the small puddle of gold into what one could, at a stretch, describe as a pool. And with the gold from Apollophanes, he was even more determined to squeeze as much benefit from every coin as he could. He knew much of the tangle of deals and alliances, feuds and petty hatred among the merchants of the city. Great misfortune alone had quenched his fire, driving him into the state she had found him. A smile tugged at her lips as she thought of how she had hustled through his door and promptly turned his life upside down. She only hoped that it would not all be for naught. The last thing she wanted was to upheave his family again – but this time for a worsened state.

Duris, too, had not made it easy. It seemed he and the other merchants had gone about Trilos speaking ill of her to other traders, leaving no one willing to share in her apparent bad fortune.

It made her furious, as each day her dwindling funds grew smaller.

It did not help that demand for Apasan goods had soared since the king's declaration, but there was little supply to be had. Those who did have stock were inundated with offers, far greater than what she could match.

She passed a table selling amulets and paused. The merchant hurried over and eagerly pointed out his different wares, what they protected against or brought to the wearer. They were of fine make, well-carved and threaded on gold, silver, and leather. 'Do you have one to help sleep come?' she asked, her fingers hovering over a gold amulet shaped like a bay laurel wreath with an arrow suspended in the middle. A symbol of Aplu.

'You are having trouble sleeping, my lady?' the merchant asked.

'Not me,' she said, glancing at Bel. 'For a friend.'

'Well, I have one of Tiur, the Mood Goddess who watches over us all. Or Artimi, for she often hunts those with wickedness in their hearts at night. Or here is Artume ...'

Mynta took the necklace bearing a sigil of the Goddess of Night. A circle of obsidian bordered by tarnished silver. Delicately carved into the stone was an owl. 'I will take it,' she said. 'And this one.' She pointed at Aplu's amulet. Pleased with her purchase, she placed them in her pouch tied to her belt.

They wandered for a little while more before pausing to rest on a seat by a fountain, portraying the triplet daughters of Laran: Glory, Praise, and Victory.

Mynta leant against the stone, enjoying the warmth of the rising sun, listening to the splash of water behind her and the bustle of the market. It was peaceful.

Her maid shook her arm. 'My lady, is that not master merchant Duris?'

Mynta's eyes snapped open, and she sat up so fast she caused her maid to stumble back.

He haggled at a stall over a rug. Laughed at something the merchant said. Her heart fluttered a little before she clamped it down; she had fallen for his smooth words and kind smile, but it had been a ruse meant to trap a sheltered girl. Tros had gathered the details. Duris made it out that *she* had brought the proposition to *him* and convinced him to rope in friends and colleagues. He even implied that she had failed in her due diligence and tricked him with silver words.

Before she knew what she was doing, she was on her feet.

She drifted to the opposite side of the stall, pretending to feel the different rugs available. At first, he did not notice her. But when the merchant turned to apologise for the wait, their eyes met. Duris paled and quickly made his excuses to the merchant before stepping away.

Mynta moved quickly, ignoring the rug merchant completely, as she rounded the stall and stopped Duris in his tracks.

'Lady Amynta,' he said with feigned surprise. 'How delightful to see you again.'

'Master merchant. How is business?'

'Sethlans has blessed me recently. One of my scouts found an emerald deposit along the cliffs of the Straits of Athamantis. With a few investors, we have successfully begun mining operations.'

'How wonderful,' she said, her voice full of bitter honey. 'I am surprised you did not invite me to enter the partnership.'

Silence hung thick between them.

She raised an eyebrow.

Drawing himself up, he was still not much taller than her. 'I did not think you would be interested after Sabate. And I was not sure if you would be able to afford the share, as it was significantly higher than for the tin mine.'

'And it would have nothing to do with you telling all of Trilos that the Sabate venture failed *because of me*?' People were beginning to look but she could not care less. 'I trusted you, and you chose to shed the embarrassment of a bad investment onto me. Explain yourself, master merchant.'

Duris' eyes flicked side to side, noticing the crowd that lingered to capture every detail of gossip to share and spread. 'This is not the time nor the place for this discussion,' he said in a low voice.

'You are a coward,' she hissed. 'And the only shame I feel is that I allowed myself to believe you were a man of values. You dishonour Tinia with your actions.'

His face grew dark. 'If you recall, my lady, we came to your home seeking your father. You were the one to ask us. We even tried to deflect your request, but you persisted. You chose to sign the contract. You chose to invest. You chose to take on the risk.' He stepped closer to her, breath warm on her face. Her guard moved forward but she waved them back. 'This is the game, my lady,' he said, brown eyes boring into her. 'You tried to dance and stumbled. Do not seek to place the blame for your ineptitude on me. Learn the steps and try again.'

Mynta moved away, face burning with shame. He was right. The mistake was hers and hers alone. 'You still did not have to lie to the other traders,' she said.

He shrugged. 'You should have lied first. Reputation and money are the two currencies we work in. Sethlans guide you, my lady.' He gave her a short bow and departed, pushing through the crowd.

Her maid came to stand beside her. 'Let us return home, my lady,' she said, glaring at the onlookers.

Mynta was led away meekly, Bel trailing. Her mind weighed upon her – there truly was none to catch her if she fell. And she wondered how many times her strength would let her rise again.

The market was half empty when Anesidora slipped out after her lady's return.

Vacant stalls were scattered between traders and merchants, as obvious as toothless gaps in a mouth. The noisy cries and chatter only seemed to make their silences echo all the louder. It was not only the Apasans who had begun to leave Trilos. Dramakian, Athanain, Thevan – all trickled out of the city.

It had been over a week since the king's ridiculous proclamation. All ties cut with Apasa. The world was growing darker by the day, and she did not think she would last until the next sunrise.

Anesidora waved to a friend buying oranges but did not stop. It was further to the palace than she remembered, and Usil was merciless in his journey across the sky. Her peplos felt like a heavy, woollen blanket wrapped around her cracking bones, and her hair was a wet mop atop her head. The blasted basket of linens on her hip was getting heavier with every step.

She eventually reached the gates to the palace; the guards simply waved her in. Few servants were ever noticed, unless their beauty caught the eye. And she had long since lost any allure her youth once held.

The riches and gilded splendour of the palace had faded from her notice long ago. As the years passed, gold lost its gleam. It only grew brighter for those in power.

Shambling through the halls, she passed nobles plotting away in small alcoves and harried advisors. Groups of priests roved the halls, greater in number than she had ever seen in the palace. It was not their place to be here. The Forge was their home.

Anesidora was a devout woman. She prayed to the gods, left offerings and lit incense, always showed respect for their power. But why they felt the need to bring their own disputes here, among those who had such fleeting years, and force them to live in their struggles and arguments, was beyond her comprehension. She sometimes wondered if to be kind was mortal and to be cruel divine.

Turan and Sethlans did not even live in the League any longer. Were Quirinale and Aventinus also at odds? Has the Empire fractured by holy decree?

She began the long climb up one of the towers. The steps were shallow and wide, arched windows offered her a rotating view of the city and sea, which helped to lessen the pain in her hip.

She saw no other path forward than this one. The daughter of her heart – the girl she had raised from the moment her mother handed the swaddled babe into her arms, still covered in the mess of birth – needed help. She could not tell Amynta that she had been quietly adding her own drachmae to the household. A nursemaid's pay was not much, but over the course of several decades, it added up to a tidy sum. Enough for an old woman to retire on. Or to cover the smaller costs of a household for several months.

But this was the right thing to do. Amynta may not be able to see that for herself, but it was the truth. The coin gathered from selling her jewellery would not stretch far enough. She needed more help than she was able to give herself.

It pained Anesidora to see how Amynta punished herself for the mine's failure, how she cursed Duris for ever darkening her hall, how she could not deny the fact that every choice had been hers and hers alone. The ruin of her fortune and the near downfall of her fledgling house.

Anesidora had cared for many children over her life. But it was with this household she had found the calling of her heart. She had thought it was with the child she first laid eyes on over forty years ago, but it turned out to have been her daughter.

And despite the years that flowed, sometimes it was still the task of a nursemaid to remind their charge of what it meant to do what was right.

Eventually reaching the door, midway up the tower, she pushed it open without knocking. A maid rushed over, her mouth open to reprimand, but Anesidora did not give her a chance.

'Move aside, child, or I will paddle your bottom, and it won't be as enjoyable as when Lord Damasos' son does it.' She swept past.

A noblewoman sat before a large, polished bronze mirror, studying her hair. 'Eudokia, who are you talking to?' Her eyes met Anesidora's reflection. She lowered her brush and turned around stiffly. 'I am surprised to see you here, my childhood nurse. Tell me, what news of my daughter?'

CHAPTER FORTY

Mynta wanted to tear up the parchment she held in shaking hands, but she forced herself to lay it on the ever-growing pile of rejections. Another supplier had declined her offer. It seemed she could not even crack into the sandal business, be it with the cobblers or the tanners.

The gold from her jewellery was dwindling. Tros did all he could to slow the tide, but eventually, she would be left stranded. She thought of Bel and Olus, the cook, her maids, the guards Sebastos had laboured to train, her ageing nursemaid. They all relied on her, their livelihood depending on her success. Their names and fortune were tied to her own.

Tros looked up as he shuffled some reports. The time he had been in her household had been good for him. His tired face had grown refreshed, despite the late nights and early mornings she asked of them all, and his frame was filling out with the food she made sure was always to hand.

'Perhaps, my lady, we need to look further afield,' he suggested.

She sat down again, filling their cups with honeyed lemon water. 'What do you mean?'

'Well,' he said, 'it is not something a novice merchant would usually attempt, but in our current circumstances, I believe the payout is worth the risk.'

She was intrigued, though frowned at being called a novice. 'Tell me more.'

Young Bel ran into the room, skidding to a halt in his new sandals. 'My lady,' he said breathlessly. 'Your mother is in the outer courtyard and requests to see you.'

Her heart sang and slumped simultaneously – Mynta had not seen her mother since she and her father had left for the palace. She had not responded to any of Mynta's messages, and did not answer when she tried to visit their apartments.

Now, she was outside, with no invitation or prior notice of her visit. What was her game?

'Run and fetch Aneisdora,' she said. 'Have her escort my mother to the small dining room, and then run to the kitchen and get some light food served. Run, my boy.'

Bel bowed and sped off.

'Shall I take my leave?' Tros asked.

'That may be best.'

She left the office, moving stately through the house, for her mother had taught her that a lady did not rush in her own home. She passed a mirror and wished for a moment she had worn something else, but viciously dismissed the thought. It was not formal, but practical – a warm yellow peplos with the sides cut out to provide as much relief from the heat as possible. It had no sleeves, though it did reach down to the floor. Her hair was piled up high on her head, and she wore simple topaz jewellery, a gift from Cela three years ago.

Her mother was already in the small dining room, Anesidora standing stiffly in the corner.

Her mother raised an eyebrow when Mynta entered. She was a classic Trilosii beauty – slim and copper-skinned, black hair shining with sweet oils, breasts plump. Her tight peplos was cinched by a dozen tiny strings so it clung to her body. Her arms were covered in gold bracelets from wrist to forearm, and a necklace strung with egg-sized emeralds covered her chest. Beauty ready to be wielded as a weapon when required.

'Mother,' she said with a small bow.

'It is customary for the host to be waiting when a guest is shown inside,' she said.

Anger flared inside her, her cheeks heating. 'And it is customary for a guest to be invited or announced prior to arrival.'

Her mother sniffed. 'I did not realise a mother had to be so formal to visit her daughter.'

Blow ceded to her mother.

Mynta gave up on the exchange and took a seat across from her. Two maids entered with trays of food and laid them out – vine wrapped lamb, thinly sliced carrots, small rosemary cakes, grapes, and other titbits. Mynta reached out for a piece of cheese, and her mother sighed.

Shame pierced her more deeply than any arrow; her hand hesitated for a moment before she withdrew it into her lap. 'How are you, Mother?'

She flicked open a fan, flapping it gently. 'Your father and I are worried. We have heard rumours that have made us uneasy.'

Mynta remained silent, holding her mother's gaze.

'Petulance?' she said, pausing her fan. 'You are not a child anymore, Amynta. You style yourself lady of this house, and yet you sulk like a girl when questioned.'

Mynta felt herself shrivelling. How was it her mother's words could reduce her so quickly? 'What rumours have you heard?' she finally asked. 'I do not listen to every whisper on the street.' A touch of iron.

'That you sought to sell this house – our home. Do not attempt to deny it, for I heard it from your maid's own lips, Helice. This house is in your father's name, as you no doubt learned from Ethausva's temple. I cannot believe your arrogance. Or your stupidity.'

Mynta's face burned. 'It was simply an enquiry,' she lied. 'I was looking into my options.'

'And that you paraded through the city selling jewellery like a destitute beggar-woman.'

'I only sold what I owned, mother,' Mynta replied. 'I required coin.'

'For what?'

Silence again.

'Another wasteful venture?' her mother asked. 'Like Sabate?'

So her parents knew. She tried to tamp down the embarrassment. Everyone had a failed investment in their life. Even her father, though she still could not find a record in the office. She would not let them shame her because she was trying to forge her own life. 'What do you want, Mother?'

The fan snapped shut. 'Your father has sent me here to tell you to stop being a fool and demeaning our family. If you choose to continue on this path, then we will not support you any further. Your stipend will be revoked, and you will need to find another home.'

Another home? They would drive her from where she had grown up because she defied them. 'Mother, please, can you not speak to Father? This is madness.'

Her mother rose to her feet, smoothing the front of her dress. 'We will await your answer by the end of the week. You can either step away from this family, or you can marry the man we have chosen for you.'

Another shock. 'Marry who?'

'Councilman Aridolis.'

It took Mynta a moment to recall him. He was the age of her father, a burly man who had been on the Council for fifteen years. He owned many trade ships and dealt mostly in Empyrean glassware. As far as she was aware, he was a kind and rich man, a more than suitable arrangement.

She felt sick.

Her attention flicked past her mother to her nursemaid. The old woman, who had cared for her more than both her parents combined, gave a slow nod.

She faced her mother, barring the way out. 'You can have my answer now. I will not give up this freedom. Aplu and Sethlans have given me the strength to seek my own destiny. I love you, Mother, and even Father, though it is hard sometimes. Know that, even as you walk out the door and away from your only daughter.'

Guilt was a two-edge blade.

'I wish you well, Amynta,' her mother said sadly. She clapped her hands. Two men carried in ironbound chests. They set them on the floor with grunts, the chest thudding heavily.

'What is this?' Mynta asked as the men left the room.

'Your father's instructions were very clear,' she said. 'We will cease your stipend when *we*,' she stressed the word, 'have heard your answer. If you say no, we will stop supporting you. If you say yes, you will wed Aridolis within the month. Regardless, we will be taking back our home.'

She paused as she passed Mynta, laying a hand lightly on her shoulder. 'In one of the chests are the deeds to a small house in the plum tree quarter. It has been purchased in your name, and cannot be taken away.' Her eyes glistened softly. 'Prove him wrong.' Her voice was barely a gossamer. She pressed a kiss on Mynta's brow, lingering as though pained to part from her.

But part from Mynta she did – with straightened shoulders, she swept from the room, calling for her escort to gather.

Mynta did not turn to watch her leave. She held the memory, clasping it gently like a swallow between her palms, afraid to break its brittle bones. Her mother's scent of spiced plum and almond flowers lingered. Mynta had not realised how greatly she missed her smell.

Anesidora approached and drew her into a hug. 'It is okay, daughter of my heart,' she said softly. 'Sometimes a lioness must wander alone before finding her own pride.'

Mynta nodded and wiped her eyes. She moved to the chests and flipped open the first lid. Both of them gasped – it was filled to the brim with gold drachmae, glinting in the sunlight of the hall. The second chest was filled with silver coins.

'Aita Below,' her nursemaid said quietly, hand on her chest.

'There must be hundreds,' Mynta said, plucking the scroll from the top of the silver chest. The deed to a house in her name. A final gift. 'But how could my father have allowed this?'

'You heard her, my lady,' Anesidora said. 'The money will stop when they both hear your answer by week's end. I think you will find your mother will delay telling Linos what you said today.'

'But he will punish her for this,' she said, gesturing at the fortune in front of her. 'He will notice the withdrawal.' She shuddered to think what mood he was already in. As Emissary to Apasa, he had lost his title and whatever influence it gave him. If what Serapion had said was true, he had gone from one of the most powerful on the Council to the least in a matter of months.

'Yes, he will notice and most likely punish her.' She gripped her arm. 'But do not diminish this act of love from your mother by wishing she had not done so. Take it into your heart and remember it to the end of your days. Do you hear me, Amynta? Remember your mother's love.'

She nodded, closing the chests, and called for Sebastos to form a guard to take the chests to the temple of Februus. She hurried to tell Tros that they had received a reprieve from their dour prospects.

Five days later, the house was in turmoil as they readied to move into the home her mother had gifted her.

Yesterday, she had the entire staff assembled in the outer courtyard. She had already dismissed the guard and maid reporting to her father. Those who remained were given a choice: they could stay in her father's employ or come with her.

Though she knew some would choose to stay, it still stung when they stepped forward. One of the maids had been with her since she was twelve. The cook did not hesitate in choosing her father, and five of the household's original guards moved forward. Mynta thanked them for their service and gifted them a gold drachma each.

She was left with her nursemaid, three maids, two messenger boys which included Bel, two male servants, and a guard of twenty-two warriors. As well as Tros and his two scribes.

The first thing she had arranged was a replacement cook.

The plum tree quarter was to the southeast of her former home, in a less wealthy but still respectable area of the city. The main street was filled with multiple varieties of plum trees that the locals picked in summer, a juicy morsel on a hot day.

Her house was set between a weaver and a wineshop. It had a narrow entrance, mostly filled by a heavy wooden door bound in bronze. The street was clean and filled with families going about their day. An automaton stood silent vigil across the way, its dread expression frightening.

'How are the preparations?' she asked her nursemaid.

'Tros' wife has it well in hand. I think it is time you name her formally as your housekeeper,' Anesidora said in a lowered voice.

'I think you're right. I will have several announcements soon.' She ignored Anesidora's quizzical expression. 'Let us enter.'

The doors opened as they approached, and Mynta let out a delighted gasp. The inner courtyard was also narrow, but was presided over by a large almond tree covered with white-and-pink blooms. A small wall of green tile surrounded its trunk, emblazoned with nature goddesses and dryads.

Past the tree, the house widened and stretched behind the two shops on either side. It was simply built, but it had a garden along the northern wall, with a fountain instead of a creek.

It had room enough for them all, along with formal and intimate dining rooms, a large kitchen, three guest chambers, an office, and a welcoming hall. It was everything she needed. And it was hers by law.

'It is magnificent.' Mynta abandoned decorum by hiking up her hem and running through the house. Anesidora called after her, but she ignored it.

She laughed as she sprinted past startled guards. She saw Bel ahead of her and called out, 'First one to the kitchen gets a honey cake!'

The boy jumped at her shout before grinning and speeding off, far faster than she could hope to run. But she put on an extra spurt of speed all the same, coming last by a full half minute, stitch burning her side, heaving as she struggled to breathe. But she shared an elated smile as she dashed the sweat from her brow. 'I think next time you need to give me distance to start with,' she said breathlessly.

He shrugged with a silly grin and stuck out his hand expectantly.

'Crown him with a honey cake, please,' she said to the new cook, who ruffled his hair.

'First and second place,' the cook said, giving them each a cake.

They left the kitchen with their prizes and found Tros' wife, Irene, giving instructions to several maids. The group bowed when they saw her approach, hand and face sticky with honey.

'My lady,' Irene said, offering a cloth.

'Thank you,' she said, wiping Bel's face before her own. 'How goes everything?'

'Wonderfully,' Irene said. Taller than her husband, with hair a light brown that seemed dusted with gold when the sun struck it, her face was weathered from a difficult life but softened with joyful lines. 'We have everything settled, though we did lose two bowls, a bottle of wine, and an amphora of olive oil in the move. '

'I would like you to join me for dinner tonight,' Mynta said.

Irene blinked. 'Dinner, my lady?'

'Yes.' Mynta continued on her way, eager to see her bedroom.

It was the perfect house for her to truly begin her new life. Her mother had chosen well. And she had saved her the stress of looking with only a week's notice of eviction. She prayed to Uni to see her mother again soon, without the distance of Linos between them.

'Show me your room,' she said to Bel. She could see her own later.

He took her hand and led her back through the house. It was next to the kitchen but was an actual room with a window looking onto the rear lane. Two small sleeping pallets were set up with a table, shelves, and stools. Now that the two messenger boys had a space to call their own, she would make sure they filled it with items they cherished. Starting with ...

'I have a gift for you.' She knelt to his height. 'I got this from the market the other day.' She drew from her pouch the necklace with Artume's pendant. Eyes wide, he gently cupped his hands. She pooled it into his palms and smiled. 'It is an amulet of the Goddess of Night. It will help you sleep when the sky is dark and the wolves are sniffing around.' She had even made the trip to Artume's temple, a small building tucked away on a street corner, as though untroubled with the fact it was nearly forgotten. The priestess had seemed surprised to find her inside, but was overjoyed to bless the amulet for Bel. She had made Mynta promise a dozen times to bring the boy to the temple in the future. Mynta would, but only if Bel wanted to, for it was a strange building for a goddess not often spoken of.

'Thank you, my lady,' he whispered, finger tracing the owl.

'I want you to wear it each night,' she said, 'but otherwise keep it safe in your room so you don't lose it going about your duties. Understood?'

He nodded vigorously.

'And look,' she said, pulling out another necklace. 'I got one too.'

He touched the golden laurel and arrow. 'Which god is this?'

'Aplu, God of Foresight and Song and Freedom.'

'Which one do you want?'

She slipped the amulet over her head, holding it between her fingers. 'Freedom.'

CHAPTER FORTY-ONE

'A little higher on the side,' Desma directed her maid, a young girl from a vineyard a little outside the city who had been thrilled at the chance to work in the palace. She was enthusiastic, though tended to be a little heavy-handed when it came to Desma's hair and makeup. But she was learning quickly.

'The ruby necklace with the rose quartz,' she said to another maid gaping at the array of jewellery before her. Desma had quickly discovered she had sizeable funds available to her which, traditionally, would be controlled by her husband. But Lycon seemed happy to let her be, preferring to avoid as much conversation as possible following his strange attack. Desma had made several jewellers and dressmakers quite wealthy, though it required several arguments and threats before they made the commissions to her designs rather than in their regular subdued fashions.

Tonight was the opening of the Celerian Games. It began with a feast held by the king in the afternoon with nobles and great lords, before the palace doors were opened at sundown and tables laid out in the street with barrels of wine and mead for the citizens.

Desma had ordered a new peplos made for the evening. Shimmering crimson of expensive silk, leaving her shoulders bare except for twin ribbons. A sculpted belt of copper beaten with myrtle and celery flowers. Her hair was swept high and back, a diadem crafted from garnet waves and golden froth nestled among her locks – a nod to her new home.

She would stand out in the room like blood among sand.

Her chamber doors burst open. The queen sent Desma's maids scurrying with a gesture. Her greying hair was strung with pearls, a rare display, but her face was darkened with displeasure. They had barely spoken since the vowing in Nethuns' temple – Desma had learned that a moment's kindness from the queen was but a feather hiding the iron.

Desma rose smoothly and bowed. 'Queen Pinaria.'

'I will not dip my toes in the waves. You have been married for months, and yet I am informed there is still blood upon the sheets. This will not do.'

Desma was momentarily taken aback, but soon found her footing. 'You were wed to the king for ten years before you fulfilled your duty. And I hear it took him less than a year to have Alnea.' She still could not believe Lycon had a sister, nor had she found the right moment to bring it up with him. The royal family had secrets tangled within secrets. How she was to navigate this mess of webs, she did not know.

Pinaria's eyes widened. 'How did you ... your crew are like snakes slithering through my halls,' she hissed.

'If you are so eager for a grandchild, *Mother*, then I suggest you talk to your son. For it is he who will not lie with me in our marriage bed. Perhaps he fears it will trigger another attack on himself ...'

'The prince is fine,' the queen said coldly, echoing the words Desma had heard a dozen times.

'So I hear.'

Pinaria opened her mouth to say something else but decided against it, turning on her heel with dignified fury and stalking from the room.

Desma let out a breath, sweat beading her brow. She was quickly finding herself without friends in the palace.

She could not be wholly angry at the queen. Desma had only been royalty for a handful of months and found it exhausting. And she was fortunate to be married to Lycon, who seemed to flit between mild support and indifference. She could scarcely imagine what it would have been like to be married to Gylippus.

There was a knock at the door.

'Come,' she called.

Cela slipped through, dressed in a beautiful, green peplos, her hair sculpted artfully, and copper adorning her skin. But Desma spied the hard leather sandals that peeked from under her hem.

Cela had told her weeks ago of her plan to help Alnea escape the palace tonight during the Games. And while she had much to distract her through the days, there was always a heavy weight in her chest reminding her.

She had stayed away from Alnea, not wanting to give the king or Kalchas an inkling of what was planned. She had even feigned ignorance of the princess' existence until just moments ago. Desma dearly wished to have spoken to her, just once, to know the woman who had also been an unwanted part of the royal family. And to tell her how precious Cela was to her.

'Everything is in place? The priest, the captain, the princess?'

'What – they all walked into a bar and ordered a drink?' Cela laughed at her own joke. 'Yes, Arete has helped us prepare. No detail has been missed.' Her smile saddened. 'Please tell the others how I will miss them, how I will never stop thinking of them, how ... how dearly I love them all.'

'Even Cosmas?'

'Kick him between the legs for me.'

Desma felt like there was a whirlpool inside her. She wanted to cling to Cela, cry how she will miss her, how she will long for the day she returns to the palace, to share memories of Apasa and their adventures one last time. She wanted to drink wine and dance in a tavern, to listen to Cela's stories of bedroom conquests from the night before, to laugh at her antics, and bask in the warmth of her golden glow.

But she only embraced her. Breathed in her apple and jasmine scent one more time. Let everything she felt but would not say slide from skin to skin, heart to heart.

'Be well, my dear friend,' Desma whispered into her hair.

'Be fierce,' Cela replied, her voice filled with spiderwebbing cracks. 'And be kind.'

'To love's end and back.'

'Always back.'

The great feasting hall burst with half-drunk lords and merchants and priests. Tables groaned with roasted boar, sour octopus, fish as large as Desma herself and smothered in herbs and lemon.

Maids wove between the tumblers and bards and musicians, pouring wine with long-suffering smiles. Wives sat stiffly beside their husbands, sharing pointed looks when Desma entered the great hall on Lycon's arm, the first touch since they had kissed. He wore a garland of celery flowers on his windswept hair, his chiton a brighter shade of green than usual with yellow stitching. He waved and called out loudly to friends and allies as they crossed the hall, taking their seat on the high table. The king had also forgone his usual black garments for the same green, his sapphire crown swapped for a laurel of celery flowers and pine needles, honouring Nethuns and the Games.

The queen refused to meet Desma's eyes.

Kalchas glowered from the end of the table. Hyllos gave her a nervous wave; she nodded politely in return.

Desma took her seat, gazing out at the assemblage. Kassandra, Arete, Delphinus, and Bion sat together towards the back. Cosmas was nowhere to be seen. She resolved to speak to them tomorrow, to break the news of Cela.

Though she sat there smiling politely, toasting when cups were raised, trying to make idle talk with her neighbours, Desma felt hollow inside. It was the emptiness of farewell, when one bids a friend goodbye, yet the future remains uncertain when next they would meet again. They had never been more than a week apart since they were babes.

She wanted to curse Turan for bringing this about, for driving their journey from Apasa to Koriithos, only to split their friendship apart with a crown. But she did not have the energy to muster the anger. She could only bear the pain of missing her friend.

'Is everything alright, wife?' Lycon's voice made her jump. He continued to smile and look out among the guests, but his eyes flashed quickly to her for a moment.

'I am fine, husband,' she said quietly. 'I had to say goodbye to a friend tonight and wish them well on their journey.' She ignored his questioning frown.

Maids came bearing golden trays with stalks of celery. Desma wrinkled her nose at the new dish. 'What is this?'

A ghost of a smile alighted his lips. 'It is slices of boar heart coated in mustard seeds and cooked in celery stems. It is customary on this night for the royal family to eat this meal, to give all Koriithos strength for the competitions ahead.'

She grimaced, but took a dutiful mouthful. The heart was tough, the seeds hot and bitter, and the vegetable bland. She finished her bite and took a large gulp of wine afterwards. Lycon seemed to enjoy his plate.

Gylippus surged to his feet. 'Hear me!' he roared, his voice strong despite his age, gravel rasping his words. 'We gather to open the Celerian Games, a proud tradition of our kingdom, and welcome any competitors from our neighbours who think they can outmatch us.' The hall made derisive noises, and Desma felt sorry for any Phoroniaan or Athanain attending. 'For the next five days—' He broke off at the sound of distant shouting. He went to speak again when the doors burst open. Actor sprinted through, sword out and a dozen men on his heels.

'Seal the hall,' he shouted. The warriors already lining the hall leapt to action, pushing guests off their benches as they heaved them across the doorway.

'War Leader, what is happening?' Gylippus called over the clamour, the room breaking into chaos.

'We are in danger, my king,' he answered, his eyes arrowing across to Desma. 'The Dirciade are attacking.'

Bile rose in her throat. She had caused this. That morning after training, when she had attacked that woman, broken her bones. Retribution had finally come. She hadn't planned to hurt her; she had only been wearied by the weight of their anger, when she had never earned it. And now the palace was under attack.

'Will you never cease causing me trouble?' Gylippus growled at her before turning to Actor. 'They are women, War Leader. Is my army so poorly trained that you cannot stand against kitchen knives and brooms?'

Actor opened his mouth to reply when his eyes went wide. His arm swung back and Desma caught the glint of his sword as it spun towards her at frightening speed. Lycon gripped her arm, shoving her aside, as the blade whipped between them and slammed the maid behind her in the chest. The young woman collapsed on the floor, eyes wide in pain, a dagger clutched in her hand – its hilt wrapped in hair dyed red.

'The maids,' Lycon roared, kicking his chair away. 'They are Dirciade.'

Desma watched in horror as dozens of maids drew weapons from within their dresses, attacking the assemblage in the room, uncaring if lord or priest, soldier or merchant. The warriors turned spears onto their own women, but were outnumbered. A third were killed before they realised who the enemy was.

Her friends.

Her eyes darted around the room. Relief hit hard when she spotted the crew backed into a corner, Bion brandishing a broken table, threatening anyone who got too close, the others gripping cutlery like weapons. Desma did not doubt their deadliness.

Actor moved to stand in front of the royal family, his men surrounding the high table. The rest of the soldiers struggled to hold back the tide of women. The Dirciade were wild, the essence of the barbarity they claimed Desma represented, screeching and clawing and stabbing recklessly at anyone close enough to their blade. Several of the noble women had picked up fallen swords and spears and turned on the surprised guards. Wine, water, and blood lapped across the stone floor.

Desma grunted at the sharp pain in her stomach. She looked down, half expecting an arrow to be protruding from her, but there was nothing. Another pang hit her, and she clutched the table to hold herself upright, but the strength fled her limbs and she fell to her knees.

'Desma,' Lycon said, concerned. He moved to help her but folded, clutching his midriff. His face had gone grey, and she knew hers must look the same. 'What is happening?'

Before she could answer, the queen also collapsed, curling into a ball as she screamed. The king was on his knees, fighting for breath.

Desma's gaze fell on the celery dish. Food served only to them. 'Poison,' she breathed before heaving, her vomit laced with coppery blood.

Lycon hit the ground and fear flashed through her. He was sick – what with, she did not know – but if he had an attack while in the throes of the poison, would he survive? Would any of them survive?

Actor was rooted to the spot, face frozen. 'Find Kalchas,' she hissed through the pain. The astronomer had vanished at the first signs of trouble. 'Get ... Hyllos.'

More vomit.

Actor spun into action. Desma slipped under the table. Her friends fought through the crowd, heading for the high table, Arete and Kassandra cutting down any maid or lady in their path without hesitation.

Her last thought, before the pain consumed her, was the hope that Cela had made it out safely.

Faint sounds of shouting drifting down the cliff to the harbour. It had been easy to sneak out of the palace, everyone too busy setting up for the communal feast to check two women carrying linen and baskets. But Cela did not think the alarm would have been raised so quickly.

Alnea wore a thick, muted-red himation, her cowl covering her veiled face. Besides Khufu, she was the only other person from the Great Lands she had seen in the city, so Cela was glad for the darkening sky to hide her complexion.

Once they were well into the city, Cela stopped at an inn. She had paid the innkeeper a silver coin to stash their packs in the storeroom earlier that afternoon. None of Alnea's clothes were suitable for an overland journey on foot – it was many days hard walking, and she doubted the princess had ever gone further than the canal bridge. Fortunately, Alnea was more than happy to produce the drachmae needed to furnish the journey.

'I have never been on a ship,' Alnea stated as she boarded the vessel, her cowl slipping as she gazed upwards at the sails and rigging.

'Cover your face,' Cela shouted, leaping forward to fix her robe. Some passersby looked towards the noise, and she made a show of fixing Alnea's cowl, the princess' face towards the city. Hopefully, those same people would be around when Actor came searching. He would easily be able to track the ship and its course to Athanai.

The palace was hard to see from this angle, obscured by the cliff face, but its presence was made known by the great glow of a thousand lights. Her crew, her friends, would be up there, partaking in the great feast before the games, and were probably wondering at her absence. Only Arete knew she was leaving them. It pained her to not say goodbye, but at least most of them would be able to truthfully deny any knowledge if questioned.

Desma would be seated with the royal family, crowned and once more shining fierce like a bonfire. Cela could only pray that one day their paths might cross again, and that both of them would have been fortunate enough to salvage some happiness. But the fates did not listen to mortal pleas. Perhaps their hurried goodbye was the final sip of their friendship, the cup empty, the amphora run dry.

'We are ready, captain,' she said, as Alnea went to stand by the bow. 'Let us away.'

CHAPTER FORTY-TWO

Mynta wandered the house where she had grown up one last time. Most of it was untouched, for she had only taken what was in her rooms and what she had purchased since her parents moved to the palace all those weeks ago.

There was the cracked paver in one of the halls where she had dropped a pretty rock she wanted to show her father. There was the shrine she and her nursemaid had erected to Horta and Esplace, when they had finally convinced her parents to stop starving her for beauty.

Her rooms were empty, their yellow stone walls echoing with a life filled with pleasures and hardships. She stopped by her parents' shared bedchamber, not stepping inside but leaning against the door frame, trying to remember when she had ever felt welcomed in the room.

The centre garden was her favourite place, and she lingered until the sun began to dip over the horizon. The fruit trees and bubbling creek, the soft grass, and colourful flowers. Her talks with Desma and Cela as they sipped wine pilfered from the kitchen. Her mother braiding her hair and telling her the history of noble families. Her nursemaid whispering lessons of strength and wit.

Tears dropped onto the grass, but she did not move to wipe them away. She would give the house the last gift of her grief, for the love it had given her.

She stopped at her father's office, a scroll clutched in her hand. She had spent half the night writing it. A message to her father. It held all the things she had never said. It had been the worst pain she had ever felt – her heart wrenched and torn and bled onto the page. She had wanted to howl the words, but she kept silent, not wanting to waken the others.

Would her father read it? Would he feel anything if he did?

She had tricked and shamed him in his own household, driving him away. She had betrayed everything he had brought her up to be, had cast aside his dreams and plans to pursue her own. In turn, he had ignored her for weeks, scrambling to save himself among the Council. She was a thorn in his side, a burn on his hand, a bramble in his robes.

She tore the scroll up, ripping over and over again until it was tatters in her hands. She let them fall to the floor, shaking the more stubborn pieces off.

Then turned and walked away. Sebastos, Tros, and Anesidora waited in the outer courtyard.

'Are you ready, my lady?' Sebastos asked.

'Let us away,' she said, folding her arm over her nursemaid's. 'Our new home awaits.'

Later that evening, they reclined on the couches in the smaller dining hall. Most of dinner had been consumed, though they still picked at the fresh fruit. The raised roof with high-set windows allowed warm air to rise and the cool, evening breeze to sweep in. The mosaic floor depicted Ethausva and Uni dining on stuffed peacocks, surrounded by dryads and fauns. A fountain set in one wall, braced by two slender pillars, gave a soft trickle as water fell gracefully from the mouth of a sea nymph.

Mynta looked around at the people she had gathered around her.

Anesidora lay on the couch next to her, eyes closed, though she knew the old woman was awake. Beside her was Sebastos. Tros had gone to take that couch, but changed his mind at the sharp glare from the nursemaid. Mynta had hidden her smile and pretended not to notice.

Despite looking relaxed with several cups of wine in him, she knew that Sebastos was never truly at rest. He was like a leopard from the Great Lands. The king's father had owned one and she had seen it once. It was sleek and languid, belying a wicked strength and speed beneath its fur.

Next to Sebastos was her trademaster, the one she'd helped toward a successful future he had nearly forsaken – and one she still hoped to claim for herself. His arm hung off the couch, gently touching fingers with his wife. Irene smiled at him – so sweetly, it pricked Mynta's heart like a hundred pins. It was a love that had seen them through tough times, had grown with each child and encompassed them in its halo; their love walked the stony paths life set before them, easing discomfort and bringing peace to trouble.

These four people were the core of who she wanted to be.

And it was time to make it official.

She rose off the couch, brushing breadcrumbs from her dress as a maid hurried over to clear the dishes from around her feet. Mynta thanked her with soft words before turning to the others, bidding them to remain as they were.

'Friends, mentors,' she began. 'I wish tonight to make several announcements, decisions I have reached because of you. Thanks to my mother for her last act of kindness, we have been given a new home, one we can truly call our own. My household is filled with people who wish to serve me for myself, and not for the man my father is. I have already made mistakes, and I have no doubt I will make more in the days to come. But that is the struggle of all mortals – we do not know what is beyond our own feet. But with you by my side, I have little to fear of my next steps.' She took a moment to quell the wave of emotion rising in her. Over a year ago, this would have been a dream that she dared not voice aloud.

'We are proud of you, Lady Amynta,' her nursemaid said quietly, tears shining in her own eyes.

'One of the most important lessons I have learned is that I do not walk this path alone,' Mynta continued. 'Though I lead the way and am guided by your wisdom, I know now that it is not my house, but all of ours. You have bound your names, your honour, your families to my service and so I, too, serve you.'

Mynta took a deep breath. 'Irene, wife of Tros, I call upon you to be my housekeeper, ruler of oil and wine, mistress of my home and its honour. I call you in Tinia's name. Will you answer?'

Irene looked at her husband in shock. She rose to her feet. 'My lady, I was simply helping where I could. I pray, I did not make any assumptions to this role ...'

'Irene, will you answer?' Mynta repeated.

Irene swallowed and glanced again at Tros, who kept his face blank. The choice was his wife's, not his. She smoothed her simple dress before clasping her hands. 'My lady, in Tinia's name I answer – yes!'

Tros let out a wild cheer as Mynta crossed the space between them, kissing her new housekeeper upon the cheeks. 'Thank you, Irene,' she whispered, before returning to her couch.

'Tros, husband to Irene,' she said, 'I call upon you to be my trademaster, lord of coins, master of merchants and papers. I call you in Turms' name. Will you answer?'

He rose from the couch. 'You saved my daughter's life and gave my family a home of which they can be proud. You have given me a new chance and honour every day I am here. My lady, in Turms' name I answer – yes!'

'Come, trademaster,' Mynta laughed, kissing him on his cheeks before sending him back to his wife, who he embraced, swinging her around.

'Sebastos,' she said. The old soldier was already on his feet, back straight as he met her gaze. 'I call upon you to be the captain of my guard, protector of all I hold dear in this world. I call upon you in Laran's name. Will you answer?'

He drew his knife, holding the hilt in both hands as he placed it over his heart. 'Though I have not served you for long, my lady, and time is still required for me to know your heart wholly, I can see both kindness and greatness in you. That is a rare doubling. For this, my lady, in Laran's name I answer – yes!'

She folded her hands over her heart as well, mirroring his salute.

Mynta then turned to the most precious woman in her life, the person her heart called family, even if her blood did not. She took up her nursemaid's hand and helped her to her feet. Gently cupping her wrinkled face, Mynta bent forward until their brows touched.

'You have walked with me every day of my life,' Mynta said, her words falling soft. 'You have guided me through joy, grief, anger, pain, womanhood. You will guide me in triumphs, failures, passions. There is no one in this world who I want more by my side. Anesidora, I call upon you to be my first advisor, speaker of wisdom, my champion in this world. I call upon you in Menrva's name. Will you answer?'

The old woman leant forwards to gently kiss her lips, tears falling onto Mynta's cheeks. 'In Menrva's name, I answer the only answer I could ever give you, my lady – yes!'

Mynta embraced her dearest friend. They held tight to each other, neither speaking, before she pulled back and called forth her maids. They brought cups filled with rich, dark wine. She raised hers up high. 'You have all answered the call. Tonight is the first gathering of my council. May Tinia's eyes fall favourably on this household.'

They all cried out with her, 'Tinia!' before emptying their cups at once and casting them on the stone floor, shattering the pottery as they sealed the promise to each other, to the household, to her.

Mynta could not keep the smile from her face as she bid them all goodnight, thanking her maids as they came in to clean away the broken cups and leftover dishes.

She wandered through the house to her new office, lighting the candles herself, though she did not take a seat at the table. Instead, she walked around, gently touching the mostly empty shelves, though some held the paperwork of her few, small business deals. The beginning of everything.

'My lady,' Tros said quietly from the doorway, startling her slightly. 'I am sorry to interrupt, but I am afraid I do not think I could sleep one more night without speaking to you.'

'Is something wrong?' she asked, concerned.

Her trademaster shook his head, his eyes gleaming. 'No, I just want to finish the conversation we began before your mother's unexpected visit, if you recall.'

He had mentioned something about looking further afield. 'Yes, of course. What is it?'

'Tell me first, what do you know of Anama?'

She frowned. Anama was an island a little larger than Konoso. It lay towards the eastern edge of the Middle Sea, beyond the boundary of the League. Its people were a strange blend of Leaguemen and the easterlings.

Anama was an island of tall hills and steep foothills, with valleys that flooded during the rains and soil difficult to grow crops. They had an abundance of copper and sulphur deposits. Trilos and Quirinale often fought each other over who could purchase the most product from the island.

Tros shook his head when she told him all she knew. 'You will need to get a tutor if this endeavour has any chance of succeeding.'

'What endeavour?'

He looked at her with a gleam in his eyes. 'Do you know about the gloaming sheep?'

Her eyes widened. All citizens of the League knew of the sheep. Found only on the island, their wool was the rarest in the world. Cerulean dye was the most expensive, a small thimbleful worth a thousand gold drachmae. A cloak of gloaming wool was worth ten times as much. Their wool was the colour of a young twilight, rich purples and greys and blacks; some sported hints of red or flashes of white. But what made their wool so coveted was that, at dawn and dusk, the fibres glowed with filaments of silver, like starlight caught in a web.

It was said that the sheep belong to all Anaman, and even the meanest farmer wore cloaks of shining wool. But when it came to trading with other kingdoms, the island people had strict requirements that nearly all failed. For the past several thousand years, only a few bushels of the wool had left the island. And the wool was more fragile than that of any other sheep, falling apart a year or two after shearing. Mynta knew of no one in Trilos who possessed any currently.

'You must be drunk,' she said, 'or taken with madness. You want to trade in gloaming wool?'

He shook his head. 'Not I, my lady. You.'

'Trademaster, please.' Dozens of people travelled to the island every year to try and pass the tests set by the Anamans, to buy their wool. And dozens were sent home empty-handed. How was she, with one failed investment and a set of rundown warehouses under her belt, to achieve what master merchants failed to do?

'My lady,' Tros said softly, splaying his hands on the table. 'You brought me into your service, for what reasons I do not know beyond simple kindness. But let me speak as your trademaster – you wish to make your mark upon this city. Duris and the others have blackened your name. I am sure that, in time, we can repair the damage they have done. But it will be hard, and slow, and expensive, and may result in little achievement. And now we have lost the Apasan markets. But this opportunity! I say, take the chance. Let us sail to Anama and take the test. If we fail, we waste a trip. But if we succeed ... riches and fame beyond any in Trilos.'

It was tempting. But to leave Trilos for the strange island and its magic sheep. She had only ever gone to Apasa, and once to Thevai.

'Let me think on it,' she finally said.

Tros deflated.

She patted his hand. 'It is not something to be rushed into, trademaster. I have been burned before with rushed decisions. Give me a day or two to think and ask questions. Be prepared to have those answers at the ready.'

He bowed with a smile. 'Of course, my lady.'

But that night, Mynta dreamt of a sky not filled with stars, but grazing sheep that shone silver.

CHAPTER FORTY-THREE

Desma was in a waking nightmare of pain and screams.

Everything was disjointed, broken by searing slices of agony in her abdomen that felt like a hot knife going in, but a rusty fishhook being dragged out. She would fade away in a grey haze, only to be brought back to consciousness by another wave.

At some point, she had been lifted into someone's large arms, cradled against a chest whose hair tickled her nose – Bion? – before being rushed from the great hall. The lumbering gait sent her into convulsions, acrid bile slobbering from her mouth, her body lacking the energy to heave it up. It soaked the chiton and chest of whoever was carrying her, her face pressed against the warm sick, but she couldn't lift her head away.

Eventually, she was placed onto something soft and chill. *A bed*, her mind helpfully suggested. Voices crackled around her, and she tried hard to focus on the words, but they came in scraps.

'... what is the poison ...'

'... we need to purge their stomachs ...'

'... idiot, Hyllos. It has already soaked into their blood and fluids ...'

'... do something, Astronomer ...'

'... we need to save the king and Lycon ...'

'... don't you dare leave Desma as a second thought ...'

'Save. Lycon,' she wheezed, her throat raw as sandpaper.

A cool hand on her brow. 'It's alright, Desma,' a dry voice said. Arete. 'We will save you all.'

She fell back into her misery as another wrenching spasm took her, leaving her gasping and soaked in sweat.

'... dead throughout the halls ...'

'... warriors have regained most of the palace ...'

'... Actor has arrested every woman ...'

A voice spoke in her ear. 'I can save you,' Cosmas whispered. 'Kalchas' suggested cure will leave the four of you dead. Trust me – I know poisons.'

Desma tried to lift her hand, but all she could manage was to wiggle her fingers.

Arete saw. 'Quiet! Desma is trying to speak.'

She licked her lips, spreading bile into the cracks and causing her to hiss. 'Listen. To. Cosmas.'

'I will not let a foreign cook touch the king and queen!' she heard Kalchas shout. 'As first astronomer, I am the only one who can speak for the king and I tell you all to get out of this room—'

'That is not true,' Hyllos said.

Desma forced her eyes open to slits. The older astronomer turned on the younger. 'Do not speak again, or I will have you thrown into the canal,' Kalchas warned.

'Desma is royalty and is the only one of the four who can speak. She has given us an order, and thus her word outranks your authority, First Astronomer.' Hyllos looked sick himself, but he stood his ground before his mentor.

'She is Apasan ...'

The door bang opened.

Desma closed her eyes as her strength faded, but she heard Actor's voice over his studded sandals on the stone. 'What is happening?'

They all fell over themselves to inform the general. Desma did not know how he could make heads or tails of their words, but he was a battle-hardened warrior used to the chaos of the field. Within moments, he was snapping orders: 'Cosmas, do what you must. Kalchas, step back, or I will have you shackled. Bion, gag him if you must.'

Cosmas touched her chest, neck, ankles, throat. She never noticed how much he smelled like river moss. She moaned as he prodded her stomach. The pain seemed to have faded, but her limbs were stone, her blood mortar being pushed through her veins. Breathing was hard, like a boulder laid on her breast.

Cosmas left her to check on the others. Time passed – whether minutes or hours, she could not say – before Cosmas' voice brought her back.

'... chimean leaf. It is not native to the League but comes from the west coast of the Empire.'

'Is there a cure?' Arete asked.

'I believe so, but I need help. We will need your fleetest runner, War Leader ...'

She faded away.

Desma walked on a stony beach, naked and uncaring, letting the waves wash over her feet. She did not know where she was but it did not bother her. It was calm, quiet. The rocks clattered gently as she stepped, the only sound beyond the lapping sea.

Someone walked beside her. A hooded figure matching her slow meander. Robes heavy and dark, a colour hard to distinguish. She could not see their face or hands, and the hem covered their feet.

She was not afraid.

They walked on in silence.

An olive tree appeared on the horizon. Desma did not quicken her pace; there was no hurry. It was an old tree, its trunk thick and gnarled, twisted by the years; tracing from root to branch made the eye dizzy. Sage and silver leaves, like thin spears, dappled the stones, even as the waves washed its roots.

The voice of the hooded figure, filled with the warmth of rising bread, echoed as though they stood in a small cave. 'This seems like a good place to part ways.'

'Thank you for walking with me,' Desma said. 'Do you have far still to journey?'

The figure chuckled, a pleasant sound. 'For me, the journey never ends. But I do like to stop now and again for rest and company. I see you have been doing the same among my people.'

Desma did not understand. The Koriithosans? This did not seem like the Nethuns she knew. 'Are you a god?' she asked.

Again, they chuckled. 'I seem that way to you, though my people do not place so great a distance between us. I will leave you with these words, daughter of love – be wary of kindness.'

Desma did not understand but bowed her head nevertheless; for she did not doubt this was a being of power, and it was always wise to err on the side of politeness. 'May the road be smooth and wine strong.'

The figure turned from her and walked up to the olive tree, patting a branch as they passed as though it were an old friend. Before her eyes, they stepped into the trunk, disappearing. All that was left was a thin wisp of smoke and the outline of the hooded figure burned into the trunk.

Desma awoke with a gasp, as though wrenched from sleep by rough hands.

A shadow appeared above her, its hood wide and deep. For a moment, she thought she was still dreaming, until she saw the twin scars on her face. Eidia.

'Easy, Princess,' the Arydorian soothed, helping her sit up. 'Your body has been in battle and needs rest.'

'What has happened?' Desma could remember some of the night's events. The feast, Actor, the maids drawing knives, poison … 'Lycon!'

Eidia took her hands. 'He is fine. He sleeps beside you.' She pointed to the bed next to her. The prince looked weak and sallow, but his breathing appeared even.

'Thank the gods,' Desma sighed. 'The king and queen?'

Eidia's eyes grew dark. 'I think you had better speak to those in power. I have accomplished my task, though I did not expect to be dragged from my bed by palace guards when I went to sleep.'

It came to her then. The hooded figure. Eidia's door. 'Thank you,' Desma said gratefully. 'And thank the Wanderer for me, as well.'

Eidia's eyes widened curiously, but she said nothing as she left the room.

Desma sank back onto the pillow, breathing deeply and feeling relieved when no pain coursed through her body. Chimean leaf – she had never heard of it, and wondered how the Dirciade could have gotten their hands on the poison.

Actor soon came in, followed by Hyllos, Arete, and Cosmas.

The general looked tired and stern. She doubted he had gotten any rest since the feast. How long had it been?

'Praise Nethuns you have recovered, Princess,' Actor said with a genuine smile.

'He had little to do with it,' Cosmas muttered wryly. Arete elbowed him.

'I am thankful to everyone,' Desma said. 'I heard enough to know you all had a role to play. And I would not be here if you had not had the foresight to bring Eidia to help, Cosmas.'

'A promise is a promise,' he said.

Like a dog with a bone, she thought. 'I know Lycon is well, but what of his father and mother?'

Darkness coated the Koriithosans' faces, and Arete's lips thinned.

Desma closed her eyes. They had not survived the poison. Gylippus and Pinaria were dead. Despite everything between them, the fights and bloodless battles, Khufu's sacrifice, the lies and secrets – they were her father and mother by marriage. Her husband's parents. Killed because their own women feared her.

She did not hide the tears that gleamed along her lids.

Lycon groaned. The room held their breath, waiting for the prince to waken. His breath quickened. Desma frowned. Something was wrong.

His eyes fluttered then shot open, blood vessels breaking until his pupils were crimson. His tongue lolled out of his open mouth, stretched open in silent pain, his every limb stiff as wood. Veins threaded across his skin, streaks of blue turning to purple.

'Lycon!' she shouted as Cosmas leapt to his side, beating the general and astronomer. His fingers flashed across the prince and Desma saw worry in his eyes.

'I do not understand,' he growled. 'This should not be happening. It is as though something has interfered with the medicine we gave him.'

Desma's eyes bored into Hyllos. 'Tell us.'

The astronomer looked about the room like a chicken before the wolves. 'The prince suffers attacks to his body. When he was a child, he fell from a balcony and hit his head. He seemed fine, but after a few days he began to have fits. Some were mild, and he would stare into the distance, ignoring everything about him. Others were worse – he would collapse, sometimes shaking and other times completely still. We summoned priests of Esplace but, for some mysterious reason, the God of Healing withheld his blessing.'

Cosmas grabbed the astronomer roughly by his robes. 'And you didn't think to tell us this before? We gave him nemera root! It cures the stomach but worsens anything wrong with the head.' He threw Hyllos away from him, sending the man crashing to the floor.

'Hold his arms, War Leader,' he commanded Actor. The general grabbed the prince. 'Arete, his legs.' The shipwright threw herself on top of Lycon.

Grabbing a bag from a nearby table, he pulled out a glass tube with tiny green berries. He broke the tube in half and poured the fruit into his palm. 'This might save him or it might kill him. But if I do nothing, then he will certainly die.' Without another word, he slapped his hand over Lycon's open mouth, massaging his throat so the berries fell.

Long seconds passed. His body stayed rigid—so still, Desma couldn't tell if he was breathing. Then, with a long exhale, he went limp. His eyes closed, and he seemed to settle into sleep.

'Did it work?' Actor asked.

Cosmas shrugged. 'We will not know until he wakes. He will either be himself or he will be like a child, simple and slow in speech.' He turned piercing blue eyes on the astronomer, who had risen to his feet. 'You better pray it is the former.' He left the room.

'I know there is much to be discussed and decisions to make. But not tonight,' Desma said. 'Before you go, could you move my bed closer to Lycon?'

Actor stood by her head while Arete and Hyllos took the other end of the simple wooden frame. They lifted it gently and tucked it beside the prince. They left quietly with promises to not be far.

Desma barely heard them as she looked at her husband, saw his challenges and struggles. The pain and fear he lived with every day. The blow to his pride when he could not fight the monster himself and then had to wed her.

She reached out and took his hand, hoping to lend what little strength she had to him.

For she knew she could not rule Koriithos alone.

Two days later, Desma finally had the strength to walk unaided.

Lycon had still not awoken but he didn't appear to have issue swallowing the cooled broth they dripped down his throat. Cosmas refused to say if that was a good sign or not.

Desma ordered for reports to be brought to her so she could know the aftermath of the attack.

The maids in the feasting hall had killed over fifty people, with half their own number slaughtered before they finally surrendered. Over three hundred women had attacked the palace doors as they opened for the citizen's feast in the courtyards. They plundered the palace rooms and halls, killing as they went. They scattered once Actor's men had recovered, driven out by spear and shield. Dozens had been arrested and crowded the cells beneath. Desma would not decide their fate today, but she did order their food and water be cut by half and no torches be left alight for them to see. They could suffer.

She ordered trade be suspended for ten days while the city recovered. The army was out in force, patrolling the streets and city surrounds, strengthening patrols on the borders in case their neighbours felt opportunistic.

She summoned the high priest of Nethuns, as well as priestesses of Aita and Phersipnai, to begin planning the funeral. Not so long ago, she had been numb during her own mother's death rites, and had been banished before she could burn her father on the pyre.

Her orders were carried out without complaint or argument. Actor and Hyllos were by her side, her chief advisors, while she kept the city running.

She no longer heard grumbles of her foreign origin or her blood crime, did not see sneering lips or disapproving eyes. Everyone was afraid. And they were happy for her to lead – blame would fall on her if anything went wrong.

And through it all, Desma did not leave Lycon's side.

She had never seen herself as the dutiful wife, but it was the least she could do for him. All this had happened because she had come to Koriithos to be cleansed. It was foolish to blame herself – many gods had a hand to play in how events turned out since she returned from Urruc – but that did not always quieten the voice inside her heart.

She was talking to Hyllos about when they would let the markets reopen when Arete slipped through the door, her hazel eyes solemn. Desma waved the astronomer to silence and waited for the shipwright to approach.

'Trouble is brewing in the megaron,' Arete said. She glanced at Hyllos. 'With Kalchas' hand on the tiller.'

The astronomer put his hands in the air. 'I know nothing of this. I am all but banished from his door since I spoke for you, Princess.'

Desma pursed her lips. Lycon had not changed in two days, except to grow thinner. She loathed to leave his side, but she could not let the first astronomer cause trouble, not after she was finally beginning to get a handle on affairs. 'Let's go.'

It was a slow journey across the palace, for she still tired easily, but with Arete's arm to support her, they soon made it to the almond tree courtyard. The doors to the throne room were open and the crowd of nobles fell silent at Desma's entrance.

Her hard stare pierced lords and merchants as they shuffled their feet, unable to meet her eye. What a change from a few days ago!

Kalchas stood before the throne, his dark robes stitched with silver, a triumphant glare on his cracked and weathered face. The queen's throne sat empty beside him. Desma was surprised to find Actor standing with him, shoulders slumped and a begging look in his eye.

'What is this, First Astronomer?' Desma called out in a weakened voice. 'It seems that in Koriithos' hour of need, you are absent. But here I find you, conspiring like a weasel in the gloom.'

'I would guard your tongue, Apasan,' Kalchas said. 'For its lies will no longer gild our ears with silver and tarnish them with rot.'

Desma drew back. 'You dare speak to me like that,' she snapped. 'I know you have served this family and kingdom faithfully for decades, but do not think it grants you any allowance.'

'As you say,' he began, eyes alighting, 'I have served with honour and loyalty for far longer than you have drawn breath. My faith is unquestionable. And so my words ring with truth when I accuse you, Desma of Apasa, of the murder of our king and queen.'

She closed her eyes, tiredness like a fog rolling over her. How much more must she endure in this room? Had she made a mistake to cast aside Khufu's sacrifice and come back for these people? The same people who hated her beyond reason, to blindness, twisting everything good about her into a monster?

She opened her eyes to look at Actor. 'He has caught you in some web where you must do as he says.' It wasn't a question.

The general looked defeated. 'Our laws state that he may accuse a member of the royal family, less the king or queen, of a crime. They are to withdraw any power or authority granted until a triumvirate is formed to verify the claim. And our laws also state that, in the absence of royalty, the first astronomer is to act as regent.'

'How tidy,' Arete said with bared teeth. 'With the death of Gylippus and Pinaria, is Desma not now queen?'

Actor shook his head. 'Only true royal blood can crown her. Lycon must speak the words'.

Kalchas called out, 'Guards, bind them!'

Desma did not move as men approached, their faces stoic. She had no fight left to give.

'Why, Kalchas?' she asked. Her words gave the guards pause.

The astronomer's eyes were bright and she was surprised to find it was from tears, gleaming beneath his glare. 'My city grieves, Desma. Its crown is soaked in blood and poison. Women, who know their civilised place, have given in to barbarity. I stood in this room and declared to my king that you were the one the stars foretold.' His voice trembled. 'But I see how wrong I was! You are the darkness between stars, the Despised Beloved. You would drown Koriithos in salt and blood. And I. Will. Not. Allow. It.' He gestured to the warriors.

Desma nodded for Arete to step away, swaying for a moment as she found her balance on weakened legs. 'My friends have done nothing. Do not include them in my fate. Here, in front of Koriithos, I order all members of my crew to raise no hand in defiance of this city. They will lend aid when asked and otherwise not interfere but to care for my family. So I speak, as my last act as princess.'

She met Kalchas' eyes. After a moment, he nodded.

'No,' Arete pleaded. Desma was grabbed roughly, her arms twisted behind her and bronze chains wrapped around her wrists.

Desma tried to give the shipwright a brave smile but it came out more a grimace. 'I must walk this road, dear friend. Even now, I cannot abandon these people. But, please, care for Lycon.'

She turned upon the nobles of the city. 'I returned to the city because of a prophecy. Gylippus believed it enough to force me to wed his only son. Fear has grasped us all by the throat but *we must not give in*. I will stay by your side, stand before you and whatever danger approaches. I will be the shield that bears fate's blows. This I swear to you. I have not forgotten my duty.' She looked to Kalchas. 'Even if some have.'

'Take her away,' the astronomer barked.

As she was marched away across the megaron, she saw a group of women standing in the back of the hall. Clad in dresses of charcoal and moss and dour red. Each held a lock of red hair, their hands stained crimson from the dye. Desma felt her throat catch. How could some of the Dirciade be allowed in the throne room after what had happened?

There was a stir at the back of the group. The women shifted aside to allow a figure to step between them. Desma twisted her head to keep them in sight as she neared the doors. The figure stopped before the Dirciade, a hand reaching up to push the hood away from their face.

Her heart froze. Her throat collapsed.

Camillus smiled, grim and dreadful, filled with a darkful glee. The bishop raised a peach to his mouth and took a bite, juice flowing down his chin and splattering the marble floor. His hands were also dyed red.

'No. No, no, no,' Desma cried out, digging her heels into the ground, but she had no strength left. The guards carried her out the doors. 'Kalchas! Arete! No!'

The doors boomed shut behind her.

Epilogue

The sound of low humming brought him awake.

Eyes blinking wearily, his lids fought him. He forced them open in the softened gloom. Gods, but he was tired. Everything ached as though he had been run over by a herd of bulls.

It took several moments for his eyes to adjust to the dim light. The ceiling was rough-hewed, with deep gouges and broken chunks missing. Like someone took hammer and claw to it.

The halls were slick with moisture that gleamed softly silver. With effort, he moved his fingers off the pallet he rested on and rubbed the floor. The stone was rough as well.

In the distance, the glow of daylight. The faint rush of water. He was in a cave. He tried to move his legs but that strength was beyond him.

He turned his head the other way and saw the cave kept going. Not a cave, he realised, but a tunnel.

But that direction did not grow darker as one would expect. Instead, it filled with a mist that sparkled. Motes of glittering colours wafted in the air, shifting in different directions, ignoring the thin breeze that whispered from the faraway entrance.

'Where am I?' he asked aloud, his voice hoarse and dry.

The humming that had awoken him came to an abrupt end.

The sound had been coming from behind him, but he could not turn himself over to see.

'Name yourself,' he called out, angry at the fear threaded within his words. He was unarmed, prone on the floor in a strange tunnel.

The person snorted. 'I have more names than you have years of life. But why settle for titles when we can be far more dramatic ...'

A golden light flooded the tunnel, and he cursed, squeezing his eyes shut. Melodies began around him, as though the stones themselves were singing. They wove and plucked and thundered, a choral paean that would drive any mortal to their knees.

'Look at me,' the voice, rich and timbral, commanded him. And he had no choice but to obey, for the words were power.

He opened his eyes and found the light, while still bright, did not burn his eyes. His mouth slacked open. They stood before and above him, golden and resplendent. Clothes of purest white embroidered in cerulean, a belt of orichalcum, a crown of laurel and cornflowers. The god – for it could be nothing else – smiled down at him.

'Hello, Khufu,' the god said brightly. 'I'm Aplu.'

The Deities Mentioned Within

The Holy Twelve

Aplu – God of Light and Prophecy and Freedom.

Artimi – Goddess of Witches and the Wild.

Ethausva – Goddess of Hearth and Home and Family.

Horta – Goddess of All that Grows.

Laran – God of War.

Menrva – Goddess of Cunning and Wisdom and Learning.

Nethuns – God of the Seas and the Deeps; Father of Monsters.

Sethlans – God of Forges and Creation.

Tinia – King of the Gods; Lord of the Sky, Storms, and Judgements.

Turan – Goddess of Love

Turms – God of Paths and Colours and Tricksters

Uni – Queen of the Gods; Goddess of Marriage, Social Order, and the Stars.

Other Deities

Aita – Under-God of the Beneath; Keeper of Souls.

Artume – Goddess of Night.

Asra and Sera – Gods of the North and South Winds.

Athrpa, Enie, Pemphetru – The Diviners, Daughters of Fate.

Charun – One of many who carry souls across the blood rivers.

Culsans – Two-Faced God; Keeper of Doors

Esia – Goddess of Peace.

Esplace – God of Healing.

Februus – God of Riches.

Fufluns – God of Wine and Laughter.

Ilithiia – Goddess of Childbirth

Mania – Goddess of Shades.

Munthukh – Goddess of Healing.

Nurtia – Corded Goddess of Fate and Chance.

Orcus – The Punishing God.

Phersipnai – She of Two Lands.

Prumathe – God of Thought

Selvans – God of Forests and Pastures; Father of Twilight and Madness

Soranus – God of Fire Beneath.

Summanus – God of Dark Lightning; Lord of Night Storms.

Thesan – Goddess of the Dawn.

Tiur – Goddess of the Moon.

Tricon – God of Currents.

Usil – God of the Sun.

Vanth – Demon-Goddess of the Beneath.

THE LOVERS
(ALL ARE CHILDREN OF TURAN)

Aminth – son of Aita, God of Requited Love; Avenger of Unrequited Love.

Erus – son of Laran, Cruel Love.

Heran – son of Uni, God of Weddings.

Leinth – offspring of Turms, Deity of the Between and the Liminal

Svutaf – son of Atunis, God of Yearning.

Tusna – son of Aplu, God of Sweet Talk.

Turnu – son of Summanus, God of Uncontrollable Desire and Impetuous Love.

ABOUT THE AUTHOR

Damien J. Coluccio is an Australian fantasy author from the South Coast, NSW. Inspired by the greats of Ancient Mediterranean literature and mythology, 2024 marked the debut of his The Wine-Dark Series.

Graduate of the University of Sydney, when not lost in reading or writing, Damien can be found wandering a botanic garden, hunting through antiques, throwing ridiculous parties for his friends, and seeking out little adventures. He currently lives in the Wollongong area with his supportive husband and sassy corgi, Obie (short for Oberon, King of the Faeries!).

Scan the QR codes below to learn more about Damien, his books, upcoming events, and more:

Visit Damien's Website

Visit Damien's Instagram

Acknowledgements

And the dream continues.

Only a year prior to this, the first instalment of The Wine-Dark Series came out in the world. Now, you are holding the second book in your hands to enjoy the continuing trials and triumphs and turmoils of Desma, Cela, and Mynta. It means the world to me that you want to read on with these tales.

My first thank you – always – goes to my husband, Andrew, for your unending love and support. You have continued to listen to me ramble on with my thoughts, dealt with my worries and anxiety, and celebrated in all the milestones and successes. Your steadfast belief has kept me going.

And to the brilliant team at Authors Own for being the reason – yet again – that this story has gone from words on my computer to the book on your shelf and e-reader. Thank you to Danikka Taylor for the company you have built for little indie authors like me, for your editorial guidance and the precious care you took with my characters, and for guiding me through the many stages of publishing. Thank you, as well, to Henry Sinclair for your insights and for teaching me more about grammar than everything I can remember from school. And to Casey Grills for creating the absolutely gorgeous artwork that graces my cover. And to everyone else at AO who, behind the scenes, helped make this come about.

And to Angeline Trevena of Step-By-Step Worldbuilding for my amazing map.

To my beta-readers for your time, your feedback and ideas, and your excitement to dive back into this world – Megan, Stephanie, and Lauren.

To Cass for your friendship and support, for all our buddy-writing sessions, and for always cheering me on.

The biggest thanks to Kim for ever standing by my side, for bolstering my confidence, and never letting me doubt myself.

To all my friends and family for sharing your support and love.

To the high school teachers and university tutors who inspired me beyond measure.

And huge thanks to the authors and editors I've met along the way who have encouraged and advised, helping me grow as a writer.

And lastly, to all the amazing booksellers, shop owners, podcasters, mentors, and members of the bookish community for your encouragement and guidance, and for giving me a chance.